"Along the way to the satisfying ending, Virgil displays the rough humor and rough justice that make him such an appealing character." —*Publishers Weekly*

"The tenth Flowers novel is a knowing portrait of small-town life layered into a very well plotted mystery. Virgil understands that, in small towns, no one ever outgrows high school, and he uses that knowledge to unravel both mysteries by dissecting the relationships and economic realities in the town. One of the very best novels in a superior series." —*Booklist* (starred review)

"The reader's quest to discover the whole truth will propel them forward, where [Sandford] has plenty of twists (and more than a few laughs) planted along the way. *Deep Freeze* is easily one of Sandford's best Virgil Flowers novels yet." —*The Real Book Spy*

"Add a gripping storyline, a generous helping of exquisitely conceived characters and laugh-out-loud humor that produces explosive guffaws, not muted chuckles, and you're in for the usual late-night, don't-even-think-of-stopping treat when Flowers hits town."
—*Richmond Times-Dispatch*

PRAISE FOR JOHN SANDFORD'S VIRGIL FLOWERS NOVELS

"Each of Flowers' cases reveals more quirks, more depth, and a wicked sense of the absurd, as well as an investigator who can be as analytical as Nero Wolfe and as tough as everybody's favorite Boston badass, Spenser. Great entertainment." —*Booklist*

DEEP FREEZE

JOHN SANDFORD

G. P. PUTNAM'S SONS • NEW YORK

PUTNAM

G. P. PUTNAM'S SONS
Publishers Since 1838
An imprint of Penguin Random House LLC
375 Hudson Street
New York, New York 10014

The Library of Congress has catalogued the G. P. Putnam's Sons
hardcover edition as follows:

Names: Sandford, John, author.
Title: Deep freeze / John Sandford.
Description: New York : G. P. Putnam's Sons, [2017] | Series: A Virgil Flowers
novel ; 10
Identifiers: LCCN 2017025620| ISBN 9780399176067 (hardcover) |
ISBN 9780698407114 (ebook)
Subjects: LCSH: Flowers, Virgil (Fictitious character)—Fiction. | Cold cases
(Criminal investigation)—Fiction. | BISAC: FICTION / Crime. | FICTION
/ Suspense. | FICTION / Thrillers. | GSAFD: Suspense fiction. |
Mystery fiction.
Classification: LCC PS3569.A516 D44 2017 | DDC 813/.54—dc23
LC record available at https://lccn.loc.gov/2017025620

First G. P. Putnam's Sons hardcover edition / October 2017
First G. P. Putnam's Sons premium edition / September 2018
G. P. Putnam's Sons premium edition ISBN: 9780399573781

Printed in the United States of America
1 3 5 7 9 10 8 6 4 2

DEEP
FREEZE

ONE

David Birkmann sat in his living room with an empty beer can in his hand and stared sadly at his oversized bachelor's television, which wasn't turned on. A light winter wind was blowing a soft, lovely snow into the storm windows. He needed to get out in the morning to plow the drive. But he wasn't thinking about that, or the winter, or the storm.

He'd gotten away with it, he thought. That didn't make him much happier.

David—he thought of himself as *David* rather than as Big Dave, Daveareeno, Daveissimo, D-Man, Chips, or Bug Boy—didn't consider himself a killer. Not a real killer.

He was simply accident-prone. Always had been.

Accidents were one reason he'd been elected as Class of '92 Funniest Boy, like the totally unfunny time when he hadn't gotten the corn chips out of the vending machine in the school's junk-food niche. He'd tried to shake the bag loose and the machine had tipped over on him, pinning him to the cold ceramic tiles of Trippton High School.

Everybody who'd seen it had laughed—the fat boy

pinned like a spider under a can of peas—even before they were sure he wasn't injured.

Even George Marx, the assistant principal in charge of discipline, had laughed. He had, nevertheless, given David fifteen days of detention, plus the additional unwanted nickname of Chips, a nickname that had hung on like a bad stink for twenty-five years.

His own father had laughed after he found out that Trippton High School wouldn't make him pay for the damage to the vending machine.

Big Dave, Daveareeno, Daveissimo, D-Man . . . Bug Boy . . . Squashed like a bug.

The latest accident had occurred that night, though David thought it was all perfectly explainable if you understood the history and the overall situation. He knew that the cops wouldn't buy it.

The history:

First, his father was the Bug Man of Trippton, the leading pest exterminator in Buchanan County. For nine months of the year, the brightly colored Bug Man vans were seen everywhere you'd find a bug. For the other three months, in the heart of winter, even the bugs took time off.

David had never been the most popular kid in school and, because of his father's rep, had been told to *Bug off* or *Bug out* when he tried to hang with the popular kids, even in elementary school. That'd become a tired thirteen-year-long joke in the trek between kindergarten and twelfth grade. He'd always laughed about it, trying to ingratiate himself with the Populars.

He wasn't laughing now.

Because, second, Birkmann had fallen in love with Gina Hemming during the summer after sixth grade, when the first freshet of testosterone hit. He'd loved her all through school—and, for that matter, his entire life. How, he wondered, could that love have put him here, empty beer can in his hand, a hole in his heart?

Hemming had been one of the Populars—too smart and arrogant to be the *most* popular, but right up there, with her gold locket, cashmere sweaters, and low-rise fashion jeans. She had a silver ring, with a pearl, in her navel. Her father owned the largest bank in Trippton, which placed her in the local aristocracy.

She was pretty, if not the prettiest; she had a great body, if not the greatest; and she was one of two National Merit Scholars in her class, selected 1992's Girl Most Likely to Succeed. People expected great things from her, but, in the way of many small-town girls, the great things hadn't quite come true.

After college, at St. Catherine's in St. Paul, she'd gone to work in Washington, D.C., as an aide to a Minnesota congressman. There, she learned that being the heiress of Trippton's richest banker didn't cut a whole lot of ice in the nation's capital. Plus, in Washington, she was only in the top twenty percent of pretty, and maybe—just maybe—the top twenty-five percent of good bodies. Those clipboard-carrying aides tended to spend time in the gym, and when that didn't work, on the operating table, getting enhanced.

After two years in Washington, she'd moved to New York, as an editorial assistant at HarperCollins, and she needed a solid input of Daddy's money to rent a barely livable apartment on the Upper West Side. One day, she was assaulted on a subway to work, or at least that was the way she thought of it, though the guy had only pushed her, probably accidentally.

Five years after graduation from college, she'd been back in Trippton, working at Daddy's bank. Two years later, she married the scion of the Trippton real estate dynasty, such as it was, in a beautiful, eight bridesmaids ceremony at Trippton National Golf Club, to which David hadn't been invited.

With her good marriage, her father's support, her Washington line of bullshit, and her New York hairstyle, she'd advanced quickly enough, from loan officer to vice president, and then to president. When Daddy choked to death on an overcooked slab of roast beef, she got, at age thirty-seven, the whole enchilada.

And at forty-two, had filed for divorce, for reasons not disclosed in the Trippton *Republican-River*. Rumor had it that the real estate guy, Justin Rhodes, had taken to wearing nylons and referring to himself as Justine. That would be fine in Washington, New York, or L.A., but not so good in Trippton. There were no children.

There she was, David's first and truest love.

Available.

What did he love about her? Everything. He loved to watch her walk. He loved to hear her talk, he loved to hear her laugh. He loved the brains and the self-confidence . . . the whole . . . gestalt.

David's own divorce had taken place two years earlier. His ex had promptly moved to Dallas—or maybe

San Antonio, he got them confused—with her lover, to start over with a fresh Dunkin' Donuts franchise. She hadn't asked for alimony, only that David purchase her adulterous lover's local Dunkin' Donuts store. David had sold off the land on the old family farm, which he'd rented out anyway, to get the two hundred and fifty thousand dollars he needed.

His ex had taken the cashier's check at a joint meeting with their attorneys, clipped it into her purse, and snarled, "I never even *liked* you, Bug Boy." Then she'd looked around the faux-walnut paneling in the law office conference room and asked, "How'd I ever get stuck in this freezin' fuckin' mudhole? I must've been out of my goddamn mind."

While all that was going on, David had inherited the Bug Man business from his father, who'd died of several different kinds of cancer. During most of his career, the old man had considered chlordane, which even smelled kinda good, to be the answer to a bug man's prayers. Turned out, it wasn't. Turned out it was a multi-faceted carcinogen.

After his father's death, David bought out a rival business that had employees trained in the elimination of pest animals—rats, skunks, and squirrels, mostly, and the occasional raccoon—and had changed the company name to GetOut!

At forty-two, he was the undisputed pest elimination king of Trippton, as well as the owner of the only local Dunkin' Donuts. There were some in town who considered that a salubrious combination. Others were not so sure—or, at least, they hoped he frequently washed his hands.

And he was still the Bug Boy.

All of that had set up the situation that left David crying in front of a blank-screen TV.

Gina Hemming, the rich, arrogant, divorced chairwoman of the board and president of the Second National Bank and the Class of '92's Girl Most Likely to Succeed, and David Birkmann, the financially okay divorced owner of GetOut! and the Main Street donut shop and the Class of '92's Funniest Boy.

On that cold Thursday night in January, they met at Gina's house with a group of Populars from the Class of '92, including the class president, the Homecoming King and Queen, the Boy and Girl Most Likely to Succeed, the Most Athletic Boy and Girl, and the Funniest Boy and Girl. A few of the most popular kids had left Trippton and never returned. They'd been invited to the meeting but had unanimously declined.

The group that met Thursday night was to begin working out the mechanisms of the upcoming Twenty-fifth Reunion of the Trippton High School Class of '92 ("Go Otters").

One of the committee members, Ryan Harney, a physician, had looked at the faces gathered in Hemming's living room and said, "Man—the more things change, the more they stay the same, huh?" whatever that meant, and later said, "Isn't it weird that we're all still here after twenty-five years?"

Nobody seemed to know what that meant, either. Where else would they be?

The committee sorted through the usual bullshit and passed out assignments: Lucy Cheever, Homecoming Queen, now owner of the Chevrolet dealership, agreed to have her computer assistant track down members of the class to get addresses, emails, and cell phone numbers; Gina would arrange to get the tent at Trippton National Golf Club for the big second-evening reunion; George Brown, the Most Athletic Boy, now owner of the bowling alley, would provide dancing and free beer at the alley on the first Fun Meet-Up night; Birkmann was friendly with the leader of the Dog Butt dance band, which, as June Moon, played softer, more romantic music, and agreed to pick up the cost of the band for both nights. Somebody else agreed to collect home movies and convert them to videos for the Fun Meet-Up. And so on.

Around eight-thirty, the committee members started drifting away. Ten o'clock was bedtime in Trippton, if you wanted to get a good start on the next day. Birkmann, though, had other plans.

He'd gotten ready for the night by dressing casually but carefully: tan Dockers slacks, high-polished cordovan penny loafers, a button-down checked shirt and green boat-neck sweater, both of the latter from Nordstrom Rack up at the Mall of America.

As he was leaving the house, he'd picked up his regular red company hat but noticed that it had gotten brushed with something black and sticky; no matter, he had a box of them in a variety of colors. He picked a yellow GetOut! baseball cap sprinkled with black dots that, when you looked closely, were deer ticks. Not everybody liked them, but David thought they were cool. And the yellow coordinated nicely with the green sweater and tan Dockers.

Anyway, he'd been looking good; casual but businesslike. When everybody but three committee members had gone, David had gotten his coat and slipped into Hemming's kitchen and out the back door. His van was parked in the street, with a layer of snow on the windshield.

He had stashed a bottle of Barefoot Bubbly Brut Cuvée in his van and it was now nice and cold. He'd watched the last three members depart, all in a group, saying good-bye to Hemming at the front door. When the last one was gone, he'd hustled back up the driveway and in the back door, the bottle of champagne in his hand.

He'd had something casual and sophisticated in mind. But it had all gone bad.

Cut to the action:

"Get away from me, you fat fuck!" Hemming screamed. She was wearing a burgundy-colored jacket and skirt, with a pale pink blouse and high heels. "You're disgusting . . . you . . . fuckin' . . . Bug Boy!"

Hemming wasn't satisfied with humiliating him, screaming at him and calling him the hated name, she had to go one step further. He'd spread his arms, embarrassed enough, trying to quiet her, and she'd stepped right up to him and slapped him on the side of the head, raking him with her fingernails. Really put some weight behind it.

Stunned, he'd swung back . . . not really thinking.

He'd swung with the hand that held the bottle. In the movies, if you hit somebody with a bottle of wine, the bottle broke and the person went down and a moment later got up, maybe with a little trickle of blood at the corner of his mouth.

When he'd hit Hemming, the bottle went *CLUNK!* as though he'd hit her with a pipe. The bottle hadn't broken. Hadn't even cracked. Hemming dropped like a head-shot deer.

For the next couple of minutes, there was a lot of calling her name, pleading, and shaking—"Gina, come on, I didn't mean it, get up. Come on, Gina, get up"—but the fact was, Gina Hemming was deader than the aforesaid deer, looking up at him with half-open blank gray eyes. Gina wouldn't be coming back until she marched in with Jesus and all the saints.

Birkmann hadn't really thought about what to do next, since it was all unplanned. He stared at her for a while, lying crumbled on the floor, then said, "Oh my God!" He thought about calling for an ambulance, but that would get him put in jail.

He already knew he didn't want to go to jail—didn't deserve it. She'd started the fight, had struck out at him. He'd not even swung the bottle, not really. He'd tried to block another blow, he thought, and the bottle sort of bumped her.

Deep in his heart, though, he knew he'd killed her.

He stood there and thought about it, turned, looking around the room, noticed the blond wooden railing of the stairway coming down from the second floor.

She'd tripped and fallen, he decided.

He swallowed back his nausea, pulled her body over to the bottom of the stairs, spent a moment arranging it. When he'd hit her, he'd literally knocked her out of her high heels. He picked them up—stylish tan pumps—carried one halfway up the stairs, left it on a step, put the other one halfway back on one of her feet.

Got close enough to notice that she still smelled good. He started to cry, tears running helplessly and hopelessly down his cheeks. He brushed them off with the sleeve of the green sweater, but, gasping with grief and fear and loathing, thought, *What else?*

Nothing else. Nothing more he could do. Wait: fingerprints on the back door . . .

Two minutes later, he was out the back door again, having carefully wiped the doorknob with a paper towel from the kitchen. He walked out to the van, settled into the seat, ran his hand through his hair . . . and it came away sticky with blood.

She'd cut him when she hit him, raked him with her fingernails. He still had the paper towel in his hand and he used it to wipe his hair. More blood, but drying. He again ran his fingers through his hair, found the cuts, two of them, a quarter inch apart. Raw and stinging now, but not bleeding much.

Because of his jobs, he kept a bottle of alcohol-based

hand sanitizer in the door pocket. He squirted some of it on the paper towel and used it to clean up his hair as best he could. When he was done, he touched the cuts again and came back with faint specks of red on his fingertips. Done bleeding, he thought.

A car went by, and he turned his face away from the headlights.

In another minute, he was driving out Maple, his mind churning. David knew his *CSI* shows: if the cops brought in somebody to check for DNA, they'd find his all over the place. And why not? He'd been at the meeting. He'd hugged Gina when he arrived. Well, he hadn't, actually, but others had, and nobody would have noticed that he hadn't. He was cool on the DNA.

At the intersection of Maple and Main, he stopped and looked both ways. To the south he saw the glittery lights of Club Gold. He almost froze at that point; almost fled home, to bury his . . . what? Angst?

He didn't do that. He touched his hair again and this time his fingertips came back clean. After a moment, he drove down to Club Gold, parked in back, and walked over to the back door. The men's room was there, and he went inside. He looked at his hair in the mirror. The cuts were invisible. He peed, zipped up, turned on the sink water, and waited.

None of it was thought out. He was acting purely on instinct. And from information gleaned from the *CSI* shows.

He waited some more and, after two or three minutes, heard cowboy boots coming down the hall. Here came a witness. He punched the soap dispenser and began washing his hands. Five seconds later, a guy named

Cary Lowe bumped through the door, said, "Hey, Big Dave, how they hangin'?" and eased up to the urinal.

"Free and easy," Birkmann said, as he rinsed his hands and dried them beneath the hot-air blower.

As Lowe continued to pee, he asked, over the roar of the blower, "You singin' tonight?"

"Does the Pope shit in the woods?"

"Good luck, then," Lowe said. "You do have the voice, my man."

Karaoke every Thursday and Saturday night at Club Gold. Karaoke and a gold-plated alibi.

Birkmann finished drying his hands, pushed out into the hallway, hung his parka on a coat peg, and ambled out to the main room. He got a beer, signed up to sing. Twenty minutes later, Bob Hart said, "You've seen him before, you've heard him before, you've loved him before. You know what's coming up now, folks. Here's Big D—Daveareeno, Daveissimo, the Bug Boy—with Roy Orbison's 'Pretty Woman.'"

David did a decent "Pretty Woman" and got a respectable round of applause from the . . . witnesses . . . and when he got off the stage went and had another beer or two. And he talked to lots of people. Because *everybody* knew Bug Boy.

He went home, sobbing against the steering wheel of his van. And at one o'clock in the morning, with a storm coming in, he sat in the living room armchair and drank a last beer of the night, staring at the blank screen of the television.

Right into those dead gray eyes.

Dead. Gray. Eyes.

TWO

Ben Potter was an old guy, unshaven half the time, smelling of fried eggs and something fishy— sardines? He occasionally walked around with his fly unzipped, mumbling to himself. His eyes were too pale, wandering and watery, half buried in the flesh of his eyelids. He was always heavily bundled up against the winter cold, a tanker cap askew on his head, fleece earflaps hanging loose. He'd inherited the cap from his older brother, now dead, who'd gotten it the ugly way, in Korea, during the war.

Potter was pushing eighty but got around all right on his two artificial hips. People paid no attention to him, except to say, "Hey, Ben," or, "Mr. Potter, how's things?"

Nobody really wanted to hear how things were.

Potter didn't have many years left, and he'd spend them alone.

On Saturday afternoon, Potter collected his fishing gear and headed out to the sewage plant. The plant was on the river south of Trippton, and he'd been told any number of times that the water coming out of the effluent canal was clean enough to drink.

He was willing to believe that insofar as catfishing was concerned. He stopped at the Piggly Wiggly for a tub of chicken livers to use as bait and drove out to the plant.

There'd been a heavy snowstorm on Thursday night, followed by light but persistent snow all day Friday and Saturday morning. The sewage plant's parking lot had been plowed clean, as he'd hoped, and he parked near the gate. He got his gear out of the back of the truck, pulled on his Sorels, his insulated overalls, and a parka. Years before, he'd epoxied a cheap thermometer to the back hatch of his camper. He peered at it now: five degrees above zero. He went back into the truck, found a face mask, and stuck it in his pocket in case it got *really* cold.

Headed downriver, a tough trek for an old guy, carrying poles with one hand and a plastic fishing bucket with a tackle box inside it with the other.

There was normally a walked-in path through the snow, but he was breaking trail now. He could see where the path was but not the individual ruts and rocks that littered it. He nearly fell twice, which he wanted to avoid at his age because getting back up was so difficult. He took fifteen minutes to make the four hundred yards down to where the warm effluent stream cut into the river's ice, leaving an oblong pool of open, steaming water.

Potter was by himself. Too cold for fair-weather fishermen. Workers at the local tree service, who liked to fish, had set up a dozen cutoff cottonwood stumps around the outflow as chairs. Potter brushed the snow off one of them and sat down to bait his hooks.

That's when he noticed the burgundy-colored cloth

floating slowly in a wide circle around in the open water. The cloth caught the eye because . . . it was the size and shape of a body.

A body?

He kept looking, but the shape was partly submerged, and what he could see was mostly bumps of fabric, now pink against the black water.

Was that a *sleeve*?

Potter watched for a minute, then looked around. No help nearby. He hadn't expected any, but he had looked anyway.

A body?

He swallowed once or twice, opened his tackle box, and found a treble-hooked bucktail. He clipped it on, hands trembling with cold and foreboding, cast and watched the bucktail fall in the open water on the other side of whatever it was. He reeled in the lure carefully until the bucktail hit the floating fabric. He set the hook and towed the thing over to his shore. There was weight to it. A lot of weight.

The closer it got, the more it looked like a body.

He got it right up to the narrow rim of ice around the open area, reached out with a bare hand, caught a bare foot, and dragged the body up on the rim of ice.

"Oh, jeez," he muttered. He was afraid, literally shaking in his boots, his hands trembling so violently that he dropped his fishing rod. He rolled the body over to look at the face.

His hook had gone into the woman's cheek, a couple inches below her eye. He didn't try to remove it. He simply gawked . . .

Then, "Gina Hemming? Gina Hemming?"

Horrified, he turned and shouted into the winter's silence, "Help! Help me!"

No response. There wouldn't be one, he knew. He stepped away from the body, couldn't help looking back, and looking again, and again, as he broke into a slow, stumbling old man's run back to the sewage plant . . .

THREE

Virgil Flowers sat uncomfortably hunched over in a camouflaged blind on the banks of the frozen Mississippi, roughly a hundred miles, as the crow flies, north of the Trippton sewage plant. He was wrapped from his chest to his stocking feet in a heavyweight sleeping bag, the lens of his Nikon D810 digital camera peeking out through the blind's front screen. His boots sat next to him, stuffed with air-activated hand warmers.

Light snow drifted over the riverscape fronting the tent, while to his left, a few hundred yards away, the Prairie Island Nuclear Power Plant pumped huge volumes of steam into the bitterly cold winter air. Virgil wasn't sure whether the snow was natural or condensed from the steam.

He'd been in the blind for two hours, and though he was wearing a parka, his lack of movement let the January chill seep into his shoulders and down his spine. He'd brought the sleeping bag to deal with that problem, and when he'd begun to lose feeling in his butt, he'd taken off his boots and pulled on the bag. Overhead, his breath was condensing into ice crystals on the inside of the tent.

Virgil was a tall man, thin, with country singer blond hair and cool blue eyes. An agent for the Minnesota Bureau of Criminal Apprehension, he was in the final two days of a weeklong winter vacation, which he was using in an effort to get photos of an owl.

As a part-time outdoor writer, Virgil liked all the Minnesota seasons; the best months were the lush August days and the brilliant blue days of February. There was hunting in the fall and spring, fishing almost year-round, and he liked to walk, to simply get out and look at the place he lived.

A birder friend had mentioned seeing a great horned owl fishing over the open water south of the nuclear plant, which they weren't supposed to do. Great horned owls ate rabbits, not fish. The birder said the owl had been around since a big cold front had come through in mid-December, fishing the whole time.

Virgil wasn't that much of an owl fancier, but he'd made some inquiries, and *Wing & Talon*, a magazine focused on raptors, had guaranteed a thousand dollars for good photos of a great horned owl taking a fish, with a short accompanying article.

At three o'clock on this sunny afternoon, Virgil still had good light, but it'd be fading quickly over the next hour and a half. He wanted to be out of the blind before sunset, which came at 4:48. Despite an air temperature of minus three degrees, the river in front of him was open, with wisps of steam rising up like cartoon ghosts. The heat came from the nuclear plant's cooling towers, which used cold water to keep the nuke from turning into a fiery hell pit of radiation and doom. From the cooling towers, the warm water flowed through canals and a couple of ponds and into the river.

Virgil's girlfriend, Frankie, had said, "You'll come back with your balls glowing in the dark."

"Wrong, ignorant farm girl," Virgil said. "The cooling water doesn't touch the radioactive part. You could drink it."

"You know that for sure?"

"Yeah, I looked it up," Virgil said. They were taking down the Christmas tree, packing the glass ornaments into boxes of Styrofoam peanuts. "Besides, if my balls did glow in the dark, I'd have some light when I get up at night to pee."

"Or, even better," she said, "you could lead Santa's sleigh if something happened to Rudolph."

She was not only an ignorant farm girl but a wiseass.

Virgil's great horned target had taken up residence in a nearby oak: Virgil could see its hulk as a dark oval through the bare branches. The day before, he'd seen it swoop down over the water twice but hadn't yet gotten a good shot, hadn't yet seen it nail a fish. The problem was, the owl didn't hunt during bright daylight hours, except for the couple of hours before sundown and the hour or so after daybreak.

To shoot at those times, he used a Nikon 400mm f2.8, paid for by the good citizens of Minnesota who'd bought it in the belief that he would use its lens to apprehend the criminal element. The lens cost something like twelve thousand dollars. Should it roll down the riverbank into the Mississippi, he'd be looking at a major hole in his retirement plan.

So here he was, sitting in a camo tent, eating cheese-and-peanut-butter crackers, a prefocused, bazooka-like camera lens mounted on a tripod. He hadn't gotten the owl yet, but he'd gotten several dozen photos of other forms of wildlife—foxes, minks, otters, bald eagles—all pulled in by the warmth of the open water and the fish roiling the shallows near the shore.

He had gotten one great sequence of two coyotes hunting mice, or maybe voles, in the snow-bent wild grass at the top of the bank. The coyotes would move silently across the snowfield, noses down, ears up, listening for movement under the snow. When they heard something, they'd rear up and come down on the mouse or vole with both feet, pinning the unfortunate rodent to the ground.

Best shot: the larger of the two coyotes passing a mouse off to the other one. Mates? Sisters? Couldn't tell. Great sequence, but great coyote sequences were a dime a dozen, as were great bald eagle shots. Dozens of bald eagles hunted the open water during the winter, and he could easily fill up a memory card with shots.

Virgil was looking at the Safari browser on his iPhone when the owl made its first move of the day. Virgil caught the movement out of the corner of his eye, went to the camera's viewfinder, picked up the bird, and turned the lens with the bird's flight and hit the trigger, which fired an automatic sequence of shots, and *BANG!*

Nothing.

The bird's talons had touched the water but come up fishless. The owl flapped its great silent wings a couple of times and returned to its perch onshore.

"Get a fish, you incompetent motherfucker," Virgil muttered. The owl sat on the branch, its head swiveling as though on ball bearings, then cocking sideways.

Virgil, under his breath: "Go, go, go . . ."

The bird made a small downward movement, as though cocking itself, and dropped back toward the water, and *BANG!* This time, it came up with a flapping fish, probably a small white sucker. Virgil shot thirty frames, starting from the owl's launching point, to the water, and back. He burned up a few more frames of the bird tearing the fish apart, sat back, and chimped the results.

Not bad, he thought, as he flipped through the images on the camera's LCD screen. In fact, excellent. One thousand American dollars, unless the good folks at *Wing & Talon* had been shining him on.

Back at his truck, he put the folded blind away and the lens back in its case, pulled his iPad out of the backseat and transferred the photos. He also kept them on the memory card as a backup and, when he got home, would move them to the Cloud as even further insurance.

He started the truck and was backing out to the road when the phone burped. Frankie wouldn't be calling, because he'd asked her not to call between three o'clock and sundown when a call could disturb the owl. He picked up the phone and looked at the screen: Jon Duncan, his nominal boss at the BCA. He was on vacation, so the call could be social. Maybe. Okay, maybe not.

"What's up?" Virgil asked.

"Man, I know you're on vacation—"

"No, no, no! Get somebody else."

"It's down in Trippton, your old stomping grounds. I've got to ask you to take a look. Do this for me, take the rest of your vacation when it's done," Duncan said. "The big boss says nobody will check if you take a bunch of undertime on top of your vacation."

"Undertime" was a concept widely used in state government: it was like overtime, but instead of working more, you worked less, while still getting paid. The real artists took undertime while on the clock for overtime, thus getting time-and-a-half for not working.

"How much undertime?" Virgil asked.

"However much you want . . . that isn't outright theft."

"I gotta talk to Frankie. We were going out tonight."

"Go out," Duncan said. "There's no point of getting down there before tomorrow morning anyway. Since tomorrow's a Sunday, you probably don't even have to get there early."

"Gimme the short version," Virgil said.

"Short version: forty-two-year-old almost-divorced female bank president disappears Thursday night and is dumped in the Mississippi, only to emerge as a block of ice this afternoon."

"How'd she emerge?" Virgil asked. "The river's frozen solid all the way down to Iowa."

"A sewage plant effluent stream creates open water a couple miles south of Trippton. Some guy was out there fishing when she floated by."

"That's disgusting."

"Yeah, I'm told it wasn't exactly pleasant."

"I meant fishing in the effluent stream," Virgil said. "Do they know what killed her? Shot, or drowned, or what?"

"The ME has her in Rochester; he says she died of a fractured skull. He finished the autopsy about ten minutes ago. Wasn't an accident, wasn't a fall or anything. She was wearing a burgundy-colored dress and was barefoot. The sheriff said that when she was last seen in that dress, Thursday night, she was wearing high heels. She wasn't walking around on river ice in four-inch heels and a Donna Karan jacket."

"All right," Virgil said. "If Frankie gets pissed, I'm gonna blame it on you."

"That's one of the fardels I must bear," Duncan said.

"What?"

"You must not be familiar with *Hamlet*," Duncan said. "You know, by Shakespeare."

"Oh, that one," Virgil said.

"Yeah. One of my ancestors is in *Macbeth*."

"I'll buy a copy, maybe you can autograph it for me," Virgil said. "I'll call you back tomorrow night about the banker lady."

"Virgil, I owe you."

"You keep saying that, but you never pay off."

"That's one of *your* fardels," Duncan said.

Virgil was two hours from home. He called and spent some time talking to Frankie about nothing in particular but including a ten-minute rumination about her sister's sexual misadventures at the University of Minnesota, which seemed designed to gain her a tenured teaching position. "Absolutely disgusting," Frankie said. "I sometimes can't believe that Sparkle and I are even related . . ."

"It's absolutely awful," Virgil said. When he got off the phone, he brought up a country music station and fantasized about a Frankie-Sparkle-Virgil sandwich, which should have made him ashamed of himself but didn't.

Virgil and Frankie spent Saturday evening at the Cine Grand Mankato watching *Hacksaw Ridge*, then went over to the Rooster Coop for a couple of beers and to chat with people they knew. Between the two of them, that included half the patrons in the place, including three out-and-out barflies and an out-of-tune Eagles cover band.

Frankie was a short, good-looking woman with pale blue eyes and blond hair, which she wore in a fat, Swedish-style single braid. She was once a smart redneck but was now the smart owner of an architectural salvage business, which meant she bought and tore down old houses that had good wood or salable fixtures in them. She also operated a small farm outside Mankato, mostly growing alfalfa.

She had recently bought, for three thousand dollars, in a dying prairie town, an abandoned mansion that had once belonged to a rich quarry owner.

The place was filled with black walnut floors and oak beams, which by themselves would have had her only breaking even on the three grand after paying her employees. The real find had been the library, where all the wood was straight, dry, turn-of-the-twentieth-century Brazilian rosewood, for which she would net an additional thirty thousand dollars from a musical instrument maker.

"You don't feel bad about screwing the former owner?" Virgil had asked when he heard about the thirty grand.

"The former owner was a Kansas City hedge funder who wanted to get rid of the house and outbuildings so he could plow over another four acres. Would have cost him ten thousand to get a wrecking contractor to tear the place down—instead, they *make* three thousand."

"Then screw 'em," Virgil said.

F rankie had a complicated history, which at times had involved minor crime, and which included five children, all boys. The oldest worked as a partner in her salvage business, while the next oldest cheerfully drifted around the United States in a series of casual jobs, good training for what he wanted to ultimately become: an author. He and Virgil talked writing whenever he was in town.

The other three boys still lived at home. The third son, a senior in high school, was in charge of the other two when Frankie spent the night at Virgil's place.

After an hour at the Rooster Coop, they went back to Virgil's, fooled around until midnight, then let Honus the Dog back into the bedroom. Honus had been deeply insulted by his temporary exclusion from the room, but he was a good-natured yellow dog of indefinite breed and gave them both a nose and assumed his spot at the bottom center of the bed.

*   *   *

At breakfast the next morning, Frankie asked, "Have you ever been to Trippton when you weren't towing your boat?"

"Didn't think about that, but I don't believe I have," Virgil said. "It's not the most inviting place in winter. In fact, it's butt ugly."

"Well, say hello to Johnson Johnson for me," Frankie said. "No point in telling you to stay away from him."

"Hey . . ."

"I know, I know, old college buds and all. But the guy ought to be declared a federal disaster area."

That was true, so Virgil changed the subject. "I've got to get going. Could be gone a few days, and it's colder than hell," he said. They both looked out the kitchen window at the snowfields around the house. "Gonna have to take the big bag."

"Any chance this is more than a one-time deal?" she asked. "The murder?"

"No idea."

"Then take your shotgun, too," she said. "I'll clean up the dishes while you pack, and I'll walk Honus out at the farm. I'll check the house every day you're gone."

"Good deal."

Virgil wrote checks for a few routine bills, put stamps on the envelopes, sent JPEGs of the owl photos to *Wing & Talon*, packed his cold-weather gear into a duffel bag, pulled on insulated hiking boots, and made sure he had two pairs of gloves, one for driving and one for outside. Watching the gear going into the big bag depressed Honus, who slunk away to sit next to Frankie.

When Virgil went back to the kitchen carrying the bag, he found a red-eyed Frankie sitting at the table, the dishes not done, a short stack of papers by one hand. She looked up, and he asked, "What?"

"You left your insurance papers on the sink . . . I wasn't snooping," she said.

"Yeah?"

"Well, I'm down as the beneficiary," she said. "And if we're both killed at the same time, my kids get it . . ."

"Yeah?"

"Stop saying 'Yeah?' Made me cry a little bit," Frankie said.

"I got nobody else who I'd want it to go to," Virgil said. "Just you and the kids."

She sighed and said, "You know, Virgil, sometimes we don't talk enough. I gotta tell you, I'd be totally up for another kid. Especially if it was a girl."

Virgil sat down because he needed to.

She said, "We don't have to talk about it now, but so you know: you'd be like the first-best dad in the world. You already sorta are."

Virgil said, "Ah, boy."

FOUR

With all that, and the fallout, Virgil left late for Trippton.

On the way, he called the medical examiner at the Mayo in Rochester to tell him that he'd be a bit later than he thought. The ME told him not to worry about it, he wasn't doing much anyway, just another murder.

With frequent snow-covered stretches on the highways, and a stop to get coffee, Virgil took an hour and a half to make the trip. Once in town, he found a parking space in a city parking structure, walked through the Skyway, and then the Subway, to the Mayo.

Since it was a Sunday, there were few people around. The medical examiner, Peter Thurston, said he'd be waiting in the cafeteria. Virgil had worked with him a number of times and had found him a congenial sort, good at his job. Thurston was sitting at a table, reading the *New York Times*. Virgil gave him a wave and continued on to the food line, where he got a piece of pumpkin pie and a Diet Coke and carried it over to Thurston's table.

Thurston was a small, dark-haired man with a sleepy look about his heavy-lidded eyes. Virgil said, "I hope this isn't too much trouble," as he sat down with his pie. "Being Sunday."

"I'll tell you what's too much trouble," Thurston said, folding the paper and pushing it aside. "Falling in love. Coming in for an hour on Sunday afternoon? No problem. Falling in love? Big problem. I was a perfectly content single guy, with a six handicap golf habit, and along came Buttercup."

"That can't be her name," Virgil said.

"No, it can't. Her name is Laurie, and she's a crazy vegetarian, yoga practitioner, feminist bitch lawyer. Unfortunately, I fell in love with her."

"When did all this come up?"

"Two or three months ago," Thurston said. "It seems like it's been forever. Like I've known her forever."

"I'm familiar with the feeling," Virgil said. "Been there myself a few times."

"A few times? Did you love them or was it the sex?" Thurston asked.

"Oh, I loved them," Virgil said. "I even married them."

Thurston thought about that for a moment, then asked, "Then what?"

"After a while, we got divorced," Virgil said. "The first divorce was bad, took some time to get over that one. The third only took about six weeks to get over."

"Three divorces?" Thurston was impressed.

"Yeah, I was . . . unsettled," Virgil said.

Made Thurston laugh. "All right. Finish your pie and let's go look at Miz Hemming."

*　　*　　*

Virgil had seen people shot, stabbed, burned, drowned, beaten to death, blown up, run over with cars, and eaten by a tiger. When Thurston rolled Hemming out of the cooler, she looked almost uninjured, if you could ignore the various dismemberments done during the autopsy. Thurston had put her roughly back together, leaving the rest for the funeral home.

Even with the autopsy work, when Virgil looked closely he could see that her head was no longer symmetrical. She wasn't bloated, like most floaters: in fact, she seemed to have shrunken, and she was pale as a piece of printer paper, except that her lips, eyelids, and the tops of her ears were a distinct blue. She showed one wound, in her cheek, but that was small and bloodless. Her breasts were flattened, her nipples so pale that they merged with the skin around them. She had almost no pubic hair.

"Death was very quick—effectively, instantaneous," Thurston said. "She was struck on the left side of her head, at her temple, and almost certainly from the front, so it's better than fifty-fifty that the killer was right-handed. She was struck with something curved and heavy—I'd say there's a good chance that it was a large, full bottle. A bowling ball or a bowling pin could have done the same kind of damage, but you usually don't get people being smacked in the head with a bowling ball or pin. Whatever it was, it was larger in diameter than a baseball bat."

"What's the cut on her face?"

"Oh, yeah. The guy who saw the body floating in the river was a fisherman; he hooked her with a treble hook and pulled her in. The cops cut the lure off but left the hook. I took it off to see if there was any other, earlier defect beneath it. There wasn't. All the damage was done by the hook."

"Is there any way to tell how long she was dead before she was dumped?" Virgil asked.

"I can't tell you exactly how long, but it was *some* time. The river water is cold, in the thirties . . . colder than a typical refrigerator. She showed substantial gravity-based internal bleeding toward her left side, which suggests that she was lying on that side for quite some time. Then the river water hit, and when she got cold enough, the bleeding would have stopped. I can't say four hours, as opposed to two—that would depend on how the body was handled—but I can say it was *some* time."

"Okay . . ."

He gestured toward Hemming's chest and stomach, which had been opened with a Y-shaped incision. "The other thing is, she'd eaten quite a lot of cheese, which she may have liked but apparently didn't agree with her. Prior to death, she'd already begun to develop intestinal gas, and that process continued after death, although it would have stopped when the body got cold enough. The cold also created some rigidity in her sphincter muscles, so she didn't pass that gas until we opened her up."

"Is there a point here?" Virgil asked.

"Yes. It was probably that gas that kept her afloat enough to wind up on top of the water at the sewage plant. If it weren't for that, she would have been at the bottom of the river."

"Okay."

Not much help there. Another man came through the door, a heavyset guy wearing a ski hat, an open parka, and a fulsome neck beard. "Sorry I'm late," he said.

Thurston said to Virgil, "Karl is our death investigator. He can give you some information on her clothing
and the recovery of the body and so on . . ."

Virgil shook hands with Karl Lone, who asked Thurston, "You tell him about the bruises?"

"Getting there," Thurston said. He took a yellow
pencil from his jacket pocket and used it as a pointer. "If
you look here, you can see that she had bruises at her
wrists . . ." He pointed to them. "And at her ankles." He
pointed again. The bruises were faint but distinct, once
you saw them, and circled her wrists and ankles like
bracelets. "She also had light striped bruising on her buttocks. They happened some time before her death—days
before, maybe a week before. Not hours. We can roll her,
and you can look at the bruises if you want . . ."

"No, no," Virgil said hastily. "I believe you. Are they
relevant?"

"It's possible that they're from B and D," Lone said.
"Bondage and discipline. She was possibly tied up and
spanked."

Virgil looked at Thurston: "Really?"

"It's the best explanation," Thurston said. "*You* can
decide if it's relevant. Some sex play may have gone too
far . . ."

"Not sex play if you whack somebody hard enough to
break her skull," Virgil said.

"But sex, alcohol, a taste for violence, a quarrel . . .
somebody brings a bottle over expecting to get laid, she
tells him to take a hike, they argue, and *WHACK!*"

"Okay," Virgil said. "It's a possibility."

Lone stepped up: "The doc won't tell you this, because he's a conservative medical doctor who's careful

about what he says, but I'll tell you what—I've seen a couple people killed by B and D during my career, and I don't know if her . . . sex partner . . . killed her, but I know B and D bruises when I see them. That's what we're looking at."

Virgil turned back to Thurston again, who said, "Umm."

Thurston said, "Possibly more relevant to your investigation . . . look closely at the fingernails of her right hand. The nails on her ring and middle fingers are cracked and slightly ripped, and that happened at the time of death or slightly before."

"How can you tell?"

"I don't want to sound too definite about that, to tell the truth, but it's what I think," Thurston said. "There was some instantaneous bleeding behind the nails at the time of the trauma, but the bleeding quickly stopped."

"Why wasn't this washed away when she was in the water?" Virgil asked.

"The blood we see is down behind the nails, which sealed up the broken blood vessels."

"And that's relevant . . . how?" Virgil asked.

"It looks to me—*possibly*—that she struck her killer with her hand and raked him with her nails. She has well-cared-for nails, and they're quite long. There was no tissue of any kind beneath the tips, but that easily could have been washed away in the water because it wasn't sealed beneath the nails."

"You're saying that the killer could have scratches," Virgil said.

"Scratches, or even nasty cuts, because she hit him hard. Now, it's also possible that she damaged her nails

some other way before she was killed, but in my experience a woman like this isn't going to walk around with
two ragged hangnails. They'll clip them, or use an emery
board to clean them up—and right away. I think the
damage happened in a fight at the time of her death."

Overall, Virgil spent an hour in Rochester, talking to
Thurston and Lone, but didn't get much more that would
help with his investigation. Hemming's body showed no
signs of a pre-death struggle, other than the nails: no fresh
cuts or bruises on the body, except the scalp; no large
amounts of missing hair, although there may be some
small bits missing around the point of impact.

Lone said that her clothing was undamaged by anything resembling violence, although it had been discol-
ored by immersion in the river. She'd been barefoot
when taken out of the water.

Back in his 4Runner, Virgil spent another hour driving
on to Trippton, moving slow through the rough rolling
terrain of the Driftless Area, thinking about the ME's find-
ings. He was thirty miles out when his phone rang: Duncan again, calling from St. Paul.

"Wanted to make sure everything's okay, that you
made it to Trippton," Duncan said.

"Not quite there yet," Virgil said. "I spent more time
with the medical examiner than I expected. I'll be there
in half an hour or so."

"Good, good. Listen, something else has come up,"
Duncan said. "Our new governor, God bless him, has
been looking around for somebody to help out on a
minor crime problem. As it happens, the center of the
problem is in the Trippton area. He was trying to deal

with it when he was the attorney general, but nothing got done, and you know he likes your ass . . ."

"The new governor is dumb as a box of rocks," Virgil said. "And that's an insult to rocks and boxes."

"Yeah, yeah, but he's governor now. And because he's dumb, he's got lots of people whispering in his ear, telling him about things he needs to do. Somebody wants him to look into this . . ."

"Well?" Virgil said. "What is it, Jon?"

"It's too complicated to talk about while you're driving," Duncan said. "There's a private investigator, named Margaret Griffin, in Trippton right now. She's from Los Angeles. She'll meet you wherever you're staying and lay the whole thing out."

Virgil had picked up traces of nervous stress in Duncan's voice and he said, "Jon, you lying lump of horseshit. You've done something to me . . ."

"Not me. The governor," Duncan said. "The governor did it. I don't even entirely understand it. Anyway, this Margaret Griffin will meet you wherever . . ."

Duncan never did tell the truth, Virgil thought, as he drove down the hill into the Mississippi River Valley and Trippton. Virgil told Duncan that he was staying at Johnson Johnson's riverfront cabin as a way to save the state some money and that he could meet Griffin that night.

As they were finishing the conversation, Duncan dropped his voice and said, "Virgil, when you're all done and back home, take a whole week off. I will not tell a single person. That's two days to make up for lost vacation, plus three days. If you work overtime in Trippton, put in for it. Is that fair or what?"

"That depends on what kind of goddamn sinkhole you've thrown me into with this Griffin woman," Virgil said. "I know something's up. I can smell it from here. I might be talking to you about a couple of weeks off even if I don't get shot or something."

"We can talk about it," Duncan had said. Then, after promising to give Virgil's phone number to Griffin and arranging for her to meet Virgil at Johnson Johnson's cabin, he'd hung up.

FIVE

Virgil and his fishing buddy, Johnson Johnson, had met while playing baseball for the University of Minnesota. Virgil had been at third base while Johnson was a catcher. Johnson had been given his unusual first name by his father, Big Johnson, an outboard motor enthusiast who'd named both of his sons after his favorite outboards, Johnson and Mercury.

"He liked to have a few drinks after his babies were born," Johnson said. "That's when he'd think up the names."

Johnson Johnson was tall and heavily built, like a proper catcher, and ran a hardwood lumber mill in the hills west of town. He'd once chivvied Virgil into Trippton to investigate a rash of dog thefts.

In the course of that investigation, Virgil had broken the dog theft ring and had uncovered both a major meth mill and a murderous conspiracy run by the local school board. The school board and the local newspaper editor were serving thirty-year, no-parole sentences at two different penitentiaries, and two other accessories were serving shorter sentences. He'd also acquired Honus the Dog.

Because of that investigation and the prosecution that followed, Virgil was well known to Trippton and Trippton was reasonably well known to him. All of which made him wary of the whole private investigator problem.

What in God's name had the town gotten up to to attract a private eye from Los Angeles in the middle of the winter?

Johnson Johnson's cabin fronted a backwater of the Mississippi, with a channel that led north to the main stream. That arrangement gave Johnson both immediate access to the water and also protection from the waves generated by the tow boats that pushed barges up and down the river during the open-water months.

The driveway into the cabin had been neatly plowed, and Johnson's truck sat parked in a clearing on the right side of the structure. Virgil parked beside it, got his bag and his shotgun, locked the 4Runner, and trudged up the steps to the front door. A sharp wind was blowing in from the northeast, which must have put the windchill in the minus numbers. When he opened the front door, he walked into a wave of heat that pushed at him like a warm mink muff.

Johnson and his girlfriend, Clarice, were standing at the kitchen sink, shucking sweet corn.

Johnson said, "Hey, man," and Clarice said, "Hi, Virgie," and Virgil asked, "Where in the heck did you get that corn?"

"Picked this morning in Florida, flown straight into La Crosse by my old buddy Hank Johnson. He brings some every time he comes back," Johnson Johnson said. "We're having pheasant stew and sweet corn."

"He a relation?" Virgil asked, dumping his bag and shotgun next to the couch.

Johnson frowned. "Why would he be?"

"You're both Johnsons," Virgil said. "And he has an airplane."

"Virgil, every third person on the river is named Johnson."

"There is that," Virgil said. He slipped his hand around Clarice's waist and said, "How about a kiss, sugar bun?"

She kissed him on the lips and said, "Maybe I'll come back after Johnson's asleep." She was a pleasant but tough-looking blonde who could more than hold her own with Johnson.

"I sleep with one eye open," Johnson said. And, "Tell us who murdered Gina Hemming."

"I do want to hear about that," Clarice said. "It was *quite* the shock."

"Give me a week," Virgil said. "Then I'll tell you. In the meantime, you guys are big gossips . . . What have you heard?"

"I'm not a gossip," Clarice said. "Johnson is, of course. I try to weed out the ridiculous bullshit he picks up, but even after that, I can tell you, there are *still* a whole bunch of suspects. Everybody's pointing a finger at somebody else, so almost everybody in town has been pointed at. Including Johnson and me."

"Really?" Virgil said. "You didn't do it, did you?"

"Not that I recall," Johnson said. "Maybe Clarice did. I can't speak for her."

"Why you guys?"

"Well, hmm. See, there's this old couple, the Masons, retired twenty years ago, got some nice timber land up on the bluffs, mortgage with Second National with ten years to run," Johnson said. "They missed some payments—one of their daughters said they were getting forgetful, another one said they might not have the money—and the bank was talking about foreclosing. Word kind of got around that Gina and her husband, Justine . . ."

Clarice jumped in. "Used to be Justin. Soon to be her ex-husband."

"Everybody in town know that?" Virgil asked.

"Yup, I think so," Clarice said. "The tip-off came when Justine got publicly lovey-dovey with another guy, Rob. Hot Latin type. I don't know his last name. Something not Latin."

"Anyway," Johnson continued, "word got around that they could force a sale and were planning to buy it themselves and sell it off as hunting parcels. Got some nice whitetails in there, a few birds, woodcock, ruffed grouse. Like that. Anyway, I heard about it, slipped in and made a deal with the Masons . . . Besides the whitetails, there's some great old walnut in there, and lots of good maple and oak. I covered the mortgage and gave them a down payment on a contract for deed. And I get to select-cut. As part of the deal, they get to stay put and pay nothing but taxes. And when the last one croaks or moves to the nursing home, I pay the rest of the purchase price to their kids and take possession. We both got a good deal."

"And that pissed off Hemming?"

"Yeah. She got up in Clarice's face down at Dunkin' Donuts. So the next time I saw her, I gave her a piece of my mind," Johnson said.

"Called her a money-chokin' bitch on wheels, is what he did," Clarice said. "That's a quote. Since he said it in the coffee shop, a lot of people heard him."

"Okay, so Johnson's a suspect," Virgil said. He yawned and stretched, and asked Clarice, "You think he could handle hard time?"

"Probably. I could run the business while he was gone and we'd get rich. And we wouldn't go wasting money on shit like airplanes," Clarice said.

Virgil looked at Johnson: "My God, Johnson, tell me it's not true . . ."

Johnson told him about the airplane, a single-engine Beaver, currently being refurbished in Seattle. "When I go pick it up in the spring, I want you to come along," he told Virgil. "Help me bring it back across the Rockies."

"Sure . . . when monkeys fly out of my ass," Virgil said. "You already crashed two planes—"

"Not 'crashes,' they were 'forced landings,'" Johnson insisted. "When I get the Beaver down here, I can run us up to Lake of the Woods on weekends . . ."

"Flying monkeys," Virgil said.

They ate the sweet corn, which wasn't as good as Midwestern sweet corn but was a lot better than no sweet corn at all, and the pheasant stew was perfect, a Northern Prairie equivalent to a Biloxi seafood gumbo. They were cleaning up the dishes, still talking about the Beaver and catching up with recent history, when Virgil took a call from the private detective.

"I can't find this Johnson place," she said. "I've been driving up and down the highway."

"If you start at the Big Bill Boozy liquor store in Trippton and drive exactly one half mile north, you'll go around a curve and see a fake yellow highway sign that says 'Raccoon Crossing' with the silhouette of a raccoon on it," Virgil said.

"I've seen that," the woman said. She had a husky voice like she'd smoked too many unfiltered Camels.

"That's the entrance to Johnson's driveway," Virgil said. "We're down here, washing dishes."

"Five minutes," she said.

Virgil had explained about the detective during dinner, and Johnson now asked, "You want some privacy for this talk?"

"No. I don't want to talk to her at all," Virgil said. "What I want to do is find Hemming's killer, drop his ass in jail, and go home."

They were still talking about nothing, still catching up, when headlights swept across the kitchen windows and Clarice said, "Here she is." A moment later, the woman knocked once on the door and pushed through, carrying an oversized brown briefcase, and said to Johnson, "I'm Margaret S. Griffin. I hope you're Virgil Flowers."

Johnson said, "Yes, I am. These are my friends Johnson Johnson and his illicit lover, Clarice—"

"Shut up, Johnson," Clarice said. She pointed at Virgil, who was drying a plate with a dish towel, and said, "This is Virgil. The big lug is Johnson. I'm Clarice. You want a beer? Or hot cider?"

"I'd kill for a cider," the woman said. She pulled off a knitted ski hat and unbuttoned her parka, which looked about two hours old. She was tall and solidly built, in her late thirties or early forties. She had dark brown hair with a flamed tint the color of an international orange life jacket. Striking, with a Mediterranean complexion and dark eyes and eyebrows. Gold nose ring, a short white scar on her chin. She was wearing skinny jeans, a wool turtleneck sweater, and on her feet the worst possible winter shoes, thin-soled flats.

Clarice picked up on that and asked, "Where're you from?"

"Los Angeles," Griffin said. She took the unoccupied kitchen chair and dropped into it. "I haven't been this cold since . . . I've never been this cold. My butt feels like an ice cube, my toes are freezing off . . ."

"If you're gonna be around here, honey, you'll need some different shoes—and I mean like right now—or you could lose those toes," Clarice said. "When you're done with Virgil, I'll tell you where you can get some."

"Thanks. I want to wind this up and get back to L.A.," Griffin said.

"What are you doing?" Virgil asked. "I didn't get an exact description of the problem."

"Virgil's down here to solve a murder," Clarice said. "It'll take him a week or so."

Margaret Griffin seemed not impressed: "A murder? What happened?"

Johnson told her, and she asked, "How'd she get in the river? As far as I could tell, the river is a solid chunk of ice."

Virgil nodded at her. "Excellent question. I will ask that tomorrow morning first thing. Now, what are you doing here?"

"Trying to serve a federal cease-and-desist order," Griffin said. "I've been here a week, and I get nothing but the runaround, including from the sheriff. I was out to where I think the target might be, a place called Carry-Town, and a man came out of his mobile home and said if I kept sneaking around I could get hurt."

"That's not good," Clarice said.

Virgil: "What are you trying to get stopped?"

Griffin said, "I represent Mattel, the toy company. Maker of Barbie dolls." She accepted a microwaved cider from Clarice, popped open her briefcase, and pulled out a Barbie doll—a nude one.

"A regular old Barbie," Clarice said. "I had about four of them when I was growing up. They broke a lot."

"Seeing one naked makes me feel kinda funny," Johnson said.

"You put your finger right on the problem," Griffin said. "It's not a regular Barbie." She turned it over to show them a series of small holes drilled in Barbie's back. And, below that, a pink plastic button.

"What does that . . ." Clarice began.

Griffin pushed the button, which operated a tiny digital recording. Barbie said, *"Ohh, God. Ohh, God. Give it to me harder! Give it to me, big boy, harder. Ohh, God, you're so big, don't stop . . ."*

That went on for a while, then Barbie's orgasm ran

out of steam, ending with a vocal *Erp*. They all stared at the doll for a minute, Johnson finally saying to Clarice, "Some sonofabitch has recorded us, babe."

"In your dreams," Clarice said.

"Battery-operated," Griffin said. "They call this one the Divine model because she says, 'Ohh, God. Ohh, God.' There's a Negative model that says, 'Ohh, no. Ohh, no,' and a Positive model that says, 'Ohh, yes. Ohh, yes.'"

Clarice said, "There's probably a fake orgasm one that says, 'Ohh, Johnson. Ohh, Johnson.'"

Johnson said, "Funny."

Clarice laughed merrily and said, "It really was. Sometimes, I slay myself."

Will you guys take this seriously?" Griffin said. She looked around at them. "Somebody up here is manufacturing these things by the hundreds, the recorder components shipped in from China. They call them Barbie-Os. We leaned on a few Internet retailers and they pointed us at Trippton. I asked around, and nobody helps much, but I eventually came up with a name—Jesse McGovern. Can't find her. Nobody seems to have heard of her. But how could you run an operation that makes hundreds of these things, in a town the size of Trippton, and nobody knows her?"

"You know what I think?" Clarice said. "I think you have the wrong town. Between me and Johnson, we've lived here most of our lives. If there was a Jesse McGovern in town, we'd know her."

Johnson scratched his forehead. "There was a Jesse that lived down at the pumpkin farm . . ."

"She's long gone," Clarice said. "That's Jesse *Hammer*. She's a nurse up in the Cities."

"Hammer doesn't seem right," Johnson said.

Clarice: "That's because she used to be Jesse *Wagner* before she got married. The Wagner pumpkin farm. She married Larry Hammer, Joe and Barb Hammer's boy."

Johnson ticked a finger at her. "That's right. I got it now." They sounded so small-town that even Virgil was impressed.

Griffin said, "That's the first Jesse I've heard of. You're sure she's up in the Twin Cities?"

"She was for sure," Clarice said. "Her folks still live here, if you want to talk to them. The Wagner farm is a couple miles south, right down the highway. There's a big orange plywood pumpkin sign out front. Can't miss it."

"I might check with them," Griffin said. "All I need to do is hand this Jesse a piece of paper. After that, I go home, and she goes to jail if they keep putting these things out. Mattel is really, really pissed. You can't go around cutting up Barbie and Ken without taking some serious heat."

Clarice: "They cut up Ken?"

Griffin hesitated, then dipped into her bag again and came up with a Ken doll, wrapped in newspaper. She pulled the newspaper off and put the doll next to Barbie.

"My God," Clarice said. "That's not something you see every day."

"They call him Boner Ken," Griffin said. Back to the bag, she pulled out the top of a Ken doll box. The regular label had been pasted over with a similarly colored patch that read "Boner Ken . . . the Ken of your dreams."

"Not very realistic," Virgil said of the doll's most prominent appendage.

"I guess that would depend on . . . your personal . . . perspective," Clarice said.

Griffin said that she was staying at Ma and Pa Kettle's River Resort, which was, she said, eight rooms behind Ma and Pa Kettle's Restaurant and Lounge.

"Stay away from the vodka," Virgil said. "It might have a few uncertified ingredients."

"I'd be happy to stay away from the whole damn state if I can find Jesse McGovern . . ."

Clarice: "Say, does Ken talk?"

Griffin said, "Some do. Not this one. But they're all special," she said. Ken's most prominent appendage was upright, and she pushed it down: another switch. Ken's head began to vibrate.

They all looked at it for a moment, then Clarice said, "Ohh!"

Virgil: "I always assumed Ken was gay. But that . . ."

"There's also a Missionary model, and a BJ model, which is their most extreme version. Those *do* have recorded messages, and they all vibrate," Griffin said. "You wouldn't want to hear what they say."

"I kinda would," Johnson said.

"He's a pervert," Clarice said to Griffin. "That's why I stay with him."

Griffin gave Johnson a testing look and said, "I can see that in him. You're a lucky girl."

"Everybody, shut up," Virgil said. To Griffin: "What exactly have you done so far?"

Griffin outlined her investigation, which had produced nothing useful, except some UPS shipping labels that came from a variety of towns, all in a wide half circle around Trippton, but none from the Wisconsin side of the river.

When she was done, Virgil said he'd make some calls to his sources in Trippton, and back her up if she found anything on her own. Clarice told Griffin about an outdoor store where she could get some boots and how to get there. "Buy some Sorels. S-o-r-e-l."

"I will," Griffin said. "I hope I can get out the driveway."

"You got a rental?" Johnson asked.

"Yeah, a Prius."

"Jeez, that's like driving an ice skate," Johnson said. "Got those hard little tires . . . You better not be on the road if it starts snowing."

Griffin finished her hot cider, pulled on her coat, said, "Back to the iceberg," and left. They watched from the window until she turned onto the highway, and Virgil looked at the other two and said, "You guys were lying through your goddamn teeth. Where's Jesse McGovern?"

"Couldn't tell you that," Johnson said. Clarice shook her head.

"What's going on here?" Virgil said. "Goddamnit, Johnson . . ."

Clarice said, "You haven't been here much in the winter. Next time you drive through town, check it out. If you don't already have a job here, there's none to be had, unless somebody dies. Jesse's found a way to bring in some money for a dozen or so folks that don't have any.

I'll tell you, Virgil, you're a good friend and all, Johnson's best friend, but you won't find out about Jesse from us."

"She's like Jesse James," Johnson said. "The outlaw heroine."

"She good-looking?" Virgil asked. Outlaw heroines in the media age usually were.

Johnson laughed and said, "Yeah, she is. She really is."

Clarice changed the subject. "What about Gina? What'd you find out, Virgil? Have you been to her house?"

Virgil told them about his visit with the medical examiner. When he mentioned the body bruising, Clarice and Johnson looked at each other, considering the possibilities. Then Clarice shook her head and said, "I don't doubt that it happens here, with the long winters, but I don't know who'd be into it."

"I experience enough pain cutting timber," Johnson said. "And if I tried paddling Clarice . . ."

"You'd have to sleep with both eyes open," Clarice said.

"I've dealt with sex crimes, but this . . . I've never done anything like B and D people, where it's voluntary," Virgil said. "I need to do some research, I guess. I mean, do they tend to violence? Or are they just playing? Or what?"

"You get a thrill out of spanking somebody hard enough to leave bruises, I think you might get excited by violence," Clarice said. "Especially if the . . . spankee? . . . is tied up and helpless. And even if that's voluntary, there's something wrong in that somewhere."

"I hear you," Virgil said.

"Got a thought for you," Johnson said. "When you're doing your research, I wouldn't go to the library and ask for a book about it. The town is not all that big, and you might not want that kind of reputation."

Virgil said, "I don't know. Could bring me some compelling new local contacts."

"Since it's B and D, it'd even be heavy on the 'compelling,'" Clarice said.

SIX

That night, in his regular pre-sleep contemplation of the mystery of God's ways, Virgil thought about the unfairness of personal appearance. When he asked Johnson if the Barbie-O maker Jesse McGovern was good-looking, he hadn't been asking idly.

Pretty people, Virgil believed, both male and female, had a totally unwarranted, unearned lifelong advantage over average and ugly people. The advantage began in their earliest years—*What a pretty baby!*—and persisted for most of their lives. Quite often, they didn't believe in their advantage. Oh, they knew they were pretty, but they took it as their God-given right rather than an unearned gift.

Jesse McGovern was being forgiven even as she apparently, and repeatedly, broke and evaded the law, even if the lawbreaking in this case seemed trivial to most people, including Virgil's friends.

Gina Hemming had also been a pretty woman and well-off since birth. Both Johnson and Clarice had described her as haughty, better than thou, assuming appearance, brains, and money not only as her righteous heritage but as weapons to be used.

Hemming might very well be dead because of all that, Virgil thought. Rich and pretty attracted attention, not all of it good.

Why would a just God allow this to happen? Was it all part of an evolutionary clockwork that God allowed to work through itself, unguided, an enormous experiment of some kind, for good reasons that humans couldn't perceive?

Not something Virgil could work out in one night.

Virgil got up early the next morning, looked out the window at the thermometer—one below zero. He could see dead brown leaves fluttering on a riverside oak, so there was some wind, too, which would make things worse. He cleaned up, pulled on his long underwear, wool socks, put on his Pendleton wool shirt, jeans, and insulated boots, parka, double-layer watch cap, and driving gloves, with his ski gloves carried in the parka pockets.

He had breakfast at Ma and Pa Kettle's—scrambled eggs, toast, sausages, and Diet Coke—and read last week's *Republican-River*. The newspaper didn't have a word about the murder, not because it was a crappy paper—though it was—but because it was a weekly and came out on Thursday mornings and Hemming had disappeared Thursday night.

As he ate, Virgil wrote down a list of names. He needed to talk to Jeff Purdy, the Buchanan County sheriff who also provided law enforcement services to Trippton; Justin (Justine) Rhodes, Hemming's husband; and, he thought, he might make a quick visit to an elderly lady named Janice Anderson. It wasn't much of a list, but it was a start.

He was finishing his Coke when Margaret Griffin came through the door, looked around, spotted him sitting by himself. She asked a waitress to bring her coffee and an omelet, sat down across from him, and asked, "What can you do for me?"

"I've been out at CarryTown before, so I know where it is," Virgil said. "This guy who warned you off . . . what trailer is he in?"

"Number 400. I don't know what his name is. I was going to ask at the post office. You want me to come along?"

"Better if I go by myself. I've got to give priority to the murder case, but when I get a break, I'll run out there," Virgil said.

"Okay. I looked you up on the Internet last night and found those stories about the school board . . . That sounded like quite the unusual situation," she said.

"Not something you run into all the time," Virgil said.

"I never ran into anything like it when I was a cop," she said.

"Where were you a cop?" Virgil asked.

"L.A. Six years on the street, and things got so rough I finally said screw it. Started off to law school, ran out of money—didn't much like it anyway—but that helped me get my private investigator's ticket, and I've done okay," Griffin said. "I do a lot of background checks for executive employment. Mattel is one of my big clients, so when they asked me to do this, I could hardly say no."

They chatted for another ten minutes, then Virgil

said, "You take it easy while you're poking around, Margaret. This woman, if she's in town, is going to hear about you, if she hasn't already, and the people out here have guns."

"You think there might be a real threat?"

"Oh, no, not really. Minnesota's generally a peaceful place," Virgil said.

"Except for a whole bunch of serial killings that you've looked at over the years, and Vietnamese spies killing people, and a school board that murders its critics, and now this woman who was murdered and thrown in the river . . ."

"Well . . . yeah. We're not perfect."

When Virgil got up to go, Griffin asked, "You don't carry a gun yourself?"

"I've got one, but it's, you know, heavy," Virgil said.

She squeezed the bridge of her nose for a moment, muttered, "Okay."

What she was thinking, Virgil thought as he walked away, was "hick cop."

Virgil pulled on his ski gloves and walked over to the law enforcement center. A balding deputy was sitting behind a panel of bulletproof glass reading a book called *Techniques in Home Winemaking*, which he put down when Virgil walked in.

He pushed an intercom button and said, "Virgil. Here to solve the murder?"

"That's one thing. Is Jeff in?"

"Yeah, he's back there. Be happy to see you, I believe. I'll buzz you in."

The working area of the sheriff's office was behind a sturdy black steel door. When the lock buzzed, Virgil pushed through and heard the deputy call, "Hey, Jeff—that fuckin' Flowers is here."

Virgil had been there before and he followed the hallway around a corner as the sheriff popped out of his office and stuck out a hand. "Man, am I glad to see you. We gotta figure this thing out right quick. The Chamber of Commerce is all over my butt. Come on back."

Virgil followed him back to his office, took a chair, and asked, "Who inherits? The husband?"

"Not quite sure. I haven't seen a will yet. Gina had a sister, but the sister lives in Iowa City with her husband—he's a doctor—and they were both there in Iowa when Gina went for the swim."

"They're out as suspects?"

"Yeah. They came up here—they're still here, at the Motel 6, waiting to see when they might have a funeral, making arrangements for running the bank . . ."

"Who's going to do that?"

"Well, Marv Hiners is first vice president over there. He's iron-clad for Thursday night and Friday—he was up at a Wild game in the Cities with his wife and kids, got back here about noon on Saturday. Anyway, the sister, her name's Ann Ryan—her husband is Terry Ryan—says they'll probably sell the bank off to Wells Fargo. Take the cash out. That's been the plan for a while, she said, so Marv knew he wouldn't be taking over the place . . ."

"Still could wind up running the bank if Wells keeps him on," Virgil said.

"Yeah, but he'd be on a branch bank salary. Even if he runs the place, he won't be getting rich. Besides . . . he was in the Cities. This whole thing doesn't look like a professional hit, which it would have to be if the Ryans or Hiners paid for it. To me, it looks like a domestic, and the killer tried to hide it."

"So . . . Justin/Justine?"

Purdy winced and shook his head. "Got no alibi, got nothing. His boyfriend was down in Prairie du Chien that day, taking a cooking class and hanging out. He and Justin/Justine have a new French restaurant. Justin said he was home reading Proust." He pronounced "Proust" as if it rhymed with "toast."

"Proust?" Virgil rhymed it with "roost."

"That's what he said."

"I understand he was still talking to Hemming," Virgil said.

"Oh, yeah, they were still friendly. Gina told me, 'No harm, no foul.'"

"Was she dating?"

"She's had some male friends over the years but wasn't sleeping with any of them—not currently, as far as I can tell. But I wasn't in charge of watching her, you know?"

"You do know about the B and D bruises?"

"Thurston told me about them. I don't know what that means. He said they were old, for one thing. And, hell, they were voluntary. I didn't spend a lot of time worrying about them even if they are real."

They spent another ten minutes talking over the background. When Virgil asked if the department's crime scene investigator, whose name was Alewort, had turned anything up, Purdy told him that Alewort was up at St. Mary's, in the Cities, drying out.

"This is usually our slow season, so it was the best time for him to go," Purdy said.

"So, basically, you haven't been able to turn up a lot."

"That's not quite true," Purdy said. "We've got a guy who's trained to fill in for Alewort, though he might not be quite as good as the real thing." He turned around to his desk and pawed through a rubble of paper, finally coming up with a single yellow sheet torn from a legal pad.

"When Gina was found, she was wearing a dressy outfit, matching burgundy-colored skirt and jacket with a pinkish blouse. On Thursday night, she had a meeting at her house, to work with a committee that's setting up the Twenty-fifth Reunion of the Trippton High School Class of '92. There were eight people there, besides her, and all eight say she was wearing that same outfit. She didn't show up for work on Friday, so we all think she was killed Thursday night before she had a chance to change clothes."

Virgil said, "Okay, I can use that."

Purdy held up a finger. "Furthermore, our investigator found a spot of blood on the carpet in the living room. Not much of a spot, but enough that it wasn't a casual cut. We've taken samples and sent it off to the lab to make sure it's human, but I'm betting it is. So, she was killed at home, Thursday night, after that meeting."

"You've checked all the people at the meeting?"

"Sort of."

"Sort of?"

"One thing we know is, the last three people who were there all left together. Of course, any of them could have gone back," Purdy said. "But it's also possible it's a total outsider."

"Anyone in particular look good?"

"I haven't pushed that aspect of it," Purdy confessed. "Soon as we pulled her out of the water, I called your folks up at the BCA and asked for help. Even if one of these people *is* the killer, I'd have to piss off seven innocent people to find that out. I knew you were coming, so I decided to leave the pushing to you. And the pissing off."

Virgil nodded. He dealt with local sheriffs all the time, and what Purdy told him wasn't unusual, although it wasn't usually stated quite so bluntly. "All right. I can push."

Purdy handed him the yellow sheet of paper. "Names, phone numbers, addresses, both home and business, for everybody involved."

"Saves me a day right there," Virgil said. "I'd like to look at the crime scene. Do you have keys?"

"I do. They're in the evidence locker. I'll get them."

"Do you know if Janice Anderson is still alive?"

"Shoot, that old biddy is never gonna die," Purdy said. "You know she wants to end high school football and replace it with art? You know what life drawing is?"

"Drawing naked people?"

"She wants high school seniors doing that—these girls seeing grown-up naked men," Purdy said.

"You think you got any senior girls down here who haven't seen a grown-up naked man?" Virgil asked.

Purdy thought it over for a while, then muttered, "Gotta be one or two."

"Maybe those two could make cookies instead," Virgil said. "Now, tell me about Jesse McGovern."

Purdy groaned. "Aw, shit, Virgil, don't hassle me about Jesse. Please."

"Where is she?" Virgil asked.

"I don't know. I don't want to know," Purdy said. "You ever run for anything?"

"Not yet."

"If you ever do, this is what you'll find out," Purdy said. "Every year, you piss off one percent of your constituents. No way around it. They'll vote against you every chance they get. I've been sheriff for twenty years, so there's twenty percent of the electorate who'll vote against me every chance they get."

"I don't think the math would work exactly like that," Virgil pointed out. "Some of them you'd piss off twice."

"Okay, okay, not exactly, but I try not to piss off influential people any more than I have to, and pointing you at Jesse would probably cost me five hundred votes," Purdy said. "So, I ain't gonna do it. You want her, catch her on your own. To tell you the truth, if I were you, I'd catch whoever killed Gina Hemming and let Jesse McGovern slide. Catching her wouldn't do nobody any good except some big corporation out in California. Which doesn't have *any* votes in Buchanan County."

He had a point, but somehow it didn't seem entirely congruent with the American Way, the Rule of Law, and all that. But a job was a job, and times were bad in the small out-of-state towns. Virgil got the keys to Hemming's house and headed for the door.

SEVEN

Janice Anderson wasn't on Purdy's list of contacts, but she'd provided key information when Virgil broke the school board case. He didn't know if she'd have any relevant information on the Hemming murder, the old lady nonetheless keeping her ear to the ground, so instead of going straight to Hemming's house, he stopped at Anderson's.

Virgil parked down the street from her house, walked the last two hundred yards—no point in advertising the fact that he was talking to Anderson—pushed through her front gate, and knocked on her bluebird orange door. He heard her moving inside, and a moment later an elderly woman with short, curly white hair and rimless glasses pulled open the inner door, pushed open the storm door, and said, "Virgil Flowers. I knew you'd come snooping around."

"You gonna leave me standing out here freezing my tits off?" Virgil asked.

"Not at all. Say, did you ever play football?"

"Yeah, in high school, out in Marshall. I was a wide receiver."

"That explains a lot," she said. "C'mon in anyway. I wouldn't want to have any frozen tits on my conscience."

Anderson had spent nearly forty-three years in Trippton as a high school teacher, and since few outsiders moved into Trippton, virtually everybody in town, forty-eight and younger, had been in one of her classes. Since she'd grown up in Trippton, she also knew almost everybody between forty-eight and seventy as friends from her youth.

She led the way into the kitchen and asked, "Coffee or hot cocoa?"

"Cocoa," Virgil said, as he took a chair at the kitchen table.

"That's right," she said. "You get your caffeine from Diet Coke." She got a can of Hershey's cocoa out of the cupboard, and as she was putting it together with milk and sugar on the stove she said, "You're here about Gina Hemming."

"Yup. What do you know?"

"A few things—which you didn't hear from me," she said.

"Of course not," Virgil said. "By the way, I've got a list for you to look at."

He put the yellow legal pad page out on the kitchen table, and when she'd finished mixing the cocoa and milk with a metal whisk, she picked it up and read down the list.

"If any of these people killed her, it was an accident," she said. "Though, I guess the cover-up wouldn't have been an accident, would it? Taking her out and throwing her in the river."

"No, it wouldn't. Killing her wasn't an accident, either, unless you'd consider whacking somebody on the head with a heavy object to be an accident."

She frowned at that and said, "I hadn't heard exactly how she was killed. So she was beaten to death?"

"I wouldn't call it that. 'Beaten to death' usually means a person was hit a whole bunch of times. Hemming was hit once, with something round and heavy, like a full bottle of wine."

"Didn't fall and hit her head?"

"She could have, I guess, and then, not thinking clearly, crawled through the streets of Trippton, down to the Mississippi, where she cut a hole in the ice and threw herself in."

"Don't be a wiseass. I'm an old woman," Anderson said.

"An old woman who's trying to close down Trippton football. It's like telling the Catholic Church to cut out Holy Communion."

"Barbaric sport. Nasty. Nasty. A hundred years from now, nobody will believe that we allowed it to go on. It's gladiatorial games, but with children," Anderson said. "Anyway, none of the names on this list exactly jump out at me. I had all of them . . . Wait a minute. Were all these people in the same class?"

"Yes. Class of '92," Virgil said. "The last people to see her alive, according to Jeff Purdy, were the members of a committee putting together the Twenty-fifth Reunion for next summer."

"Hmph. There is a lot of potential violence in class reunions. Old wounds never healed, and maybe even exacerbated, over the years, especially when they're all in the same pressure cooker, like Trippton," she said. "You look at most reunions, there's usually at least one fist-fight among the men, one hair-pulling spat among the women, and more. There've been whole brawls . . ."

"Really?"

"Oh, yes. Remember, these people, at their twenty-fifth, are all well into their lives and careers, and they're all the same age, in the same pond," Anderson said. "They've married each other, they've had affairs with each other, they've had business clashes and disappointments, the loving couple in senior high wound up marrying other people—and somebody got dumped. Brutal stuff, when you think about it."

"You're making this sound harder than I want it to be," Virgil said.

She looked him over for a few seconds, then said, "You know, you originally struck me as the lazy sort who wouldn't go out of his way to work too hard. I now know that's purely dissembling on your part. A mask. The last time you were here, you arrested the entire school board and the newspaper editor for murder, cleaned the meth heads out of Orly's Creek, broke up a dognapping ring, and even got Johnson Johnson to stop drinking, which was probably the biggest miracle of all."

"He stopped himself," Virgil said.

"That's not what Johnson told me," Anderson said. She poured a large cup and a small cup of cocoa at the kitchen sink, reached into another cupboard, took out a bottle of Grand Marnier, added a jolt to each of the cups of cocoa, shook in a bit of nutmeg and cayenne pepper, and gave him the big one. "Anyway, I now see you as a person with a very deceptive personality. I believe that to be calculated, although I suppose it's possible that it's

slightly schizophrenic. Of course, that's neither here nor
there . . . Let's talk about Gina."

et's," Virgil said, in relief. The cocoa smelled wonder-
ful, but was hot enough to set fire to his face, so he
put it down to let it cool for a while.

"How much do you know about her?" Anderson
asked.

"What Jeff Purdy told me—and I've seen her body, so
that I know that she was pretty."

"Jeff Purdy—there's an Olympic-level brownnoser for
you. I gave him a D in sophomore English. Not going to
set any land speed records for honesty, either, in my
opinion."

"Gina Hemming," Virgil said, pushing her back on
point. He took a sip of the cocoa: still too hot.

Gina Hemming, Anderson said, had been one of the
brightest students in her class, one of two National Merit
Scholars, and was also pretty, popular, and stuck-up.
"She stayed that way, right until she was killed. Lucy
Cheever, who is on your list, was the most popular girl in
the class . . . She was Homecoming Queen. Also smart."

Anderson filled in a quick history for the dead woman,
including her fraught marriage to Justin Rhodes.

"Justin was a year older than Gina, and he's had a
question of sexuality hanging over his head since high
school. I once walked in on him necking with a trom-
bone player named Ralph Filson back in the boys' dressing room when the place was supposed to be empty.
Ralph was definitely gay, everybody had known that
since he was in third grade, but I hadn't known it about

Justin . . . if he is, in fact, gay. I think there's some possibility that he's only gay in reaction to his father, who is an enormous, brass-plated asshole and homophobe. In other words, a feature, not a bug.

"On the surface, though, the marriage looked pretty good," Anderson continued. "They obviously liked talking to each other, you'd see them out on the town, and they both liked to dance. Justin's family is the biggest local Realtor . . . So they seemed to be cruising along. Then, through hard work, nepotism, and the timely demise of her father—he choked to death down at the steak house—Gina took over the bank and became important on her own."

Rhodes was currently experimenting with the name Justine. He and Hemming had separated a year earlier but hadn't yet divorced.

"I knew most of that from Johnson," Virgil complained. "I came to you for the good stuff." The cocoa was now perfect. He added, "This is the best cocoa I've ever had in my life."

She nodded and took them back to the topic of Gina Hemming. "Here's some of the good stuff: before she and Justin separated, Gina had an on-and-off affair with a brute named Corbel Cain."

Virgil nodded. "Really. C-o-r-b-e-l C-a-i-n?" He wrote it down.

"That's correct. Corbel is a tough guy. Though not dim. He's smart enough. I believe I gave him a B-plus in English. He's a heavy-equipment operator, not somebody that you'd think would be in Gina's wheelhouse. Corbel and his wife are one of those high school couples that didn't break up. He married his sweetheart right after graduation, and they're still married, though he's beaten her up a few times—enough that his wife's father once put a shotgun to Corbel's ear and said if he did it again, he'd blow his head off."

"You think he would?"

"Yes. Janey Cain is the apple of her father's eye. Her father is a farmer down south of town, and a man who means what he says," Anderson said.

Virgil picked up a vibration in her voice, looked at her for several seconds, not responding, sipping on his cocoa. She suddenly blushed and said, "Goddamn you, Flowers."

"You got this information from your farmer friend, right? Might have had a couple of interesting reunions yourself?"

"Shut up. Anyway, I happen to know that Corbel and Gina had an off-and-on affair for years. I know Corbel drinks and I know that he has a violent streak," Anderson said. "If you asked me if I thought he did it . . . I would have said yes, before you told me a few minutes ago how she died. To tell you the truth, I can't see him hitting her with a heavy object. He'd use his fists. He's been in enough fights over the years that he knows how to channel his anger."

"When was the last time you think they were . . . seeing each other?"

"It's probably been a couple of years now. They started and stopped a few times, I believe. They could have started again. Corbel is quite a . . . vigorous type, somewhat attractive in a rough way, and he's not a braggart. He wouldn't have talked about their relationship. I suspect that when Gina needed a sexual outlet, she turned to Corbel."

"If he didn't talk, and she didn't talk, how do you know about it?"

"Because us old people talk to each other even if nobody else pays attention to us. People think when you pass sixty-five, you suddenly turn stupid. Anyway, we see things, and we used to see Corbel sneaking into Gina's house. And people have seen them sneaking into the Days Inn over in La Crosse. This was two or three years ago, though. Maybe even longer."

"Got it," Virgil said. "Where can I find Corbel?"

"He's got an equipment yard down on the river, on the south end of the marina. You know where the marina is?"

"Yes."

"And you didn't hear it from me," she said.

"Of course not."

"And you don't know I might have had a farmer friend," she said.

"I've already forgotten about it," Virgil said. He drank the last of the hot cocoa. "Though, to tell you the truth, Janice, when you've had a serious relationship with a person, and at your age . . . why not put everything else aside and go for it?"

"His wife is still alive," Anderson said.

"A lot of people . . ."

"His wife is my sister," she said.

"Ah," Virgil said. "The twists in the social fabric of Trippton never fail to astonish me."

"Let it go."

One other thing," Virgil said. "Do you know where I could find Jesse McGovern?"

A wrinkle appeared in her forehead. "I don't . . . I don't believe I know that name."

"Liar."

"You're right, I am." She rapped the table with her knuckles. "Stay away from her, Virgil. I know about this private detective who's wandering around town. If you found Jesse, anything that happened would lead to a tragedy."

Virgil felt a little sneaky about it, about the misdirection, but he did it anyway and asked, "Say . . . Jesse McGovern's not in this same class, the Class of '92, is she? She wouldn't be connected somehow?"

"No, no, she's several years younger. She's your age," Anderson said. She told Virgil how to get to Gina Hemming's house, which was only a few blocks away, a little higher on the hill.

EIGHT

Hemming's house was set higher than the street, a robber baron's well-preserved Victorian mansion that looked out over the town, like a proper banker's should. A redbrick driveway, perfectly cleared of snow, ran straight up past the house to a parking circle in back. A detached three-car garage, all yellow clapboard with a circular window above the center door, sat next to the parking area. A covered, fifty-foot-long swimming pool was visible on the far side of the lot, edged with now barren lilac bushes.

Virgil was impressed by the Victorian: a beautiful house, if you liked that style, yellow with blue trim, a level of snazz you didn't often see outside of San Francisco. Hemming had spent some time getting it right, he thought.

He let himself in using the keys he'd gotten from Purdy.

Of the crime scenes Virgil had visited, Hemming's house was one of the neater; even better, it didn't carry the common odor of death or the disruptions of a crime scene crew. The kitchen did smell faintly of old food—

garbage. There were two empty wine bottles and one half full, plus two empty beer bottles on the kitchen counter with a half dozen wineglasses showing traces of red wine. A wooden tray held a couple of Triscuits and two dried slices of white cheese.

Virgil checked a tall drawer in the counter and found a bag-lined garbage can with a crumbling cylinder of coffee grounds on top. There'd been little effort to clean up after the party, but there'd been some. Given the general tidiness of the house, it suggested that Hemming had been killed shortly after the party ended . . . but some time afterwards.

In the living room, Virgil found a blood spot on the carpet, no bigger than a quarter. She'd bled a bit from her ear canal, Thurston had said, accounting for the small size of the stain.

Nothing much in the living room to look at—a Steinway grand, one of the small models, furniture that was elegant but not particularly eye-catching, and nothing that might have been used as a club and then put back.

The room looked like a stage setting, as though it were only used by rare visitors. He found an office in the back, with a wide antique desk, an iMac computer, and a file cabinet. He turned on the computer, which asked for a password. He left it on, hoping he'd find a password as he went through the desk and files.

The first drawer of the cabinet was precisely arranged, red, yellow, and blue hanging files all carefully labeled— Car Insurance, House Insurance, Vanguard, Tax Estimates, Charitable Deductions, Expenses—and so on. Another drawer was half filled with boxes of used check duplicates, another filled with office supplies.

Nothing that looked like a password. He really wanted to get into the computer, so he called Duncan at the BCA and asked for a crime scene crew and a computer tech.

"Is the scene sealed up?"

"Can be, yeah," Virgil said. "The locals have already walked through it, though."

"Seal it, then. Bea's out west, and Sean's crew is all the way up in Grand Marais and won't be back for at least a couple of days. I'll get them going when I can, but it'll be a couple of days anyway."

"Do what you can," Virgil said. "I'll talk to the sheriff and put some tape on the doors, but sooner is better than later."

Off the phone, he continued prowling the house. There were two identical doors in a hallway off the kitchen. Virgil popped the first one open and found a laundry room, along with a wall lined with pegs on which were hung a variety of coats and jackets. Three pairs of boots and one pair of moccasins sat under the coats, and two umbrellas were propped in a corner.

He closed the door. There wouldn't be much in there, he thought, and he'd leave it for a qualified crime scene crew.

The second door revealed a set of steps to a basement. He turned on the lights, and at the bottom of the stairs he found a narrow room that had been fitted out as a gym, with a Livestrong elliptical machine facing a wall with an older flat-screen TV. A weight bench sat nearby, with some light dumbbells, and a yoga mat stretched out on the floor by the dumbbells. Another door led into a mechanical room. Again, nothing to catch the eye.

*   *   *

Virgil went back upstairs to the second floor, where he found three expansive bedrooms with en-suite bathrooms. All three had views of the frozen river and the bluffs of Wisconsin on the far side. Two rooms were apparently for guests: a pair of double beds in each, made up but unused-looking, bathrooms with toilets that showed a bit of sediment at the bottom of the bowls.

Hemming's bedroom featured a king-sized bed, with an elaborate bathroom, including a sauna, and a walk-in closet with a dressing table. Virgil worked through the closet, looking for anything of interest, though he had no idea of what it might be. He saw some men's neckties lying in a roll on a countertop and they made him wonder if a man were spending enough nights here to warrant leaving neckties?

He unrolled them, found four inexpensive ties, not especially attractive, all nylon rather than silk, like you might find in a discount store. Something was missing. Four ties, but no other male clothing. Odd.

He put the ties back and worked around the rest of the bedroom, found nothing that particularly interested him except a large, and empty, jewelry box, and an empty wall safe with an open door—had the sister taken the jewelry? Probably. Surely the sheriff's investigator would have noticed the empty box and safe, and Purdy would have mentioned it if it were important.

Maybe.

The dressing table had a stack of drawers on each side. There were three electric outlets on the top of the table, with a phone charger still plugged into one. The top

DEEP FREEZE   73

drawers were everyday clothing, though a lot of it, while the bottom drawers were filled with specialized gear—summer swimsuits in one, with swimming goggles, and ski clothing in the other. The bottom drawers felt too heavy when he pulled them open. He tried to pull them all the way out of the cabinet but couldn't do it without breaking off the trim around the drawers.

He pushed on the back panel of one of the drawers, which didn't move, but as he was doing that his fingers hit a protruding lump on the bottom of the drawer. He lifted out the layer of ski clothing covering the lump and found a pinky-finger-sized metal knob. When he pulled on it, the wooden bottom of the drawer came up, revealing a hidden space below, two and a half inches deep.

Inside were a chrome .38 caliber revolver, fully loaded; ten gold coins in separate square plastic boxes; and three banded stacks of twenty-dollar bills. Virgil had a vague idea that the coins would be worth more than a thousand dollars each for the gold alone, but these, he thought, might be for collectors. The banded twenties, if she hadn't removed any of the bills, were worth two thousand dollars each.

He crawled on his hands and knees to the other drawer, found a similar knob, and lifted out the overlying stack of swim gear. In the space below, he found several sex toys—but not a vibrating Ken doll—and a whip. The whip had a black handle and foot-long strands of leather but didn't look dangerous or even particularly punishing.

He called Purdy and told him about what he'd found, and Purdy said, "Goddamnit. We should have found that stuff. What do you want to do with it?"

"Why don't we put the gun, coins, and cash in your evidence locker until the crime scene people clear them and then you can turn them over to the sister?"

"All right. I'll have a car there in a few minutes to pick them up. What about the sex stuff?"

"I'm going to leave it for crime scene. Could have DNA."

"All right," Purdy said.

"Did you guys, or the sister, clean out the jewelry box and safe?"

"Yeah, the sister did, with Gina's lawyer," Purdy said. "They moved the stuff to a bank safe-deposit box until the will's settled."

Virgil took the coins and cash out of the drawer and stacked them on the dressing table, added the revolver to the collection—had Hemming been worried about her personal safety?—and pushed the drawers back in. He checked the dressing room door: solid oak, with a heavy dead bolt. A safe room, with a revolver, and a spot for a cell phone.

It occurred to him that he hadn't seen a purse or the phone. He called Purdy again. "No, we don't have them. I should have mentioned that—I noticed it the first night when I went over to her house."

Virgil ended the call, walked out of the dressing room into the bedroom, went back and looked at the ties again. They'd been bothering him, and after looking at them a second time, he knew why. Men's ties got wrinkled on both sides at the front of the neck, where the knot would be, with the short section that went around the back of a man's neck smooth. These ties, all four of them, were badly wrinkled near the ends.

They had been used, Virgil thought, to tie somebody up—but tie her up comfortably.

Back in the bedroom, he dropped to his knees and looked under the bed. There were several boxes, with a variety of things inside them—the leaves for a table, Christmas ornaments.

He put the stuff back in the boxes and shoved them under the bed again.

One door in the upstairs hallway didn't lead to a bedroom but to an attic instead. The stairs smelled musty and showed a layer of dust, without footprints, so he left it for the crime scene crew.

He continued prowling the house—checked the refrigerator, because women liked to hide things in the freezer, and checked the drawer under the stove—but found nothing more of interest.

He was about finished when a deputy showed up, and they counted out the coins and the cash and the deputy wrote a receipt for them and took them away. Virgil took a last look around, locked up, got some crime scene tape from his truck and put it across the exterior doors.

The house had more or less confirmed what people had been telling him: an impulsive killing by somebody who knew Hemming. Not a robbery—nothing out of place, with valuables left behind—but with some effort to delay discovery, with the removal of the body, phone, and purse.

He got out Purdy's list, found the cell phone number

of Hemming's sister, and called it. The sister answered on the second ring, and Virgil identified himself and asked when and where they could meet. The sister suggested that Virgil come to their motel. Now would be fine.

Ann and Terry Ryan and their two boys had two connecting rooms at the Motel 6, Trippton's premier hostelry. The boys, watching TV in the second room, looked up at Virgil and went back to the TV. The Ryan adults and Virgil talked in the first room. The Ryans seemed less distraught than tired, and worried, until Virgil mentioned the gold coins.

"Oh, thank God," Ann Ryan said. She looked like her sister but a few years younger, strong-chinned and blond, close-cut hair. "Those are St. Gaudens twenty-dollar gold pieces. I got ten, and Gina got ten, when Dad died. They're the rarest ones, and in perfect condition, and worth quite a bit. I didn't want to mention them to anybody until . . . Well, we were worried . . ."

Terry Ryan stepped in. "We were afraid that if some sheriff's deputy found them, we'd never see them again. We were going to search the house ourselves."

Virgil opened his mouth to say something defensive, decided against it. Ann Ryan had grown up in the town and probably had fairly accurate ideas about local law enforcement. Instead, he asked, "Do you have any ideas of who might have done this to Gina? Anything at all, any hint?"

They were both shaking their heads before he finished asking. "We came up here for a week every summer, around the Fourth of July, but other than that we didn't see Gina that much. She liked the boys, but . . . she had a different life than ours," Ann said.

"A couple people have mentioned that Gina took the bank over when your father died . . . Is your mother still alive?" Virgil asked.

"Oh, no, she died of breast cancer when she was forty-two. I was ten, Gina was thirteen. Dad never re-married."

"So . . . who inherits?"

"Oh, boy . . . we looked at the will," Ann said. "Gina hadn't changed it since she and Justin broke it off. She didn't expect to die. The way it works, Dad left the bank to Gina and me, equally, but it was in a trust, and Gina was the sole trustee. So, I owned a third of the shares, and she owned a third, but she got to vote both thirds—she had control. Every year, she'd declare a dividend, and I'd get some money, and the other stockholders would get some money, but she controlled everything. When she died, I became the trustee. I get Gina's stock and control two-thirds of it. We'll probably sell the bank . . ."

"But that fuckin' Justin gets the real estate," Terry Ryan said. He was a tall, thin man, intense; looked like he'd spent a lot of time on a racing bike.

"Language," Ann Ryan said to him, glancing through the door at the two boys in the other room. To Virgil: "Gina owns her house, and a condo down in Florida—a very nice condo, in Naples—Justin inherits those. She also had large cash investment accounts—I get those. She and Justin were talking to lawyers about a divorce, but she hadn't changed her will. She simply didn't think she was going to die . . ."

"Do you think Justin . . ."

Ann was shaking her head. "I've known him forever. He wouldn't hurt a fly. But he has this boyfriend . . ."

"Rob Knox," Terry Ryan said. "Justin moved out of Gina's house last summer and he and Knox moved in together. Knox is a vicious little snake. He also thinks he's got a great investment mind and he decided Trippton needed a French restaurant." Terry snorted. "Can you believe that? A French restaurant? He hired some chef from down in Prairie du Chien, and they started a restaurant up here, with Justin's money. I understand they're in the process of losing their shirts."

"You don't know that," Ann protested.

"Yeah? Garlic butter snails in Trippton? Are you kiddin' me?" Terry said. "Truffled squab in sauce le orange? More like fuckin' bridge pigeons, if you ask me. A hundred dollars a plate? In Trippton? I don't think so."

"Language," Ann said. Virgil decided not to correct the "le orange/l'orange."

Terry Ryan continued. "You want a tip, Virgil? Rob Knox is an ass"—he glanced at his wife—"a jerk. Would he kill Gina to get the real estate money? Yes. In a New York minute."

"How much is the real estate worth?"

Hemming owned her house free and clear. The Florida condo had a mortgage on it—but if it were sold, the takeout would be about four hundred thousand dollars, Terry Ryan said. The house would be another six hundred thousand, even in Trippton.

"Altogether, Justin will clear around a million," Terry Ryan said. "There's no estate tax on the trust because of the way it was set up. Since the rest of her estate comes in under five mil, there'll be no estate tax at all. He'll get the whole amount tax-free."

Ann said, "We sound greedy. We don't want to sound that way. We're not greedy, really. Terry's a surgeon, and I'm a clinical psychologist, and we have an excellent income, especially for Iowa City. I've inherited a bunch, Terry will inherit from his folks when they die. We don't need the money. But they were getting divorced . . ."

"And Knox is going to get the money from Justin and piss it away," Terry said. "A guy who had nothing to do with Gina. Nothing."

They had more to say, and Terry said it with more language to corrupt the boys, but what they said wasn't of any help to Virgil.

But the inheritance . . . that was more than interesting.

Back in his truck, Virgil called Rhodes Realty and was told that Justin Rhodes was out on a call. He thought about Corbel Cain, supposedly Gina Hemming's rough, on-again, off-again lover.

Time to pay him a visit.

NINE

Corbel Cain's heavy-equipment yard had a variety of yellow John Deeres and Caterpillars lined up at one edge of the two-acre lot, including a huge excavator with a claw at the end of its boom instead of a bucket. Probably used for demolition, Virgil thought. If you needed a house ripped apart, right now, that would do it. A sprawling gray metal building stood on the back of the lot, and two men in battered canvas work clothes were working on a bulldozer's hydraulics, pumping steamy breath out into the cold air as they worked.

The company office was inside a low, unadorned concrete-block building with narrow barred windows. Virgil went to the front door and pushed through, found two women and a man working behind a wooden service counter. The place smelled of diesel exhaust and multi-purpose cleaning liquid.

"Can I help you?" one of the women asked.

"I need to talk to Corbel Cain," Virgil said. "Is he in?"

"Can I tell him what it's about?"

"It's private," Virgil said. He held up his ID. "I'm

with the state Bureau of Criminal Apprehension and I'm hoping Mr. Cain can help me out."

"Really? Well, hang on a minute." She picked up a phone and said, "Corbel, you're needed in the office." As she spoke, Virgil heard her voice ringing through a speaker outside. She hung up and said, "He ought to be here in a minute or two."

On the way across town, Virgil had called the duty officer at the BCA and had given him Corbel Cain's name. "Don't know his birthday, lived his life in Trippton, Minnesota. I do have an address, which should give you his DOB from his driver's license."

The duty officer called back as Virgil was leaning on Cain's shop counter. "We show three arrests involving domestics, no convictions, two DWIs, paid fines on both of those, the last one was in 2010. Not a lot of detail on the domestics, but it appears that the charges were withdrawn by the victim."

Virgil rang off, and five minutes after the woman had called for him, Cain pushed through the front door. His face was red from the cold, and he was wearing a heavy yellow canvas work jacket over a hoodie and cloth work gloves. He nodded at Virgil and said, "I'm Corbel. Can I help you?"

Virgil repeated what he'd told the woman, and Cain said, "Well, come on back." He led Virgil through a door at the back of the building and into an office that smelled of cigarettes and was decorated with a couple of stuffed muskies, a twelve-point deer head, and an ancient, carefully preserved Snap-on Tool calendar.

Cain stripped off his jacket, dropped it on the floor,

sat behind his desk, pointed at a plastic visitor's chair, and asked, "What's this about?"

"About Gina Hemming," Virgil said, as he settled into the chair.

"I don't want any shit about that, from you or anybody else, especially that dipshit Purdy," Cain said. "I'm really serious. I liked her, she was an interesting woman, and I'm more than a little pissed about what happened."

"I don't know yet if I'm going to give you shit, Corbel, but I've got some questions and I need some answers," Virgil said.

Cain was an inch or two shorter than Virgil, but wider and thicker. He had a strong-boned face, and wore his hair longer than Virgil's, halfway down his neck. His face and hands were heavily weathered, and he had a piece of paper medical tape stuck to one cheek over the hint of a nonstick pad. He put a leg up on a corner of his desk, the cleats pointed at Virgil's face, scowled, and said, "If you're here, you know I used to sleep with Gina. I haven't for years. The murder's got nothing to do with me."

Virgil said, "A couple of people have mentioned that you and Gina had an off-and-on sexual relationship. You also have several domestics on your record, so . . ."

Cain shook his head. "I don't know who told you about the affair, but they must not have told you it's been over for quite a while. We broke it off three years ago, and I've hardly seen her since—never, except on the street. When we saw each other on the street, we usually had a good laugh. I never would have hurt her. I never would have. I liked the pussy, but we were never like a big passion or anything."

"Three years?"

"About three . . . except it was in the summer when we broke it off . . . It could be two and a half, could be three . . . Let me think." He scratched at the bandage and said, "Three. Yup, three years. Three and a half. I didn't have to shut her up to hide her from my wife or anything stupid like that because Janey already knew about it. You can ask her, if you want."

"Purely out of friendly curiosity, where did that bandage come from? On your face?"

"Why? Did she fight back and cut somebody?"

"Where—"

"She did, didn't she? She was a tough girl. Good for her." Cain reached up and touched the bandage. "Mohs surgery, they cut out one of those basal cell panorama things. Takes six or eight weeks to heal up. I can give you the doctor's name and all kinds of people have seen it on me, for three weeks now. Looking at you, by the way— you're gonna get some real-time experience with the Mohs. Blond and too much sun will do it every time."

Virgil asked him a few more questions—Cain said he had no idea of who else Hemming had dated recently. Virgil mentioned the signs of a B and D relationship, and Cain's eyebrows went up. "Really? That's something new. I mean, that girl really liked to get moved around, if you'll pardon the expression, but she never even hinted she'd be interested in anything like that."

"When you say that Gina liked to be moved around . . ."

"She liked it that I was big. And I'm strong. So . . . I could pick her up and turn her around and move her. She was pretty big herself, and she said I made her feel like a girl . . . that's what I meant. She was married to this guy . . . Justin . . . he didn't move her around much. If at all."

"You weren't exactly sweethearts," Virgil suggested.

"Like I said, not a big passion. I was having trouble with my wife . . ."

"Involve a shotgun?" Virgil asked.

Cain flinched, then smiled. "Damn, you've got some sources there, Flowers . . . Nobody there for that except me and the old man. There wasn't a shotgun, the time I'm talking about. What I was going to say is, I was having trouble with my wife, I was living at Ma and Pa's for a couple of weeks. I called up Gina and she blew me off— she was packing for a trip. I got down to pleading with her. Didn't do any good, she blew me off anyway. Another time, she called me up, but I was going deer hunting and I didn't want to miss the party we have the night before the season opened, so I blew *her* off. Made her unhappy. We were like that: we liked the sex, but we weren't all that romantic about it. Or committed to anything."

Okay." Virgil pushed him on the charges of domestic violence, but Cain claimed they came in the wake of brawls with his wife, brawls that went both ways. He claimed that she'd attacked him more often than he ever smacked her, and she usually came after him with something that would hurt, like a coffeepot.

"The cops always charge the guy, and after everybody talks to the sheriff and the judge, they usually let it go. That's what happened with me," Cain said.

"Don't do that anymore," Virgil said.

"What am I supposed to do when the woman comes after me with a coffeepot?"

"Run," Virgil said. "Seriously. It's the best answer."

Cain almost laughed. "Probably the best idea. Last time, though, she had me cornered in the bedroom."

When Virgil finished with the questions, Cain had a few of his own. "How was she killed?"

"Struck once with something heavy," Virgil said.

"She wasn't thrown in the river and drowned?"

"No."

Cain made a twitchy movement with his hands. "You know where Orly Crick is?"

"Yes."

"I went through the ice there, when I was a kid," Cain said. "Almost got pulled downstream, under the unbroken ice. I've had nightmares ever since, about getting stuck under the ice, trying to break my way up . . . Good she was dead before she went in."

"Well . . ."

Cain asked, "Have you figured out how she got in the water? River's froze solid for miles."

"I don't know where she went in, but her body came up at the sewer plant outflow," Virgil said.

"I heard that. You know, the sewage plant has a couple of cameras up there on the roof. I did some work for them once and they said it was okay to leave the Bobcat because there were cameras covering it twenty-four/seven."

Virgil said, "Thanks for the tip. I'll go take a look."

"One more question," Cain said. "Does Rhodes inherit? They weren't divorced yet."

Virgil said, "That's really private . . ."

"Right. The sonofabitch does get something, doesn't he? I heard a rumor about that. About how he gets the house."

"I don't know."

"You lie with a straight face. That's good if you're a cop, I guess," Cain said. "I'll tell you something, Virgil. I did like that woman. A lot. And I'm not one to lay around yanking on my dick when there's work to be done. I know all about when you were down here the last time, and I guess you're good at it, the cop shit, but I'm gonna look into this myself. I been thinking about it all day."

"Corbel—"

"Fuck it. I'm gonna kick some ass and take some names. If I find anything out, I'll call you."

"Stay away from Justin Rhodes," Virgil said.

"That's something I can promise you," Cain said. "I'll stay away from Justin Rhodes."

They sat there, staring at each other, and Virgil was at a loss: he had nothing to use as a crowbar, and Cain had answered all his questions. Still, Cain had the look of a brawler about him, and, by his own admission, *was* a brawler. If Hemming's death was an accident, a brawler might be exactly the person you were looking for. Virgil had a feeling that Cain had been telling the truth, that he wasn't involved in the murder, but Virgil wasn't yet ready to label him nope. After a moment, Virgil said, "I'm going to hold you to that. Don't mess with Justin."

"Justine," Cain said.

"Rhodes."

Virgil stood up, and Cain said, "We gotta catch the motherfucker who did this. Gina could be a pain in the ass, but you don't get the death sentence for that."

"No, you don't," Virgil said. "I don't want you messing around with this, Corbel . . ."

"I'm a free man and I do what I want," Cain said. "I'll be seeing you around."

He stuck out a hand as Virgil was leaving and Virgil took it. Cain's hand was like a rock, but not big enough a rock to have made the dent in Hemming's skull.

Out in the office, with Cain a few feet behind, Virgil asked, "Say, does anybody know where I can find Jesse McGovern?"

The two women and the man behind the counter, and Cain, all shook their heads.

"I didn't think so," Virgil said. He turned back to Cain. "You take it easy, there, Corbel."

"You, too, Virgil."

He worried a little about Cain, but Virgil had heard that kind of revenge talk before from friends of victims. Nothing had ever come of it, not in Virgil's experience.

He went to his truck and sat a moment. A video of the body being thrown into the Mississippi was too much to hope for. Virgil knew that, even as he started the truck and drove south through town to the sewage plant.

And he was right. He talked to the plant superintendent, who told him that the cameras were pointed at the chain-link front gate, which was locked shut at night. The effluent channel was several hundred yards farther south.

The superintendent, a burly man in striped coveralls, said, "She wasn't thrown in there anyway. I knew who she was and she probably weighed one-forty, one-fifty. You would have had to walk a half mile on a bad slick-icy path in the middle of the night with a hundred-and-fifty-pound body on your back. In a blizzard? No way."

"You have to walk it?"

"Yup. You park in our parking lot here, and there's a path that runs along the river. Not a government path, not a sidewalk—a path that's been walked in."

"How do you know it was in the middle of the night?" Virgil asked.

The guy cocked his head. "You think somebody walked a half mile down a slick-icy path in the middle of the *day* with a hundred-and-fifty-pound woman's body on his back?"

"Well . . . no."

"There you go," he said.

"The guy who found her . . . he fish down there much?" Virgil asked.

"Ben Potter? Yeah, once or twice a week, year-round. He's probably eighty. Saw her jacket, snagged her with a lure, pulled her in, called the cops."

"He doesn't have any problems with the idea of fishing, you know, in the effluent stream?"

"Hey. When it goes out of here, that stuff is as clean as springwater," the superintendent said. "You could drink it."

"You ever do that?" Virgil asked.

"I'm confident about our water quality, but I'm not crazy."

"You know Jesse McGovern?"

The guy's eyes went flat. "Who?"

On his way back through town, Virgil stopped at the public library, where a chubby blond librarian said,

"Virgil Flowers! Welcome back. Are you here on the Gina Hemming thing?"

She'd helped him out on a previous case, and he appreciated it. Virgil said, "Yeah, I am. You know her?"

"Sure. I mean, I've talked to her a time or two. She mostly knew my folks; they had a mortgage from the bank. We had a little ceremony when the folks paid it off, and Gina gave us the paper in person."

"Huh. All right. Let me ask this: do you have yearbooks from the high school?"

"Sure. I've heard rumors about the reunion meeting. You'd want Class of '92," she said. "Let me show you."

She took him back in the stacks and showed him two shelves that, between them, contained fifty or sixty high school yearbooks. Virgil said, "Thanks, I can take it from here."

"Class of '92 right here," she said, touching one of the books. "If you need more help, ask me."

When she'd gone, he pulled off a book a foot farther down the shelf than the '92, cracked it open, and looked at the index. Janice Anderson had been right: Jesse McGovern was in the same class as Virgil. He found her senior picture, spent some time looking at it—the photo was in color, and McGovern had a thin, foxy face, freckles, and auburn hair—until he was sure he'd recognize her, then put the book back.

He hoped Janice Anderson never figured out what she'd given away. She was a nice old lady, and he liked her. She'd be upset if she knew he'd played her.

*   *   *

On the way out the door, the chubby librarian leaned across the checkout desk and asked, with a lowered voice, "What happened with Gina? You can tell me—I won't tell anybody else."

Virgil had long disagreed with the usual cop technique of keeping everything quiet about an investigation. The people of a small town—he mostly worked in small towns—knew more about their places than any outsider ever could. He often went to the locals for help even when that meant filling them in on the investigation.

Virgil looked around. The library was empty except for one old man reading a newspaper, so he told the librarian what he'd gotten so far. She lit up when he mentioned the possibility of bondage. "Ooo. That's *interesting*."

"Really?"

"Yeah. She was so proper, she was almost stuffy. I mean, even when she laughed it was like 'Ha-Ha-Ha' like she'd practiced it in a mirror. Getting tied up and spanked? That's a whole new thing right there."

"I'd very much like to know who her partners were," Virgil said.

The librarian wiggled her eyes at Virgil. "Me, too."

Made him laugh, which made him feel a little guilty, too. It was, after all, a murder investigation. He said good-bye to the blonde and headed for the door. As he got there, he turned and said, "Say, how would I look up Jesse McGovern?"

She shook her head and said, "Never heard of her."

"There's a surprise," Virgil said.

The Jesse McGovern question was like a bad joke.

TEN

Virgil's next stop was at Rhodes Realty on Main Street. He angle-parked and went inside, where a blue-haired woman was poking at a computer keyboard and looked nearsightedly at Virgil when he came through the door. "Can I help you?"

The receptionist was sitting in a little corral, maybe ten feet across. A hallway went down one side of the office, with doors leading off to a half dozen individual offices. Some of the doors were open, some closed. Virgil said, "Is, uh, Justine Rhodes in?"

The receptionist lowered her voice and said, "In the office, he's *Justin*. Are you one of his friends?"

"I'm an investigator for the Bureau of Criminal Apprehension," Virgil said. "Is he in?"

"Yes. Let me call him. He's very upset about Gina. He's been crying for three days straight."

She called Rhodes, who poked his head out of one of the offices and called, "Come on down."

His office was a bit larger than the receptionist's cor-

ral, but not much. He had a compact desk with two visitors' chairs, one of them occupied by a sallow-faced
Hispanic man with shoulder-length black hair and dark
eyelashes. Virgil looked from one to the other. The Hispanic man didn't offer to leave, and Rhodes pointed at
the other chair and asked, "Isn't this awful? Isn't this terrible?"

Virgil said, "Maybe we should talk privately."

Rhodes shook his head. "I don't keep anything from
Rob. And you might want to talk to him, too, so he
might as well be here . . . Rob Knox . . ."

Knox said, "Yeah. But we reserve the right to get an
attorney." He may have had Hispanic ancestors, but his
accent was straight Minneapolis.

Rhodes was a tall man, with a short straight nose, a
square jaw with a dimple in his chin, a heavy shock of
brown hair slicked straight back with gel, and brown eyes
rimmed red. He was wearing a pale blue suit, which
seemed a little summery for January, and a red necktie
that matched the rims of his eyes. He was also wearing
the faintest hint of makeup. Virgil told him about the
investigation, asked him where he was when Hemming
was murdered.

"I was at her house for the meeting, I'm sure you
know that, and then I was at home. By myself. Until ten
o'clock or so, when Rob got home. I know that's not a
good alibi, but that's where I was. Rob was down in Prairie du Chien, at a class on French cooking, with people
who know him. Every winter, when it becomes intolera-
ble here, I read boring books—last year it was *Moby-
Dick*, this year it's Proust. I know that won't hold much
water with you people . . ."

"We run into it all the time—people with no alibis," Virgil said. He wanted to encourage Rhodes to talk, so he added, in a friendly way, "They're usually innocent, because guilty guys try to fix up an alibi for themselves. The more elaborate they are, the more suspicious we are."

Virgil looked at Knox. "And you were . . . where? At a class?"

"Yeah. In Prairie du Chien. I didn't get home until late. After ten o'clock."

"Were there a lot of people at the class?"

He shrugged. "Six or seven, I guess, not including the two instructors. I talked to most of them. I've got some names for you, if you need them."

"I will," Virgil said. "I really have to check everything. How long did the class run?"

Knox looked away. "Three hours. Mostly in the afternoon."

"The afternoon? Why were you so late? Can't be more than an hour from here."

"It's more than an hour even without the snow. More like two hours, and, with the snow, longer than that. I lived there for a couple of years, I hooked up with some friends and we hung out at their restaurant."

"Gonna need those names."

Knox was sullen. "You can have them. Check away."

Rhodes had watched the interplay and now opened a desk drawer and took out a Kleenex tissue, huffed his nose into it, and threw the tissue into a wastebasket. "The thing is, Virgil, Rob really doesn't know Gina," he said. He looked at Knox. "I mean, have you even talked?"

Rob said, "Yeah, we talked that one time at the farmers' market. When we got those pies."

"That was five minutes," Rhodes said. "God, why did they kill Gina? It must have been jealousy . . . Or maybe some crazy farmer who wasn't paying his debts."

Virgil: "When you say jealousy . . ."

"Gina was a fabulous-looking woman. She was smart and successful . . ."

"And you were married to her."

"Yes. We loved each other, but at some point I became . . . confused . . . about exactly who . . . inhabits this body." He slipped his hands down his chest. "My body. We didn't clash over it, we didn't argue about it, I think she sensed the problem even before I did. Oh, God . . . Anyway, we were going to get divorced so we both could explore alternative realities, but we remained the closest of friends."

"I have to ask you this, but it's a little embarrassing," Virgil said. "Did you and she ever engage in . . . rough sex?"

Rhodes had started to slump but now straightened. "Was she . . . did somebody . . . before she died . . . ?"

"Sometime before she died. A week or so."

"Well, it wasn't me," he said, his voice indignant. "We haven't had sex for a long time. When we still slept in the same bed, I sometimes . . . helped her along."

Virgil pushed him a bit, and Rhodes was willing to explain—actually, seemed happy to explain—until Virgil finally cut him off. He really didn't want to hear it, and Rhodes said that their last active sexual engagement, which did not include intercourse, had been two years earlier.

Virgil skipped away from the sex to ask, "Do you know who will inherit?"

Rhodes put his elbows on the desk, knitted his fingers together, and looked at Virgil over his hands. "I suppose . . . we never did estate planning when we were married, we were too young . . . but I suppose her sister. I don't know anything about Gina's will. I know Rick James was her lawyer. He'd know."

"Don't lie to me, Justin," Virgil said. "It makes me feel bad, and makes you look guilty."

Justin flushed and said, "Ah, God, I knew somebody would get on me about that. I guess I have something coming. I've thought maybe I should decline. Should I decline?"

"I was told by somebody who knows you that you wouldn't hurt a fly," Virgil said. "They weren't so sure about your friend Rob. Do you think Rob could find a use for that money?"

Knox said, "Fuck that. Fuck that."

A spark appeared in Rhodes's eyes. Anger? He leaned across the desk and said, "No! Rob is an angel. An angel! He would never!"

Knox settled back in his chair.

Virgil took out the list of people who'd been with Hemming the night she disappeared, showed it to Rhodes. "Yes, they were all there. All respectable businessmen and -women . . . Do you think she was killed by a man?"

"That's my operating theory. Her body had to be moved a substantial distance, no matter where she went into the river. The killer had to be somebody with some strength, unless there were more than one of them."

"Huh. Well, Ryan Harney is very fit; I see him at the gym. Dave Birkmann is too fat; he'd probably have a heart attack. He might be sorta strong, though . . . I don't know. George Brown is strong; he could have carried her across the river. Barry Long is fit, I think, but I can't even imagine why he'd hurt Gina." He looked up, his eyes unfocused for a few seconds, then said, "Everybody likes Barry. He was the class president for three years, and he's been in the State Legislature forever. But I'm not sure he's . . . sexual. He's not gay, for sure, but I'm not sure he's heterosexual, either. Huh."

He looked back down at the list. "None of the women could have moved a body. Margot Moore would be the strongest, but she's too small. So . . . you know what I think?" He slid the list back toward Virgil. "I don't think it was any of them. Or me or Rob. For sure, not me or Rob."

Virgil: "Then . . ."

Rhodes held his hands up, a dismissive gesture. "You're looking at the wrong people. The economy around here has never recovered from the crash in '08. We used to have seven Realtors working out of this office, now we have three. A lot of businesses are still in trouble, a lot of places closing down because of Internet sales. Gina had a lot of loans out. *A lot*. She's the main source of loan funds around here and she's had to make serious decisions about people who can't make payments."

"I'd thought about that, but it opens up a whole universe of suspects, which is a problem," Virgil said. "Is there anybody in particular who you think couldn't pay and might be dangerous?"

"Nooo . . . The people at the bank could help you with that," Rhodes said. "Now that I think of it, most people would suppose that their problem is with the bank, not with Gina. Kill her and the bank would still collect. Of course, as a decision maker, maybe the anger was aimed directly at her. Lots of people are plain stupid."

Virgil talked with Rhodes for a few more minutes—Rhodes told him that Hemming was a "fussy dresser" and that she would never have gotten up in the morning and put on the same outfit she'd worn the night before—and despite Rhodes's lack of alibi, Virgil was nearly ready to cross him off the list of suspects.

The fact that he'd been crying didn't mean much—lots of killers cried after they'd offed their wives—but Rhodes seemed so nakedly open that Virgil believed him. Faking both openness and innocence at the same time wasn't easy; most hardened sociopaths couldn't pull it off.

That was not true of Rob Knox, who sat in his chair and smoldered, watching Virgil from the corners of his eyes.

Before he left, Virgil had Knox give him a list of names, the people he'd been with in Prairie du Chien.

As Virgil walked back to his truck, he was thinking about a grilled cheese sandwich. He'd gotten a good one at Shanker's Bar and Grill the last time he was in town, so he went that way. At Shanker's, he pulled into the parking lot, stopped in the second row of spaces, and climbed out of the truck.

As he did, a red pickup was pulling past him into the first row of spaces right outside the back door. He waited until it was stopped, noticed one of the stickers in the back window that showed a cartoon family: husband, wife, five kids—two boys and three girls, in a variety of sizes—two dogs, and a cat.

Frankie had a sticker like that in the back of her truck, with a single woman and five boys, and, lately, a slightly askew sticker of a dog that actually resembled Honus, as much as any cartoon could.

As Virgil walked toward the bar's back door, a woman got out of the passenger side, wrapped up in an old-style parka with a heavy snorkel hood that left nothing visible but her eyes.

As Virgil passed the truck, another woman got out of the backseat on the passenger side, and as he walked up to the door, he found that the truck had held four women, all bundled heavily against the cold. He didn't think about the fact that the truck would be heated, and they certainly wouldn't have needed the hoods inside it . . .

He got to the back door of the bar and politely held the door open, and the first woman coming through, half turned away from him, whipped back toward him, leading with her fist, and knocked him on his ass.

He was still sitting up, surprised as much as stunned, when the other three piled on, what he later estimated to be roughly six hundred pounds of woman flesh, and he tried to roll over but could barely move, felt the breath being squeezed out of his lungs.

Then they beat the hell out of him.

He couldn't hear much, except a soprano voice squeaking—"You fucker, you fucker, you fucker"—keeping time with the blows.

They didn't exactly know what they were doing, and

his ribs did have some padding from his parka, or they would have hurt him much worse, but, as it was, they hurt him badly enough.

He kept trying to roll so he could get to his knees, but they kept hitting him in the face and knocking him flat on his back. He got in a couple of short punches, but the heavy parkas on the women soaked up the impact.

The woman in a blue parka did most of the hitting, with her big, hamlike fists, while the other three kept him pinned, one of them struggling to her feet and starting to kick him in the hip and legs. The woman in the blue parka broke his nose, and blood went everywhere all over his face, and one woman actually squealed at the sight.

Nearly blind now, he got his hand inside one of the hoods and grabbed some hair and yanked it out of the woman's scalp, and the woman screamed and rolled away from him, but Ham Fist hit him in the forehead, and someone kicked him some more, and finally a woman with a nice soprano voice said, "Stay away from Jesse, you prick."

The weight suddenly lifted, leaving him lying on a dirty crush of snow and ice, trying to catch his breath. The women ran back to the truck, one of them saying, "He yanked my hair out, I'm bleeding," and then the four doors slammed shut. The truck started crunching across the gravel lot, but he couldn't see it because of the blood in his eyes, and he was afraid they were going to run him over, so he blindly rolled toward the building until his back was against the concrete-block wall. He was low enough that the bumper couldn't get him, close enough the wheels couldn't get him . . . he hoped.

If he'd had a gun, he might have tried to shoot at the truck, but he didn't have a gun. A few seconds later, the truck was gone.

Virgil wiped the blood from one eye, ran his tongue along his teeth. None seemed broken or loose, though he could taste blood. He found with some probing that his lower lip was cut, apparently on his own teeth.

He managed to get to his knees and crawl to the back door of the bar but couldn't reach high enough to get hold of the handle. He scratched at the edge of the door until he got his fingers around an edge and pulled it open—smeared blood on the glass, found both hands were bleeding from the gravel in the parking lot. He crawled into the back hallway, where he fell flat again.

A man came out of the men's room and stepped over him and said, "Hey, buddy, you had a little too much there . . . Oh, holy cats." And the man started shouting, "Shanker! Shanker!"

A minute later, the bar owner was there, and he looked at Virgil and said to somebody Virgil couldn't see, "This is Virgil Flowers. Get an ambulance. Get an ambulance . . ."

Everybody in town knows me, Virgil thought vaguely, and, safe for the moment, he let himself relax and let other people take care of him.

He was aware of the transfer to the ambulance, although he felt himself to be some distance from that event. Once in the ambulance, he tried to sit up but found that he was held down by a safety harness. A man's face loomed over him and said, "Easy, there. Stay down."

A minute later, they were at the Trippton Clinic, not his first visit. When they rolled the gurney inside, a familiar doc looked down at his face and said, "Virgil fuckin' Flowers. How are those stitches holding in your scalp?"

Virgil said, "Aw, jeez . . ."

The doc said, "Good. You're talking. I'm going to wash your face here."

He did, and Virgil could see from both eyes, and again tried to sit up, but the doc put a hand on his chest and said, "Count backward from ninety-five by sevens."

"I couldn't do that unhurt or sober," Virgil said.

"Okay, good, you're not too concussed . . . but you're going to have amazing black eyes. I've got to do something about your nose . . . Do you hurt anywhere else?"

"Hip." Virgil had one hand free enough that he could pat his right hip.

The doc said to somebody Virgil couldn't see, "Let's get his clothes off," and to Virgil, "We're going to give you something to relax you. You'll feel a little sting . . ."

When Virgil woke up, he was in a small room with a lot of electronic equipment, some of which was attached to him. He had a needle at the crook of his elbow, and a tube that led back to a bag on a rolling rack. A nurse stuck her head in the door and said, "You're awake."

"I could use some water," Virgil said, his voice sounding like sandpaper on Sheetrock.

"I'll get the doctor."

Virgil didn't know exactly how long it took before the doctor showed up, but it was long enough for him to realize that his nose hurt so bad that his upper teeth hurt as well. He wiggled his teeth with a finger, but everything felt solid. The doc came in with a bottle of water with a straw, held it while Virgil took a sip, and asked, "How do you feel?"

"Hurt."

"You've got a displaced septum—not the nasal bones—the septum, the cartilage, which has been pushed off to the left. I can't do much for you now except put a gel retainer on it to hold it in place until the swelling goes down. In two or three days we can take another look and come up with a permanent solution, which will probably involve wearing a brace for a while. In a few weeks, everything ought to be back to normal."

"Goddamn them," Virgil said. He would have ground his teeth, but that would have hurt too much. He took the water bottle from the doc and swallowed another sip.

"Yeah, whoever 'them' is. We've got a deputy hanging around waiting to speak to you."

"Bunch of women," Virgil grunted.

"Women?" The doctor's voice had a query in it as though he suspected Virgil might have taken a harder hit to the head than he'd believed.

Virgil took another pull of the water, added, "Four of them. Red pickup. Caught me behind Shanker's. Could have hurt me a lot worse. Must've weighed six or seven hundred pounds . . . piled on."

"Ah, I see," the doctor said, reassured by the detail. "One of them also spent some time kicking you in the right hip and leg. Your leg looks like somebody was hitting you with a baseball bat. No bones broken, but you'll hurt for a while."

"Can I walk?"

"Oh, sure. Want to take it easy at first, to make sure all the ligaments and tendons and so on are still hooked up where they're supposed to be, but we did some X-rays and range-of-motion tests while you were asleep and I don't see a problem. Wouldn't want you using any aspirin or other blood thinners for a while."

When the doctor ran out of diagnoses, Virgil asked, "When can I leave?"

"If you're concussed, it's not too bad. I'm told you never completely lost consciousness, although you got your bell rung pretty good. I want you to take it easy here the rest of the day and overnight."

Virgil didn't protest because he really felt like he could use the rest. The doctor said, "I'll check in on you every once in a while, but, right now, go to sleep."

"Gimme my cell phone," Virgil said. "As long as my tongue isn't crippled, I need to make some calls."

The doc said, "That's the first thing everybody asks for when they wake up . . . Goddamn cell phones make me tired. Guy's in cardiac arrest, he wants his phone . . . I'll give it to you, but don't use it any more than you have to—you really need the sleep."

Virgil got the phone, called Johnson Johnson, and told him what had happened. "I need you to get my truck out from behind Shanker's. You know where the backup key is. There's guns and other stuff in there, and I don't want anyone breaking in. Don't take it to the cabin—take it up to your place, where you and Clarice can keep an eye on it. Then, get my iPad out of the seat pocket and bring it down here."

Johnson: "Wait a minute. You say a bunch of *women* beat the shit out of you?"

Virgil said, "Johnson, get the fuckin' truck, okay?"

When he had Johnson moving, he called Jon Duncan at the BCA and told him, and Duncan said, "Holy crap, Virgil. What are you into now?"

"It's that goddamn Barbie doll thing you put me on," Virgil said. "Doesn't have anything to do with the murder. I'll be moving again tomorrow. Do not tell Frankie about this or she'll jump in her truck and come running over here, all worried. We don't need that."

"You need Jenkins and Shrake?" Jenkins and Shrake were the BCA house thugs.

"No. Not yet anyway. What I need is some sleep. I'll call you tomorrow morning and tell you where I'm at."

"Take it easy, Virgil. Don't push it. Do what the doctors tell you. If you need more time to recover, take it."

"Yeah. Call you tomorrow."

While he was talking to Johnson, a woman in a sheriff's deputy's uniform stepped through the door. They spent five minutes talking: he gave her what details he had on the attack, and she said she was sorry, they'd try to find the truck. And she went away.

Virgil dropped back on the pillow, thinking about the women who'd attacked him, and about the mysterious Jesse McGovern. From the reactions he'd gotten from Trippton people, he'd begun to push McGovern further down his list of priorities.

As an experienced cop, he was completely aware of the tragedies that sometimes followed a too-slavish application of the law. His own girlfriend had lived on the edge of the law for years, sometimes tiptoeing over the border. But she was a good mother, maybe a great mother, with five kids and no husband. If she hadn't supported them, if she'd been trucked off to jail, her kids would have been screwed.

What do you do about those situations?

He'd nearly decided to let McGovern slide; the women who had beaten him had convinced him otherwise. If he could find the four of them, they'd be trundling off to the Shakopee women's prison, and Jesse McGovern could suck on it.

ELEVEN

Johnson Johnson walked into the hospital room with Virgil's truck keys, stopped, and said, "You got a blue squid on your face."

"Holding my nose together," Virgil said.

"Yeah, well, the word's out that you got beat up by a bunch of women, but I'm doing the best I can to squash it," Johnson said. "I'm telling everybody you were once ranked third as a light-heavyweight fighter, and there's no way . . ."

"Well, it's all true," Virgil said. "All except the light-heavyweight part."

"You have your facts, I have mine," Johnson said. "Virgil, I got to tell you, you look like a fuckin' raccoon. A raccoon with a blue squid on its face."

"Thank you."

"It's no big deal," Johnson said. "Anybody who's worth a damn has had his nose broken at least once . . . Though, how many is this for you? Three? That's bordering on too many. Does Frankie know about it?"

"No, and she better not find out," Virgil said. "In the meantime, I'm looking for somebody associated with

Jesse McGovern, who drives a red double-cab pickup and has one of those family stickers in the back with a husband, wife, five kids, some dogs and a cat."

"Huh. Ford, Chevy, or Dodge?"

"I don't know. Could be a Toyota, as far as I know."

"Not in Trippton, it couldn't be. I'll tell you what. I don't want you messin' with Jesse, but this doesn't sound like her," Johnson said. "She's a vegetarian, and vegetarians don't go around beating people up. Probably one of her contractors. I'll check around. What else can you tell me about them?"

"They wear parkas."

"That's a great fuckin' clue right there," Johnson said. "Too bad it's not August, you could pick them right out."

"That's all I got," Virgil said.

Johnson hung around for a while, and Virgil recounted his conversation with Justin Rhodes and Rob Knox about the Hemming murder, and concluded with his belief that Rhodes hadn't done it but he wasn't willing to make a judgment on Knox. Johnson agreed with that. "Justin's not a bad guy, and he's too mellow to hurt anyone. Besides, he's got a contact for the best California pot you ever smoked. Knox, though, is an asshole. What's next?"

"Talk to the guy who's running the bank now and then go on down the list," Virgil said. "To tell you the truth, I'm not sure the killer is somebody you'd call a bad guy, not without knowing what he did. I might be looking for somebody you all consider a good guy."

"I'll think about that," Johnson said. He offered to smuggle in some pork chops and beer. Virgil declined, and Johnson went home. And Virgil went to sleep. He woke up a couple times during the night with an odd kind of headache: it didn't actually throb, but his head felt hollow, and it was disconcerting. In the morning, he felt better: instead of the hollow-head feeling, his face hurt, his hip and leg hurt when he moved them, and he was stiff all over, but the pain was local, and nothing he hadn't felt before.

A nurse came in to check on him, and later to bring breakfast, and after he'd finished his Jell-O, he eased out of bed and took a few steps around the room. His balance was okay, the pain was tolerable.

The doc showed up and checked him over and said he'd release him if he would take it easy for a few days. Virgil said he would. The doc gave him some Tylenol, and told him not to fight any more women. Said he'd do the paperwork, and somebody would sign him out.

A nurse said the paperwork should be done "any minute," but it wound up taking two hours. Virgil got dressed and lay back down on the bed to wait, and when the forms finally came in, he signed off and called the town taxi. The nurse insisted that she push him out to the parking lot in a wheelchair.

The cold air hit him as soon as they got to the lot. Felt good. The taxi driver, another morose Tripptonite, said, "Bad night at the Bunker, huh?"

The Bunker had a reputation as the worst bar in Trippton, but Virgil had never been in it. He said, "No, I fell down on my way into Shanker's for a grilled cheese sandwich."

"I'm not sure the wife'll believe that," the cabbie said.

"Fuck her if she can't take a joke," Virgil said. Ten minutes later, he was back at the cabin. He checked his watch: noon. He wanted to talk to Marvin Hiners, the VP at Second National, but the banker was probably at lunch, so Virgil decided to lie down and try to relax a bit. He did that, and when he woke up, he woke in darkness. He fumbled for the bedside lamp switch, turned it on, looked at his watch: ten minutes to six. He'd blown the whole day.

He hurt when he sat up. His hip was the sorest, but he also had some pain in his right shoulder, his punching arm. His mouth tasted foul, and maybe a bit like blood and chicken feathers, so he brushed his teeth, set the shower to the volcanic setting, and spent fifteen minutes standing under the near-boiling water. He was pulling on his shirt when headlights swept across the cabin windows. Johnson and Clarice came in a moment later, carrying food.

"Everything you like, as long as you like barbeque ribs and mac and cheese," Clarice said. Virgil realized that he was starving. "We brought your truck back."

"I ran into that private detective down at the Kettle," Johnson said. "I told her what happened. She was going to come by right away, but I told her to hold off a day or two."

"Thank you," Virgil said.

"So who killed Gina Hemming?" Clarice asked.

"Not there yet. I didn't have anything to think about before I got clobbered," Virgil said. "She was found in the same dress that she wore to a meeting on Thursday night. I asked Rhodes about it and he said she was a fussy dresser: she would never wear the same outfit two days in a row. That means she was killed between the time the meeting ended and before she had a chance to go to bed.

The sheriff's office didn't do much of an investigation but did find out that she almost always got to the office before the bank opened and usually stopped at The Roasting Pig for a latte before she went to work. That all suggests that she was usually up and getting dressed before eight o'clock in the morning . . ."

"No later than that," Clarice said. "She always had good makeup; I never saw her without it. That takes a while. If she got to The Roasting Pig at eight-thirty, let's say she left her house at eight-fifteen. I think no less than forty-five minutes to go to the bathroom, shower, do the makeup, get dressed . . . and that would be fast. Now you're at seven-thirty for getting up. If she ate breakfast at home, checked the news on her laptop . . . she was getting up at seven o'clock. Or earlier."

"With that kind of routine, she was probably going to bed at eleven o'clock at night. Good chance that she was killed between nine o'clock and eleven o'clock," Virgil said.

"Unless she stayed up late to argue with somebody," Johnson said.

"Even so, she was probably talking to the killer before eleven o'clock," Clarice said.

Clarice had plates out on the cabin's kitchen table and spooned out a helping of mac and cheese and dropped a half slab of ribs beside it, while Johnson Johnson opened a bottle of California Cabernet Sauvignon. "Thought you were totally off alcohol?" Virgil said.

"That wasn't working. I'm totally off all alcohol except wine, which I never get drunk on," Johnson Johnson said. "Clarice says if I start going over the edge again, she'll warn me off and I'll quit the wine."

"Hope that works, but I gotta tell you, I'd be happier if you didn't drink at all," Virgil said.

Johnson: "I would be, too, but that ain't gonna happen yet. I can hold it to one drink, though."

Virgil let it go, something to worry about later. He spent a few minutes eating and thinking, then said, "Rhodes brought up the idea that somebody who owed money to the bank might have killed her."

Johnson shrugged and said, "I don't know," and Clarice said, "That doesn't sound right."

"Doesn't sound right to me, either," Virgil said to her. "Why doesn't it sound right to you?"

"From what you told us, it sounds more like an accident than something deliberate—hit once and killed," Clarice said. "If somebody was really, really angry with her, they might beat her up and wind up killing her, but that didn't happen, right?"

"Doesn't seem that way. She didn't show anything in the way of injuries, except the one that killed her, and some broken fingernails," Virgil said. He thought about what Corbel Cain had told him about brawling with his wife. "Although it's possible that she attacked first . . . and the guy was actually defending *himself*."

"Some defense," Clarice said.

"If somebody went there intending to kill her, they could have found a more efficient way of doing it than whacking her on the head, especially if it turns out she was hit with a bottle. Sounds more like a . . . lover. Seems impulsive. Could be that somebody was waiting for the reunion people to leave, she let them in, because they know each other, they argue, and *WHACK!*" Virgil said. He had been focused on the food as much as on the crime and looked up from his plate and said, "Holy cats, these are great ribs. Did you make these, Clarice?"

"I did," Johnson said. "Clarice bought the wine."

"What are you going to do next?" Clarice asked Virgil.

"Jack up the Class of '92," Virgil said. "They probably knew her better than anyone. See if I can find a close female friend who might know about a relationship."

By the next morning, Virgil still hurt when he walked, still had the squid on his face, but wasn't dysfunctional. As he was carefully pulling his pants over his aching black-and-blue ass, Margaret Griffin called. "I heard."

"Yeah. I haven't got anything on Jesse McGovern, I haven't really had time to look. But you be careful. It looks like there are some people who are extremely protective of her if they're willing to beat up a cop."

"Heard they were all women."

"Hard to tell with the parkas, but I think so," Virgil said. "Could have been a short guy in the mix. I didn't have time to check for testicles."

"How'd they do it, exactly? Rush you?"

Virgil told her about it, and she asked, "Are you all right now?"

"I'm better, I'm going back to work," Virgil said. "If I get anything, I'll call."

"If they come after me, they better bring a gun," she said. "I carry a baton with me when I travel. I've got it in my coat pocket now. They give me one second to react, they'll find out what an L.A. cop can do with a steel pipe."

"Jeez, Margaret, take it easy."

"I don't need a bunch of trailer trash putting me in the hospital," she said. "If they hurt *you* bad enough to give you a concussion, they might have cracked my skull. Nope, that ain't gonna happen to Margaret S. Griffin. If somebody's going to the emergency room, it won't be me. I'll whip their asses right down the street."

On the way into town, Virgil worried about that. Trippton was the biggest town in the area but was isolated, the best part of a half hour from La Crosse, the nearest larger city. Given that, Trippton was turned in upon itself: everybody knew everybody else—and everybody's business, relationships, history—and all the local news when it happened. Rumors ran through the place like grease through a goose.

Everybody knew Virgil, or about him, and by now, with her inquiries, everybody would know Margaret Griffin. Somebody might go after her—and having been an MP in the Army, Virgil was quite aware of what a trained cop could do with a metal baton. Griffin was a big woman and appeared to be in good shape. If she'd spent her cop years on the street in L.A., as she said she had, she would be formidable in a fight.

Virgil's first stop that morning was at Hemming's Second National Bank. When he walked through the door, he was spotted by a stout white-haired man named Marvin Hiners, the bank's senior vice president. They knew each other from Virgil's investigation of the school board murders, and Hiners hurried over and said, "Let's talk in my office" and "What's that on your face? The blue thing?"

"Nose support—I got beat up," Virgil said, as he followed the man to his office.

Hiners shut the office door, and they both sat down, and Hiners said, "I heard something about that, but I didn't know it was so bad. Jeez, I'm sorry."

"Not even the murder case," Virgil said. "Nothing to do with Gina Hemming."

"Isn't this awful? Gina? And, no, I don't think it was a customer who killed her. And I didn't do it, either, so I could get her job."

"Thanks for clearing that up," Virgil said. "Tell me why it wasn't a customer."

"I'm not saying it *wasn't* a customer, because everybody in Trippton is a customer. I'm saying it didn't happen *because* the person was a customer." He explained that—the apparent lack of aggression in their overdue accounts. "I've been through every one of them since this happened, trying to figure out if there was any danger to the rest of us. We've got some serious goobers out there, but I don't see any of them doing this. Or Gina letting them into her house. I wasn't there that night, but I understand that Jeff Purdy looked at the house and found out that nobody had broken in. In fact, it was all locked up, nice as you please. Like she'd gone out for a walk."

Virgil sat back. "Is that possible? That she'd gone out for a walk? A little too much booze, decides to clear her head, somebody grabs her on the street?"

"As far as I know, she didn't go for walks," Hiners said. "She had an exercise room with an elliptical machine, and a place where she did her yoga . . ."

"I saw that, down the basement," Virgil said. "I was thinking of a walk to get some air . . . stretch her legs."

Hiners mumbled, "Where was I? Okay. Now, it was drop-dead cold that night and she was wearing a skirt . . . If Donald Trump had grabbed her by the . . . you know . . . after a walk that night, he would have gotten frostbitten fingers. She didn't have a coat on when they pulled her out of the river. I think she was killed at her house, by somebody who knew her. In fact, that's what everybody thinks."

"If she let somebody into her house, who would that have been? Somebody here at the bank? A boyfriend?"

"Not at the bank—she was very strict about intra-bank relationships, though we've had a few. Her motto was 'Don't get your honey where you get your money,' and I believe she followed that herself. Besides, we only have seventeen employees—if she was seeing one of them, I'd know about it. She wasn't."

Hiners was a smart guy, so Virgil asked the obvious question: "Who do you think the killer is, Marv?"

Hiners pulled at his lower lip for a moment, then said, "Don't know, Virgil. But Gina had a number of sexual relationships over the years, and there was no reason to think that her . . . impulses . . . had cooled off. When you find the person who did this, I believe you'll find out that it was a boyfriend that none of us know about."

"None of you? Nobody in town? Is that even possible?"

"Difficult but possible. They could keep it in motels up in the Cities, or even in La Crosse or Rochester," Hiners said. "Wouldn't be much fun that way, but maybe the only thing they could do if the guy was married. So, possible. If it were somebody prominent who was already married and they quarreled, and Gina threatened to go public . . ."

"I like that, Marv, thank you," Virgil said. "Another possibility: what if one of your employees is stealing, and something Hemming said, or did, hinted that she suspected, and he went over there to talk to her about it?"

Hiners pulled at his lip some more, flashed his blue eyes up at Virgil. "I don't believe it. For one thing, Gina wasn't that much into the numbers. That's my job, and they would have killed *me*. But, I guess it's a possibility. I'll get an outside audit going. Like right now. I'll be on the phone before you get out the door."

"How long will that take?"

"A few days. To know for ninety percent sure. The other ten percent will take a while. But if that were the case, we'd be looking at a complicated form of theft— manipulating investment accounts and so on. I don't think we've got people who could pull that off. Even if they could, Gina wouldn't be the one who'd discover it, know about it."

"Did she have any close female friends she might have confided in?"

"Didn't like other women so much, but she did have one old friend. Maybe Margot will know about others. You should talk to Margot Moore. She was the Most Athletic Girl, Class of '92, and she and Gina had been tight since high school. She was at the Thursday meeting. Margot's father owned Moore's Funeral Home, sold it out to a chain a few years ago. Margot runs Moore Financial—she's one of those certified financial planners. Does quite well at it."

"Where's Moore Financial?"

"Go out the door, take a left, walk two blocks. You'll see a barber pole, and it's the next door down the street."

People on the street were hustling along, shoulders hunched, puffing steam into the frigid air, but, all in all, looking reasonably happy with themselves. One or two of them nodded to Virgil, and one, a dog owner, said, "Hey, Virgie. Investigating Gina Hemming?"

Virgil said yes, and after the man expressed bewilderment about the murder, Virgil asked after the man's Labrador retrievers and got a two-minute lecture on the care of dogs' paws in sub-zero weather. Moving on down the street, trying not to limp, Virgil spotted the barbershop, waved at the man behind its single chair, and turned into Moore Financial.

A receptionist sitting behind a high counter, typing, smiled at Virgil and said, "You're Virgil. I heard about the black eyes and the blue thing. You're here to talk to Margot. She thought you might be coming around."

"Is she in?"

"Yup. I'll tell her you're here."

Margot Moore was a forty-two-year-old gym rat, short, thin but not delicate, with carefully cut hair wrapped tightly around her oval face. She was wearing narrow black computer glasses. She had three computer screens on a side desk, and an expansive center desk stacked with paper files in different colors. She took off the glasses and stood up when Virgil walked in and shook his hand.

"Sit down, Virgil. Isn't this unbelievable?"

"You know who did it?" Virgil asked.

"Of course not or I would have called you up. I suspect somebody told you I was Gina's best friend, which is true enough. But this . . ."

"Was she seeing a man? Somebody who would not be happy to have that get out?"

Moore swiveled in her chair, looked out the window behind her desk, swiveled back, and said, "I really don't know for sure . . ."

"You think she was," Virgil said.

"No, no, I really don't know. I really don't know if she was seeing a man, or, if she was, who it would be."

"Let's not focus on what you know for sure. Give me your opinion. Was she seeing a man?"

Moore hesitated, then said, "No. Not in what you'd call a real relationship."

"Did she talk about her relationships?"

"Oh, sure. With me anyway. The thing she was most private about was money. She wanted people to know that she was rich but not how rich. For one thing, they might have thought she was a lot richer than she really was and she wouldn't want them finding out she wasn't as rich as they thought. People think she was the richest person in town, but if she was, it wasn't by much."

"Did she ever talk to you about Corbel Cain?"

"Corbel . . ." She half laughed, rubbed her forehead with her middle three fingers. "Yeah, she told me about Corbel. About everything. Corbel wouldn't hurt her, though. If you wanted a good, rousing fuck—excuse the language—Corbel was the man to see. Nothing fancy, meat and potatoes, but he knew how to dish it out."

Virgil studied her for a moment, said nothing, and she added, "Yeah, yeah, Corbel and I had a thing, too, right after my divorce. I sort of borrowed him from Gina, who thought that was hilarious."

"You were close enough to . . . borrow. Was there anyone else?"

"No, no, no . . . Corbel was sort of our girl thing."

"I'm a little surprised that Corbel's wife hasn't shot somebody," Virgil said.

"Corbel's wife takes care of her own self," Moore said. "I once knew for sure that she was banging the guy who has the diesel fuel franchise here. She came in for the annual investment tune-up, and, since we were friends, I said, 'Janey, there've been some rumors going around, you got to be more careful,' and she waved me off and said, 'Keeping two men happy is the only way I can stay happy myself.'"

"This place . . ." Virgil said.

"Is exactly like every other place," she said.

They sat for a minute or so, Virgil mulling it over and then asking, "How long has Gina been involved in B and D?"

For the first time in the conversation, Virgil realized he'd delivered a shot. Moore's eyes opened wider, and her forehead went red, and she said, "Gina doesn't . . ."

"Yes, she does," Virgil said. "I'm wondering if her partner . . . or partners . . . might have gone too far, or maybe Gina said something that freaked him out and he hit her a little too hard."

"My God, Virgil . . ." Her eyes slid sideways, and Virgil understood that she was about to tell a large, whopping lie, and she said, "I don't believe that she would ever have been involved with anything like that."

"I found a whip under her bed, along with a couple of sex toys. I've got a crime scene team coming down to check it all for DNA," Virgil said. "The medical examiner found light bruising on her wrists, ankles, and buttocks consistent with being tied up and spanked."

"Virgil . . ."

"You don't know anything about that?"

"No!" A little anger this time.

"The reason I ask is that if this . . . partner . . . killed her, he might want to make sure that nobody who knows about the relationship talks with the police. If he thinks you might know about it, you could be in trouble."

"That's ridiculous. Don't go speaking poorly of the dead, either. She was a very successful businesswoman in Trippton. And if you start spreading this around—"

"It won't hurt her a bit," Virgil said. "You know why? Because she's dead."

"Virgil! Stop!"

They went back and forth for a couple of minutes, Moore insisting that she had no idea of who the B and D partner might be, Virgil nearly certain that she was lying. When there was no more to be said, he asked Moore about money. Moore said that Hemming was going through a midlife reassessment, that they'd talked extensively about the possibility of selling the bank.

"She controlled two-thirds of the bank stock through

a trust. She owned a third of that outright herself, another third is owned by her sister, but the trust controls all of it and Gina controlled the trust. The other third of the stock is owned by probably a couple dozen people. Some of the others were pushing her to talk to Wells Fargo and U.S. Bank about selling out because a sale could generate a nice premium on top of what the stock was worth on the market."

"Was she going to do that? Sell out?"

"I think she might have—but she hadn't decided yet. The problem was, if she cashed out, she wouldn't get much more from her investments than she was getting from salary at the bank. And she wouldn't have the perks of being a bank president, either. There were two kinds of return in owning that bank stock: one was her salary, which she essentially set herself, and she did very well; the other is the power you have when you're the biggest banker in town. That part, the power locally, would go away if she cashed out. The thinking was, she'd take four to five million out of the bank, there are other opportunities for somebody like her with four or five million in cash, and the bank was beginning to bore her."

"What kind of opportunities?"

"Investments . . . moving out of Trippton. She has a condo down in Naples, Florida . . . If she hadn't gotten involved with this reunion thing, she'd have been down there right now and would still be alive," Moore said. "Anyway, she'd talked about moving down there, about the opportunities to meet eligible men. Not many of those in Trippton. Not desirable ones anyway."

"Huh. I've been told that her sister will probably sell out. Should I be looking at one of the other stockholders who might have been anxious to move the sale along?" Virgil asked.

"Nah. The biggest of them has maybe a quarter million in stock. He might get three hundred thousand if Wells or U.S. Bank bought them out, and that's before taxes. After taxes, the buyout would net him less than an additional forty thousand, more than he'd get from a private buyer. I know him and he doesn't need the money."

"No boyfriend that you know of, or will admit to, and not a stockholder. Who, then?"

"I don't know enough about the murder—only rumors. Tell me about it," she said.

Virgil told her about it—everything he had. When she'd heard him out, she said, "You know I was at the meeting the night she disappeared."

"Yes. I have your name on a list. Most Athletic Girl."

"I've been thinking about the people at the meeting and there's not a single one of them that I'd suspect of killing her. If she was killed that night—"

"She almost certainly was," Virgil said.

"—it was somebody who showed up later."

"That doesn't help much," Virgil said.

She shrugged. "That's the way it is."

When Virgil got up to leave, he said, "I'll tell you, Margot, I believe you're lying about knowing her B and D friend." She opened her mouth to protest, but Virgil held up a hand. "I'm not going to argue about it because I've got no proof. If you deliberately withhold information I need to conduct this investigation, you could find yourself with deep legal problems. If the killer knows that you know about him . . . you could be in even more trouble."

She said nothing for a moment, then asked, "Do you have a card?"

"Yes." He fished one out of a pocket, wrote his cell number on the back of it, and said, "The sooner you call, the better. Don't wait until it's too late."

TWELVE

Lucy Cheever was standing in the glass cage of the manager's office at Cheever Chevrolet when Virgil went by on his way to interview Hiners at the bank. She recognized his 4Runner because, for one thing, it was probably the only 4Runner in town.

"There goes Virgil Flowers. I wonder what he's finding out?"

Elroy Cheever sat behind a wide metal desk, going through a stack of invoices. He was a big man, easily large enough to carry a hundred-and-fifty-pound woman down to the effluent outflow and throw her in. He also had a ferocious five o'clock shadow, even early in the morning. When put together with his large square jaw, he looked like an enforcer for the mob.

"Nothing about us," Elroy Cheever said.

"He might think it's suspicious that Gina Hemming looked like she was going to turn us down for a business loan and, two minutes later, she gets killed," Lucy Cheever said. She chewed on her lip for a moment, then said, "Wonder if she told Marv Hiners? Marv all but said we were clear for it."

"Don't think she would have had time," Elroy Cheever said. "He was up in the Cities at a hockey game. Technically, she hadn't turned us down yet."

"Marv might give it to us if he's running things now."

"Lot of money," Elroy Cheever said. "Makes me nervous."

"Shouldn't," Lucy Cheever said. She had the money brain in the business; Elroy was sales, and was good at it. "The question is, should we go talk to Marv now? That might make him suspicious. Especially if they'd talked. Might make Virgil Flowers suspicious of us."

"Maybe we ought to go back to the Wells guy in Rochester."

"It'll cost a percentage point, maybe a point and a half," Lucy Cheever said. "God, I don't know. A million dollars . . ."

"Lot of money," Elroy said again.

"If we get it, we've got Trippton cornered. Heck, we've got the whole Minnesota side from La Crescent down to the Iowa line. Dodge will be gone in a year; they're having a hard time selling a truck anymore. If only that bitch hadn't turned us down . . ."

"You know what? Flowers is going to suspect that one of us killed Gina. Because of all the money."

"You're right. We'll have to talk about how to handle him."

David Birkmann knew Virgil Flowers by sight from Virgil's involvement in the dog-snatching, meth-cooking, school board murders cases. Virgil had been on the witness stand down at the courthouse for parts of two days, an SRO crowd, and Birkmann had been there for the whole thing.

He'd gotten the distinct impression that Flowers was not a man to be fooled with. At the same time, he'd heard that Flowers was going around town asking only the most routine questions and hadn't a clue about what had happened to Gina Hemming.

Birkmann was on a stool at his Dunkin' Donuts outlet when Virgil came ambling down the sidewalk on the other side of the street and went into Moore Financial. He was interviewing the reunion committee, Birkmann thought.

On the previous Sunday, with the murder three days in the past, Birkmann, nursing a vicious hangover, had driven into the Dunkin' Donuts. His store was one of the few places in town that was open early on a Sunday morning, and he desperately needed a coffee and a sugar fix. When he pushed through the door, his counter-woman, Alice, was gawking at John Handy, who worked for the city's buildings department. Alice pivoted toward him, her mouth still open in astonishment, and sput-tered, "John . . . Tell Dave."

Handy, with the intensity of a man delivering news that was bad, but more *interesting* than personally bad, said, "Somebody killed Gina Hemming. Threw her body in the river. Ben Potter spotted her down by the sewage plant, snagged her with a Rapala, and pulled her up on the bank."

Birkmann was astonished. "What?"

Handy had the details: half a dozen city employees had been involved in the recovery and transportation of the body, and sheriff's deputies had spent half of Saturday evening checking out her house. There was now word that Virgil Flowers of the BCA was coming back to town to take charge of the investigation.

Birkmann barely registered the part about Virgil: *She had been pulled out of the river? What the fuck?*

At the moment, he'd staggered backward onto an empty stool and blurted, "But I saw her Thursday night."

Handy said, "Oh, yeah—you were in the Class of '92?"

Birkmann nodded dumbly. *Pulled out of the river?*

"Well, Flowers gonna be on you like white on rice," Handy said. "Word is, she was probably killed that very night you all were meeting."

Birkmann stood up and muttered, "I gotta go . . . walk around."

Alice asked, "You all right, Dave?"

Birkmann ran his hands through his hair and said, "This is awful. I knew her since we were in grade school. Since kindergarten."

Handy and Alice nodded sympathetically, and Birkmann wandered semi-blindly out the door. *What the fuck? In the river?*

On that Sunday, reeling from the shock of the discovery of Hemming's body, Birkmann went back home and sat in front of the TV for most of the day, tried drinking some more, and fell into bed in a full-out stupor.

The next day, Monday, he steamed himself out in the shower, dressed neatly for work, chose a yellow hat from his box of GetOut! complimentary hats, and headed downtown.

His Dunkin' Donuts store was Trippton's epicenter of

the latest news, rumor, and blind conjecture. There was a load of all of it, on Monday morning. Most of the medical examiner's report was on the street by Monday, and Hemming reportedly had been beaten to death before she was thrown in the effluent stream.

He spent the rest of Monday on the routine chores of a small business operator—writing checks, approving invoices, worrying.

The news stream was even richer on the next day, Tuesday. Flowers had been badly beaten on Monday afternoon and had been taken to the clinic and held overnight and might be out of it for good with permanent brain damage. There were rumors that the BCA was planning to flood the town with agents; that Flowers had been attacked by people who were making the Barbie-O dolls; that the attackers were all women; that Gina Hemming had planned to foreclose on the boot factory and that she'd been killed to stall the foreclosure; that Flowers's friend Johnson Johnson had sworn to kill Flowers's attackers; that one of the murderous school board members who'd gone missing had returned to town and had organized the attack on Flowers as revenge for her friends' imprisonment; that Gina Hemming's heart had been cut out of her body and placed on a satanic altar found near the sewage plant but that the sheriff was covering it up until the cult leader could be arrested, that the sheriff denied that, but was obviously lying, and might be involved in the cult himself.

"Jeff Purdy in a satanic cult? I don't think so," Birkmann said.

Alice said, "But wouldn't it be the person you'd least suspect?"

Another donut eater jumped in to answer that: "Maybe, but Jeff is too damn dumb to be in a satanic cult. He has trouble starting his car."

"You got me there," Alice said.

Now, on Wednesday morning, here was Flowers leaving Moore Financial and heading straight across the street to the donut shop. Birkmann wasn't ready for that and retreated to the kitchen, where he could hear what was being said but couldn't be seen from the counter.

And what was said was . . .

Alice: "What is that on your poor face?"

"Nose brace," Flowers said. "I got beat up."

"You must be Virgil. I heard about that," Alice said. "Told it was a bunch of women."

"Yeah, it was. They're gonna enjoy their visit to Shakopee. Lots of time to discuss their problems and become emotionally engaged. You know, do all that women stuff."

Alice: "Why would they be going to Shakopee?"

"'Cause that's where the women's prison is," Virgil said. "They should have read section 609.2231 of the Minnesota Statutes before they jumped me. Assaulting an officer of the law and doing a demonstrable injury is a felony. Does this blue thing"—he pointed at his face— "look like a demonstrable injury?"

"Looks like a blue squid," said one of the donut eaters. "A small blue squid. Like one of them things they've got down at Ma and Pa Kettle's on Friday nights."

Alice: "Calimari?"

"Before they're fried."

"Calimari aren't blue," Virgil said.

"You apparently ain't been down to Ma and Pa's and looked at the squid," the donut eater said. "I stay away from them, myself."

Alice turned back to Virgil. "What can I do for you?"

"Give me two peanut . . . no, *one* peanut and one Boston crème . . . and a Diet Coke."

"Sure. Gotta charge you for the Coke, but the donuts are on the house for all our first responders."

Donut eater: "We've been told on good authority that Gina's heart was cut out with a surgical tool and placed on a satanic altar by the sewage plant. Is that true?"

Virgil: "What do you think?"

"I think it's horseshit."

Virgil: "You're a lot smarter than you look."

"Thank . . . Hey!"

Alice: "I put an extra donut in the sack for you, honey. That'll be a dollar eighty-seven for the Coke."

When Flowers had gone, Birkmann stepped out of the kitchen and watched as he walked up the street, munching on a donut, back the way he'd come. When he was a full block away, Birkmann pulled on his coat, told Alice, "Good move with the extra donut," and headed across the street to Moore Financial.

Margot Moore kept him waiting for five minutes. When she finally called him in, she looked as though she'd been crying. Birkmann dropped into a client's chair and said, "You look like I feel."

"Virgil Flowers just left," she said.

"I was over in the donut shop and saw him coming

out. I figure he must be interviewing all of us on the re-union committee."

"That's what he's doing, but he . . . I don't know, Dave. He's asking about some things . . ."

"What things?" Birkmann asked.

"I don't want to talk about it. It's rather private," Moore said.

"He's gonna ask me anyway, isn't he? We're both in the same place."

Moore opened a desk drawer and took out a pink tissue, blew her nose with an unfeminine *HONK!* and said, "Well, he says they have evidence that Gina was involved in B and D."

The letters meant nothing to Birkmann. Sounded like a railroad: riding the rails to Frisco on the old B & D. He asked, "What? What's that?"

"You know, whips. Getting tied up."

Birkmann still looked blank, and Moore said, "For sexual purposes, for Christ's sakes, Dave. Bondage and discipline. B and D."

"Whips?"

"Not real whips, play whips. Flowers said he found one in her bedroom."

"Play whips? You've seen them?"

Moore backtracked. "I assume they're play whips. I talked to Gina every day, and we worked out together at the Y, and I never saw any whip marks on her. Must be play whips."

Birkmann didn't entirely buy that, the backtracking, but had no place to go with it. Instead, he asked, "Who was tying her up? Somebody from Trippton?"

"I suppose . . ."

"From *Trippton*?"

"Dave, Dave . . . try to pay attention, okay? I mean, you can buy vibrators at Target. People in Trippton do more than the missionary position."

"I didn't know that," Birkmann admitted.

"Maybe that's why your wife ran off with a donut shop guy," Moore said.

"You don't have to be offensive," Birkmann snapped.

"Sorry. I didn't mean that. I'm really upset. Maybe we ought to talk about this some other time."

"Tell me what Flowers asked you," Birkmann said. "If I have some time to think about it, maybe I'll figure something out."

"Well, he wondered if anyone on the committee might have killed her," Moore said.

"That's ridiculous."

"That's what I told him . . ."

She outlined her conversation with Virgil, and five minutes later Birkmann was back in the donut shop. "Give me two chocolate-frosteds and don't tell me about my heart," he told Alice. "Give me the fuckin' donuts."

A cross the street, Moore was back on the phone with a man who had a deep voice. "Dave doesn't have any idea of what happened," she said. "If somebody blew his brains out, it'd take him two weeks to notice."

"You can see where this is going. I mean, it's freakin' me out," the deep voice said. "I've had problems with the law, and if Flowers gets to me, he's gonna hang me up like a piece of Sheetrock. I'm like a cop's dream. I got a beard, a tattoo on my neck, I got a Harley, I done time for assault. You put that together with whips and chains, the fuckin' jury gonna airmail me to Stillwater prison. I gotta do *something*."

"Don't panic. I put him off. Who else could give you up?" The silence on the other end of the line lasted a couple of beats too long, and Moore's voice went cold as she half repeated what she'd said: *"Who else could give you up?"*

"You . . . weren't my only clients."

"Clients? Clients? What are you talking about? We didn't *pay* you." More silence. "Did we *pay* you?"

"Gina . . . helped me out from time to time."

"Oh my God, you're a hooker," Moore screamed. "Have I got AIDS?"

"No, you don't fuckin' have AIDS. I'm not a hooker. I'm a sexual therapist, registered by the State of Minnesota. Listen, I gotta think about this. This is a murder case, and running won't do me no good . . . not if my name comes up."

"Maybe . . . Maybe you should go talk to Flowers. He's supposed to be a good guy. You could say it was you and Gina, and you never hurt her, and you wouldn't have to say anybody else was involved."

"Are you deaf? Beard, tattoo, a Harley Softail, assault convictions, whips and chains? Are you shittin' me? He gets my name in connection with Gina, I'm SOL."

"Listen! Think of something else, if you can. Think about the possibility of going to Flowers. I saw him in action a couple of years ago and he's a smart guy. If you're straight with him, he could believe you. Tell him it was playacting. Tell him where you were Thursday night . . ."

"Thursday night? Thursday night? I got an alibi for

every night except Thursday night. Ain't that the way it is? Every fuckin' night but Thursday."

He hung up.

Moore spent the afternoon obsessing about the conversation. He was going to get caught, she thought. The therapy sessions—that's what she and Hemming had called them—had been arranged by email, and Flowers would have access to Hemming's computer. Sooner or later, he'd track the guy down.

If he confessed that Moore was involved in the whole B and D thing, it'd get all over town. How would she handle that? Every single thing she had on earth came out of her business . . .

THIRTEEN

Virgil talked to Lucy Cheever, the Homecoming Queen, and Barry Long, the Homecoming King, got one good alibi and one reasonable one for Thursday night after the meeting.

Cheever had gone home after the meeting and put the kids to bed after checking their homework to make sure it all got done.

Cheever said that she'd left the meeting at nine o'clock, one of the last three people to see Hemming—the other two being Rhodes and Moore.

"We all left at once," she said. "Of course we've all thought about who might have done it, and we've talked about it, too, along with everybody else in town. That's about all we talk about anymore. Who would hurt her? We mostly liked her. Maybe a couple of people didn't see eye to eye with her, especially her politics, but they wouldn't kill her, for God's sakes. They didn't even argue with her."

Cheever's alibi seemed solid to Virgil for a couple of reasons: she was a small woman and would have had a hard time moving Hemming's body; and, according to

Johnson Johnson, she and her husband were "richer than Jesus Christ and all the apostles," which took the money issue out of it.

Clarice said that Cheever and her husband, Elroy, had been partners and lovers since high school, and that she felt it was highly unlikely that Cheever's husband would have had a relationship with Hemming, creating a revenge motive.

Virgil hinted at the possibility, and Cheever picked it up immediately and laughed. "Elroy's never wanted anybody but me and I've never wanted anybody but him. Even if he did want somebody else, he couldn't hide it from me. I've known him since he was two years old. We got caught playing doctor when we were seven. I mean, no . . . he didn't have an affair with Gina, and I've never had an affair, either. Elroy and I are going the whole route."

When he finished with the Cheevers, Virgil went out and stood on her porch for a minute and scratched his head. What he really needed to do, he thought, was think. And maybe take a couple of non-blood-thinning painkillers for his nose. Instead, he headed for Long's greenhouse.

Long was a tall, sober man with an engaging smile, but a smile with some distance to it, as though he did it only professionally, which he did. His hand was narrow, bony, and cold, as Virgil imagined an undertaker's might be.

"I never really had much to do with Gina, not even back in high school," Long said. "Can't really tell you why. We didn't click, I guess. Our politics are different enough that we spent a lot of time being polite to each other. She's given money to my opponent in every single election."

"Because she didn't like you?"

"No, because Washington made her into a Democrat and I'm a Republican, and never the twain shall cross. She was one of Mr. Obama's few advocates in Trippton."

After leaving Hemming's house on Thursday night, Long said he had been working alone at his greenhouse office on issues for the State House of Representatives, which had already convened, although it was temporarily in adjournment. He offered Virgil a raft of emails with time and date stamps on them, indicating that they'd been sent Thursday night between nine o'clock and eleven o'clock, when he'd gone home.

Virgil didn't know whether or not the time and date stamps on the emails could have been faked. He suspected that a hacker could do it, and Long had that semi-geek attitude and appearance suggesting a familiarity with technology. He'd seen the same geekiness in men who had a problem relating to women. Long wasn't married, but, as Rhodes had said, neither was he gay. He simply seemed to have one passion and that was politics.

Although he was considered a serious political power in the Republican Party, he didn't make any effort to impress his authority on Virgil; he was polite, and spoke in complete, well-parsed sentences.

Before Virgil left him, Long said, "I watched you when you were investigating the school board. I found that . . . interesting. Do you think you'll find Gina's killer?"

"Yeah, I do," Virgil said. "I think he or she will be somebody who was either there that night or somebody who's attached to the people who were there. Who do you think did it?"

Long thought about the question, then said, "I don't know. I've thought about it, but I haven't come to any conclusion. And I agree with you: it was somebody who was there that night or somebody attached to them. Somebody who knew about the meeting and wanted to speak with Gina. Most likely . . . not an accident, but un- intentional. There have been some rumors about the possibility that a vagrant riverman did it, somebody off a barge, but I don't believe it. No, Gina was killed by somebody who knew her and probably was welcome in her house."

When he left Long, Virgil continued down the street to the offices of Trippton Medical and Surgical, where he caught Ryan Harney as he finished with a pa- tient. There were two more patients waiting, but Har- ney's nurse told Harney that Virgil was in the office and Harney had him shown in.

"I don't have a lot of time, I've got people waiting, but you sort of caught me between anuses."

"Won't take much of your time," Virgil said. "I'm here about Gina Hemming . . ."

"I don't know who killed Gina. Or why they would. I don't even suspect anyone. If I suspect *anything*, it's that somebody snuck in a back door to rob her, maybe some guy off the river, and picked up something handy and hit her with it."

"Didn't find that, whatever it was," Virgil said. "What exactly is your relationship with Gina anyway?"

Harney shrugged. "I don't have one. We went to high school together; we both belong to Trippton National, we're somewhat friendly; but she's a pretty woman, and I'm married. So there's that. I have a checking account at Second National, but my savings and investments are through the Edward Jones office."

"Essentially, no regular contact except out at the club? You guys play golf or tennis, or something?"

"I golf. I've never seen her on the course. I think she might be tennis, but I don't pay too much attention to those people. Gina and I don't . . . didn't . . . hang out with the same people at the club. We're friendly, but we're not close."

"You think that's how other people in town would characterize your relationship?" Virgil asked.

"Sure. Talk to people at the club, if you want. Tell them I sent you up," Harney said.

"Did you finance your business through the bank?"

"No, never did. Our partnership borrowed money for the building here—we own it—from a specialist medical financing company twelve years ago. We've never needed additional financing. And we've got the medical care business here sewn up. There are five partners, we're all on staff at the clinic when we're needed there, and there are three more docs down there who aren't partners. But it's all . . . sewn up."

Virgil nodded. "After you left Thursday night?"

"Went home. Our office hours start at eight, I get up at six to exercise, catch the morning news, get cleaned up, help get the kids ready for school. I was one of the first people out of there. I'll tell you, Virgil, the meeting was really boring—I wouldn't have gone if I didn't think

I had to. And I'll tell you this: there was no tension there, at the meeting. Nothing that I could see. Nothing at all."

Virgil could tell when he wasn't making headway, so after a bit more talk, he let Harney get back to his work. As he was leaving, Harney said, "Get up here on my table. I want to look at your nose."

"I got a doc down at the clinic," Virgil said.

"Let me look."

Virgil let him look, and when he was done, Harney said, "You live in the Cities?"

"No, over in Mankato."

"There's a Mayo branch there. Get one of their ENTs to take a look. There's still quite a bit of swelling, but I don't like the way the end of the septum looks right now. You might need a little more work there."

"Well . . . okay. If they do something, it'll hurt, won't it?"

"Oh, yeah."

Virgil called Johnson, who was nearly unintelligible with one of his sawmills working in the background, but managed to get Clarice's phone number. Clarice worked in the office, and when she came up, Virgil said, "If I wanted to buy some whips and chains, maybe a couple of vibrators and so on, could I do that in Trippton?"

"Nope. Not as far as I know. Why would anybody do that?"

"Because maybe they wanted to get vibrated?"

"Hang on one second, Virgil . . ." Virgil hung on for ten seconds, then Clarice came back and said, "I put 'sex toys' in the search field at Amazon. They sent me to their

'Sexual Wellness' category, where they list entire departments: Condoms and Lubes, Performance Enhancers, Bondage Gear, Sex Toys, Exotic Apparel, Novelties, Men's Toys, Sex Furniture, and Sensual Delights. Those are all *departments*. I am clicking on 'Sex Toys' . . . and the first two entries are the 'Utimi Upgraded Silicone Ten-speed G Spot and Clitoris Vibrating Vibrator,' which is right next to the 'Utimi Ten-speed Silicone USB-charging Vibrating Anal Butt Plug Prostate Vibrator.'"

Virgil said, "You didn't make that up?"

"No, I didn't. By the way, they're all eligible for Amazon Prime."

"That's a relief. I'd hate to wait for three days," Virgil said. Getting no response, he said, "You're telling me that a sex toys store in Trippton would be superfluous."

"That's my belief, yes," Clarice said. "If you bought something here, everybody in town would know in eight seconds. If you buy from Amazon, maybe it's an electric toothbrush or a rubber dog bone, and it comes in a brown box."

"I'm sorry to have bothered you, Clarice," Virgil said.

"And I'm sorry if I embarrassed you, Virgil," Clarice said.

Virgil hung up. Anal butt plug and prostate vibrator? What the hell was happening in the world? Somebody with a man bun and a skateboard in Portland, Oregon, might be able to explain how it was all very natural and healthy, but he wouldn't find that guy in Trippton.

He called Johnson again and Johnson shouted over the whine of the circular saw, "She help you out?"

Virgil said, "Yeah. I need your expertise on the Hemming murder. You got someplace close that we can talk?"

"How about the Cheese-It? I could get a sandwich, and you could get a Diet Coke. I could be there in twenty minutes."

"See you there."

The Cheese-It was one of the lesser restaurants in a town full of them—lesser restaurants, that is. Virgil had once ordered a BLT at the Cheese-It and they'd forgotten to put the "B" in between the two pieces of soggy white bread. Johnson alleged he'd once sent an open-face roast beef sandwich back to the kitchen because it moved. On the other hand, there was nothing wrong with their Diet Cokes.

He got a Coke, and a table, and Johnson arrived a few minutes later, ordered a grilled cheese sandwich and a Sunkist Orange Soda, dropped into the chair opposite Virgil, and asked, "What's up?"

Virgil said, "It's Thursday night and it's snowing, and you've killed Gina Hemming, maybe more by accident than by plan, and you decide to get rid of the body to delay the discovery of her death. Maybe to obscure the exact time of death . . . Maybe hoping nobody will ever find the body."

"You dump her in the river," Johnson said.

"Right. How do you do that in the first week of January with the river locked up tight? Who could carry her down to the effluent outflow at the sewer plant? It's too far, and she was too heavy. The snow was really coming down, but there were also people working at the sewage plant—you, or your truck, could be seen."

"I could have carried her," Johnson said.

"Not many guys with your kind of strength," Virgil said. "If you killed her and wanted to throw her in the river, would it even have occurred to you to park down there at the plant and walk a half mile with a body on your back and throw it in . . . and not expect somebody to see either you or your truck?"

Johnson shook his head. "No. It wouldn't occur to me. It could be the guy wasn't half bright and so he did it and got lucky. It was snowing like hell, so from his point of view, that might have been a good thing. If he thought somebody might have been coming, he could have stepped a few feet off the trail and not been seen . . ."

"True," Virgil said.

Johnson scratched his neck and said, "I don't believe it. He's kinda frantic, he's kinda panicked, he wants to get rid of her, he thinks of the river. Why? He could haul her up in the woods and stick her in a snowdrift and nobody would find her until the end of March."

"You ask the right question: why?" Virgil said.

Johnson slapped the tabletop and said, "Because he knew the river. It was the first thing that popped into his head."

"Why would he think that? The river's locked up."

"Because he's a river rat. Because he's got an ice-fishing shack out there, and a ten-inch auger. Cuts a couple three holes, hooks them up with a chisel, shoves her under. Like a hole you cut when you're pike fishing. Hopes she doesn't show up until spring, down in Dubuque. Or maybe never."

"If you did that, somebody might still be able to see that big hole, right?" Virgil asked. "If somebody looked? Like us?"

"If I were doing it, I'd cut nice clean holes, the smallest that would take the body. I'd shove her as far down as I could, so the body wouldn't get stuck under the ice right away. You could do that with the ice chipper, do it right, not afraid to get your arm wet, you could get her eight feet down. I'd let the holes freeze over. The river water wouldn't come right to the top of the ice, so you'd have to pour more water in after the first freeze. Scuff some broken ice over it, drill another hole or two . . ."

"Probably still see where it was," Virgil said.

"Not after you scuffed it up a little, packed some snow on it, got some fish blood on it. Dragged some fishing stools over it . . ."

Virgil thought about it for a couple minutes, then asked, "You still got those sleds?"

"Absolutely. When do you want to go?" Johnson asked.

"This afternoon? I'm gonna have to get some warmer gear on. How many shacks out there?"

"Maybe fifty, in two groups, and a few scattered," Johnson said. "Some of them will be locked up. Most of them not. Won't be too many people out there in the afternoon—things don't really get going until after dark."

"Let's do what we can. I gotta think if the guy's a river rat, and if he has a shack, he'd have used his own place . . ."

"Meet you at the cabin," Johnson said. "Hot dog. This is gonna be fun. I'll bring my .45."

"Johnson . . ."

"Fuck you, I'm bringing it. I got a concealed carry permit now."

"That's . . . really good," Virgil said.

"I thought so," Johnson said. "Gives me a certain status."

They rendezvoused at the cabin, Johnson trailering in two Polaris snowmobiles. Virgil, now dressed in his camo deer-hunting suit with ski gloves and a hood, let Johnson unload them. Johnson handed him a helmet, said, "All gassed and ready to go. Follow me out, but try not to run over my ass."

"I'll do that," Virgil said. His suit's hood wouldn't fit over the helmet, so he pulled the helmet on and yanked the drawstrings of the hood tight around his neck, making a seal around the bottom of the helmet. As he settled onto the sled, which was already turning over, he hooked the kill switch cord to his suit belt. Johnson lurched down the bank and onto the frozen river, made a wide left turn, and leaned on the throttle.

Virgil followed, and they settled into a steady sixty miles an hour over the relatively smooth, snow-covered ice. The sky was a brilliant pale blue to the east, over Wisconsin, with a sullen gray cloud bank moving in over the bluffs above Trippton, to the west. A good day to ride, but maybe not a good night.

A mile north, they turned out onto the main river, where the ride got rougher, with windrows of snow like soft speed bumps running perpendicular to their tracks. Virgil opened up the machine a bit more, pulled even with Johnson, a hundred feet to one side, as they headed toward a cluster of ice shacks three or four miles down-river.

Though the day was still bitterly cold, he was comfortable enough with the heated handles and the wind-proof suit; the ride was exhilarating, and he could have done a few more miles, almost regretting it when Johnson swung into a circle that would slow them into the first fishing village.

And it *was* a village, maybe like something that would have been built on the frontier a hundred and fifty years earlier. There were several shacks that were built as mock-upscale houses, with porticos and pillars; a few like tiny barns, a couple with quarter moons like outhouses; one painted to resemble a brick house, another a bar, and a dozen that were unpainted plywood boxes. There were several tents. There was also an ordinary travel trailer with a couple of tubes extending down from its floor to surround the ice holes beneath; it had a TV antenna on the roof. As they came in, two snowmobiles headed down-river, away from them, and they could see a third one coming out from the direction of the Trippton marina.

Johnson steered them to a shack built to look like a log cabin, with smoke coming out of a narrow tin smoke-stack, and dismounted and killed the engine. Virgil got off his snowmobile, and Johnson said, "We get out of here early enough, we ought to make a run up the river. For the ride."

"Good with me," Virgil said.

As they walked toward the shack, Virgil noticed a small person—couldn't tell if it was a man or woman—walking toward a semitransparent plastic tent. The person glanced at them once, and again, and again, and disappeared inside the tent, though Virgil could see the body shape moving around behind the plastic sheeting.

Johnson said, "Hey."

Virgil turned back and found he'd left Johnson behind at the door of the log cabin. "Sorry. Got distracted," he said, as he crunched back across the ice. "Who's this?"

"Rick Thomas," Johnson said, as he led the way to the cabin door. "He's the mayor of the ice town, and he's usually around. He sleeps out here, half the time."

He pounded on the door, and a man shouted, "Who's there?"

"Johnson Johnson," Johnson shouted back.

"Go away. I'm getting laid."

"With whose dick?" Johnson shouted. "Yours ain't worked since the Carter administration."

The door popped open, and a man, who looked like a skeletal Santa Claus, peered out at them and asked Virgil, "What's that on your face?"

"A squid," Virgil said.

"Huh. Some kind of religious thing, then?"

The cabin was snug, warm, and comfortable, with four holes in the floor and four chairs facing one another, two by two, either side of the holes. A single bunk bed, an easy chair, a shelf of books and magazines, and an electric stove and heater made up the rest of the place. A rack of storage batteries occupied the back wall, fed by a diesel generator that sat outside. The place smelled of fish, both raw and cooked.

"I hope you got that generator isolated or you're gonna gas yourself to death out here, Rick," Johnson said.

"I'm all caulked and sealed. I worry about it since what happened to Jerry," Thomas said. "I got a new CO detector on the wall, too."

Johnson said to Virgil, "Jerry got all fucked up on fumes. Damn near died. He has one of the better spots out here, too. If he'd croaked, there would have been a hell of a fight over his spot."

"That would have been a shame, the mourning and all," Virgil said.

So what's up?" Thomas asked.

Johnson introduced Virgil, who first explained the blue squid, then the murder problem, and Thomas said, "Well, it won't be one of the big places out here. Has to be one of the small ones."

"Why's that?" Virgil asked.

Thomas pointed at the floor. "Because the big places have wood floors. You'd have to drill a hole through the floor. Or you'd have to move your whole outfit, and you can see if that's been done, and nobody out here has moved since before Christmas. Lot of the smaller places don't have full floors."

"That helps," Virgil said. "If you know all the people out here . . . where's the first place you'd look?"

"I'm not sure you'd look in an ice house at all," Thomas said. "Even if the guy is a rat, why wouldn't he haul the body out to his house, pick up the auger, and go on up the river where nobody can see him, drill some holes, and drop her in there? It was snowing hard Thursday night—I wasn't out here, I was in town, but I was out with my snow blower for a while . . . real pretty night.

Anyway, in that storm he could have driven out on the river, a pickup or a sled—either one—and drilled a few holes lickety-split, dropped her in, been back to shore, nobody the wiser."

"Well, fuck me," Johnson said. To Virgil: "It was all so clear in my mind."

"That's gotta be an unexpected change," Thomas said.

"You still might be right," Virgil said to Johnson. He turned to Thomas. "You see any tracks going up- or downriver?"

"Yeah. About a million of them. Everybody's been out riding."

Johnson: "That's true. Shit."

"Still worth a look around," Virgil said. He said to Thomas, "There's a translucent plastic tent out there, a big one . . ."

"Duane Hawkins's place. Supposed to get thermal gain—lets the sunlight in, got a dark fabric floor to soak up the radiation, mirror on the inside so it doesn't radiate back out . . . free heat."

"Does it work?" Johnson asked.

"I guess. He's got a kerosene heater in there, too, thermal gain cuts the kerosene use by about half, he says. 'Course, doesn't work worth a damn at night. But he's not out much at night, and during the day the plastic lets in all the light you need, so it's not a bad setup . . . Haven't seen it in a real high wind yet."

He looked back at Virgil. "Why? Can't think Duane's involved with Gina Hemming in any way?"

"Don't particularly think he was," Virgil said. "A plastic fishing tent . . . something I've never seen before."

They chatted a few more minutes, but Thomas didn't

have much more information. And clearly wasn't a suspect: Gina Hemming would have kicked his ass in a struggle.

Back outside, Virgil zipped up his suit and said to Johnson, "I want to take a look at that tent. Talk to the owner."

"Oh-oh. What'd I miss?"

"The person going in there kept looking at me . . . there's a kind of thing that happens when people look at cops and keep looking back," Virgil said. "Attracts the eye. A cop's eye, anyhow."

"How'd he know you're a cop?"

"Could be a she—couldn't tell from the parka—and I got the squid on my face. And the hair, when I took off the helmet."

"You think . . . ?"

"Dunno. Let's go ask. Do you know this Duane Hawkins?"

"Yeah, I see him around from time to time. Works out at the Kubota dealer, mechanic or something," Johnson said.

They tramped across the ice to the tent, probably fifty yards, but when they got there, there was no one inside.

"Shoot," Virgil said.

"No lock on the door," Johnson observed.

"Still would need a search warrant to go in," Virgil said.

Johnson: "I'm not a cop. I'm an old buddy of Duane's."

"Johnson . . ."

Johnson pushed the door open and stepped inside, as Virgil hoped he would. Virgil didn't go in but stood outside and watched. The tent was furnished with four orange molded-plastic chairs and a wooden gun rack that, instead of holding guns, held erect an array of short ice-fishing poles, ice skimmers, and a chipper. A well-used, gas-operated eight-inch auger lay on an unpainted board. The chairs were made more comfortable with fabric floatation pillows.

Two cardboard boxes sat behind the chairs.

"What's in there?" Virgil asked.

"Nothing. They're empty."

Virgil scanned the village: nobody in sight. He stepped inside, glanced around, and was about to step back out when he saw what looked like a silver coin on the floor attached by wires to a brown plastic disk about the size of three quarters stacked on top of one another. Virgil picked it up, turned it over in his hand. The silver coin was a battery inside a thin holder; the brown disk showed a hole the size of a pencil eraser and, at its bottom, a shiny copper strip.

"What do you think?" he asked Johnson.

Johnson peered at it for a second, fished in a pocket, produced a mechanical pencil, and used it to push on the copper strip.

The brown box spoke to them. *"Oh, yes, oh, yes, give it to me harder, big boy. Oh, yes, you're so big . . ."*

"Goddamn. Must have been out building them Barbie-Os," Johnson said. "That'd keep you busy while you're waiting for a bite."

"That was a woman who went sneaking off. She knew who I was. If we'd come here first, I would have had my hands on one of the women who put the squid on my face," Virgil said.

"Quit whining. What are you going to do?"

"Nothing. Not yet. Call up Margaret Griffin, suggest she talk to Duane what's-his-name . . ."

"Hawkins . . ."

"And, in the meantime, we ought to check around with the people out here and see if anybody saw anything Thursday night. Or a truck go by. I'd like to find the hole the killer stuffed the body through."

Over the next hour, they talked to a dozen fishermen, got a lot of shaking heads; went farther south, checked a couple of isolated shacks but found nobody home; hit a second, smaller fishing village, talked to a few more fishermen. One of them said, "Let me call Rusty Tremblay. He might know something. He saw a weird hole Friday night."

A minute later, they had Tremblay on speaker, and he said, with a mild Quebecois accent, "Yah, I seen a hole, too big even for pike guys. Let's see . . . Friday night, I might have had a couple three or four drinks, so I was not one hundred percent. I was going over to Rattlesnake, but I aimed too far north . . . You know how that works, pissed as a newt and snowing an' all . . . There's a light on a pole outside the Lutheran church. I was aiming at that, thinking it was Rattlesnake, and I almost run over the hole . . . Yeah, you could have shoved a body through it . . . Thinking about it now, had to been done either Thursday night or Friday, 'cause somebody had scraped snow in it and it wasn't completely froze up yet."

"Good information, Rusty," Johnson shouted into the phone. "We'll go over there. How's Booger?"

"She's fine. Getting trained now. I got her bringing my shoes."

"Great. Good for you," Johnson shouted. "We're

gonna go look for this hole. And my assistant here, Virgil, might want to come talk to you later. That okay?"

"That's okay, Johnson. I'll be at Wyatt's after eight o'clock."

On the way back to their sleds, Virgil asked, "What kind of fuckin' idiot would name his dog Booger? You can see him, out in the neighborhood, calling her in: 'Here, Booger' . . ."

"Not his dog," Johnson said, as he straddled his sled. "She's his granddaughter. Gotta be two years old now."

He fired up the sled and took off, Virgil trailing behind.

They took an hour to find the hole. They started by lining up the Lutheran church, which was on a road along the river, north of the Rattlesnake Country Club, and the boat ramp at Trippton, which was where almost everybody got onto the river.

They made the mistake of looking too close to the Wisconsin side, tracking back and forth, and finally stumbled on it less than halfway across and south of their original line. The newly refrozen hole wasn't much to look at, maybe two and a half feet long and twenty inches wide, made with six auger holes, and connected by chipping out the area between the holes with an ice chipper.

"That's got to be it," Johnson said, scuffing at it with his boots. "No reason in hell that somebody would cut a hole that size out here by itself. You might catch a mud cat down there, but there's no walleyes or anything good."

"Okay." Virgil looked around and picked out a reference point on the Wisconsin side that lined up with the hole and the Trippton boat ramp. "You know what?

Suppose you killed a woman and wanted people to think she might have gone off someplace with her purse and shoes and all that shit . . . what would you do with that stuff? You wouldn't want to get caught with it."

Johnson checked the hole again and said, "Yeah. I'd throw it in the hole. The river's low and slow, it's probably right down there."

"Maybe with the murder weapon," Virgil said. "We need an ice diver."

"Don't know of one," Johnson said, "though I imagine they're around."

They headed back to the cabin, letting the sleds run two or three miles north of the turnoff to Johnson's slough, a wildly enjoyable ride on a darkening afternoon. At the cabin, they parked the sleds next to it because Virgil thought they'd probably need them again, and Johnson said, looking at the sky, "If you're gonna find a diver, you better get going. A quick eight inches of snow would cover that hole right up."

"Is it supposed to snow tonight?"

"Not supposed to . . . or not much . . . but still . . ." He looked up at the oncoming cloud bank.

Virgil called Jon Duncan, told him what he'd found.

"I know there are divers around, I'll find one," Duncan said. "What's happening with the, uh, Barbies?"

"Got a name on that—I'm going to feed it to this private eye, hope we get clear," Virgil said.

"Good. Good. I'll tell the governor. His weasel called this morning. I told him you were all over it."

"You can count on it," Virgil said.

*   *   *

After ringing off from Duncan, he called Margaret Griffin and gave her Duane Hawkins's name and said that he worked at the Kubota dealership. "I'll be all over his credit history in five minutes; I'll be collecting his ears by ten o'clock tomorrow morning," she said. "Virgil, thank you."

When Virgil hung up, Johnson made a dusting-his-hands motion and said, "We done good. I'm thinking burgers and fries."

"I need to finish some interviews," Virgil said. He took a slip of paper from his jeans. "What do you know about David Birkmann?"

"Bug Boy? He's kind of a sissy," Johnson said. "His wife got it on with the owner of Dunkin' Donuts, and they split up, and she made him buy the donut shop so she and lover boy could buy another Dunkin' Donuts in Austin. Or maybe Houston. I get them confused. That's the story anyway."

"Why's he called Bug Boy?"

"He owns the pest control company, bugs and rodents and skunks and so on," Johnson said.

"And the Dunkin' Donuts."

"Right. You can talk to him, but I kinda don't think he did it—killed Gina. He *is* sort of a sissy."

FOURTEEN

David Birkmann lived in an American foursquare farmhouse a mile west of Trippton, above and west of the riverfront bluffs. The house was basically a two-story clapboard cube painted a grayish white with a pyramidal roof, and a dormer centered over the wide front porch.

The front lawn, going up to the porch, was a plateau of unmarked snow. A narrow barn-shaped building sat to the left side, in back, with newer garage doors. The driveway had been plowed back to the garage and up to the side door leading into the house. Snow was starting to fall; not heavy yet, but with the slanting, serious feel that would leave behind at least a few inches by morning. The yard was lit by a sodium-vapor pole light that threw a flickering orange glow on the falling snow, the plowed snowbanks, and the side of the house.

As he drove up the driveway, it occurred to Virgil that if it had been a scene from a Stephen King movie, somebody was gonna die and it was gonna be ugly.

He parked at the side of the house, considered for a moment, knelt on his seat, opened the lockbox in back, and took out his backup pistol, a small Sig 938 in a flat, front pocket carry holster. He slipped it into his jeans pocket, as a porch light came on next to the side door, and got out of the truck and walked over.

The chubby, balding dark-haired man stood behind the half-open door, wearing tan slacks and a plaid shirt, the shirt open at the throat, the sleeves rolled up to his elbows. He called, "Can I help you?"

Virgil said, "I'm an investigator with the state Bureau of Criminal Apprehension. Are you David Birkmann?"

"Yes. You must be Virgil Flowers."

"I am," Virgil said. "I need to speak to you about Gina Hemming."

"I was expecting you," Birkmann said. "Come on in."

They walked up a short flight of steps into a kitchen, with an old linoleum floor, that smelled of fried eggs, grease, and maybe oatmeal. Birkmann asked, "You want a beer or a Pepsi?"

"Thanks, I'm good," Virgil said, he being a Coca-Cola snob.

Birkmann led the way out of the kitchen through a squared-off arch into the dining room and through another arch into the living room, where a couple of easy chairs faced an oversized television. He pointed Virgil at one of the chairs, which turned out to have a revolving base, and he took the other, and they rotated toward each other.

Birkmann said, "Ask away, but I don't think I can help you much."

"You last saw Gina Hemming Thursday night?"

"Yeah. I left there about eight forty-five. I sat in my truck for a minute, wrote down some stuff from the meeting—when we were supposed to meet again; what I was supposed to do, exactly; the deadlines and stuff. There were still a few people there when I left . . ."

"Then you went home?" Virgil was checking Birkmann, saw no signs of any fingernail damage to his bare face or arms.

"No, not right away. I went down to Club Gold— that's a bar downtown. They have karaoke on Thursday. I drank a couple beers and sang a couple of songs. I was there for a while . . . I don't know exactly how long. I walked out with Bob Jackson, he's a post office clerk. He might have a better idea about the time, but I'd say . . . it must have been close to eleven. From there, I came straight home and went to bed. I never even heard about Gina until Sunday morning, down at the donut shop. I couldn't believe it."

"What'd you do on Friday and Saturday?"

Birkmann shrugged. "The usual. I have two businesses, and most of my job is keeping the books, making appointments, making sure the guys are on time and are doing the work, and ordering stuff. I take complaints, if there are any. I've got an office on Main Street—actually, it's in a building on Main Street, but I'm in the back. I did the usual stuff on Friday, I guess, because I didn't know that anything had happened to Gina, and nobody told me. I worked a half day Saturday, came back here, plowed the driveway, and, later in the day I ran up to La Crosse. Went to a bookstore, bought some movies, got back late, got up early Sunday, went downtown to the donut shop, and that's where I heard about Gina. Freaked me out, man. I mean, really. I've known her since we were both five years old."

"Did you see anybody you knew at the bookstore?"

"No . . . but I did charge the movies on my Visa card. That'd give you a time and date, I guess, if you wanted to check."

Virgil nodded. "Of the people on the committee, who'd be most likely to have killed her?"

Birkmann leaned back in the chair. "What? None of them. Listen, Officer . . . Agent . . ."

"Virgil," Virgil said.

"I have a hard time believing any of this, Virgil," Birkmann said, waving a hand to indicate "any of this." "If you want to know what I think, I think she went out somewhere after we were all gone, maybe got hit by a drunk driver, and the guy panicked, and, you know . . . put her in the river."

"Her car was still parked in her garage and it was really cold—not much place to walk to from where she lived. She had some boots, but they were sitting by the back door."

"Maybe somebody . . ." Birkmann trailed off in thought. Then said, "You know what? I don't *know* what happened. I don't have any idea. I can't even guess."

"Do you have a ten-inch ice auger?" Virgil asked.

"I don't have any auger. I don't do that . . . ice fish. Or regular fish. I don't have a boat or a snowmobile, or anything. Before I got divorced, I used to deer hunt, but I don't do that anymore, either. Mostly what I do is work."

"Dating anyone?" Virgil asked.

"No. To be honest, I'd like a few years of peace and quiet," Birkmann said. "I've had some of the local gals flirting with me, but I'm not making another mistake like the last one."

"You wouldn't know anyone involved in bondage and discipline, that kind of sexual practice?"

Birkmann chuckled—a dry, tired sound—rubbed his face, and said, "You know what, Virgil? I talked to Margot Moore and she said you had asked her about B and D. That's what she called it, and I had no idea of what it was. The initials. I knew people tied each other up and played with whips and so on—I'm not stupid—but I didn't know what you called it. I was kinda embarrassed she had to explain it to me. I mean, the sexiest thing I ever looked at was a *Playboy* magazine. This tying people up . . . I didn't know."

"Just had a similar experience," Virgil said. He felt sorry for Birkmann: as Johnson had suggested, he was a bit of a schlub. "I asked a woman if there was a place you could buy B and D stuff in Trippton and she told me no there wasn't because anybody with any brains would order straight from Amazon, where they've got everything anybody would ever want."

Birkmann made the same tired chuckle sound again, his head dropped, and he rubbed his forehead, shook his head, and said, "That's not entirely . . . true."

"It's not?"

"There's a place downtown, Bernie's Books, Candles 'n More. Books and magazines and candles and knick-knacks," Birkmann said. "Bernie's dead, but his son, James—Jimmy—runs it now. A friend of mine said he once took a peek in the back room while Jimmy was talking to a customer and there were porno mags back there and some rubber . . . penises and sex toys and stuff. Apparently, you've got to get invited to go back there."

"You haven't been invited?"

"I never wanted to be. I'm not very sexually . . . adventurous, I suppose you'd say. Margot suggested that's why my old lady ran off. Maybe she's right."

"What time does Bernie's close?"

"Eleven o'clock, Monday through Saturday. Closed on Sunday."

Virgil continued to bounce questions off Birkmann and Birkmann bounced back answers. He hadn't been that close to Hemming, he said. They didn't socialize, they didn't talk, except about business, although they'd stop for a word if they ran into each other on the street.

There was something not quite right about him, Virgil thought—it didn't feel like guilt, and, after a while, he decided that it might be depression or possibly even confusion. Virgil was asking questions that implied that Birkmann might be a suspect in a murder, but Birkmann couldn't seem to focus on that; his attention seemed to keep drifting away.

After a while, Virgil asked, "You okay?"

Birkmann seemed to slump deeper in the chair. "Huh? Why?"

"I don't know. You seem a little off center. Bummed-out?"

Birkmann sighed and nodded. "Yeah. This whole thing about Gina got me down. You know, she's dead, murdered, and we're the same age. Why's she dead? That's what I can't get over. Why? And I've made my whole life out of killing things, at least until I bought the donut shop, which doesn't do anyone a lot of good, either. I'm forty-two years old, forty-three next month, and this is what I got? Another thirty years of killing skunks and bugs and I drop dead from eating one too many donuts? No wife, no kids? I'm not even a good drunk, so I don't have that. What the hell am I doing, Virgil?"

"Maybe you need a minister. Or a counselor. They can help you think things through, if they're good," Virgil said.

Birkmann showed a spark of interest. "You think so?" He considered for a moment, said, "You must see a lot of sad stuff in your job . . . maybe you've even killed people, I won't ask. What do you do with all the sad stuff? Doesn't it get you down?"

"Of course it does, sometimes . . ." Virgil hesitated, then added, "What I do is, I talk to God before I go to sleep at night. Talking about it, and thinking that maybe there's somebody on the other end, seems to help."

Birkmann waved that away. "I'm not religious. Going to church—it's a magic show, in my opinion. Don't tell the Chamber of Commerce I said that."

"I'm not talking about religion. I'm talking about God," Virgil said. "I'm a Lutheran minister's kid, and, believe me, there's a difference between a religion and God. I sorta cut out the middleman."

Birkmann sighed again and asked, "Are we done?"

Virgil got up. "I think so. For now. I'll leave you a card. Call me if you think of something."

"Yeah. Hey, thanks for the God tip, I'll try it. Not gonna bum me out any more than I already am," Birkmann said. "What should I do if He answers?"

Virgil grinned and shook his head. "Maybe that's where you start to worry." On the way out, he added, "Take care of yourself, Dave."

Birkmann said, "You, too, Virgil." He showed the

first hesitant sign of a smile. "Don't go fighting any more Trippton women. They're man-eaters, I'm telling you."

"I hear you," Virgil said.

After the interviews with the Homecoming King and Queen, Virgil thought, "Nope." They probably hadn't done it. He didn't think that about Birkmann, because Birkmann was too stunned by Hemming's murder. People die all the time, even if they're not murdered, and a death of somebody he wasn't all that close to shouldn't have brought him down quite as much as it obviously had. On the other hand, maybe it was like he said: one component of an incipient midlife crisis.

Most bothersome, though, was Birkmann's claim that he didn't fish—no boats, no snowmobiles for winter. Not a river rat. Those were claims easily checked. He was, he said, a former hunter. A hunter, Virgil thought, would take the body out in the woods, not out on the river, especially if he didn't have something he could use to cut ice.

Still, Birkmann wasn't yet a nope.

Virgil began a mental tap dance. He should be a nope because, one, he didn't look like a guy who could carry a large woman anywhere, and because, two, he had an alibi that could be easily checked with the list of witnesses Birkmann said had seen him at Club Gold.

Virgil mulled it over for a minute. While his brain might have been ready, his gut wouldn't yet let him stick the nope label on Birkmann. The guy was a little too emotionally wrought.

*   *   *

The snow was falling harder, the roads were turning slick. Virgil dropped back down the hill and into town, taking it slow. Johnson called and said that he and Clarice would be going out for a pizza, did he want to go?

"Give me until seven o'clock, and I'm not going to Ma and Pa's."

"We're going to Tony's Chicago Style. I'm looking at the radar, and this piece of snow will be out of here in forty-five minutes. The back end is already through Caledonia, but there's another big chunk coming after that. We got maybe an hour or two break between them."

"All right. I'll see you at seven. By the way, tell Clarice she was wrong."

"About what?"

"That's private. Just tell her."

Bernie's Books, Candles 'n More was at the south end of Main Street. A sand-and-salt truck was making its way down the street, yellow lights flashing in the night. Virgil had to follow for two blocks before he could get around it and spent the time thinking about how much additional corrosion it'd put on his aging 4Runner.

Bernie's was a corner store, with big windows both on Main and the side street, the windows crowded with useless crap. Beeswax candles, leftover Christmas decorations at fifty percent off, a notice for a book signing by Trippton's favorite author, which had happened three days earlier, and a sun-browned sign that said, "Explore Your Home Scent Design . . . *As seen on TV.*"

Inside, it was candles and knickknacks for the first twenty feet, smelling of cinnamon and jasmine, then a candy rack and a glass-fronted refrigerator case full of soda, three rows of paperback book racks, and finally a magazine rack.

There were three other people in the place, one of whom was talking to a tall, thin gray-faced man behind the counter who was wearing a University of Minnesota hoodie; he glanced at Virgil as he went by and made Virgil think of a vulture sitting on a branch. Virgil walked all the way to the back rack, where he picked up an outdoor magazine, glanced at a feature entitled "Swamp Gobblers in Your Sights," and checked out the store. In the back, the scent of cinnamon had faded, giving way to the pleasant odor of newsprint.

There wasn't much to see—nothing unexpected—but there *was* a door leading farther into the back, as Birkmann said, right next to the magazine rack. He'd read the first three badly written paragraphs of the "Swamp Gobbler" story and was exchanging it for a tattered copy of *Automobile* when a man dressed in a red-checked hunting parka walked through the store to the back, looked suspiciously at Virgil, reached up above the door and pushed what must have been a hidden doorbell button—Virgil heard a buzzer bleep at the front of the store.

An electronic lock snapped on the door, and the man in the red-checked coat pushed through. Virgil stuck out a foot to block the door from closing and followed the man into the back.

Through the door, he found himself in a narrow room with a magazine rack on the wall filled with pornographic magazines and DVDs. There was a third man in the room, in a tan canvas coat, deeply engrossed in a copy of *Big 'Uns*. Nobody looked at nobody else.

Virgil spotted a "Novelties" sign at the end of the magazine rack, went that way, and turned a corner. The store didn't have much, but what they had was low quality: the usual sex toys, including some for men; edible underwear; and, best of all, a box containing a whip that appeared to be exactly like the one he'd found in Hemming's dressing table.

He took down the box, found another box behind that: two whips, so maybe a regular item. On the bottom shelf was a row of bondage magazines, fresh enough that there must actually be a regular clientele.

He put the box under his arm, poked around to see if he could turn up a modified Barbie, but didn't. On the way out of the back room, he said to the man still studying *Big 'Uns*, "That's not something you see every day, huh?" and went on out.

James Barker was alone at the front of the shop. He peered out from his hood, taking in Virgil and his box, and said, "I don't know you. What were you doing back there?"

"Gathering evidence," Virgil said.

"Say what?"

Virgil held up his ID case. "Virgil Flowers, Bureau of Criminal Apprehension. I'm trying to trace down purchasers of this model of whip. I need to know who, exactly, bought one."

"Hey, that ain't right. You can't come rockin' in here and poke around. First Amendment, dude," Barker said.

"The First Amendment guarantees your freedom of religion, speech, and press, that you can assemble with other people and petition the government for redress of grievances," Virgil said. "It doesn't mention whips, bondage and discipline, or withholding information from the police. Of course, you could take the Fifth, but that would imply that you have something to hide. Do you have something to hide?"

"Of course not," Barker sputtered. "But . . . I'm not the only one selling stuff outa here. I might not know who bought what."

Virgil looked around the store. "You're telling me you have staff?"

"I have a woman who works the mornings . . ."

"Somebody bought a B and D whip from a woman in the morning?"

"It could happen," Barker said.

"Yeah, but it didn't, did it, Jimmy? You sold a whip to a guy, maybe more than one. I can see it in your face. And this happens to be a murder investigation."

"Gina Hemming?"

"Yeah. Did you sell one to Hemming?" Virgil asked.

"No . . . Women don't go back there," Barker said. "They don't know about it."

"So, who bought it, Jimmy?" Virgil asked. "Or, maybe . . . you held one out for yourself?"

"No, no, no, no . . . But if I tell you, the guy's gonna kill me."

Virgil smiled, brought out all the teeth. "This is great,

because it tells me two things: the guy is violent, and you know who he is. That means if you don't cooperate, I can charge you with accessory after the fact in a murder."

"Jeez, man, you don't have to be an *asshole* about it," Barker said.

"The name?"

"Fred Fitzgerald. He's a biker guy. He's got a tattoo shop out on Melon."

"Thank you. Don't go calling Fitzgerald or I'll bust your ass. Listen, since you're in this deep . . . does Fitzgerald buy any other stuff involved with bondage and all that? Or sex toys?"

"Yeah, from time to time. Nothing that would hurt anyone. Handcuffs, butt plugs, stuff like that."

"Is Fitzgerald a fisherman?"

"I don't know. A lot of people around here are . . . I know he has a snowmobile for when he can't ride his Harley."

When Virgil emerged on the street five minutes later, he'd successfully scared the shit out of Barker, who wouldn't be talking about the interview, and Virgil believed he'd made serious progress.

Fred Fitzgerald had a primitive website that Virgil and Barker looked at on Barker's laptop. That gave Virgil an address, and, after leaving the store, he called the duty officer at the BCA, gave him the name and address. The duty officer came back with a rap sheet.

"He's a bad boy but a small-timer," the duty officer said. "Couple of small burglaries, lots of fights and assaults, a DUI four years ago, charged with theft of motorcycle parts out in Sturgis, did a little time on that. Let me see . . . I'd say an assault back in 2009 is the worst of it. Went after a guy with a pool cue, broke his arms, did a year less a day in the county jail. Apparently, part of a deal where he put a tattoo on a guy and misspelled something and the guy went around bad-mouthing him."

"Smells like a loser," Virgil said.

"Maybe. But I'll tell you what, Virgie. The guy's got a bad temper and a violent streak. You want to have somebody with you when you go to see him."

"Gotcha. Talk to you later."

Virgil met Johnson Johnson and Clarice at Tony's Chicago Style, and Johnson said Fitzgerald was not a bad guy. "He's made some mistakes."

"Busted up a guy with a pool cue," Virgil said.

"Well, who hasn't?" Johnson asked.

"You and Virgil," Clarice said, "for two. Don't give me any of that tough-guy bullshit, Johnson, you've never busted anyone up with anything, except maybe you punched a couple of guys in the nose."

"You're harshing my buzz, man," Johnson said to Clarice.

"He do your ink?" Virgil asked.

Johnson had full sleeves. "No way. I got primo work by one of the godfathers of art tattoos. Fred's not a bad guy, but he's second tier."

The pizza came, a lot of pepperoni swimming in a lake of extra-sharp cheddar, all of it scooped out on top of a sugar-free piecrust. Nothing like it had ever been served within a hundred miles of Chicago.

"To get back to Fitzgerald . . . He *is* a bad guy, Johnson," Virgil said. "The question is, would he have killed Hemming if he felt the need?"

Johnson considered and then said, "No. It would have been an accident. He wouldn't have thought about it."

"I can buy that," Virgil said. "She was probably hit only once, in the head. Like somebody got mad, swatted her with a bottle."

"You know, I can't even see him doing *that*," Johnson said. "He's been in enough fights that he'd know that he'd hurt her bad. I can see him twisting her arm, maybe choking her a little, slapping her . . . Not hitting her with a bottle. Not cracking her skull."

"You're not helping here," Virgil said.

"I'm telling you the truth, though."

They gnawed through a few slices of the pizza, which turned out to be tougher than it looked. Clarice asked Virgil, "So . . . you found a place that sells sex stuff?"

"Back room at Bernie's Books."

Her eyebrows went up. "Really? I didn't know that— but I guess I'm not surprised. Jimmy's always been a sleaze dog. A friend of mine told me he was coming on to her daughter when the daughter was fifteen. He was thirty-four."

"That's called statutory rape in Minnesota," Virgil said.

Johnson: "You can't rape statues anymore?"

Clarice ignored him. "They hadn't slept together before the mom found out. He might have introduced the daughter to reefer madness, though. My friend went down to the sheriff's office and talked to Jeff Purdy and Jeff had a word with Jimmy. That ended that."

Johnson asked, "When are you going to talk to Fred?"

"Tomorrow morning," Virgil said, "if I can get out of your driveway."

"Well, if you can't, Fred's place is on Melon, right where it comes down to the highway. You could ride one of the sleds down there, if you aren't ascared to walk across the railroad tracks."

"We'll see what happens," Virgil said.

Johnson looked at Clarice. "What do you think?"

"Don't know him that well," she said. "From a woman's perspective, though, I can put him with Gina if she was sleeping with Corbel. Fred's good-looking, has got the same kind of rough-trade vibe that Corbel has. If bad boys did it for her, Fred would fit the bill."

"The duty officer at the BCA called him that," Virgil said. "Bad boy."

FIFTEEN

Corbel Cain didn't drink every day, or even every week; but once in a while, when the weight of the world grew too heavy, he'd go off on what he called a run and what his doctor called a binge. During the run, Corbel told the doc, he'd likely get screwed, stewed, and tattooed—and, more than likely, correct some grievous wrongs.

He didn't win all the fights, because he tended to pick on even larger brawlers, but he won most of them.

"The problem with that is," his doc said after the last run, "somebody will eventually kick you to death. Or cripple you. Or you'll forget to stop sometime and you'll hurt somebody bad and wind up in prison. You got to cut this shit out, Corbel."

Cain thought about it, and seriously, but hadn't gotten there yet.

As Virgil was getting ready for bed that night, Cain was disturbing the peace at George Brown's bowling alley.

After Brown cut him off, Cain struggled out into the

parking lot, where, with his oldest pal, Denwa Burke, at his side, they mutually agreed that they needed more excitement in their lives, because, honestly, when you thought about it, too much was never enough.

Driving drunk usually provided solid entertainment. Because bars were such a large part of Trippton's economy, the cops generally stayed away from drivers who might have an extra cocktail under their belts as long as they didn't run into anything too expensive or uninsured.

Cain got in his Jeep Rubicon, fired that mother up, and five minutes later launched himself and Burke onto the frozen Mississippi River. Once clear of the first ice village, he aimed the truck north and dropped the hammer. The Jeep bucked and thrashed and occasionally went airborne off the windrows of snow, Burke screaming his approval—and chipping a tooth on a bottle of Stoli—until they hit the main channel, where the wind had cleared most of the bumps.

There, running the Jeep up to fifty, Cain cut sharp left, and the Jeep spun down the ice like a top. He did it again and again, then the snow came, and they were essentially flying blind, but still working the ice, until Burke shouted, "Stop, stop!" and Cain yelled back, "You pussy!" and Burke shouted, "No, stop, stop!" Cain got the Jeep stopped, and Burke popped open his door, got out, and barfed most of several beers, a pint of Stoli, and four or five hot dogs onto the ice, got back in the truck, wiped his chin with his parka sleeve, and said, "I'm good."

"'Preciate that," Cain said, and, "Pass the bottle."

Denwa passed it, Cain took two long swallows, passed the bottle back, and dropped the hammer.

Once, a few minutes before he'd gone out on the ice

with his truck, a deputy asked him, "Why do you do that, Corbel? Drink and fuck around on the river?"

Cain answered, "Because that's what we do. We've always done that."

Off the ice, but no less hammered, Cain pulled the Jeep to the side of the street and said to Burke, "I gotta tell you something, Denwa. Not exactly a secret, but kinda like that."

"Go for it," Burke said.

"You know Ryan Harney?"

"The doctor? He did my hemorrhoids," Burke said. "What's the secret?"

"A few years back, he was fuckin' Gina Hemming."

Burke looked at him slack-jawed, puzzled by the importance of this secret. "Yeah? So what?"

"So what? So everybody in town knows he's got trouble with his wife, and what I think is, Gina told him she was gonna come out with the news, and his wife was gonna find out, so he killed her and threw her body in the river."

"No shit," Burke said. He held up the bottle of Stoli, realized there was less than half an inch left. He finished it and threw the bottle out the window, where it shattered on the street. "What're we gonna do about it?"

"Go kick his ass," Cain said.

"Let's do it," Burke said. "Motherfucker can't go around killing our women."

Cain dropped the hammer, and the Jeep lurched away from the curb.

"Say," Burke said, "Didn't I hear from somebody once that you used to fuck Gina? Might have been your wife said it."

"Yeah, but I didn't kill her. She needed me, because . . . Justine."

"Huh. Justine," Burke said. He burped. "You know, if he gets the operation, I could go for a piece of that."

"What?"

"Good-looking woman . . . or whatever," Burke said.

Cain didn't want to hear it. And had an idea that he wouldn't remember it anyway. That was a good thing.

They showed up at Harney's house, a sprawling tan-brick affair with a three-car garage and a couple of bay windows poking out on either side of the recessed front door. There were lights on at both ends of the house. Cain pulled into the driveway, killed the engine, the two men piled out, and Cain led the way to the door. He rang the doorbell and pounded on the door, and a minute later the door popped open, and Harney was there in a robe and slippers, the open robe showing the top of a pair of blue pajamas.

He asked, "Somebody hurt?"

"You motherfucker," Burke shouted. "You killed Gina Hemming. You motherfucker . . ."

Burke seemed to have lost the thread at "motherfucker," and Cain stepped up. "We know all about it, Harney," he said. "Gina was going to turn you in, to your wife, and you decided to shut her up."

"You guys are drunk."

"Damn right," Burke said.

Harney's wife, Karen, showed up in a robe behind Harney and asked loudly, "Ryan, what's going on?"

"There she is," Burke shouted. "Your old man killed Gina Hemming because he was fuckin' her and he didn't want you to find out."

She crossed her arms. "What?"

"Not true, not true, none of it's true, they're drunk idiots," Harney said. As Cain shouted, "Who you callin' idiots?" Harney turned to his wife. "You know everything that happened, it was years ago, and these assholes are drunk . . ."

"Who's an asshole?" Cain shouted, and he punched Harney in the forehead. Harney went down in the entry-way, and his wife stumbled over to the entryway closet and began throwing coats at Burke and Cain, who fought through them, undamaged, until she pulled the five-foot-long dowel rod out that the coats had been hanging on and swung it like a baseball bat. Cain managed to duck, but the rod hit Burke in the teeth, breaking off several of them and knocking him down.

"You bitch," Cain shouted.

He moved on her, but Harney tripped him and he fell down. From the back of the house, a young boy was screaming, "Mom? Dad?" and Cain began to get the feeling that he might have screwed the pooch.

He tried to get up, but Karen Harney hit him, hard as she could, across the back, and he went down flat, and Ryan Harney sat on his head and told his wife, "Call the cops."

"If we call the cops . . ."

Cain said, "If you don't call the cops, we'll go away."

"Call the cops," Harney said.

His wife said, "I'm talking to Taylor first thing in the morning." Taylor Miller was their divorce attorney.

"Call the cops," Harney said. Burke had struggled to a sitting position; blood was pouring out of his mouth and down his chest. Cain shouted, "Get the fuck off my head."

"Call the fuckin' cops," Harney said. He felt really, really tired.

His wife went to call the cops.

The snow that night came through in ten-mile-wide pulses, accompanied by occasional thunder. Virgil didn't sleep well in the strange bed, with the wind blowing through the eaves and thoughts of the murder investigation prodding him awake.

The first wave of snow had already gone through when he got back to the cabin, and he could see stars overhead. He got out his iPad and opened up Fred Fitzgerald's criminal file, as downloaded to the BCA site by the duty officer. The details were unique to Fitzgerald, but the pattern was familiar enough—a small-town biker thug whose proclivities led to bar fights and minor crime.

He finished the file, made a couple of notes on the iPad, then spent some time reading Thomas Perry's *The Old Man*, talked to Frankie for a while—it was snowing at the farm, and her third-oldest son would be getting up at five a.m., before school, to plow a dozen driveways—and finally went to bed at midnight.

He woke three times during the night to look out the bedroom window. Twice it was snowing, once it wasn't, and when he got up in the morning, he found a sullen gray sky and six inches of new snow on the front porch and covering the truck.

He put on his camo suit, spent fifteen minutes shoveling off the porch and steps and brushing the snow off the 4Runner. His leg and hip still hurt, but the pain in his nose seemed to be going away. When he was done clearing snow, he went back inside and ate an oversized bowl of oatmeal, with cinnamon and raisins, and read the news and weather on his iPad. The National Weather Service said the day would be cold and windy, as would the rest of the next week, with a chance of snow every night.

As Virgil was shaving, Jon Duncan called from the BCA. Virgil put him on speaker, and Duncan said, "Bea Sawyer is on the way down to take a look at the house and she's bringing Bill Jensen with her to look at the computer. Clay Danson—he's a diver—is on the way down with a dive crew. Danson is costing us an arm and a leg. With the snow on the highway, they might take a while."

"They got my number?"

"They do, and they'll call as soon as they get into town."

Beatrice Sawyer was the lead crime scene tech for the BCA; Virgil had never heard of Danson.

A few minutes later, Jeff Purdy called. "We got Corbel Cain and his friend Denwa Burke in jail. They went over to Ryan Harney's house last night and attacked him. They were trying to force him to admit that he killed Gina Hemming."

"Oh, boy. Anybody get hurt?"

"Denwa got some teeth broken off, Harney got hit on the forehead and has a bruise the size of a pancake, Cain's been pissing and moaning about his back and neck. Karen Harney hit him with a dowel rod from a closet—you know, that thing they hang the coats off of—the same thing she used on Denwa. Denwa and Corbel got terminal hangovers. That's about it."

"Why did they think—"

"Seems Ryan had an affair with Gina Hemming, years ago. Corbel thinks he killed Gina to keep Gina from telling Karen, but it seems that Harney confessed all, years ago, and Karen knew about it. But now that it's come up again, kinda publicly . . . Karen's talking divorce."

"Harney had an affair with Hemming? He told me he barely spoke to her."

"I don't know how much they talked, but they apparently spent some serious time screwing each other."

"I'll be down to the jail to talk to Corbel. Can you hold him until I get there?"

"Yeah, he's got to wait for Sam Jones to order bail, and bail hearings don't start until eleven o'clock, so he won't get out until after noon. We've got him here in a holding cell; we haven't transferred him to the jail."

"I'll be down right away," Virgil said.

Corbel Cain looked fairly discouraged when he was retrieved from his holding cell and brought out to an interview room, where he dropped into the plastic chair. He nodded at Virgil, rubbed the back of his neck, and said, "That didn't work out so good."

Virgil was sitting across the interview table. "What

were you doing, Corbel? I understand the Harneys beat
the shit out of you and your pal . . ."

"*Mrs. Harney*. Mrs. Harney—she ambushed us with a
baseball bat . . ."

"It was a stick, Corbel. A dowel rod from a closet, for
Christ's sakes," Virgil said. "Jeff Purdy says your friend
looks like a vampire, with all his broken teeth . . ."

"Yeah, he took it bad. That fuckin' Harney tripped
me, and Mrs. Harney hit me with that baseball bat . . ."

"*Stick* . . ."

"Felt like a baseball bat," Corbel said. "I might have
to go to Harney to fix me up because he sat on my head.
I don't think my neck's gonna recover for a month. You
ever try to lift up your head when there's two hundred
pounds sitting on it?"

"No, I never have," Virgil said. "Now, tell me what
you were doing."

"I will if you'll get me a bottle of water. My mouth
feels like the Sahara Desert . . ."

Virgil got a deputy to fetch a bottle of water, and
Cain said, "Well, when I was fooling around with Gina,
it came out, I don't remember how, that she'd had a
thing with Ryan Harney. She made me promise not to
tell anyone, but what I figured was, they had this party,
for the class reunion, or this meeting, whatever it was,
and she said something to Harney that made him think
it was all gonna come out. So he left, waved good-bye to
everyone, and he came back and killed her. Or maybe
she was friendly at the party, and he came back, thinking
he was gonna get laid, that they could start up again,
and she told him to fuck off, and he picked up a wine
bottle they had there and whacked her with it."

"How do you know they had wine bottles?"

"Hell, everybody in town knows everything that happened at that meeting. They were drinking heavy."

"Not from what I've figured out," Virgil said. "They had eight people there, and when Jeff Purdy went in Saturday night, there were two empty wine bottles on the kitchen counter, and one half full. Maybe fifteen glasses of wine split up between eight people over an hour and a half or two hours? They weren't drinking much. I've asked them: nobody thinks anybody else was drunk."

"Did you ask that question specific about Harney?"

Virgil hesitated, then said, "Okay. He might have had a little more than the others."

Cain leaned across the table. "See, that's what happened. Harney's got an unhappy home life. He's already been caught fuckin' around on his wife . . ."

"How do you know that?"

"Found it out last night. Kinda came out in . . . the conversation."

"The fight."

"Whatever. Anyway, he gets loaded at the party, comes back. She tells him to fuck off. He's drunk and pissed and whacks her with a bottle." His eyes narrowed as he thought about it. "Now, Virgil, you really think eight people only drank two and a half bottles of wine in two hours? In Trippton? You got a missing bottle there. Nobody would have walked away with one, you can't steal from the hostess, somebody would have seen it. He whacks her with the bottle, takes it with him when he goes to throw the body in the river."

"Does Harney fish?"

"Well . . . not that I know of. But I don't know all the fishing people here," Cain said.

"Does he have an ice-fishing shack?"

"Well, no, I don't think so."

"Snowmobiles?" Virgil asked.

"Uh, jeez . . ."

Virgil sent him back to the holding cell, asked Purdy whether Denwa Burke was worth interviewing, and Purdy said no. "He's got no idea of what happened at that meeting. He's a hell-raiser and a shovel operator for the port. When I say shovel operator, I mean the kind with a wooden handle."

Virgil called Harney's office to find out if he was in and was told that he was ill and was at home. Virgil called, Harney answered, and Virgil told him they needed to talk.

"Yeah, I figured you'd be calling. Listen, could you stop and pick up a couple of large lattes at The Roasting Pig? We've been up all night and we're starving here . . ."

Virgil stopped at The Roasting Pig for the lattes, walked down the block to Dunkin' Donuts and got a half dozen donuts—two chocolate-frosteds, two glazed sticks, two original sticks, in a bag, and a jelly to eat on the way over to the Harneys'. The counter clerk offered him the donuts free again, but Virgil paid. A couple of donuts was okay; seven was a bribe.

When Harney popped the front door open, he looked as though he'd spent the night in hell. His hair stuck out in all directions, he had a large blue bruise in the middle of his forehead, and he looked like he'd gotten exactly no sleep. He told Virgil to come in, took the two large cups of coffee and handed one to his wife, who'd come up behind him, and they all went into the large kitchen to sit at the dining bar.

Harney said, "I guess Corbel told you that I had a thing with Gina years ago."

"He didn't say when it was," Virgil said. He glanced at Karen Harney, who looked fairly relaxed; he wondered about the possibility of a Xanax or two.

"Five years ago," Harney said.

"While I was pregnant with our second child, you asshole," Karen Harney said.

Virgil to Ryan Harney: "You let me think you hardly knew her . . ."

"I really messed up the middle part of my life when I fell in bed with her," Harney said.

"You betcha," Karen Harney said.

Harney continued. "But I broke down and told Karen, and we put things back together, after a rough time, and I . . . well, I thought the fact that we'd had an affair, so long ago, wasn't really relevant. Then that fuckin' Corbel showed up last night."

Virgil told him Cain's theory that Harney got drunk— and Karen Harney interrupted to say, "He does drink too much"—and got violent after being turned down for sex. "He'd never get violent," Karen Harney said.

Harney said, "We've been up all night here. This whole thing . . . we're going to change our lives. We're not happy here. I'm going to start looking around for a job in the Cities, or in Rochester. Maybe even Denver.

Maybe an emergency room gig: get some regular hours, for a change, spend more time with Karen and the kids."

"I do love him," Karen said. "But Trippton's never been right for us. We need a bigger place."

They talked some more, and the Harneys ate four of the pastries and Virgil ate one (chocolate-glazed), and the two Harneys so casually dismissed Cain's theory as crazy that Virgil decided he wouldn't get anywhere with them without more facts to back him up.

As he was putting on his coat to leave, Harney said, "Virgil, you know, I didn't want to say anything about this because it's so minor . . ."

"Nothing's minor in a murder," Virgil said.

"When we were leaving, I was out at my car, and Justin and Margot walked down her porch steps, and Gina was up there alone with Lucy Cheever, and there was something really . . . tense . . . about their body relationships. They looked like they were arguing. But this was only a glance as I drove by. It's probably nothing."

"I'll ask," Virgil said. "I'll keep you out of it."

Driving away, Virgil thought a bit about Karen Harney. She'd dropped both Burke and Corbel Cain, two well-known brawlers, with a closet rod. There was a willingness to use violence . . . although it could have been simple fear and anger.

Still . . .

Betrayed by her husband, worried that he might be straying again . . .

*   *   *

At nine o'clock, he eased into a freshly plowed parking spot on Main Street in front of Margot Moore's office at Moore Financial. The secretary said Moore was not in yet but was expected any minute. "Probably over getting a cup of coffee."

Virgil waited in the lobby, reading an old copy of *Modern Farmer*, a magazine aimed at yuppies ("The Complete Chicken Guide"), and ten minutes later Moore came in, stomping her diminutive L.L. Bean rubber mocs. She saw Virgil, stopped, and said, "Oh, shit."

Virgil asked, "Is that nice?"

"Come on in." To the secretary she said, "Jerry Williams is supposed to be here at nine-thirty. I should be done with Virgil by then, but, if I'm not, stall him. I don't want him to go away."

"Yes, ma'am."

Moore led the way back to the office, hung her parka on a hook, and asked, "What now?"

Virgil sat in the client's chair and asked, "Was there some tension at the reunion meeting between Lucy Cheever and Gina?"

She tapped her lips with a forefinger, thinking, and said, "Maybe."

"Why was that?" Virgil asked.

"Don't know. They're both about money. If there's something there, you should probably talk to Marv Hiners."

"But you said, 'Maybe.'"

"Gina and Lucy are sort of rivals for the title of richest woman in Trippton. Lucy's empire is growing. Whenever you'd see them together, they'd be a little gushy like they were the best of friends. They weren't doing that

Thursday night. If anything, they were cool with each other."

"Okay," Virgil said.

"That's it?" Big smile.

"No . . . How often were you and Gina Hemming getting together with Fred Fitzgerald?"

Moore stared at him for a few seconds, sputtered, "What? What?"

Virgil said, "Hey, Margot—don't bullshit me. I not only know about you guys, I actually bought myself a whip at the same place Fred got his."

She sat in mortified silence, a tear leaking out of one eye. "This could ruin me."

Virgil said, "Doesn't have to. I'm looking for information, not publishing it. I can promise you, nobody will hear about you from me, nothing that you give me confidentially."

She yanked open a desk drawer and pulled out a Kleenex, dabbed at her face. "I bet you made me wreck my makeup."

"Yeah, well, Margot, I'm not trying to make you cry—I'm investigating the murder of a woman who was probably your best friend and you're holding out on me. Don't tell me about your fuckin' makeup."

"We . . . Gina and me and Fred . . . were playing. That's all. And when I say Gina and me, I don't mean we were all in bed in a pile," she said. "Fred would come over to my place or I'd go over to his. He always went to Gina's, because his place kinda scared her. We were playing. He had this little whip, he'd spank our butts a little, he'd put on handcuffs, and . . . do stuff. It was all pretend."

"I don't need the details on that, except . . . did the handcuffs ever leave marks on either of you?"

"A couple of times . . . you'd kind of struggle around. It was all play, but the handcuffs were metal, and sometimes you'd get marks. Did Gina have marks when you found her?"

"Yeah, but they were older, not from the night she died," Virgil said. "How often would the two of you get together with Fred?"

"I was seeing him maybe . . . once a month. Gina more often, once a week."

"Last Thursday?"

Another silence, then, "I know that Thursdays were good for her. Fridays and Saturdays are party nights in Trippton, out at the club, especially in the winter. She didn't miss those because she was kind of lonely; she liked the social aspect of the club. Sunday was the night before she had to be back at work."

"You're telling me that Fred might well have gone over there Thursday night after the committee meeting."

"I know he did on other Thursdays," she admitted.

"Have you talked to Fred since I talked to you?" She looked away, and he knew what the answer was. "That looks like a yes."

She nodded. "Yes, I did. I told him you were investigating, and I worried that you'd find him and that he'd mention my name. He was worried that no matter what happened, if his name came up, that you'd figure he'd killed Gina. He says he didn't have anything to do with it but that you'd . . . frame him. Because of his prior record."

"We don't do that," Virgil said.

"He doesn't believe that you don't do that," Moore

said. "He thinks you'll do whatever is convenient, that you'll be taking a lot of pressure to get this solved and he's the best target."

Virgil: "Do you think he did it?"

"No. I don't. He really seemed panicked about having it pinned on him," Moore said.

"You think he's in the wind?"

"'In the wind'?"

"Do you think he's run away?" Virgil asked.

"Oh . . . No, I don't think so. He's probably out at his shop."

"Is he an ice fisherman?"

"Yes. He's talked about it . . ."

"I gotta tell you, he's looking good for this," Virgil said. "He's got a history of violence . . ."

"He wouldn't hurt Gina. He knows exactly what our relationships were with him, that he was our . . . boy toy. We had fun. He wouldn't *have* to hurt Gina, unless she tried to shoot him or something. He's a strong guy. If she went after him for some reason, he could wrestle her down with one hand. He wouldn't even hit her with his fist."

They went back and forth for another five minutes, then Virgil jabbed a finger at her and said, "Margot, you're standing on the edge of a legal cliff. You have no further contact with him. You don't call him, you don't tell him about this conversation. If he calls you, you tell him that you can't talk. Do you understand?"

"Do I need a lawyer?" she asked.

"I can't advise you on that. I'd say not yet. And if you hire one locally, that increases the chances that your . . . relationship . . . will become public knowledge."

She leaked another tear. "I don't know, I don't know . . ."

*   *   *

When Virgil left, Moore was on her way to the rest-room to wash her face and redo her makeup. Virgil drove down to the sheriff's office, found Purdy around at the fire station, and told him about Fred Fitzgerald. "I'm going down there to talk to him and I'd like a deputy to come along."

"You think there might be trouble?"

"I don't know him. He has a history," Virgil said.

"Okay. I'll send Luke Pweters with you. He used to wrestle for the U over at Mankato. He's out in a car right now. Let me find out where he is and ask how long it'll take him to get back."

The answer to that question: ten minutes.

They'd walked back to Purdy's office, Virgil told Purdy about the whip he'd found in Hemming's dressing table and about the identical whip he'd bought at the magazine shop, and how he'd gotten Fred Fitzgerald's name.

"I knew Jimmy was selling a little porno out of the back room, but that's been going on for fifty years," Purdy said, his feet comfortably up on his desk. "His old man did the same thing—a friend of mine in middle school snuck in there and grabbed a couple of magazines and smuggled them out, that's how I learned the ins and outs of sex . . . so to speak. Never hurt anybody that I know of."

"Kinda like ditch weed," Virgil said.

"Yeah, like that," Purdy agreed. "Everything has gone to hell since those days, Virgie. No more ditch weed.

The pot that's out there now, it's like hitting yourself on the head with a hammer. Same with porno. Not just big titties anymore; now it's stuff you can't even think of on your own."

"Somebody else told me that same thing," Virgil said.

Pweters showed up, a big, affable blue-eyed man in his late twenties or early thirties who looked like he could pull your arms off. He had a large nose, broad shoulders, and a Ranger buzz cut. "I know Fred," he said. "He wrestled for a year in junior high, but he started smoking and that was the end of him. Didn't have the wind. Think he was at one hundred and fifty-two, but he's put on some fat since those days."

"Will he be trouble?" Virgil asked.

"Don't believe so. If he is, he shouldn't be a problem for the two of us."

"I don't fight," Virgil said. "I leave that to my assistants."

"Heard that about you," Pweters said. "It's an admirable position, in my opinion. But it leaves open the question, why do you have a blue thing stuck to your face?"

Virgil followed Pweters out to Fitzgerald's tattoo parlor. Fitzgerald lived above the shop, Pweters had said. When they arrived, they found the front sidewalk and stoop still covered with snow. They parked in the street, climbed the steps, and Pweters banged on the door. A moment later, a window opened on the top floor, and a man shouted down, "Who is it?"

Pweters backed up into the street, looked up, and shouted back, "Luke Pweters. You got a minute, Fred?"

"Yeah, yeah. I'll be down."

The overhead window banged shut, and a couple of minutes later Fitzgerald banged down an interior staircase. They could see him pulling up a pair of jeans as he walked to the door. He pulled open the front door and said, "Goddamnit, Pweters, you didn't tell me Flowers was with you."

"Well, here I am," Virgil said. "We need to talk to you about Gina Hemming."

Fitzgerald glared at them for a moment, and Virgil thought he might slam the door in their faces. He didn't but said, grudgingly, "Come on in."

Fitzgerald was a medium-sized man, with some muscle, though the muscle was indeed covered with a layer of fat. He had shoulder-length black hair, a tightly trimmed spade beard, and a gold hoop earring in one ear. Tentacles of black ink poked up over the top of his black T-shirt. Because he was wearing a T-shirt, Virgil could see that he had no visible cuts on his face, arms, or hands, although he supposed a cut could be hidden by the beard or head hair. He was probably ten years younger than Hemming or Moore. Fitzgerald could have made it on an HBO miniseries, Virgil thought, if he hadn't been stuck in Trippton.

The ground floor of Fitzgerald's tattoo parlor was divided in half, the front half being the waiting room, the back half housing the tattoo parlor gear, including a reclining black-leather barber chair. Fitzgerald waved at a couch and dropped into an easy chair and grunted, "What?"

Virgil asked, "What time did you leave Gina Hemming's house Thursday night?"

Fitzgerald's face closed down. He said, "I haven't seen Gina in three weeks. I sure as hell wasn't there Thursday night."

Virgil: "Fred, with your kind of history, you shouldn't be lying to me. Lying to me makes you at least an accessory to murder, if you didn't actually murder her yourself."

Fitzgerald sat up, clenched a fist, but didn't quite wave it at Virgil. "I knew this was gonna happen. You find out I knew Gina, and you find out I ride a bike, that's all you needed to come over and give me shit."

"That and about ten arrests for everything from burglary to assault and a couple of years in jail, along with the fact that you and Hemming had some kind of bondage relationship and you'd go over there and handcuff her and whip her with a black leather whip you got down at Bernie's," Virgil said.

"That turd Jimmy told you about me, didn't he?" Fitzgerald asked.

"I don't know Jimmy. What I know I got out of Hemming's diary," Virgil lied. "She has a complete record, but she never got a chance to finish Thursday's entry because she got murdered first. But you went over there on Thursdays, didn't you, Fred? Because the parties on Friday and Saturday were a little too high-toned for the likes of you, she'd never let you go to those . . ."

"That's horseshit. Besides, I'd never go with her anyway, those fuckin' polo shirt assholes out there," Fitzgerald said. He reached over to a side table and picked up a gel hand-exercise ball and began squeezing the life out of it, the muscles bulging in his forearms.

Pweters jumped in. "I'll tell you, Fred, when Virgil asked me to come along, I told him no way you'd kill her on purpose. I said if you had killed her, it was an accident and you probably panicked. I mean, an accident is an accident, and that's way different than murder."

Fitzgerald rolled his eyes. "Shut up, Pweters. I didn't kill her any which way, murder or accident or any of it. She's the one who came on to me. She found out from Corbel Cain that she liked stuff a little rough, and I was a little rough."

"How did Gina find out you were a little rough?" Virgil asked. "You put an ad in the *Republican-River*?"

Fitzgerald looked away. "Probably from a friend or something," he muttered. And, "Listen, I know you don't got nothing on me because there's nothing to be got, except I knew her and I got in trouble years ago . . ."

"And you used to beat her up," Virgil added.

"I *didn't* beat her up," Fitzgerald said. "I spanked her a little with that fake whip, and maybe a Ping-Pong paddle sometimes, but I never hurt her. That's not the whole point of the thing . . . All she ever had to do was to tell me to quit and I would have quit it. I didn't have a *thing* with her. If she told me to leave and never come back, that's what I would have done. No hard feelings. I'm a therapist, not a torturer."

"We can put you there on Thursday night," Virgil said, lying again. "I can't get you yet for the murder, but I think I eventually will, unless it turns out somebody else was there. Is there any way you can prove that you left her there alive?"

"I don't have to prove shit," Fitzgerald said, his voice rising to a near whine. He fumbled the gel ball and it rolled across the floor to Virgil's left foot. "I can't prove shit because I wasn't there Thursday night."

Pweters turned to Virgil and said, "Looks like he's going to stick to that weak-ass story. You want to bust him now? Or wait?"

Virgil thought it over and finally said, "I don't know. I can't believe that the guy . . . I can't believe that the person who saw him got it wrong. Plus going out on the river on his sled." He tossed the ball back to Fitzgerald.

Fitzgerald suddenly looked more confident. He stood up and said, "Fuck this. I'm not talking to you no more. I know you're gonna try to frame me and I ain't sitting still for it."

Virgil said, "Fred, if I were trying to frame you, you'd be framed and on your way to jail. What I'm trying to do is make sense of what we've got so far. You're a big piece of that."

Fitzgerald threw the gel ball at the wall, snagged it midair as it bounced back to him. He made pistols out of his forefingers and thumbs, poked them at Virgil, and said, *"I didn't kill her. I didn't kill her."*

Virgil asked, "What did you do?"

"Fuck you," Fitzgerald said. "I want a lawyer."

Virgil and Pweters spent another five minutes issuing threats and listening to denials, then Virgil said to Pweters, "Let's go." To Fitzgerald he said, "Don't run. We'll find you in ten minutes, and running would be as good as pleading guilty."

"I'm not going nowhere," Fitzgerald said.

He followed them to the door and slammed it and

locked it as soon as they were outside. Pweters looked back at the door and asked Virgil, "What did we get?"

Virgil said, "I don't know, exactly. I wasn't expecting a confession, but I picked up something in there. He knows something that he doesn't want us to find out. But I messed up—we had him sweating and then he wasn't."

Pweters said, "I got that. I also got the feeling that he didn't kill Gina."

Virgil smoothed the squid over his nose and said, "Yeah, I got that feeling, too. The other thing is, he was throwing and catching the ball with his left hand, and Hemming most likely was killed by a right-hander . . ."

Virgil explained what the ME had told him about the blow that killed Hemming, and added, "I wonder if Fred might have an idea of who did kill her and he's trying to cover that up? You know anybody he might associate with who'd fit the bill?"

"The town is small enough that all the douchenozzles know all the other douchenozzles, so it's possible."

"Give me a couple of names of people he talks to—I'll go see them," Virgil said.

"Sure. I'll come along, if you want . . ."

Before they got in their separate vehicles, Virgil asked, "You're a smart guy. When are you going to run against Jeff Purdy?"

"Five years. He runs again next year. He'll get elected for four more and then he'll retire, and then I'll run," Pweters said. "It's a done deal."

"What if he changes his mind and doesn't retire?"

"I'll run anyway and beat him. I know it, and he knows it," Pweters said. "That's why the deal is done."

*   *   *

Inside the tattoo parlor, Fitzgerald watched from be-hind the window until Virgil and Pweters had driven away, then walked through the back room to an old-fashioned hardwired telephone and tapped in a number.

"Jimmy, you cocksucker, you sicced that fuckin' Flow-ers on me, didn't you?"

Jimmy Barker squealed, "Did not. Did not. He came in here yesterday and snuck in the back room, and he found one of those cat-o'-nine-tails and took it with him. Somebody told him about them, but I didn't tell him jack shit."

"If you didn't tell him, who did?"

"Somebody else you whipped," Barker said. "That's what I'd think."

SIXTEEN

Before Virgil had a chance to talk to the other town lowlifes, Bea Sawyer called and said she was coming down the hill into town. Halfway to Trippton, she said, she'd stopped at a café to get coffee and had run into the dive team and their truck.

"Clay said they'd be here by noon; they're moving slower than I was."

"Do you have the address for Hemming's house?" Virgil asked.

"Yeah, we do, and I've spotted it on my iPad."

"I'll see you there," Virgil said.

Sawyer hadn't yet gotten to Hemming's house when Virgil arrived. He peeled the crime scene tape off the back door, went inside, and walked around, looking for anything he might have missed. There wasn't anything in particular, except awkward traces of the dead woman. It wasn't the first time he'd been struck by the unexpected interruption of murder: you leave the wine bottles by the sink, thinking you'll put them in the recycling in the morning, and a week later here they still are because you're dead. Here's the silence of the house, with a couple of socks on the bathroom countertop, maybe to wear to bed, and there they still are.

But Hemming's shade was going away: the most resonant aspect of a woman's sudden death was often her perfume. Perfume was so personal, and so enduring, that it often lingered like a ghost at a murder scene. Then, after a while, it began to fade, like memories of the murdered person.

Virgil was walking back downstairs when he heard Beatrice Sawyer's truck pull into the driveway. He walked out the back door to meet the crime scene crew.

Sawyer was wrapped in a heavy blue North Face parka. A cheerful, middle-aged woman, she'd worked with Virgil on several cases, and didn't miss much. Her regular partner, Don Baldwin, looked like the farmer in Grant Wood's *American Gothic* painting, tall, thin, with watery blue eyes. His major non–Grant Wood aspect was his signature pair of black plastic fashion glasses, bought for the vibe they gave him in the punk revival band he led on his nights off.

Virgil had seen Bill Jensen around the BCA technical area but didn't know him well. A short, thin man with a goatee, he carried a leather portfolio with him, and he said that unless Hemming had done something unusual with her computer, he should be able to get by her password.

"Main thing we want to look at is emails," Virgil told him.

"I'll call you when I get them," Jensen said.

*　　*　　*

How much have you messed up my crime scene?" Sawyer asked.

"Not so much, but the sheriff's office has a half-trained crime scene substitute who went through the place," Virgil said. "Found some blood in the carpet, but that's about it. I found some B and D paraphernalia in a dressing table up in the main bedroom, which took me to the guy who used it on her. He's my number one guy, at this point."

"All right, we'll handle it despite the mess you guys probably made. Whatever happened to Alewort?"

Alewort was the sheriff's office regular crime scene man, and Sawyer had met him during the investigation of the school board murders. "He's up at St. Mary's, drying out," Virgil said.

"He did like a drink—most any time of day," Sawyer said. "Ask me how I knew that."

"I know how. You're a highly trained crime scene technician."

"That's correct," Sawyer said.

"Call me the instant—the instant!—that you find anything," Virgil said. "Progress here has been sorta slow."

"Yeah, yeah," Sawyer said. "Take off, hoser."

Virgil was sitting in his truck when the divers called and he directed them to the marina, where they could drive down the boat ramp to the river. They said they'd meet him there, and Virgil called Johnson and asked him if he could come along to the dive site. He could. "I wouldn't miss this for all the canaries in the islands," Johnson said.

They met at the cabin, got the heavy-weather gear on, cranked up the sleds, ran out to the main river, and turned south to the marina. When they got there, they found a Ford F-350 Super Duty sitting on the ramp, a large camper top on the back, fat snow tires at the corners, and three large men hanging around it. Virgil and Johnson pulled up and introduced themselves, and Clay Danson said, "Lead the way. Got about four hours. We don't dive when it gets full dark."

Virgil and Johnson got back on the sleds and led the way out onto the river. Johnson had worried that a snow-storm would cover the hole, but with Virgil's triangula-tion from the first trip out, they found it in ten minutes, in a patch of wind-scrubbed ice.

Danson, a bulky man with a gold mustache, brought a depth finder from the truck, scraped off a piece of ice and put the transducer on it, and turned it on. A mo-ment later, he said, "Nine meters. Thirty feet, more or less." He turned to the other two men and said, "All right. Let's get it going."

Danson and a man named Blue got in the camper and shut the back door, while the third man, Ralph, brought out an ice auger, a chain saw, and a pair of ice tongs. Vir-gil and Johnson stood around, being useless, as Ralph drilled a hole through the ice and used the chain saw to cut out a square five feet on a side, with cuts spaced roughly a foot apart. He used the ice tongs to pull the blocks of ice out. It was heavy work, and Johnson volun-teered to help, but Ralph said, "Naw."

He stacked the blocks of ice to one side, and Johnson said, "You could build a pretty good igloo with those."

Ralph said, "Go ahead."

That ended the conversation until Danson and Blue climbed out of the back of the camper wearing dry suits, which covered them from head to toe in heavy black neoprene, with the exception of a small oval around the face.

Ralph got a thick yellow nylon rope out of the truck, lashed one end of it to the truck's bumper, as Danson and Blue pulled on single-tank scuba outfits and rounded up lights and swim fins. Before Virgil felt quite ready for it, they were dangling their feet through the ice into the freezing river water and sealing up their face masks.

Danson grunted, "Ready?" and Blue said, "Yup," and Danson dropped the end of the rope, which was tied to a rusty, fifteen-pound dumbbell, into the river and followed it down. Blue was ten seconds behind him and immediately out of sight. Ralph got a heavy-duty, sealed plastic bubble out of the truck, with its own lead weight. It turned out to be a battery-powered LED light, and he clipped it to the rope and dropped it in the water and it slid down the rope and out of sight.

"Muddy water," Ralph said.

They all stood around and looked at the hole for a while, Ralph as quiet as the Sphinx, until Johnson said, "I bet you guys have some really great conversations in the truck, huh?"

Ralph scratched his nose and shrugged and said, "Oh . . . no."

Two minutes after that, one of the divers—impossible

to tell which—surfaced and threw a dark object onto the ice, and went back down. Virgil squatted over it: a woman's purse with a metal clasp. He opened it and found it full of the usual female junk, including a wallet. He opened the wallet and found himself looking at Gina Hemming's driver's license.

"Son of a bitch," Johnson said. "This really is the place. I sorta didn't believe it."

A diver surfaced again two minutes later and threw a high-heeled shoe out on the ice, and went back down.

"Well, she wasn't kidnapped when she went out for a walk," Virgil said, as he looked it over. "She wouldn't have been walking in that, not on that night."

Twenty minutes passed, and Ralph went to the truck and brought back a ladder like those that are hung off the back of sailboats except this one had spikes at the curled top end. He stuck it into the water and jammed the spikes into the ice. Another five minutes, and one of the divers surfaced and climbed the first two rungs of the ladder, and Ralph grabbed him by the shoulders and helped him up the rest of the way.

Danson took off his face mask and said, "I think that's gonna be about it. We did a grid ten to fifteen yards up-river, twenty yards down, ten yards on either side, and that's what we got. Don't think there'll be any more."

"You got what we needed," Virgil said. "This is where she was dumped."

"Yeah, I figured that when I spotted the purse," Danson said. Blue surfaced, and Ralph and Danson helped him up the last steps.

Johnson said, "How cold are you?"

Danson shrugged. "Not cold at all."

"This is cool," Johnson said. "I'm gonna try it."

"Lots of people tell me that, but then they don't," Danson said.

D anson and Blue went back to the camper and climbed inside to change back to street clothes, as Ralph piled up the gear at the back of the truck. Ralph also got them a black plastic bag for the purse and shoes, began slotting the blocks of ice back into the hole he'd cut.

"Always do that?" Johnson asked.

"Yup."

"How come?" Johnson asked.

"Liability."

"What . . ."

Ralph gushed, "Guy comes zooming across the lake on a snowmobile going ninety miles an hour, hits a big pile of ice blocks, wrecks his snowmobile and kills himself, and his old lady sues our butts for everything we got. Liability."

"Got it," Johnson said.

V irgil and Johnson hung around until Danson and Blue were back out of the camper, and Danson said, "We'll bill you."

"Do that," Virgil said. "And thanks."

"Easier and better than our usual calls," he said.

Johnson bit. "What are your usual calls?"

"We're usually looking for bodies."

*   *   *

When all the equipment was stowed, the three men got back in the truck and took off for St. Paul, and Virgil and Johnson rocketed back to the cabin on the sleds. When they got there, they found Griffin sitting in her car, the engine running, reading the *Republican-River*.

As they pulled in and killed the engines of the sleds, she got out of her car, walked over, and said, "Well, I've now read the worst newspaper in the country, from top to bottom and end to end. The most important thing I found was that if you act now and buy one turkey at full price, you can get a second turkey of the same size or smaller at half price."

Johnson said, "For real? At Piggly Wiggly?"

"I thought the name was a joke, but that's what the paper said." She turned to Virgil. "You've got to help me out. The guy who owns the ice-fishing house, or tent or whatever it is, this Duane Hawkins, where you found the voice recording, has gone on vacation to Florida. So his neighbor says. I don't believe it."

Virgil said, "You know, Margaret, I've got a murder case . . ."

"You've also got a governor who told my boss at Mattel that you'd make it a priority to help out, and you've got a case of assault on an officer of the law that needs to get solved. That would be your case. You could probably solve it all at once by driving out to CarryTown and talking to the guy in trailer 400. Besides, tell me what you'd do on the murder case if you didn't spend a half hour round-trip-driving out to CarryTown?"

Johnson said, "She's got you there, Virgil. You ain't got shit on the murder."

Griffin said, "See? Even this lunk thinks you ought to help out."

Johnson: "'Lunk'? I represent that comment."

Virgil: "Jesus, Johnson. The line is either 'I resent that comment' or 'I resemble that comment,' but it's not 'I represent that comment.' Could you try to keep that straight?"

"Okay," Johnson said. "I'm sorry."

"You only say you're sorry to make me feel bad."

Griffin said, "You sound like teenage girls."

They all went in the cabin, Johnson and Virgil stripped out of their snowmobile gear, and Johnson said, "I like that diving shit. I did a few tanks down in the Virgin Islands one winter. I'd be more interested in looking for sunken boats, though. Not so much bodies."

"I believe if you'd asked him, he'd tell you that you can see about four feet down there. It's not the Virgin Islands," Virgil said.

"Yeah, well. You might be right. Did it help you at all?"

"Might," Virgil said. "It's another place and time that I know the killer was at."

"As an experienced big-city police officer, I can tell you that what you found doesn't mean anything unless you have a specific sighting of the guy driving out there with a body on the back of his snowmobile," Griffin said. "Since you wasted that time, why don't you take a few minutes to drive out to CarryTown? I'll not only be out of your hair, I could be out of Trippton entirely."

"Okay, okay. Let me call my crime scene crew and see

if they need me for anything. If not, I'll drive out there and see what's what," Virgil said.

"I'll follow you," Griffin said. "And please—please!—put a gun in your pocket."

Virgil called Bea Sawyer and found that she had been trying to call him, but he hadn't heard the phone ring or felt it vibrating through the thick snowmobile gear. When she answered, she said, "Virgil. Bill has the computer open. And we have an anomaly."

"You know how I like those, Bea," Virgil said.

"Then you'll like this one. You want to come by? It's easier to see than it is to explain."

"Ten minutes," Virgil said. He hung up and turned to Griffin and said, "Clue."

"Ah, shit. Well, I'm still coming with you. After you look at this so-called clue, we can still go out to Carry-Town."

At Hemming's house, they left their vehicles in the street, and Griffin followed Virgil up the driveway and around to the back door. In the kitchen, he introduced Griffin to Sawyer, explained that she was a former cop, and they all stepped into the living room, where Baldwin had set up a camera tripod and was photographing what looked like a piece of vacant green carpet.

Bill Jensen was sitting in a corner, reading a Surface Pro.

"Okay," Sawyer said. "You know about the blood on the carpet over there." She pointed at four pieces of yellow tape that isolated a four-inch square of carpet. "Don't get near it. Anyway, that's the blood that the guy from the sheriff's department found. What he didn't find was a smaller bloodstain of the same type at the bottom of the stairs. That's what Don's taking pictures of. What we know from the ME is that Hemming sustained a skull fracture when she was struck, and that can result in bleeding from the ear canal."

"You think she crawled?" Virgil asked. "I was told that death was instantaneous."

"I've been told that. What I do know is, the first bloodstain is quite a bit more substantial than the second one, but their 'character' is the same. The first one looks like she bled from her ear into the carpet—from one point source, the ear canal, dripping blood onto a small area on the carpet, which, given the carpet fibers, wound up creating a bloodstain that's about the diameter of a pencil, extending straight down into the carpet and pooling at the bottom of the fibers. The second stain is smaller in diameter but also extends straight down into the carpet and pools at the bottom. But, they both look like they could have come from the same drip of blood. If I didn't know better, I would have thought it was possible that she fell down the stairs, cracked her head on the bannister on the way down, and landed here at the bottom, then crawled to the second spot, where she died."

"And somebody threw her in the Mississippi why?" Griffin said. "To tidy up?"

Virgil looked up the stairs and shook his head. "I don't think the ME would buy that idea—the bannister's got those edges on it, and she was hit by something large in diameter and smooth, like a bottle."

"So the guy kills her, doesn't notice the bloodstain, drags her body over to the stairs to make it look like an accident," Sawyer said.

"Then dusts off his hands, picks up the body, and throws it in the Mississippi," Griffin said. "I like your murders. They give you something to think about. In L.A., it was *BANG! BANG! BANG!*, two dead, one of them a gang member, the other a five-year-old girl on her way to buy a Popsicle. Simple, in-your-face nutcake homicide. Here, you've got to 'detect.'"

Sawyer and Virgil and Baldwin were all looking at Griffin, and she said, "What?"

"Nothing," Virgil said.

Sawyer said, "I like our way better."

"You find anything else?" Virgil asked.

"Cracked Ping-Pong paddle; could be more B and D," Sawyer said. "We can check it for DNA, if you want to put in for it. Bill's got the email up on Hemming's computer."

"This way," Jensen said, putting down the slate. He led the way back to Hemming's office, tapped the Return key on her keyboard, and the mail came up. "It's all yours."

Virgil sat down, and Griffin asked, "How long is this going to take?"

"Probably a while," Virgil said. "Give me an hour, and I'll go out to CarryTown with you."

She went away, and Virgil looked at the message count at the bottom of the screen. Hemming's in-box showed 8,406 messages, with 3,502 in her out-box.

He started typing in names, beginning with Ryan Harney. There were two recent messages, one to Harney and one back: a notification of the meeting and a note saying he'd be there. There were seventy more messages between them, but they went back five years. Nothing sexual, nothing that would necessarily say "affair," but they were meeting a couple of times a week, always at Hemming's house in the late afternoons.

There were far fewer messages to the other people who'd been at the party, with one exception: over the years, she'd sent hundreds of messages to Margot Moore, most of them quick notes setting up more meeting times. There were references to Fred Fitzgerald, but always in a kind of coded language that an outsider might eventually recognize as referring to sexual events: "Had a good time Thursday night, F brought a new toy. Ask him about the 'mouses.'"

Virgil scrolled through dozens of the notes from Moore to Hemming, both sent and received, and from Fred Fitzgerald to Hemming. The most recent note from Fitzgerald confirmed a nine-thirty therapy session. No date or day was mentioned, but the message had been sent the Sunday before Hemming was killed.

But the most interesting of all the notes was from Hemming to Lucy Cheever, sent on Wednesday afternoon, the day before Hemming was murdered.

Lucy,

I'm afraid that we might have to go another direction on the business loan. Frankly, a million's too large a commitment for our bank, at the moment. I will talk to Marv on Monday, when he gets back from the Cities, and see if he has anything to say that may change our minds, but I don't think

> *this will happen. You told me that you'd explored the
> idea of a loan with Lew Andrews up at U.S. Bank
> in St. Paul, and I did make a quick call to Lew and
> they are still quite interested in talking with you.
> Best of luck with that.*
>
>   *Gina*

Virgil found Marv Hiners's phone number and got him on the line.

"Has the bank turned down a major loan for Lucy Cheever?"

Hiners said, "No . . . In fact, it's on its way to approval. I was talking to Elroy Cheever this morning, who wanted to see what effect Gina's death might have had on their application. I told him that as far as I was concerned, we were good to go. It has to be approved by the loan committee, but that shouldn't be a big problem. How'd you hear about it?"

Virgil thought about telling Hiners about the email from Hemming to Cheever but held his tongue. Instead, he said, "The possibility came up in all the stuff I've been looking at. Thanks, Marv."

Off the phone, Virgil thought about what Hiners had told him. Hemming was planning to turn down the Cheevers' loan application, but Hiners hadn't known that. The Cheevers hadn't mentioned it, and Hemming's successors at the bank were about to approve it. For the Cheevers, Hemming's death had paid off—big-time.

When Virgil was working as a St. Paul homicide cop, he'd known of two separate killings done for single eight balls of cocaine. An eight ball, at the time, was worth maybe a hundred and fifty dollars. Kill somebody for a million? No problem. No fuckin' problem at all.

G riffin stuck her head into the office and said impatiently, "It's been an hour and a half. I'm waiting patiently."

"I've got some things to think about," Virgil said.

"Why don't you think on your way to CarryTown?" Griffin suggested. "It's a nice, relaxing drive out there."

V irgil had once solved a case involving an Israeli spy, during which he'd been given the definition of "nudnik." A nudnik, he was told, was like a woodpecker sitting on your ear, pecking at your skull. Like Margaret Griffin. When neither Bea Sawyer or Bill Jensen had any more to tell him, he went out, got in his truck, and drove out to CarryTown, with Griffin close behind him.

CarryTown wasn't actually a town but rather a collection of mobile homes that had been put up around a country convenience store called the Cash 'n Carry, six miles south of Trippton.

The mobile homes didn't look too bad under a pristine layer of snow, but when they got out of the vehicles Virgil could smell the unmistakable scent of a badly backed-up septic system. Griffin didn't seem to notice. She pointed at one of the mobile homes and said, "His name is Joseph Anderson. I was told that he may have gotten some supply packages for the altered dolls."

"Who told you that?"

"A little birdie . . . to whom I paid one thousand of Mattel's hard-earned dollars."

Virgil heard what she said but was focused on a red truck parked at a mobile home three down from Anderson's: it was almost certainly, he thought, the truck driven by the women who'd beaten him up, right down to the husband-wife-kids-dogs-cat sticker in the rear window.

Griffin picked up the fact that he wasn't paying close attention to her and asked, "What? What's going on?"

"That truck," Virgil said. "When I got beat up, I think the women were driving that truck. No, wait: I'm *sure* they were driving it."

"Then we've got a second stop . . . You put your gun in your pocket?"

"No, I didn't think it was necessary. Let's go knock. And, Margaret, be nice."

Virgil led the way to Anderson's trailer, which had a couple of concrete blocks for a step. Virgil stepped up, knocked a couple of times, stepped back down as he heard feet hit the floor inside, a heavy person walking toward the door, oil-canning the home's aluminum floor as he/she walked across it.

A hulking, square-shouldered man pushed the door open, looked past Virgil at Griffin, and growled, "What'd I tell you about coming back?"

Before Griffin could reply, Virgil said, "I'm a cop. I'm looking for information about the people doing unauthorized and illegal alterations of Barbie and Ken dolls."

"Wouldn't know nothin' about that," Anderson said. "Now, get out of my fuckin' yard. You want to talk to me, get a search warrant." His brow beetled, and he said, "You know, I know all the cops in Buchanan County, and you ain't one."

"I'm with the state," Virgil said. "I will be back with a search warrant. We'll cuff your ass, sit you in the county jail until we have time to talk to you—could be a couple of weeks, with everything else going on—and tear your home apart, see what we find. If we find anything, of course, we'll be talking prison time."

He paused, waited for an answer, but Anderson simply looked confused and, after a moment, asked, "Virgil?"

"Yeah, Virgil. Instead of doing all that other shit, you could talk to us for a couple of minutes."

Anderson put an earnest look on his face and said, "Listen, I don't know nothing about this, Virgil. The lady behind you came and knocked on my door and said I got some UPS packages with illegal stuff in them. Well, I don't know nothing about illegal stuff. My neighbor wasn't home, and I told her I'd take the packages for her."

"Which neighbor?" Virgil asked.

Anderson ducked his head and pointed to the next trailer down. "Jesse McGovern. She was in the process of moving out and said it was too late to change the address on the UPS packages, so I took them for her. She come out and picked them up a couple days after they got here."

"She's moved?" Virgil asked.

"Oh, yeah. She's been gone a couple months now. Heard she moved to . . . New York."

Griffin said, "Oh, bullshit. He's lying, Virgil. The

boxes came *here*, not to the next trailer. They had Anderson's address on them. She's still around here someplace."

"It's a 'manufactured home,' not a 'trailer,'" Anderson said. "And I hate to break the news to you, but there's only one address here. None of these lots are legal addresses—it's all one lot, and one address."

"You're still lying about Jesse," Virgil said. "I'll tell you, Joe. I may have to come back out here and take your ass to jail. You don't look like a bad guy, and I'd hate to do it— but, not to put too fine a point on it, Mattel has asked the governor to stop this crime and the governor has agreed."

"The fuckin' governor? Why would he give a stinkin' wet shit about this deal?"

Virgil looked to his left, to his right, then back at Anderson, shrugged, and said, "I don't know the details."

Anderson said, "*Oh, I see.* Somebody paid the little prick, didn't they? *Donated to his campaign*, or whatever they call it now."

"That's entirely unwarranted speculation," Griffin said.

Anderson said, "Well, maybe we both have warrants in our future—me and the governor. Come and get me when you've got mine."

He stepped back inside and closed the door.

Griffin, her arms akimbo, asked, "Well, what are you going to do, Virgil?"

Virgil said, "If you can come up with enough for me to get a search warrant, I'll come back, like I said. We're not there yet."

They'd turned back to their vehicles when a door slammed down the way and they both looked, and a large woman in a parka was standing on her stoop, her back to them, locking the door of her mobile home. The mobile home with the assault wagon parked outside.

Virgil went that way. "Hey."

The woman turned, looked at him, and said, "Virgil fuckin' Flowers." She came down off the steps and added, "How about I kick your ass again?"

Virgil opened his mouth to reply—something soothing and noncombative—but that apparently wasn't how they did it in L.A. Margaret Griffin, standing next to him, flicked her hand, and a two-foot-long steel wand snapped open.

Griffin said, "Come and get us, bitch."

Something about Griffin caused the woman to step sideways, circling to her left, which gave her a clear shot at Virgil, and suddenly she was moving more quickly than her size would have suggested, with newly painted and pointed fingernails flashing with Dior's Victoire 758 right at Virgil's face.

Virgil had his feet set, and he punched her.

A lot of great punches were thrown in the twentieth century. One of the most famous was captured in the painter George Bellows's iconic work *Dempsey and Firpo*, also known as *Dempsey Through the Ropes*, in which Luis Ángel Firpo, the "Wild Bull of the Pampas," knocked Jack Dempsey entirely out of the ring in the first round of their 1923 fight.

Then there was Rocky Marciano's 1952 knockout of Jersey Joe Walcott in the thirteenth round of their heavyweight fight, called a one-punch knockout by everyone, though there were really two; to say nothing of Muhammad Ali's 1974 knockout of George Foreman in what some people call the greatest boxing match ever.

Virgil's punch, though nearly a century after Firpo's, was on that scale. The woman came straight at him, talons flashing, the brightest thing around under the sullen winter sky, but Virgil had five inches' reach on her and had had time to set his feet.

He focused the punch two inches *behind* her nose, and she walked straight into it. The punch was so clean, straight, and pure, with Virgil's wrist and elbow locked up tight, a perfect line of bone between his shoulder and his knuckles, that the woman went down on her back like a wet sack of fertilizer.

Off to the side, Griffin said approvingly, "Whoa!"

The woman on the ground was swinging her arms back and forth as though she were making a snow angel while spraying blood from her nose all over the snow wings; a bloody angel, and making loud gasping and crying sounds. Virgil said, "Keep an eye on her. I've got some cuffs in the truck."

When he got back, the woman had flopped over onto her stomach, bleeding heavily into the snow. Virgil grabbed one wrist, and she tried to push up with her other hand, but Griffin stepped over, put her heel on the woman's cheekbone, and pushed down. The woman squealed, and Virgil said, "Don't hurt her," and Griffin asked, "Why not?"

Virgil said, "She's hurt bad enough already." Virgil got the woman's other wrist and locked it up, and said to Griffin, "Help me get her into the backseat of my truck."

They lifted the woman to her feet, and Virgil said,

"Hold on a second—keep her steady," and he went back to the truck and got a large-wound bandage from his first aid kit, which looked like an old-fashioned Kotex pad but twice as large, and pressed it against the woman's nose. The woman screamed and said, "Hurts," and Virgil said, "Yeah, I know. That's why I got a blue squid on my face. Remember that?"

"I'd do it again, fucker," the woman mumbled through the pad.

They helped her get into Virgil's truck, and Virgil put a leg-iron around one ankle and clipped it to a steel loop welded to the floor. When she was settled, Virgil asked, "What's your name?"

"Carolyn Weaver," the woman said.

Virgil said, "Okay, Carolyn, it'll help if you get some cold on your face to hold down the swelling. I'm going to give you a big chunk of snow to put on it. I'm going inside your trailer to get something to wrap it in. Do you hear me?"

She nodded, and Virgil said to Griffin, "Hold the pad against her face until I get back."

Virgil went to the trailer, where Weaver's keys were still in the lock. Inside, the first thing he saw were large cardboard boxes full of Barbie dolls and smaller cardboard boxes full of the tiny voice boxes. He looked around, found a box of garbage bags, took one outside, put a couple of pounds of packed snow in one of them, carried it over to the truck, and said to Weaver, "Lean forward. I'm going to put the bag of snow against the back of the front seat. Push against it with your face—but keep the pad pinned to your nose, too. We want the pad to stop the bleeding, the cold to stop the swelling. You got that?"

"Yeah."

They did that, and Virgil said, "I'll get you into the clinic in ten minutes. You have to hold it there until then. Hold it with your face."

"'Kay."

Virgil shut the truck door and said to Griffin, "The trailer is full of Barbie dolls and those voice things. She was making them here."

"Terrific," Griffin said. "You've made my day, Virgil. I'll get a deputy with a search warrant. And, goddamnit, that was one of the best punches I've ever seen. *Ever.* That was like . . . totally *awesome.*"

"Thank you. I thought it was a good one," Virgil said. "I better go lock the trailer."

Virgil went back to the trailer, and Griffin said, "Give me a peek."

Before Virgil could say yes or no, she climbed the stoop and pushed the door open. In the next second or so, as Virgil was climbing the stoop, she snapped a few photos with a small Sony point-and-shoot camera, until Virgil told her to stop—"Technically, you shouldn't be in there."

"I'm in shock from the fight. I wasn't thinking. When I saw the contraband, I reacted instinctively to take the pictures," she said. "That's my story, and I believe the court will accept it. Where are you headed now?"

"Into the Trippton Clinic," Virgil said.

"I'll follow you. As soon as Weaver is done with the doc, I'm going to drop some paper on her."

The trip to town took fifteen minutes in the snow, and, on the way, Virgil said to Weaver, "I locked up your trailer."

"Manufactured home," she said. She began to cry, and hadn't stopped when they arrived at the clinic.

SEVENTEEN

Birkmann sat frozen with fear in The Roasting Pig, thinking about what Margot Moore had said. Moore didn't know what she knew—but if Flowers went back to her and she blurted it out, even in confusion, Flowers would be on that one simple fact like a duck on a june bug, and he, David Birkmann—Daveareeno, etc., Bug Boy—would be fucked.

So Birkmann sat in the coffee shop, running through a list of fantasies about how it all could be explained. Came up empty. As the sun disappeared behind the bluffs and the night came down like an Army blanket pulled over the head, the question occurred to him, *What if Margot died?*

Moore was some kind of health nut and obviously wasn't going to drop dead on her own, so there was no point in pretending. If she was going to die, she'd have to be murdered.

An ugly word.

Murdered.

More fantasies, in which she died all on her own . . . And finally a dark, tickling thought, persistent, unavoidable: a perfect murder weapon was at hand. Something nobody else in town had access to . . .

Birkmann's father had dealt almost entirely with bugs. Insects. On a rare occasion, one of his clients might ask him to take care of an errant raccoon or skunk. Or an obstreperous possum, a too-visible rat. For those occasions, he carried a .22 caliber Ruger pistol in his van. The notable thing about the pistol was that it was made specifically for exterminators. And was silenced, so as not to disturb the peace when used in urban settings.

The pistol was in a wooden box at the back of a storage closet. The weapon had been purchased before all the current paperwork was required, probably forty years before. There was no sentimental value to it. But who threw away a gun? They were serious chunks of metal that, with even minimal care, would last forever. A '70s gun in a common caliber was as good as a gun bought yesterday.

Birkmann dug it out, carried it up to the living room, and sat and stared at it. Worked the action . . .

Margot Moore's second guest, Sandy Hart, came through the front door at seven o'clock, brushed a few snowflakes off her shoulders and out of her hair, pulled off her coat, and said, "My golly, when will this cold go away? It's been a week, and I don't see an end to it."

Moore took her coat to put on the bed and said, "Don't worry, we've got something to warm you up."

"Margot's hot toddy?"

"Exactly. Gonna send you home drunk on your butt. Belle's in the kitchen, setting up the board."

"She's probably hiding some tiles under her chair," Hart said.

Belle Penney called from the back of the house: "I heard that."

Moore took the coat into the bedroom, and when she walked back into the kitchen, Hart and Penney were seated at the kitchen table, turning the Scrabble tiles facedown in the game's box top.

Moore went to the stove, where the toddy had been steeping for five minutes. She poured the fiery liquid into tall mugs, sniffing the pleasant steam from the cloves, cinnamon, and the three ample shots of Jack Daniel's.

She put the cups next to the other two women and settled into a third chair. "Mix those babies up good. Remember last time, Belle kept getting those 'Q's."

"Hey . . ."

Old friends, playing Scrabble, on a cold, snowy night in Trippton.

The impulse to kill almost seemed to have its own horsepower, like a runaway truck. The elimination of one person would cut through an immediate, otherwise unsolvable threat. Birkmann drove into town, the gun in his coat pocket, snow coming down like a favor from God, muffling sounds, obscuring trucks, with cars moving slowly in the night, all eyes on the slippery roads.

An odd coincidence, which Virgil would notice later.

Belle Penney came through with the word "MUR-DER," five letters hooked through the letter "u," which

Sandy Hart had left in the open with her down word, "chateau." They'd had a brief argument about whether "chateau" would qualify because, basically, it was a foreign word, but an online check said that, yes, it was acceptable for English-language Scrabble.

That settled, Penney tapped her finger on the word, hushed her voice by a few decibels, and asked Moore, "Have you heard any more about Gina?"

Moore shook her head. "God, it's been a nightmare. I've been questioned twice by Virgil Flowers, but he knows I didn't have anything to do with it. He doesn't have anything to go on, so he's questioning everybody who went to the reunion meeting, and all of Gina's friends, people at the bank—everybody. Really putting on the pressure."

"He's supposed to be tricky," Penney said. "You think he can be trusted?"

"He's about a hundred miles better than Jeff Purdy," Moore said. "If Jeff was investigating, we'd have a mystery for the ages. Nobody would ever know who killed Gina."

"Might not be a bad thing," Penney said, "depending on who did it and why."

"Had to be a sex thing," Hart said.

"Or a money thing," Penney said.

"Or a random attack," Moore said. "That's the problem—Flowers can't even figure out the motive."

"Believe me, it was sex," Hart said.

Penney: "I think people get more angry and violent about money, especially here in Trippton. Hard times." She turned to Moore. "Who'd he talk to about money stuff? Other than you?"

Moore filled them in on Virgil's investigation, without mentioning whips or handcuffs. Or Fred Fitzgerald.

Moore had been buried in a client's investment wish list all afternoon and hadn't heard the rumors about Corbel Cain, Denwa Burke, and the fight at the Harneys' house, but Hart worked at the courthouse and had pieces of the story.

"Do you think Corbel could be right?" Penney asked after Hart laid it out. "Ryan Harney . . . that seems too unlikely."

"Corbel supposedly told Flowers that Ryan had an affair with Gina," Hart said. Hart and Penney both looked at Moore. "You think that's true?"

Moore said, "I really don't want to talk about it."

Hart said, "Margot . . . it's *us*."

Moore said, "You can't tell anyone."

"Of course not," Penney said.

"They had a relationship, but it was years ago," Moore said. "Completely over with. Gina says that Ryan told Karen about it and she forgave him."

"I don't see *that* happening," Hart said.

Penney said, "From what I've heard, Flowers thinks that one of the people at your meeting must have done it. Who do you think?"

Moore was shaking her head. "No one. It must have been an outsider. I mean, maybe somebody here in town, but nobody from that meeting. Something else is going on that we don't know about."

"That makes it even more scary. A killer on the loose, with no known motive," Penney said. "What if he's a nut? He could come after anybody."

Hart said, "Single women, living alone."

Moore: "I've got a gun under my bed."

Penney said, "Mine's in the side table. A nine-millimeter. Kelly Brenner showed me how to shoot it and load it and all. It kinda scares me, knowing it's there. It's like looking from a high bridge and thinking you might jump."

Hart said, "Maybe I should get one. I've never shot one. Is it easy to learn?"

"Point and shoot," Moore said. "An idiot can use one. Look at the news . . . anytime."

Birkmann had parked his truck on a side street two blocks away and had walked through the snowstorm with his head down, an anonymous nylon-wrapped blob trudging up the sidewalk in the dark.

Birkmann had been in Moore's house a few times on extermination missions—she'd once had a major plague of Asian ladybugs—so he knew the layout. Moore was in her kitchen, the only brightly lit room in the house. As he approached, he thought, *Is this really necessary?* It was only *possible*, perhaps not even *probable*, that Moore would tell Flowers what she knew.

Then a new thought: thrown in the river? How had Hemming gotten in the river? Had he been thrown into some weird mental state by the killing? Had the trauma wiped his memory? Such things were possible.

That whole line of thought took another two or three

minutes, but he finally shook it off and refocused on the house.

Still no light, except from the kitchen windows. No real sign of life, either. Maybe she wasn't home, maybe she'd had left the light on as a security measure or because she didn't like to get home in the dark?

A shadow moved across the kitchen curtains . . .

A sigh, the gun in hand, a fumbling check of the mechanism. A round in the chamber, a bright spot of golden brass in the steel mechanism of the gun. Birkmann walked up the front steps, reached toward the doorbell . . . paused, fled down the steps, stepped behind an evergreen, obscured in the night and the falling snow.

He stood there for a full three minutes, not really thinking, simply frozen. Another sigh, and he climbed back up the steps.

This time, he rang the doorbell.

A moment later, Moore walked through the front room to the door. Gun up, face down, until the last minute. Moore opened the door, a question on her face— her last question—then recognition, and the gun right there, three quick shots.

Moore toppled backward, landed on the front room rug with a muffled thud.

Was she dead? She had to be.

Penney and Hart didn't immediately react to the gunshots. Penney had gotten up to pour more hot toddy for the three of them, and Moore's body dropping to the floor sounded like somebody had dropped a package or a sack.

Only after a minute or two, when they didn't hear Moore speaking, did Penney call out, "Margot? Margot? Everything okay?"

Hart walked over to the door that led down a short hall to the front living room and felt the draft of cold air from the open front door. "Margot?"

She didn't see the body immediately because it was in the dark space below the storm door and a streetlight was shining in through the glass in the door. She stepped farther into the hallway and saw the lump on the floor, like a rolled-up rug . . .

"Margot? Margot?"

A fter the shooting, Birkmann ran for a half block, seeing nobody in the storm. He slowed, found himself panting. She had to be dead, because she recognized him, he thought, in the split second before he pulled the trigger, and if she wasn't dead, then he was. So she had to be dead. He hurried down the second block, got in his truck, and, as he was about to pull the door shut, heard the first of the sirens.

What? Had he missed her? No, he hadn't; he'd actually seen the bullets impact her forehead and her legs failing as she slumped toward the floor. Another witness? My God, they might be right behind him.

Birkmann, near panic, rolled up the hill and around the corner and headed for home.

T he cops didn't come for him, so Moore must have been dead. Although, he supposed, she could simply be so injured that she couldn't speak . . . at least, not yet. The Dunkin' Donuts opened at seven o'clock, to catch the going-to-work crowd, and he'd be there right at seven, to see what the latest news was.

In bed that night, Birkmann remembered what Virgil had suggested about talking with God. He tried it. He tried confession, as he'd heard the Catholics did it. He contemplated the meaning of the two deaths: in the world, in the town. He never got an answer to anything. It didn't make him feel better. There was no peace to be had.

When he closed his eyes, he didn't see anything but the little orange things he always saw when he closed his eyes.

Talking to God. Might work for Flowers, but for the Bug Boy it was just more nerve-jangling horseshit. Better to sit up and watch the late show.

EIGHTEEN

Virgil had spent the late afternoon processing Carolyn Weaver through the Trippton Clinic and filling out arrest forms when, he thought, he should have been raking the Cheevers over the coals.

The doc said Weaver's injury was only superficially like Virgil's. Weaver's injury was much worse. She would need surgery to realign the nasal bones at the top of her nose, which had been broken, and to reestablish the contour of the nasal cartilage at the tip. To get that done, she would have to be shipped up to Mayo in Rochester.

When the doc had finished evaluating her, he put her to bed, and a sheriff's deputy put a cuff around one of her ankles and locked it to the bed to keep her from running off. The doc took a look at Virgil's face, said that he was doing fine, and that the squid could be removed . . . "But don't hit anything else with your nose."

Virgil promised to not do that, and the squid came off. He checked himself in a mirror and said, "I've lost my luster."

"If you had any in the first place, it'll come back," the doc said. "You can talk to the admission clerk about insurance."

While he was doing that, Griffin sidled up to Weaver's bed, dropped a sheath of papers on her stomach, and said, "You've been served."

On the way out, Virgil asked if serving Weaver would be good enough. Griffin said, "I'm talking to our lawyer about that, but I think I'm still gonna have to find that goddamn McGovern. I'm going back with a deputy to Weaver's place, and we'll seize those dolls and the parts. I'd like to get that done tonight, if I can."

"Stay in touch," Virgil said.

As Virgil was driving over to the Cheevers' Chevrolet dealership, Johnson Johnson called to find out what had happened in CarryTown.

"I know Carolyn," Johnson said after Virgil filled him in. "Her old man ran off to Canada a couple years back. She's a tough old bird, and she needs the money, so I'm not surprised she was working with Jesse."

He asked if there was anything new about the murder, and Virgil said there wasn't, but he was planning to talk to a couple more people who'd been at Hemming's party. "I've got to tell you, Johnson, I don't expect much. I still think Fred Fitzgerald had something to do with the murder, but I've got nothing to pin him with."

"Do what you can until seven o'clock," Johnson said. "Clarice is making Norwegian lasagna."

*   *   *

Virgil went over to the Chevrolet dealership to talk to Lucy Cheever about the loan problem she'd had with Gina Hemming, but a salesman said that she and her husband had gone to La Crosse to do some shopping and catch a movie and wouldn't be home until late.

Virgil still had a name on his interview list, a divorced guy named George Brown, who owned and operated the town bowling alley, with a summer-only beach volleyball court in back.

Virgil talked to him in his office at the bowling alley, and Brown, a lazy-looking blond guy with a chunk, claimed to have been behind the bowling alley bar after the meeting at Hemming's house. He'd been there until closing, at one o'clock. He did have a snowmobile but said he didn't ice fish and didn't have an ice auger.

Virgil pushed Brown about a possible relationship with Hemming, but Brown said, "She was far too good for me back in high school, and she was still too good for me. I run a bowling alley, Virgil, where I allow people to illegally smoke cigars, and I've got a minor but persistent drinking problem. In the winter, I sit in the back and drink beer, and, in the summer, I watch twenty-one-year-old girls in bikinis playing volleyball. Sometimes I hit on them. Sometimes they say yes."

"You never dated Gina? Never asked?"

"Never asked. If I had, she'd have told me to get lost," Brown said. "She was also too old for me. My dateline is moving up, but, right now, it's twenty-one."

"Really?" Virgil said. "Mine's thirty, and I'm six years younger than you are. I mean, if I were out dating."

"You lack ambition, Virgil, you really do. If I was your age, my date line would be seventeen," Brown said.

"Couldn't do that," Virgil said. "She'd be listening to bands like Scouting for Girls." He shivered.

"There is that," Brown admitted. "The last chick I dated didn't know who the Eagles were. But Gina Hemming? No. Nope. No way. The chemicals were all wrong. You ought to check out David Birkmann. He was there that night and he's been in love with Gina since forever."

"Really? David Birkmann? I interviewed him, and he seemed all shook up by her death. You think he'd hurt her?" Virgil asked.

"Oh, jeez, I don't want you to think that," Brown said. "I mean, I spoke out of turn right there. Bug Boy's always been in love with her, but he's always been, well, Bug Boy. He had less chance with her than I did and he knew it."

"Still . . ."

"If he'd gotten physical with her, she'd have stuck her hand down his throat, grabbed his nuts, and pulled them out his face. David was not an athlete. He was the class clown, for Christ's sakes."

"Class clown . . . There could have been a lot of resentment built up there," Virgil suggested.

"You've been watching too many chick flicks, man," Brown said. And, "Listen, I heard that Corbel Cain got in some kind of fight at Ryan Harney's place last night, and it was about Gina. Is that right?"

"Right enough, I guess," Virgil said.

"I kicked Corbel out of here last night, cut him off. Didn't see the Harney thing coming, though."

"Probably wasn't drunk enough at that stage," Virgil said. "Corbel says they took a bottle of vodka with them, out on the river, and that's where they decided to go interrogate Harney."

"I heard Harney kicked his ass."

"Mostly Mrs. Harney, but, yeah, Corbel and his pal didn't do well. That Denwa guy lost about five teeth."

"Denwa is a piece of work. Somebody ought to get a court order to keep those two apart," Brown said. He glanced at his watch. "Say, it's after six. You wanna get a drink somewhere? Like here?"

He wasn't a nope, but he gave Virgil so many names of patrons who'd seen him behind the bar on Thursday that he thought Brown probably hadn't done it.

Virgil left the bowling alley and drove up to Johnson Johnson's place in the woods, a sprawling, self-designed ranch-style house. Johnson explained that when he designed it, he'd forgotten a few things, which had to be added, and then when he hooked up with Clarice she'd wanted a few more things—like a big bathroom off the bedroom. The result looked like a collection of children's blocks laid out on a rug, but giant-sized.

There was a barn out back for Clarice's horses, which she trained and endurance-raced, and an addition to the barn, which housed Johnson's collection of vehicles.

When Virgil arrived, Clarice was ready to shove the lasagna in the oven.

They ate and drank a bottle of red wine—Johnson was only allowed his single glass—and talked about the Hemming murder and the hunt for Jesse McGovern, about movies and possible summer fishing trips, and the past deer season and the possibility that whitetails from Wisconsin would cross the frozen Mississippi and spread chronic wasting disease into Minnesota, and how Clarice wanted to go to Palm Springs, California, at the end of the month, and possible alternatives to that, and about flying the Beaver back from Seattle.

They were having such a good time that when Virgil's phone rang and he saw that it was Jeff Purdy calling, he hated to answer. He did anyway.

"Jeff, goddamnit . . ."

"I'm sorry, Virgil, but something awful has happened," Purdy said. "Somebody shot and killed Margot Moore."

"What!"

"Yup. Right in her front room, while two of her friends were sitting in the kitchen at the Scrabble board. I think you better get down here."

"I'm on my way," Virgil said. "I'll be ten minutes. Gimme the address." He wrote the address on a notepad that Johnson handed him. "Listen, Jeff. Keep your crime scene guy out of there."

Clarice, her eyes wide knowing the news would be bad, asked as soon as he'd hung up, "What happened?"

Virgil told them, and Johnson said, "Shit!" and Clarice said, "Oh, God . . ."

"Why would somebody kill her?" Johnson asked. "You already talked to her, right? You said she didn't know anything."

Clarice said, as Virgil was pulling on his parka, "Maybe it doesn't have anything to do with Gina."

"Pig's eye," Johnson said.

"Maybe she knew something but didn't know she knew it," Virgil said. "Or maybe she found something out."

*   *   *

On the way down the hill, Virgil decided that if Moore had found something out, she would have called him almost immediately. She hadn't—so it was something else. Maybe something she'd hidden, something involving Fred Fitzgerald. He'd stop at Moore's place, he decided, but if there was nothing that he needed to do immediately, he was going to jack up Fitzgerald as fast as he could find him.

Bea Sawyer . . . He fumbled out his cell phone and called her.

"What?"

"Bea, did you go back to St. Paul?"

"No, I'm at Ma and Pa Kettle's resort. So's Don. In a separate room."

The implication there, that she and Don might be suspected of sharing a room, sidetracked Virgil's whole line of thought for a few seconds, and she prompted him with, "So, what's up?"

"We've got another murder," Virgil said. "Apparently, in the last half hour or so."

"Ah, poop. Give me the address . . . Is it still snowing?"

"Yeah, about the same." Virgil took the piece of notepaper out of his pocket, turned on the overhead light, and read it to her.

"We'll get there as quick as we can. If you get there first, keep people away from the body."

"I will. Thanks, Bea."

Virgil got to Moore's house four or five minutes later. There were six sheriff's cars in the street, two at either end of the block with their flashers going. Virgil was waved through, parked, and hustled up to the house. A cop on the front porch told him that Margot Moore was lying in the doorway and directed him around to the back.

Purdy and another deputy were in the kitchen with two stricken-looking women; both were crying off and on, seated over the beginnings of a Scrabble game. As though God had taken him by the hair and twisted his head to make him look, Virgil noticed that one of the words spelled out in the game was "MURDER," seventeen points, the "M" and "E" on triple letter scores.

Purdy said, "Good, you're here. C'mon."

He led the way through a short hallway into the living room, where Moore's body was flat on its back, three small bloody holes in the middle of the forehead, along with dime-sized powder burns. The crime scene crew would tell him better, but it appeared to Virgil that the gun had been only inches from Moore's forehead when she was shot.

He looked at the body for a moment, growing increasingly pissed off, then told Purdy, "Keep everybody away—our crime scene crew is on the way."

"Okay."

Virgil walked back to the kitchen, pulled out a chair, got the womens' names, and said, "Tell me what happened."

They told him, with details—but no good details.

Sandy Hart said, "She went to answer the doorbell. I was trying to figure out a word—"

"So was I," Belle Penney said.

Hart continued, "—and we heard her open the door. There was this sound; it sounded like somebody clapping hands, like she'd gotten a FedEx or something. We both heard a kind of clunking sound—we told Jeff about it— we think it might have been her, falling down, but we didn't know that . . ."

"We heard the door close," Penney chipped in. "We were sitting here, looking at the board, and after a minute or two, when Margot didn't say anything and didn't come back in, I called to her. I said, 'Margot? You're up.' She still didn't say anything, so I got up and walked in there, into the front room, and saw her on the floor, and saw her head . . . I started screaming . . ."

"When Belle screamed, I ran in there and saw Margot, checked her pulse. I used to be a nurse and I knew she was dead. I ran back to my purse and got the phone and called nine-one-one," Hart said.

"Did you touch her?" Virgil asked.

"Yes. I knelt down and I touched her shoulder and her neck, to see if she had a pulse, but that's all. I touched her shoulder, kind of pushed her, and her neck, but there was no pulse, and I ran and called nine-one-one."

"I didn't do anything," Penney said, "except scream."

"You didn't hear her talking to anyone?"

"No—we told Jeff—no, there wasn't any talk. Three claps and the door closed. And then . . . nothing."

"Do you know what time it was?"

"I . . ." Hart said, cocking her head, "I called nine-one-one. Probably one minute after she was shot."

"Longer than that," Penney said. "Five minutes."

Hart shook her head. "No, it wasn't, Belle. Think about it. We were sitting here—we thought she'd be right back—we didn't hear her walk or say anything, and we didn't wait too long before you went to look. Maybe not a minute, but not two minutes, either. Quicker than two minutes."

Purdy came in from the living room and said, "I heard that. We got the call at nine-one-one at seven-fourteen. So, probably, in the couple of minutes after seven-ten."

"Good enough," Virgil said.

Bea Sawyer stepped into the kitchen and said, "Don's getting our stuff. What do we got?"

"You're running the scene," Virgil said. "It might be the freshest murder you've ever been to. I've got to take off, talk to a guy."

"You need help?" Purdy asked.

"Is that Pweters guy working?"

"He can be," Purdy said.

"He knows Fred Fitzgerald, the tattoo guy, pretty well. I'd like him to meet me at Fitzgerald's shop."

"I'll call him," Purdy said. "He'll meet you there."

Pweters called Virgil as Virgil was driving south on Main. "I was in class. I'll be there in ten minutes."

Virgil parked across the street from Fitzgerald's shop. There was light coming through a white curtain on the second floor, but the shop itself was dark. Virgil sat and watched as the light played off the curtain: somebody was either watching television or had left a television on. If Fitzgerald was the killer, he was cool and already home.

He'd been waiting for five or six minutes when Pweters pulled in behind him. Virgil got out of his 4Runner and said, "Let me guess: computer programming."

"What?"

"Your class," Virgil said.

"Oh. No. It's a class in how to carve and paint decoy ducks," Pweters said.

"Huh. Cool. I write outdoors articles, you know? For magazines . . ."

"I've googled a couple," Pweters said. "They weren't terrible."

"Thanks. Maybe I could get something out of a duck-carving class . . . if the ducks are decent."

"They're actually *very* good; the instructor is in that folk art museum in New York City," Pweters said. He looked up at Fitzgerald's window. "Jeff told me what happened . . . Damnit, Margot was a nice lady."

"You know her well?" Virgil asked.

"Not well, but I knew her from the coffee shop. She always seemed nice, always had a good word for cops."

They walked across the street toward the shop, and Virgil said, "Stay loose."

"I've actually got my hand on my gun; it's in my parka pocket," Pweters said.

Virgil stopped and said, "Shoot. Hang on here a second."

He went back to the 4Runner, popped the back door, got his Glock out of the gun safe, and stuck it in his parka pocket.

When he got back to Pweters, the deputy said, "Remind me not to call you for backup."

Virgil stepped up to the shop door, pressed a doorbell, then pounded on the door for a few seconds.

Pweters asked, "Honest to God, did you forget to take your gun?"

Virgil took his gloves off, shoved them in the other pocket, and said, "Maybe."

*   *   *

A window popped open overhead, and Fitzgerald shouted, "We're closed. *We're closed!*"

"It's Pweters," Pweters shouted back. "Come on down and open up. Me'n Virgil need to talk to you again."

"About what?"

"Open up, and we'll tell you."

The window slammed shut, a light came on in the shop area, and a moment later they heard Fitzgerald stomping down the interior stairs. He turned on another light, and they could see he was wearing a sweatshirt and cargo shorts and leather slippers.

"Hand on the gun?" Pweters asked out of the side of his mouth.

"Won't need it," Virgil said, as he watched Fitzgerald approach the door. "This feels wrong. He's too . . ."

"Disheveled," Pweters suggested. "Psychologically unfocused."

"That's it," Virgil said. "He might have killed Hemming, but he didn't do Moore."

"So what are we doing here?" Pweters asked, as Fitzgerald fiddled with the door lock.

"Wrong question," Virgil said. "The right question is, 'What *did* he do?' I know he did *something*."

Fitzgerald was physically, if not psychologically, disheveled, and sleepy. He opened the door, heavy-eyed, scowling, and asked, "What do you want now?"

Virgil asked, "Where were you an hour ago?"

"Here," he said, "watching TV. I was asleep, with the TV on, when you started banging on my door."

"Anybody with you?"

"No . . ."

"What was on?" Virgil asked. "What was on TV? What were you watching?"

"CNN . . . the talking heads," he said.

Virgil asked, "What was the first news story you saw?"

"Donald Trump, some new tweet . . . Obama . . . Let me see . . ."

He rolled out an explanation, and Virgil interrupted to ask, "You got Sirius radio in your car?"

"My car is a 1992 Jeep pickup truck. The fuckin' steering wheel barely works. You're askin' if I got Sirius radio?"

"Just askin'," Virgil said. He turned to Pweters and said, "Dunno."

"What the fuck is going on?" Fitzgerald asked. "Did something happen?"

Pweters looked at Virgil, who stared at Fitzgerald, shrugged, and said, "Somebody shot Margot Moore and killed her. From what you're telling me, once again, you don't have an alibi. You were watching TV by yourself."

Fitzgerald gaped at him, sputtered, "Margot? Somebody shot Margot?"

Virgil rubbed his forehead with his left hand, said, "Oh, boy," and then, "Fred, I know goddamn well you had something to do with killing Gina Hemming. Sooner or later, I'll prove it, and you're looking at thirty years. Since you had something to do with killing Gina, I believe you had something to do with killing Margot. That's how it is. What I don't know is exactly what you had to do with it, but I'll figure it out."

"Fuck you!" Fitzgerald stepped back and slammed the door. A couple of seconds later, he opened it again and said, "I didn't have a fuckin' thing to do with *killing* either one of them."

"What *did* you do?" Pweters asked. "I've known you for a while, and Virgil thinks you killed them or got one of your buds to do it. I personally am willing to believe you didn't kill them. But you did *something* . . . I can hear it in your voice."

"I'm calling my lawyer," Fitzgerald said. He stepped back and slammed the door again. Two seconds later, he opened it back up again and said, "My lawyer'll call you in the morning."

"Who is it?" Pweters asked.

"Don't know yet," Fitzgerald said.

Virgil and Pweters glanced at each other, and Virgil said, "Lawyers cost money, Fred. If you don't have it, I can fix it so that a public defender takes it for free. He'll be your lawyer, and probably be as good as anyone else you can get. Margot's murder's only an hour old, and we've got to get on it. Every minute we lose is a problem. If you think you might have something to say to us, I'll crank up the public defender and get him over here right now."

Fitzgerald looked between the two cops for a minute, then asked Pweters, "Who's the public defender?"

"Ann McComber. She's good."

"If you can get her to come over, I'll talk to her," Fitzgerald said. He edged the door closed. "Tell her to call first . . ."

He closed the door one last time.

* * *

Ann McComber wasn't interested in leaving a date to talk to a tattoo artist until Virgil explained that Margot Moore had been murdered and her prospective client might have something to tell the cops about it.

"All I wanted was a third glass of wine and a little romance," McComber complained. "But . . . Fred's down at his shop?"

"Yeah. He wants you to call. I'll get your county attorney involved, so if there's a deal to be made, he can sit in on it," Virgil said.

"Well, phooey. Okay. I'll call Fred. I'm not sure I want to go down there by myself, though."

"If you want, me and Pweters can sit where we can hear you scream. If you scream."

"Let me call Fred."

Virgil got the county attorney on the phone, a guy named Bret Carlson, who agreed to meet with McComber that night if a deal was necessary. "But not after eleven o'clock."

Virgil rang off and said to Pweters, "If we can get McComber off her date and Fitzgerald off his dead ass and Carlson before he goes to sleep, we might work something out."

"McComber's on a date?"

Virgil heard the interest. "You got something going with McComber?"

"Not yet, but the thought has crossed my mind more than once. If I got that girl in bed, I'd turn her every way but loose."

Virgil said, "Oh-oh," and "How old are you?"

Pweters said, "Thirty-one. Why?"

"If you want to jump McComber . . . that suggests to me that she's about five minutes out of law school. Is she gonna know enough to work a deal? Or is she gonna blow us off?"

"Ah, she's been out of law school for three or four years, and she's smart. She knows how it works."

Virgil said, "Okay. I'll have to trust you on that."

As they were walking back to their cars, Pweters asked, "Why did you ask Fred if he had Sirius radio?"

"Because on TV cop shows, people get questioned about what shows they were watching when the crime occurred," Virgil said. "People think that might be an alibi because of the shows. But if you're halfway smart, you know that some TV shows are also on the radio— and the show that he was 'watching' is on Sirius. He could have been listening to it, could have driven over to Margot's, killed her, and driven back here without missing a thing."

"But not if he has a 1992 Jeep."

"No, but he could have been driving something borrowed. Something he borrowed from some other dipshit. But I don't really think that. I think he knows something, but he didn't kill Moore. Hemming maybe, but not Moore."

"Why do you think that? Hemming maybe?"

"Because he's all I got."

NINETEEN

Ann McComber turned out to be a moderately attractive frosted blonde with a haircut like some Olympic ice-skater that Virgil once saw in an Ice Capades show that his second wife made him go to. She was curt with Virgil, slightly less curt with Pweters, and told them that they were not permitted to wait inside Fred Fitzgerald's shop even though they had to keep Virgil's truck running to keep their asses from freezing off, a clear waste of gasoline and an environmental hazard, and even though they promised not to eavesdrop on the attorney/client discussion.

"Get a sleeping bag and huddle up together," she said. "The shared body heat should keep you alive."

"I'm not sure she's all that impressed with you," Virgil grumbled an hour or so later, as he watched the 4Runner's exhaust fumes drift down the street. The insides of the windows were frosting up from their breath.

Pweters was reading a tattered copy of *Garden & Gun*, which Virgil had stolen from his dentist, in the light from the overhead lamp. "Bullshit. She could hardly hold back from throwing me on the floor and having her way with me right there in the foyer."

"I didn't notice that," Virgil said. He checked his cell phone for the time. "Man, they've been in there for a long time."

"That's good, right? They must have something serious to talk about."

"Could be," Virgil allowed.

A few minutes later, an SUV, with its high beams on, pulled up behind them. Virgil asked, "Who's this?"

"Don't know, but the asshole has his brights on."

"Why don't you get out and look?" Virgil suggested.

"I'll do that. With my hand on my gun," Pweters said.

He did, and a moment later stuck his head back inside the truck and said, "It's Bret Carlson. McComber called him to come down."

"And didn't call us? Left us out here?"

"Okay, she's the bitch from hell. I'd still turn her upside down," Pweters said.

Virgil tended to agree. "Bitch from hell" and "Turn her upside down" were two distinctly different categories.

Carlson was out of his truck, and Virgil got out, and Carlson, whose face appeared no larger than a saucer in his parka hood, said, "Agent Flowers. Causing more trouble, I see."

"It's the town, actually," Virgil said. "It's absolutely murderous. I'm only here to help out."

"I'm sure our previous school board would disagree," Carlson said. He was wearing leather gloves, and he clapped them a couple of times and said, "Let's get out of the cold, shall we?"

The school board members had been convicted of murder in the county court by a special prosecutor appointed by the state attorney general. Carlson had been asked to step aside because of his close relationships with *all* the board members. He'd done that but hadn't been happy about it.

Carlson led the way to the shop door, where they knocked once and went inside. McComber and Fitzgerald were on the second floor, and McComber called, "Bret, come on up."

All three of them climbed the stairs, and McComber said to Pweters, "I see you survived," and Pweters snapped, "No thanks to you, Ann," and Virgil saw a spark of surprise on McComber's face. She'd thought she had Pweters safely tucked away for possible use at a later date.

"Well," she said, "let's go see Fred. He's in the living room."

She led the way down a dark, unadorned hallway that smelled of onion rings, ketchup, and reefer and into a small living room, where Fitzgerald was perched on a soft, low-backed chair.

When they were all seated except Pweters—he was the junior official, and they'd run out of chairs, so he propped himself in the doorway—Carlson said, "What's going on, Ann? I have not been briefed on this, except that it has to do with Gina Hemming and Margot Moore."

"Yes. The situation is, my client has done something he shouldn't have, for fear of the police—specifically, Agent Flowers. His transgression is relatively minor but probably not without consequence. I've already done some online research, and Fred could possibly be charged with a gross misdemeanor, if you chose to prosecute him. I've advised him not to speak to you, or the police agents involved, unless we can make a no-pros deal with you. I have reason to think that the information he would provide could be helpful in the investigation of the death of Gina Hemming."

Carlson's eyebrows went up. "But not Margot Moore?"

"No. Not Margot."

Carlson looked at Virgil. "Ann is usually truthful enough, if not always. She has been known to cut things fairly thin when she's defending an indigent client . . . but she doesn't usually tell an outright lie."

Virgil: "If Fred didn't kill the women, I don't care about a misdemeanor. Even a gross misdemeanor. I'm here to catch an active killer."

Carlson said, "Okay . . . Ann, I'll want to record this . . . Virgil?"

Virgil had two high-fidelity recorders in his truck. He went down and got them, set them up in the living room, ran a quick test. The lawyers talked lawyerly bull-shit for a couple of minutes, then McComber said, "Fred, you can tell them what you told me."

Fitzgerald: "I don't go to jail?"

"Not if what you tell them is limited to what you told me. If it turns out you actually participated in the murders . . . no, you wouldn't be protected."

"I didn't do nothing but what I told you," he said to McComber.

She said, "Then . . ." and made a "Let's roll" motion with a hand.

* * *

Fitzgerald exhaled and looked at Virgil and said, "On Thursday night, I was supposed to meet Gina for a little . . . session."

Virgil: "A sexual encounter involving what they call bondage and discipline?"

Fitzgerald: "Yeah, I guess."

"Wait . . . You guess? Was that what it was or was it something different?" Virgil asked.

"Ah, that's what it was. Nothing harsh. She liked to get . . . restrained . . . and spanked a little bit. Hey, this is kinda embarrassing with a chick sitting here."

McComber rolled her eyes.

"She's familiar with these things, I'm sure . . . in her job," Pweters said.

"I am," McComber said, as she stabbed Pweters with a glare.

Virgil said to Fitzgerald, "Okay, go ahead. You went there for a sexual encounter."

"Right. Anyway, she told me to come over around nine-thirty. She said she had a meeting that night, for her class reunion, but she said she'd get everybody out of there by nine o'clock. I was running a little late when I got there. I parked behind the house—she always wanted me behind the house instead of where people could see my truck—and I went up to the door and knocked. Nobody answered, but all the lights were on. I knocked some more, but she never came, and I thought she might be upstairs in the bath. She was kind of a clean freak, you know? Everything had to be scrubbed up . . ."

Pweters said, "You mean, your bodies. For sex."

Fitzgerald nodded, and Virgil said, "Mr. Fitzgerald

has nodded, indicating that he means to answer yes to Officer Pweters's question. So, Mr. Fitzgerald, what happened next?"

"Nobody answered, so I tried the doorknob. It was unlocked. I was kinda surprised because it had never been unlocked before. Anyway, I went in," Fitzgerald said.

Once Fitzgerald started talking, he sank back and closed his eyes, and the words rolled out like a repellent dream, riveting Virgil, Pweters, McComber, and Carlson in their chairs, viewers at a horror movie.

Fitzgerald dressed carefully for his assignations, he said: tight jeans, black T-shirt that would show his muscle, black leather jacket, heavy black boots by Daytona. Black thong underpants. He enjoyed looking like a movie biker, but the movie bikers he emulated tended to ride in Southern California or Arizona. If he stood outside in Trippton in the winter in his Southern California assignation gear, he'd freeze his nuts off.

He thought about that as he drove to Gina Hemming's house. He liked messing with Hemming, and he liked the two hundred and fifty dollars she paid him for each therapy session, but he didn't want to freeze his nuts off. Would she still be hot for him if he showed up in a North Face parka and hood, in trapdoor long johns and fleece-lined rubber boots? Maybe not.

He took his Jeep up the incline to Hemming's back drive, parked, got a plastic baggie with a couple of joints from under the front seat, hustled up the back steps of the house, and knocked. He was shivering from the cold when he finally tried the doorknob, which, to his surprise, was unlocked. He pushed inside, into the warmth of the kitchen. "Gina?"

No answer. She was upstairs in the bathroom, he guessed, and he went that way. "Gina?"

And found her body at the bottom of the stairs.

He froze, called to her across the twenty feet that separated them. "Gina? Gina?"

Trembling in the sudden presence of death, he stepped across to her, squatted next to her body, touched her neck with a knuckle: still warm but obviously dead, one side of her head crushed flat.

She'd only been dead for a few minutes, he thought. He stood, took his phone from his pocket to call the cops. And then thought twice about that.

Nobody had seen him arrive; it was snowing hard enough that he could probably get away clean. If the cops found him here, they were likely to think that her death had been something more than an accident. His reputation in town was not the best, and that prick Jeff Purdy would be happy to get rid of him for whatever reason.

Then he noticed the blood. A spot of blood marred the carpet, five feet from Hemming's head. He wasn't a doctor, and he thought for a moment that it was possible that she'd fallen, hit her head on the stairway bannister, and had landed where the blood was . . . had staggered somehow out into the room. What—and pushed herself backward to where she now lay? Not likely, not with the damage to the side of her head.

And, finally, he noticed the shoe.

One high-heeled pump lay on the stairs, as if it had

come off when she'd fallen. The other was still on her foot. But the shoe on her foot was on the wrong foot—like it had been put there by mistake, by somebody hastily faking the fall.

By the killer.

Fitzgerald looked around, suddenly frightened. She had been dead only a few minutes. Was the killer still in the house? Maybe upstairs, looting the bedroom?

He carried a switchblade, which were legal in Minnesota. He clicked it open, listened, and heard nothing but the wind. After a few minutes, he crept up the stairs and into the bedrooms, a chill between his shoulder blades as he waited for the killer to jump out of one of the many closets, nooks, and crannies of the old Victorian.

He'd never stabbed anyone . . .

But the house was empty.

As he worked through the house, he realized that his trouble was deeper than he'd first supposed: his fingerprints were on the outside doorknobs. Had he touched Hemming with his fingers? He knew from watching television shows that fingerprints could sometimes be taken from bodies, along with DNA. And he'd definitely touched Hemming's neck . . .

Downstairs, he thought about it some more and finally decided he had no choice: he had to get rid of her body. It'd be a mystery, what happened to her. The cops might eventually find out about their relationship, but if a motive couldn't be found, he should be safe . . . except for those prints.

He had to get rid of the body.

He first made very sure that Hemming was really dead. He checked her breathing and then saw the blood marks on her face, the blood slowly being dragged down by gravity, no longer pumped by her heart.

When he was sure, he went back up the stairs, into a guest bedroom, and took a plaid blanket off a cedar chest, carried it back down, and wrapped her in it. He was trembling again. He carried her in his arms out to the truck, put her in the truck bed. He returned to the house and wiped everything he might have touched with his hands. At the last pass through the house, he spotted her purse and decided to take it—maybe somebody would think she'd gone off by herself. Same with her shoes.

That done, he drove carefully back to his shop, got his auger and his ice chipper, and drove out on the Mississippi. The snow was thick, but he could still see the lights of the lowest level of Trippton when he stopped. Cutting through the ice went quickly enough, and, ten minutes later, he slipped the body into the water and pushed it down. As he did, the blanket floated off. He pushed that under, too, and threw the shoes and the purse after it. When everything was gone, he used his boots to push loose snow into the hole.

Still wearing the leather jacket and T-shirt, and on the edge of frostbite, he drove back to the lights of Trippton. Gripped with fear. A fear that had never gone away.

The cops would be coming, he knew, and he had to work through Hemming's death, change his fear to puzzlement.

He could handle the cops, he thought, but he wasn't entirely sure he could handle Hemming's murder. She'd been the most beautiful woman he'd ever slept with, the most high-toned . . . the prize of his life.

I figured she wouldn't pop up until spring, if she ever came up, and then nobody would remember who was doing what when she died," Fitzgerald told his audience. "I wouldn't have to pull some goofy alibi out of my ass. I could say I was out of town, or whatever, if anybody asked."

Virgil said, "I'm still not clear on why you didn't call the sheriff's office. Or walk away from it."

"Because Jeff Purdy would slap me in jail and call it a day. I'd be good enough for him—another fifty votes for solving the murder so quick. Purdy wouldn't give a shit about who really did it. All he'd care about would be getting somebody in jail. Anybody. I'd be perfect. If I'd walked away and left her, same deal—he'd find out that we were involved . . . sexually . . . from somebody like Margot, and I'd be in jail."

"I don't think you're being entirely fair to Jeff," Carlson said. The prosecutor's forehead was beetled in a frown. "There's no evidence that we don't treat all murders with utmost . . ."

"Oh, shut up, Bret," McComber said.

Virgil: "So you're saying that when you showed up, about nine-thirty . . ."

"A little later than that, but not much. It wasn't even nine forty-five. I'd guess . . . maybe nine-forty."

"At nine-forty, she already had those little blood things under her skin," Virgil said.

"Yeah."

"What's that mean?" McComber asked.

"It's something that happens after somebody dies, blood stripes under the skin, the beginning of the lividity process. That doesn't take long, but it takes a little while," Virgil said. "Unless Fred is lying, she must have been killed right after the meeting ended . . . unless the people at the meeting were lying and she was killed while they were still there."

Carlson shook his head. "You don't get to do that again—take down a bunch of good citizens."

Virgil, annoyed: "Bret, the school board killed several people and stole millions of dollars from the schools. From the kids. Even if they were your good friends, they *weren't* good citizens. They're doing thirty-year sentences for their rotten citizenship."

"Well, except for that, they were okay," Carlson muttered.

McComber leaned across to him and whispered, "Bret, this is being recorded," and Carlson shut up.

Virgil, Pweters, Carlson, and McComber continued to push Fitzgerald on the details of his discovery of the body, but after half an hour, there wasn't much more to learn. Virgil was interested in Fitzgerald's observation about the shoe, which struck him as very real reportage and not something a killer would extemporaneously think up as part of a cover.

When they were done, Pweters arrested Fitzgerald for interfering with a dead body, a gross misdemeanor. He would be booked at the county jail, Carlson explained, where he would be held overnight, but, at Carlson's directive, would be released on his own recognizance the following day—after Virgil had gotten a search warrant from a county judge.

Virgil and Pweters took Fitzgerald down to Pweters's patrol car, and when Fitzgerald was locked in the backseat, Virgil said, "He doesn't know anything else?"

"I don't think so," Pweters said.

"You remember the last time we talked to him and I screwed something up? All of a sudden he wasn't sweating anymore? That's because I said somebody saw him on a sled—and he'd driven out in his pickup. He knew I was bullshitting him."

"Ah. I didn't pick that up."

Virgil pulled his gloves out of his pocket and put them on. "You want to get the warrant and help search the place tomorrow?"

"Sure. After breakfast? Meet you at Ma and Pa's for pancakes?"

"I guess. Damnit, you know what this means?"

"Could mean a lot of things," Pweters said, "but tell me."

"I'd eliminated a lot of the possible suspects, like Lucy Cheever and Margot Moore and Sheila Carver, because they were too small to carry a body as heavy as Hemming's. Turns out, they wouldn't have had to. All they would have had to do is hit Hemming with a bottle and, probably, be mean or crazy enough to shoot Moore with a handgun. I'm starting again at zero."

Virgil went back to Moore's house, where Sawyer and her partner were still at work. "I've got nothing much, except we picked up two .22 long-rifle shells from outside the door, in the snow. Haven't found the third one.

But, the shooter was using an autoloader. We'll look at the firing pin marks, et cetera, maybe get you a make on the pistol. We'll run the shells for prints, but I don't see any. That's about it. You'll get my report in the morning, but there won't be much in it other than that. We should get the body off to Rochester, let the ME look at her, and dig out the slugs—no exit wounds. That might get you a little more on the make of the gun."

"Okay." Virgil hung around for a while to see if anything amazing came up, but nothing did.

TWENTY

At the cabin, Virgil hooked a pair of earphones into his iPad and called up a shuffle of country blues. He'd just closed his eyes to think when the phone rang. Johnson Johnson was on the other end and said, "You're gonna get a phone call."

"What?"

"You're gonna get a phone call. You won't recognize the number. Answer it anyway."

"Johnson . . ."

"Answer the phone, dummy. Probably next five minutes . . ."

He clicked off, and Virgil didn't bother to call him back. Johnson moved in mysterious ways sometimes—or in ways that seemed mysterious to outsiders, especially when he crashed one of his boats, trucks, cars, motorcycles, airplanes, four-wheelers, or snowmobiles and yet survived to run a thriving business. Virgil had learned that lesson through the years and so was content to wait for the phone call.

It came in three or four minutes later, in the middle of

J.J. Cale's "Call Me the Breeze": a sulky woman's voice, a little whiskey in it. "Is this Virgil?"

"Yes, it is. Who is this?"

"This is Jesse McGovern."

"Jesse." Johnson did indeed move in mysterious ways, sometimes. "I've been trying to look you up."

"Yeah, I know. For that Griffin woman who's trying to shut us down. What's it to you, what we're doing?"

"Nothing, except I guess it's illegal," Virgil said. "Even then, I wouldn't much care, but . . . I'm supposed to stop illegal stuff."

"Because somebody got to the governor, is what I heard," McGovern said. Johnson also ran his mouth, sometimes.

"Look, all Margaret Griffin wants to do is serve you some papers," Virgil said. "We're not trying to arrest you . . . yet . . . unless you beat somebody up . . . like me."

"I didn't know that was going to happen. Carolyn Weaver and some of her CarryTown pals got a wild hair, is all. Anyway, I talked to Johnson about you," McGovern said. "He said that you're open to . . . arrangements."

"If you're talking about a bribe . . ."

"No, no, no. I asked Johnson about that, and he said you don't take bribes," McGovern said. "Unlike certain other law enforcement officers I could mention."

Virgil didn't want to go there and instead asked, "So, what do you mean 'arrangements'?"

"My people could help you with the Gina Hemming case, if you lay off us."

Virgil sat up and said, "If you have any information about Gina Hemming, I need it. If you have it and don't cough it up, I'll put your ass in jail."

"Yeah? You can't even find me, how are you going to find me *and* prove I knew something about Gina? It's all in my head; it's not like I wrote it down on a piece of paper and put it in my purse."

Virgil didn't have an answer for that except a limp "I'll find you. And to tell you the truth, I don't need a bunch of amateur Sherlocks running around town, trying to turn up clues."

"It's not that. It's something specific."

Virgil decided to make an emotional appeal for justice; he had a few pre-canned: "Jesse, if you have something specific, it's your *obligation* to tell me. We're not talking about some button on the back of a Barbie doll. We're talking about Margot Moore getting shot three times in the forehead while she was playing Scrabble with a couple of friends. A woman who went to the same high school that you did. You probably knew her, right? I looked into her open, dead eyes, and it seemed to me like she was pleading with me to find the killer. You gotta think about that. You gotta help me."

"I heard about Margot." More silence. Then, "Johnson said you might try to pull some ethics shit on me."

"He was right."

"You did that really good. Made me feel guilty. The dead eyes thing," she said.

"Thank you."

Even more silence; the woman apparently didn't feel the need to fill every crack in the conversation with the spoken word. Finally, "There's all kinds of rumors going around, about who was at that party at Gina's on

Thursday night and what time that broke up. Some people say it broke up at nine o'clock."

"That's right."

"I don't know if this will mean anything, but a friend of mine—honestly, a friend, not me, and not somebody involved with the Barbie-Os—said a GetOut! truck was parked outside Gina's house at nine-thirty."

"A GetOut! truck? David Birkmann?"

"Definitely not David. My friend said it was a blond-headed man. The man may have seen my friend looking out the window at him and turned his face away, but he was a blond for sure."

"That's it?"

"Isn't that a lot?"

"It could be," Virgil said. "If it pans out, I'm going to need your friend's name . . . I'm sure you know that."

"If it pans out, this person will talk to you," McGovern said.

"Jesse, I appreciate this . . ."

"You gonna lay off us?"

"I'm not going to spend a lot of time trying to catch you. But if somebody sticks some Barbie doll stuff in my face, I'll probably have to do something. And Carolyn Weaver is going to jail for a while, for beating me up. If I can find out who her helpers were, they'll go with her."

"I got nothing to say about that, except what I already said: I didn't know what they were planning, and, if I had, I would have shut it down," she said.

"So . . . how are sales?"

"Starting to tail off," McGovern said. "Another three months and we'll have to move on to something else."

"Try to pick on a smaller company, okay?"

"We're thinking Apple," McGovern said.

"Oh, man, not a good idea, Jesse. Anyway, any fake Apple product is going to be expensive to make . . . Uh, what is it?"

"An app. We hired a programmer, put the app together, and we're field-testing prototypes."

"An app. There are a million apps out there; it'd have to be unusual."

"You know how an iPhone vibrates when you get a text message or a phone call comes in when you've got the phone set on silent?"

"Yeah?"

"What if it vibrated for ten minutes?"

Virgil had to think about it for a minute. "Jesse, please . . ."

"We're thinking, 'iPhone-eeeO: The Lady's Happy Helper' . . ."

"What is it with you guys and the sex toy thing?"

"Sex sells. It's nothing personal," she said. "You been here before, you oughta know: middle of the winter, there's nothing to do but look out the window, watch HBO, and fuck. And if you can only afford the basic package, it's look out the window and fuck. So, there's a market. We think iPhone-eeeO will go big."

"C'mon, Jesse . . ."

The whole idea was nuts, but Virgil liked to hear the woman talk, the sound of her voice.

When he got off the phone, Virgil went into the bathroom and checked his face in the mirror. He still looked beat up, and, from experience, thought he'd look that way for another three weeks or a month. He was pleased that none of his teeth were loose: dental work was a whole different problem, and way more unpleasant.

When he was done with his inspection, he undressed and got in the shower and steamed himself off, carefully washed as much of his face as he could get to. The air was so cold and dry that the humidity of the bathroom felt terrific. He got out of the shower and was toweling off when somebody began banging on the door.

Johnson's cabin was a full-service establishment—Johnson had somebody staying in it half the weeks of the year, he'd said—and Virgil pulled a robe off a hook, wrapped it around himself, and hurried out to the front door, pausing only to open his gun safe and put his main pistol, a Glock, in the pocket of the robe.

At the door, he flipped on the porch light and peeked out a window to the left side of the porch. Margaret Griffin was standing there, and as he looked out the window, she knocked on the door again.

He went over and opened the door and motioned her inside and said, "You caught me in the shower."

"Sorry. I stopped to tell you that I papered Duane Hawkins down at the Kubota dealer. He didn't go to Florida at all. Everybody's lying to me. Anyway, he says he didn't know that anybody was putting together the dolls at his fishing shack."

"It's actually a tent, and since it's transparent, and since he supposedly goes out there almost every night, that sounds like a fib," Virgil said. "Not that I could prove it without some surveillance."

"That won't happen—this is a townwide conspiracy," Griffin said. "I need to know whether you're making any progress on the murders. I don't want to get involved there; I just want to know if you're going to be able to get me some time to run down Jesse McGovern."

Virgil considered for a moment, then said, "Listen, Jesse called me tonight, out of the blue. I don't know how she got my phone number, but lots of people in town have it. She actually had a tip on the murder investigation—but she also told me that sales of the dolls are dropping off, and they're getting ready to move to a new product that has nothing to do with Mattel. A few more weeks and there'll be nothing to investigate, no reason to serve papers on anyone."

"That's not the entire point here," Griffin said. "We don't only want them to stop, we want people to see that they get punished. Jesse McGovern especially. We don't want people messing with the Mattel product lines."

Virgil said, "Margaret, I'm sorry, but I've got two murders on my hands. I don't have time right now to mess with Jesse McGovern. If I break these murders in the next day or two . . . I'll do what I can."

Griffin left, still grumpy.

She might have to look elsewhere for help, she said.

TWENTY-ONE

The next morning, Virgil met Pweters at Ma and Pa Kettle's. They both ordered pancakes and link sausages and extra syrup, and Virgil told him about an anonymous phone call from the night before, with the tip about a blond guy in a Get-Out! truck.

"You gonna talk to Birkmann about his employees or hit Fred Fitzgerald's place?" Pweters asked. "I'll tell you, Fitzgerald will be back on the street before noon."

"Then let's do his place first—maybe he's got something about this B and D ring he had going. Maybe there were more people involved than Hemming and Moore."

They talked about that, finished breakfast, and headed for Fitzgerald's. On the way, Virgil called Jeff Purdy and asked, "You know that we're gonna search Fred Fitzgerald's place this morning?"

"Yes. Pweters has the warrant."

"I know, we just had breakfast. Anyway, Fitzgerald's got a computer up there, and the warrant covers it. Could you send somebody down and ask him what the password is? So we don't have to break into it?"

"Get back to you in five minutes."

He did, and Virgil wrote the password—Tatooine—on a piece of paper and put it in his pocket.

The day was dark and cold, the wind whistling down the Mississippi from the northeast, but there was no snow. Fitzgerald's place was right across the street from the railroad tracks and the river, and a squadron of snowmobiles went by on the river as Virgil was pulling up.

Pweters had the warrant and Fitzgerald's key ring, which had been confiscated at the jail, and they let themselves in. They spent twenty minutes on the first floor—the work area—not expecting to find much, and didn't, except for a gun safe. The safe was keyed, and the key was on the key ring; when they opened the safe, they found no guns but, instead, a collection of action figures.

Virgil took out an eighteen-inch-high Joker figure, shook it a few times to see if something might be concealed inside, but it seemed solid. Pweters pointed him at the comic-book posters on the shop walls: Star Wars stormtroopers, Wonder Woman, Serpentor, Aquaman. "He's a comics guy."

They climbed the stairs and took in Fitzgerald's living quarters more carefully. While Virgil scanned the bedroom, Pweters looked at an aging Apple iMac. He tried a couple of passwords but nothing worked. "I got no ideas," Pweters said. "I've tried one, two, three, four, five . . . his initials . . . his name . . . tattoo . . ."

Virgil said, "Let me in there."

Pweters moved, and Virgil tapped in a few letters into

the password space, and the machine opened up. "Look at his emails, see who he's talking to," Virgil said.

"Holy shit, how'd you do that?" Pweters demanded.

"Password was Tatooine—you know, the Star Wars planet, and a pun on 'tattoo.' Couldn't miss it, with those posters on the wall downstairs."

"Hey, I'm fuckin' impressed, man."

"Routine, when you know what you're doing," Virgil said.

Virgil found a collection of B and D equipment, including some crappy handcuffs, in a box in a living room closet; also a folding massage table and several books on massage. Fitzgerald appeared to have a variety of sidelines, but that wasn't unusual in an isolated small town.

"Got something here," Pweters called.

Virgil went over to look as Pweters clicked through a list. "I put 'spank' in the search field, which would cover 'spanking' and other variations, and I got seventeen emails up. Looks like four or five different women . . . although, some of the emails could be guys, I guess . . . Jeez, I bet that's Janet Lincoln, the JLinc one."

"You know her?"

"Yeah, everybody does. She runs the Sugar Rush; it's a candy store downtown. And ice cream and so on. She's a little chubby . . ."

"Guess chubby people like to get spanked, too," Virgil said.

Pweters laughed. "I was hoping to find McComber on the list."

"Didn't seem to go all that well last night," Virgil said.

"Ah, I got her," Pweters said. "She pushed me and I pushed her back. Now she's worried that I'm not interested. So she'll flirt with me next time and I'll be cool. A little distant. Eventually, I'll get her. I mean, she doesn't have a lot of choice down here—last night she was out with a guy who does satellite TV installations."

"You're walking a thin line there, Pweters. Women *do not* like rejection."

"Oh, I won't reject her—I'll make her work for it. I know she basically wants my body." Pweters tapped the computer screen. "Say, look at this one. Cripes, I wonder if that's Lucille Becker."

"Looks like a Lucille Becker to me. What else would LuBec be? You know anybody else in town whose name would crunch down like that?"

"No, I don't. Huh."

"What does she do?" Virgil asked.

"She's a fiftyish English teacher up at the high school. Had her my senior year, gave me an A. I could see her in black vinyl."

"Let's try to stay professional," Virgil said. "By black vinyl, you mean the kind with cutouts over the butt?"

"Exactly," Pweters said. He looked up and said, "I'm starting to feel a little dirty doing this. Violating their privacy."

"Really?"

"No, not really." He went back to the computer.

"Attaboy," Virgil said. "Part of the job. Get those email addresses, check the letters for anything that might apply to the case, and put 'whip,' or something, into the search field."

"I can do that."

*   *   *

Virgil continued to prowl the apartment, stopped period-
ically to suggest new search terms for Pweters, but they
found nothing that would tie Fitzgerald to the murders—
nothing like a club that would match the one that must
have been used on Hemming. And no guns at all.

He would have gotten rid of the gun, of course . . .
The gun. He had to think about the gun. What had the
witness said? The gunshots sounded like Moore had
been clapping her hands? Twenty-two CBs, both shorts
and longs, were quiet, but Bea Sawyer had recovered .22
long-rifle shells. If the inner door had been closed, or
mostly closed, when Moore was shot, the sound might
have been muffled.

"Hey, Pweters?"

"Yeah?"

"You know anybody who has a .22 pistol?"

"You mean, besides me?"

Virgil called the sheriff, asked him to round up Sandy
Hart and Belle Penney, the two women who'd been
playing Scrabble with Moore when she was murdered,
and take them back to Moore's house. "We'll meet you
there in an hour."

He and Pweters finished with the search, and Virgil
lugged Fitzgerald's computer out to his truck; they had
nine names of possible B and D clients and had found
ties both to Hemming and to Moore. Hemming had dis-
guised herself by using a masked account name on Gmail
but had slipped up by signing one of her emails with a

lowercase "g," and in another, from the same Gmail account, mentioning that he couldn't come over at the regular time because she had a meeting that wouldn't break up until nine o'clock.

Moore had used her regular email account.

In some of the emails, there'd been quite explicit suggestions for upcoming events; Hemming had mentioned neckties, which confirmed what Virgil had thought about the four men's ties he'd found in her dressing room.

"Doesn't really help," he told Pweters. "We're confirming what we already knew."

"Can't believe Fitzgerald had nine clients," Pweters said. "I mean, how would they find each other?"

"Maybe some kind of female underground communications system?"

"You think?"

Virgil scratched his head. "You know . . . Corbel Cain told me about a guy who knew about some B and D stuff over here. Can't remember his name—I've got it in a notebook—but there are some guys who know about it, too. You're just not one of them."

"As far as you know," Pweters said.

Virgil shook his head. "You're far too much of a Dudley Do-Right to know about that kind of thing."

Jeff Purdy, Sandy Hart, and Belle Penney were waiting when Virgil and Pweters got to Moore's house. Pweters had made a quick stop at his apartment to pick up his .22, and Purdy had collected a stack of undistributed newspapers at the *Republican-River* before going to Moore's.

Virgil explained what he planned to do, put the two women at the kitchen table, stacked the newspapers on Moore's porch, closed the inner door all but a crack. Pweters had loaded three rounds into the gun's magazine; Virgil jacked one into the chamber, and when everybody was ready, fired three quick shots into the pile of newspapers.

That done, he took the magazine out of the pistol, checked the chamber to make sure it was empty, handed the gun and magazine to Pweters, and went back inside to the kitchen. "What do you think?"

"Way louder," Penney said.

Hart nodded. "Nothing like what we heard." She clapped her hands quickly, a golf clap imitating Virgil's three gunshots, and said, "That's what we heard."

"Guy's got a silencer," Purdy said. "Remember when you were here the last time? The guy selling silencers?"

Virgil said, "Yeah. Goddamnit, that doesn't sound like . . . I mean, the first killing seemed like an accident. This sounds like, I dunno . . . a professional. Or a semi-pro anyway."

Pweters began, "That guy"—he glanced at Purdy and the women, veered away—"who, uh, made the silencers. Did you get a list of people who bought them?"

"No, but he's available. Up in Stillwater for another three years. If we need him," Virgil said.

They thanked Purdy and the two women, and Purdy picked up the stack of papers, Pweters went to lock the gun in his truck. Purdy asked if they'd come up with anything at Fred Fitzgerald's, and Virgil said they hadn't found anything useful. With Purdy gone, Pweters said,

"I almost blurted out that tip you got about a blond guy in a GetOut! truck."

"I thought that might have been it," Virgil said. "Good catch. We'll keep that to ourselves for now. But I'm going to go talk to Birkmann about it."

"You want me to come? I like this detecting shit."

"Naw. Take Fitzgerald's computer somewhere and read any email that looks like it might be something. Don't think you'll find much, but we can't let it go. I'm gonna go find Birkmann."

He was on his way to Birkmann's office when he took a call from Jenkins, who, with his partner Shrake, made up the BCA's muscle. Jenkins said, "We're on our way down. You gonna be there?"

"Be where?"

"On the raid," Jenkins said. "You know, these Barbie-Os. That's your case, right?"

"Not really. I'm not going on any raid that I know of," Virgil said. "What the hell is going on?"

Virgil heard Jenkins and Shrake talking in their truck but couldn't make out what they were saying, then Shrake came up and said, "Virgil, we got a search warrant from the attorney general's office to search a farm down there in Buchanan County. Specifically, the barn. There's a PI down there who's hooked into the governor's office . . ."

"Yeah, yeah, Margaret Griffin. I talked to her last night and she was at a dead end. How did this get going?"

"I don't know exactly, but she got a phone number

for the ringleader of the Barbie-O people and got a GPS reading for this barn."

"When did all this happen?"

"Well, we got the call at nine o'clock this morning, so it was before that. We went over and picked up the search warrant from an assistant AG, got it signed, and hit the road. We'll be there in an hour and a half or so, if my nav system is correct. We thought you knew all this."

"I didn't know any of it," Virgil said. "I probably won't be on the raid—I've got these murders. Listen, guys, take it easy."

"Heard something about you getting beat up," Shrake said.

"Yeah, I did. The people who hurt me were a bunch of women who are making these dolls. These are people who are desperate for income. I don't think they'd fight you, but take care. This could be more complicated than knocking on a door."

Shrake said, "Huh. We were led to believe it was a door knock."

"It probably will be. But be careful, for Christ's sakes. Don't hurt anyone. They're mostly housewives."

"We'll take care," Jenkins said.

"If you're still down this evening, have dinner with me," Virgil said.

"See you then," Shrake said. "Keep your ass down."

"You, too."

Virgil sat in his truck, heater running full blast, getting madder and madder. He thought he knew what had happened: he'd told Margaret Griffin that he'd gotten a call from Jesse McGovern, and Griffin, as an experienced PI, had a hacker somewhere who could look at phone records.

They'd gotten into Virgil's and had spotted the incoming call from the night before. He'd known that could happen—in theory, at least—and every PI he'd ever met had ways of getting into supposedly confidential, law-enforcement-only online records. It was illegal, but so common as to be ordinary. He shouldn't have mentioned McGovern's call to Griffin. He'd screwed up.

He had to think for a moment before he remembered where he'd seen a pay phone—there was one in Brown's Bowling Alley—and he went that way, still thinking about what he was going to do. If he got caught, he could lose his job. But Griffin had betrayed him.

The bowling alley was mostly deserted; only three alleys were in use, but there was a gathering at the bar. Virgil, coming in the door at the far side, stopped at the pay phone, thought about it some more, and dropped in a quarter.

McGovern answered a moment later, and Virgil said, pitching his voice up and without identifying himself, "Your barn will be raided in the next couple hours. Somebody may be watching it right now. The phone you're talking on is being tracked. Take the battery out. The main thing is, make sure nobody gets hurt."

He hung up. McGovern might have recognized his voice, but if asked, he'd deny it. Lie. He liked his job and wasn't ready to go for full-time writing.

What worried him most was the possibility that somebody would get hurt in the raid. The people making the dolls had shown a willingness to assault cops—there were still three of them on the loose—and if any of them had a gun . . .

TWENTY-TWO

David Birkmann was out on bug patrol, according to the woman who sat in his office, just off Main Street. The office was a simple Sheetrock cube with off-white walls on which were hung a whiteboard, with assignments and messages written on it, and three separate corkboards with all manner of paper litter pinned to them. The place smelled a little funny, Virgil thought, a combination of body odor and bug-killing chemicals.

The woman's name was Marge, and she said, "This is prime time for Dave, so he'll be a little hard to catch. Rest of the year, it's all about servicing the accounts, which our technicians take care of. January is when Dave signs up the accounts for another year, figures out fees and all of that, and he does most of it personally."

"Maybe you can help me," Virgil said. "How many vans do you have?"

"Maybe you should talk to Dave." She gave him Birkmann's phone number. When Virgil called, Birkmann said he was out of town, up on the bluffs. "I could be back in a half hour."

"I need the answer to a routine question—how many vans do you have?" Virgil asked.

"Vans? Six. One for each technician. Can I ask why you're asking?"

Virgil ignored the question. "Do the technicians leave the vans at the office or do they take them home?"

"They drive them home. They check in with their mileage every night before they get off; Marge reads it."

"Are they allowed to drive the trucks when they're off duty?"

"We discourage it," Birkmann said. "But they do. No out-of-town trips, but, you know, they'll stop at the Piggly Wiggly on the way home or run out to a store at night. It's not really a problem. A small town, it's only an extra mile on the truck . . . Does somebody think one of our vans was involved in the murders?"

"We have a witness who says one was parked on the street near Gina Hemming's house the night of the murder."

"That was me," Birkmann said. "Right at the end of her driveway, off to the right? I was there from about seven o'clock to eight forty-five."

"Don't think it was you, Dave. It might have been someone else, and later than that."

"Well . . . do you have a van number?" Birkmann asked. "A license plate? Do you know what the driver looked like?"

"Not exactly. Are your guys licensed in any way? Do they carry IDs?"

"Oh, sure. They all have a plastic ID card, with the business name on it and their photos," Birkmann said.

"Are there copies of the photos here in your office?" Virgil asked.

"Yup. I'll tell Marge to let you look at them, if you want," Birkmann said.

"That'd be great," Virgil said.

He was about to hang up, but Birkmann said, "Listen, all my guys are good guys. Are you sure it was one of our vans? And, if it was, I'll bet it was mine. Is it possible that your witness got the time wrong? I mean, my truck was out there for almost two hours . . ."

"I can't answer that," Virgil said. "I'm not putting you off—I really can't answer the question."

He gave Marge his phone, and Birkmann told her to show Virgil the file photos of his drivers. They rang off, and Marge called up a file on her computer, with pictures of all six. Two were blond. Virgil wrote down the names, with their addresses and phone numbers, and put check marks by the two blonds.

Virgil spent the next hour and a half worrying about the raid of the barn used by the doll makers and trying to track down Birkmann's pest control technicians.

The first one, Randall Cambden, wasn't on the job, and Virgil eventually found him working part-time for a carpet company. "I'm only part-time with Dave in the winter, three days a week," he said. They were in the back of the carpet salesroom. "I go back to full-time in April."

In the meantime, he spent two days a week pulling out worn carpeting and working as an assistant to an installer.

On the Thursday night that Gina Hemming was killed, he said, he'd been league bowling, which is why he could answer the question without thinking about it. "I bowl every Thursday. And also every Monday, but that's a different league."

"At George Brown's place?" Virgil asked. Brown was the guy who drank too much and tried to date twenty-year-olds.

"Yeah, that's the only place in town. George keeps the league records and scores," Cambden said. "I talked to him a couple times that night, and he'll have my score sheet. We start at eight, finish up around ten-thirty."

Virgil would confirm that with Brown but knew that Cambden was telling the truth. Cambden said that he was home with his wife when Moore was killed. Virgil asked him, "Do you guys carry guns in your trucks?"

"No. Why would we?"

"Well, you do animal control . . ."

"We trap them with Havaharts. Squirrels, coons, skunks. If we have a problem with a dog or something, we call the cops. Dave Birkmann shot a deer once but said he wasn't going to do that again. Too many liability problems. One bad ricochet, killing some guy on the street, and he gets sued and loses the company. If we need to get rid of a deer, we usually have the homeowner contact a bow-hunting club in town. They've got a couple guys who can take care of the problem."

"You wouldn't carry .22s."

"Nope. I guess the old-timey guys did, but there are so many rules and regulations now . . . You can get busted for firing a gun inside the city limits, you know. So, no guns. Sorry."

The second blond, Bill Houston, was a fifty-five-year-old bachelor and had no specific alibi for nine o'clock on

Thursday. "Thursday is church night for me. I never miss, but I'm there only from four to eight. We run a food bank from four to seven, then we have the service, and we get out around eight. After that, I walk back to my apartment and watch TV and go to bed."

"So you're religious?"

"Somewhat religious. The pastor runs a program for alcoholics, and they got me to stop drinking twelve years ago. I'm grateful for that: they gave me my life back. So, church every Sunday and Wednesday, plus the food bank and the short service on Thursdays."

Virgil thanked him and left, scratching his head. He'd check, but he was sure that neither Cambden nor Houston had killed Hemming.

A fter thinking it over for a moment, he took his phone out and called the number that Jesse McGovern had used to call him—and got nothing. She'd pulled the batteries on her phone. He called Jenkins and asked, "Where are you guys?"

"We're out west of Trippton, setting up to go into this farm. You want to join in?"

"I'm thinking I might. When are you gonna hit it?"

"We're sitting here in our truck, talking to Margaret. We're only about a half mile away . . . probably two or three minutes."

"Give me the location, I'll meet you there. See what you get."

*   *   *

The farm was seven miles west of Trippton, up beyond the river bluffs and back in the hills of the Driftless Area. The farmhouse was a shabby ranch style, with yellow siding overdue for paint. The barn behind it was as shabby as the house, but dirty white instead of yellow. The snow outside the barn's main doors was covered with tire tracks, but none of the tracks went into the barn. A small access door to the right of the main doors appeared to have a lot of foot traffic.

The farm's fields were actually cut into the hillside behind the house; a small apple orchard stretched along the road.

When Virgil arrived, Jenkins, Shrake, and Griffin were standing outside the barn, and a woman in a heavy sweater, arms crossed over her chest, was walking away from them. When she saw Virgil getting out of his truck, she stopped, glared at him, and went into the house; one of the women who beat him up, Virgil guessed. Virgil bumped gloved knuckles with Jenkins and Shrake, said hi to Griffin, and asked, "What'd you get?"

"To use official law enforcement terminology, 'jack shit,'" Shrake said.

"There's a big bare spot in the middle of the barn, and a dozen chairs, but not a single doll in sight."

Jenkins said, "We talked to Miz Homer there, but all she said was she wants a lawyer. End of story."

Griffin was fuming. "You can tell something was going on in the barn. All those chairs?"

"There's a propane heater in there, but the heater's cold and the barn's cold, so if that's where they were working, they weren't working for a while," Jenkins said.

"The farm lady said they had a barn dance, is why they have the chairs."

"She's lying, it's obvious," Griffin said. "Who's going to a barn dance here in the middle of winter? That's crazy."

"Probably. What are you guys going to do?" Virgil asked. Relieved in a couple of ways: nobody got hurt, and he was going to get away with it.

Jenkins shrugged. "We're here overnight. It's a bad trip down, the highways are a mess. We're still good for dinner if you are."

"I am. I'll get Johnson Johnson, and we'll make a deal out of it," Virgil said. To Griffin: "How the heck did you find this place anyway?"

"Got a tip," she lied. "I've been spreading some money around."

Virgil played along. "Get back to your source. I agree that this was probably one of their assembly sites, if this farm lady is already talking about a lawyer. If your guy knew about this one, maybe he'll know about another. The boys will be here overnight, if you can find the next spot . . ."

She nodded. "I'll try. Christ, it's cold. It's like Siberia. Why the fuck would anybody live here?"

"We like it, that's why," Jenkins said. "Every March, me'n Shrake fly into LAX and drive over to Palm Springs to play golf. No offense, but L.A. is a shithole. Minnesota isn't."

On that note, they broke up, with Griffin still fuming, Jenkins and Shrake unfulfilled—they liked nothing better than a screaming raid—and Virgil satisfied that he'd worked things through. On his way back to town, Jesse McGovern called. All he saw on his phone was "Unknown," but he'd wondered if she might call.

"We got raided this afternoon," she said.

"I was there," Virgil said, putting a little gravel in his voice. Maybe she was checking his voice to see if he was the man who tipped her. "We know goddamn well that you were building dolls down there. Give it up, Jesse."

"You tracked me on my phone, didn't you?"

"I can't reveal law enforcement techniques, you gotta know that," Virgil said. "If you'd stop making those dolls, we wouldn't be having this conversation."

"Tell that woman that we're almost done."

"I told her last night," Virgil said. "She used to be a cop, and she's getting paid for being here. I don't think she's gonna quit until she hands you the paper. You know, you could stop doing the dolls now, knock on her door down at Ma and Pa's, take the paper, and she'll be out of here. She doesn't like the winter. If you can show that you've ceased and desisted—take a vacation down to Florida—you'd be in the clear."

"I'll think about it," she said.

"I got a question for you about that van your guy saw," Virgil said. "Is it possible that whoever saw it saw it a little earlier than you say?"

"No."

"That sounds pretty definite."

"She gets off work at nine o'clock, I won't tell you where," McGovern said. "She stopped at Piggly Wiggly to get a rotisserie chicken and some potato salad, which probably took ten minutes, and then saw the van when she was driving home. Probably between twenty after and nine-thirty."

"She got off at nine o'clock for sure?"

"Where she works, they don't go a minute past nine. Her replacement doesn't start a minute *before* nine. That kind of place. She walked out no later than nine-oh-one, or however long it took her to put her coat on."

"I need to talk to her."

"I'll tell her," McGovern said and hung up.

Virgil drove into town, thinking it over. The woman had a job and got off at nine. She had a replacement, a swing-shift worker. That probably meant that the job was either a two-shift or a full twenty-four hours a day. The clinic? A possibility. What else was open those hours in Trippton?

He called Johnson Johnson and got a list. The clinic, one convenience store, three restaurants, two liquor stores, the bowling alley. Bernie's Books was open until eleven, but nobody would be working a two-hour shift. And Jimmy worked until it closed, Johnson thought . . . The sheriff's office . . . The boot factory had once had two shifts but now was down to one, seven to three, and even that shift was light . . . Other than that, nothing.

The list was short enough that Virgil ran through it in a hurry. The clinic had regular hours: seven to three, three to eleven, and eleven to seven. The restaurants ran two shifts, as did the liquor stores. No shift at any of the places started or ended at nine o'clock.

The convenience store . . .

Virgil found the pear-shaped assistant manager there, and a plumber working on a compressor for a cooler, and the assistant manager, whose name was Jay, said, "Yeah, Bobbie gets off at nine. She works Wednesday, Thursday, and Friday."

"What's Bobbie's last name?"

"Cole. What'd she do?"

"Nothing," Virgil said. "Where can I find her?"

"She's standing behind the counter, wearing a red sweater."

Virgil introduced himself to Bobbie Cole, a short, stocky woman with chromed hair who was rearranging the candy stacks in front of her cash register. A half-eaten PayDay bar sat on the counter. She said, "Didn't take long to find me. How'd you do that?"

Virgil ignored the question and asked, "How sure are you that you saw a GetOut! truck outside Gina Hemming's house? After nine o'clock?"

"Positive." She crossed her arms defensively. "I get off here exactly at nine on Thursdays. I drive past her house every night after I get off. I saw the truck."

"There was for sure a GetOut! truck there earlier . . ."

"But I wasn't," she said.

"How sure are you that the guy inside was blond?"

"Positive. I was coming up behind him when he must've put his foot on the brake pedal, because the brake lights came on. And that made me sort of jerk, because I was afraid he was going to pull out. I went past and looked over and could see a man in the front seat.

And he was looking at something over in the passenger seat, because his back was turned to me, and his hair was bright yellow. I seen it. And that's that."

"No idea about his age or anything? Or anything about the truck . . ."

Jay, the guy who'd been working on the cooler, had come up behind Virgil, stopping back in the Hostess pastries section. Virgil didn't see him until Cole looked past him and said, "Jay, you still have the time clock cards from Thursday, right?"

"Sure."

"Virgil here doesn't believe me when I say I got off at nine." She looked at Virgil. "The time card will show you the exact minute. My guess is nine-oh-one."

Virgil: "It's not that I don't believe you . . ."

Jay said, "Let's go look." There were people out at the gas pumps, and he added, "Bobbie, better stay up here with the register."

Jay didn't have an office so much as a closet, with a time clock and a couple of file cabinets and a chest-high bench. He pulled the time cards for the previous week, ducked his head back out the door to check on Bobbie. In a low voice he said, "Officer . . . uh . . . You gotta be a little careful with Bobbie."

Virgil's heart sank. "In what way?"

"Everybody who comes in talks about Gina getting killed, and now Margot what's-her-name . . ."

"Moore . . ."

"Yeah, Moore. Bobbie made herself into the local expert on it, she's heard every rumor there is. I didn't know about her spotting the GetOut! truck until yesterday—I mean, a week after she saw it. She never mentioned it before. So . . . anyway, there's this medical truck that goes around from town to town, they've got a machine that checks your neck artery to see if it's getting clogged up or anything. You know what I'm talking about?"

"Yeah, the ultrasound truck."

"That's it. Anyway, it's a drop-in thing. And my doc keeps telling me I ought to get one 'cause, you know, I kinda let myself get out of shape."

"Okay."

"Last month, I came in, and Bobbie was behind the counter and says, 'Jay, the ultrasound truck is down in the Hardware Hank parking lot. Weren't you supposed to do that?'"

"And I say, 'Absolutely.' I leave her in the store and go down to the Hardware Hank, no truck. I went inside and asked at customer service, and the truck was there the day before . . . She'd seen it the day before."

"Oh, boy," Virgil said.

"I'm not saying she's wrong, I'm just sayin'."

"Got it," Virgil said.

Jay had been going through the time cards for the previous week and held one up. "Here's her time card. Out of here at nine-oh-one."

"So she's accurate about that," Virgil said.

"Sure, but . . . she was out of here at nine-oh-one on Wednesday and nine-oh-three on Friday," Jay said, peering at the card. "People don't stick around after work, and if their replacement comes in late, the counter people can get nasty about it. Feet hurt, knees hurt. I hate to say it, but it's sort of a shit job. Nobody gets here late—and everybody gets out of here on time. Every time."

Virgil ran into unreliable witnesses all the time, and Cole seemed like a classic. People could be a close-up eyewitness to a robbery and not be able to tell you whether the robber was black or white, whether he had a gun or a knife. When they were more distant from the event but had been prepped to talk to the cops through rumors and media reports, their information was often useless or, worse, completely misleading.

But not always. Sometimes, they were right on.

At the moment, though, he was at a dead end on the blond GetOut! van driver. He'd needed to talk to the Cheevers since the day before, and he left the convenience store and headed over to the Chevrolet dealership.

TWENTY-THREE

Virgil's concept of the Hemming murder suggested that it was a spur-of-the-moment thing related to the reunion meeting at her house. The killing blow—and there had apparently been only one—had the feel of improvisation. If the murder had been planned, it would have been done with something more efficient, and more sure, like a gun, as with Margot Moore.

He'd originally dismissed the idea that Lucy Cheever had done it, because she was too small to have moved the body—but now that they knew that the killer hadn't moved the body, she was back in the picture. You don't have to be large to swing a bottle, if the murder weapon was a bottle, as he suspected it was.

Elroy Cheever was sitting in his glassed-in office when Virgil arrived and he did a double take that told Virgil he'd been recognized. Cheever, a burly man with dark hair, deep-set eyes, and a potato nose, pushed himself to his feet and stepped over to his office door. Another salesman was talking to a couple looking at a Chevy Equinox, and Cheever waved Virgil over to his office.

When Virgil stepped inside, Cheever said, "Better close the door."

Virgil pushed it shut and said, "I guess you know who I am."

"Virgil Flowers, investigating the murders. Lucy isn't here, she's at home, but I can have her here in five minutes."

Virgil said, "That'd be good. Might as well talk to both of you at once . . ."

Cheever made the call as Virgil sat there, then put the phone down and said, "Five or six minutes, depending on whether she hits the light. You want a Coke or a 7UP?"

"No, thanks," Virgil said. "If we're waiting, maybe I'll go out and look at that Tahoe."

"Sure, let me show it to you . . ."

In the five or six minutes they were waiting for Lucy Cheever, Elroy Cheever demonstrated that he knew about everything there was to know about his products, and was an excellent salesman: he was quick, picked up on Virgil's requirements, and asked about a trade and about the ownership of his current truck.

"I own it," Virgil said. "Ninety percent of the mileage is on state business, and I get fifty-three-point-five cents per mile this year . . ."

"You'd need to drive it about one hundred and ten thousand to one hundred and twenty thousand miles to cover your replacement cost—that doesn't count gas . . .

but this baby will handle that, no problem. You'll get two hundred thousand miles out of it without breaking a sweat, if you keep up with the maintenance, and by that time you'll have covered the gas and insurance."

"So I'd sorta get a free truck."

"That's one way to look at it," Cheever agreed.

"What's the other way?" Virgil asked.

"The other way is, you loaned the state government fifty-five thousand dollars for five years at zero percent interest."

By the time Lucy Cheever showed up, Virgil was about sold on the truck; if, that is, it turned out the Cheevers were still out of prison when the time came to replace his 4Runner.

"Better go back to the office," Virgil said as Lucy walked in.

When they were all three in the office, with the door shut, Virgil said, "You know what I'm investigating. It's possible that the person who killed Gina Hemming was at the class reunion meeting. I think that because we've evolved a very narrow time envelope for the actual murder, putting it shortly after nine o'clock." He looked at Lucy Cheever: "You told me you left right at nine o'clock. Or shortly after."

She nodded. "That's correct."

"One of the other people at the reunion told me that you seemed to be having an argument with Gina Hemming at the door as you were leaving. Is that correct?"

Her forehead wrinkled. "Who told you that?"

"Doesn't matter. Is it true?"

She stared at Virgil for a second, as though she were running the math behind her eyes. Then she said, "It wasn't an argument because there wasn't anything to argue about. We'd applied for a business loan, and she intended to turn it down. She'd told me that earlier in the day, in an email."

"For a million dollars, is that correct?"

"A million one," Lucy Cheever said. "A million one hundred thousand."

"We'd use it to buy the Ford dealership here," her husband said. "We don't know why she decided to turn us down. She would have had plenty of collateral in the Ford dealership. It's worth half again what we're paying . . . or would be, if it were run right."

Virgil looked down at his hands, temporizing. He'd wanted to catch the Cheevers in an evasion by dropping his knowledge of Hemming's email on them, but Lucy Cheever had brought it up herself.

Instead, he said, "In my world, a million dollars is more than enough reason to kill somebody . . . And, with Hemming gone, I understand that you have a good chance of getting the same loan approved by Marv Hiners, now that he's running the place."

Lucy Cheever nodded. "We talked to Marv. We even told him that Gina seemed to have been getting cold feet and that we'd be willing to drop the application and go to Wells Fargo, if he thought that would be . . . prudent. Given the circumstances. He said that wouldn't be necessary."

"Why did Gina turn you down if you had plenty of collateral and if Marv is willing to give it to you?"

Lucy Cheever opened her mouth to answer but Elroy Cheever interrupted. "It was sort of a pointless demonstration of power," he said. "We were all in the same high school class, but me and Lucy started out as poor kids, and now we're overtaking her, building a new house up the bluffs. It was pointless because we know we can get a loan, it'd just cost us an extra point or point and a half."

Virgil poked at them for another ten minutes, essentially asking the same questions in different ways. If one of the Cheevers had murdered Gina Hemming, it would have to be Lucy, because Elroy had been executing what he called a drop-and-drag sales technique that night.

He had a potential customer who'd come in to look at a Suburban but hadn't taken it for a test drive. With a drop and drag, Elroy Cheever explained, he would drop in on the customer at home, explain that he happened to be passing by with the Suburban, and ask if the customer would like to get his wife and go for a quick trip around the block. "If you can get them driving the truck, you can sell it to him," he told Virgil. He gave Virgil the customer's name and phone number and said that he'd dropped by at eight o'clock—"We try to get them after dinner, when they don't have a good reason for saying no." The customer had bitten, and Elroy had been at the customer's house until after nine o'clock.

Virgil thanked them, did another quick walk-around of the Tahoe, and left.

In his mind, Lucy Cheever wasn't entirely in the clear because all it would have taken to kill Hemming was a quick swat. That would have taken no time at all. On the other hand, Cheever showed no sign of fingernail scratches, or any other damage, and had been so up front about the loan that he tended to believe her.

He'd gone back to his truck and looked at the crumpled list of names and addresses that Jeff Purdy had given him the first day. He still hadn't interviewed one of the people on the list, Sheila Carver. He thought about that for a moment, went back inside the dealership, where the Cheevers were still in the office, talking. He stepped inside the office and asked, "What about Sheila Carver? I haven't talked to her yet, but other people have told me she's harmless. How'd she get along with Gina?"

The Cheevers glanced at each other, then Lucy Cheever said, "I can tell you that she didn't like Gina—not like she hated her or anything—she just didn't like her. Sheila hasn't had a happy life. She and her husband haven't done real well financially. Gina never wanted for anything, of course, and I think she treated Sheila poorly. Sheila once had a part-time job up at the club, doing bookkeeping, and so she was like a staff member. Gina treated her that way. Like a low-level employee instead of an old friend and classmate."

"Do you think . . ."

Lucy Cheever was already shaking her head. "They didn't have anything to do with each other, especially since Sheila went to work at the boot factory. I can tell you that Sheila kept looking at her watch during the meeting, and I asked her if she was in a hurry, and she said her kids

didn't like to go to bed without her. She took off before
about anybody else. Maybe . . . eight-thirty or eight forty-
five. I think she walked out with Dave Birkmann."

Virgil swung by the boot factory anyway, a gray cinder-
block building that sprawled along the river alongside
the railroad tracks. Carver had a small cubicle off the
main office, and when she saw Virgil through the window
of her cubicle, she went to the door and called him in.

Her space had a single chair for visitors, and she pointed
him at it and said, "I wondered when you'd come by."

She didn't know the exact time she'd left the meeting,
she said, but it was early. "I went home to put the kids to
bed. My husband was making fudge, and they were all
waiting on me."

"The old 'I didn't do it because I was making fudge'
alibi," Virgil said.

"Yup. That's what it is," she said, and made Virgil
smile.

She didn't care for Hemming, she admitted, and said
it went back to high school when Hemming ". . . didn't
even bother to treat me like dirt. It was like I was invisible or something. Most other people were nice, even if
they weren't good friends."

Hemming's attitude derived from the fact that Carver's father worked on the docks as a laborer—"He carried stuff"—while Hemming's father was a banker. "My
dad drank too much, too, especially in the winter, when
there wasn't a lot of work around. He'd usually get laid
off in November and get picked up again in March, and
if my mom hadn't had a job here at the boot factory,

we'd have been in real trouble. My dad did sometimes fill in as a driver for the factory."

Virgil understood by the end of the talk that Carver actually didn't hate Hemming, not with any heat. She simply despised Hemming's attitude.

"You know what always got my goat? She was always better than thou. Me and my husband don't have a lot of money, but we do volunteer work, like we're always bell ringers for the Salvation Army. Gina would give a thousand dollars to this charity and a thousand dollars to that one, but it wasn't really that much, not for somebody who made as much as she did. When it came right down to it, we gave more value in actual dollars with volunteer work than she did in cash, and we didn't get any deductions for that, and nobody ever much put our names in the newspaper for bell ringing or working at the All Saints food bank . . ."

She went on for a while, letting the resentment out, but she didn't kill Hemming, Virgil thought.

As he was leaving he asked, "You walked out of Gina's house with David Birkmann, right?"

"Yes." She smiled. "Dave's the only exterminator around Trippton, and we had a rat problem at the factory—don't tell anyone that I told you. The big boss was complaining about the bill for cleaning the place up, and Dave looked her in the eye and said if she was really not satisfied, he could return her rats . . . which I thought was funny, knowing the boss. If a rat ever showed up in her office, she'd have been climbing up the chandelier, screaming her head off."

"Somebody told me that Dave Birkmann had been in love with Gina," Virgil said.

Carver narrowed her eyes. "I can see that. Dave's family goes back a long time in Trippton—his grandfather had a farm up above the bluffs and his father owned the extermination business, before he died and David inherited it. I think David always identified with the kids whose parents ran the town—but, you know, his father was an exterminator. That's not like being a doctor or a lawyer or a minister or a banker. I think . . . I dunno . . . I like him. He's a good guy . . . He might have *yearned* for her . . . but I don't think he'd ever do anything about it."

"How about the Cheevers?"

"Good people, too, as long as you're not standing between them and something they want. Lucy is polite to everyone, and I think she's real about that. She's polite because that's nice and it makes people happy, and she wants to do that."

"But you wouldn't want to stand between them and something they wanted."

"No. No, I wouldn't. Elroy could sell ice to Eskimos, but it's Lucy who's really got the hard nose. If the Eskimos didn't buy the ice, she'd slit their throats."

"In a nice way."

"Oh, yeah. They'd all be smiling while she did it."

Another question occurred to him. "Of all the people at the meeting, who do you think would have the worst temper? You know, who'd really go off on somebody?"

She had to work that around in her head for a moment, then said, "Well . . . Gina."

"Who'd be next?"

More thought. "Probably . . . Margot Moore. Or Lucy. Maybe Ryan, in a doctor way. An impatient way."

*   *   *

Virgil said good-bye and headed for the exit, but Carver grabbed her sweater and caught him in the hallway. "I knew you'd come to see me, but I wondered if you had a thought . . ."

"Like what?"

She said, "You think Margot was killed by the same person who killed Gina, correct?"

"Yes."

"What if Margot was killed by somebody who *knew* that Margot had killed Gina? Margot and Gina were friends, but it wasn't always lovey-dovey. Ask around, you'll find out."

"But why wouldn't they come to me and tell me about it instead of killing Margot?"

"This is Trippton, Virgil," Carver said. "We're so far away from everything that we're used to handling our own problems. If somebody who loved Gina knew something about Margot . . . it could happen. You need to find out who *doesn't* have an alibi for killing Margot."

Virgil went out to his truck, deciding on his way that he didn't believe that. He couldn't believe it. If Margot had killed Gina, and Fred Fitzgerald came along and dumped the body, and somebody else killed Margot out of revenge, he was screwed. He'd never get to the bottom of this.

TWENTY-FOUR

The day was getting old, and Virgil felt like he'd been running in circles. What he needed more than anything, he thought, was a couple hours of absolute silence so he could sort out everything he knew about the two killings.

Jenkins called and asked if they were still on for dinner. Virgil suggested the steak house at seven o'clock, and Jenkins said okay and added that Margaret Griffin had told them that she'd come up with a new idea for solving the Barbie doll problem but wouldn't say what it was.

Johnson Johnson said he and Clarice would meet them at the steak house and also said that the arrest of Fred Fitzgerald, and the reason for it, was all over town. "That boy's gonna have to pack up and leave," Johnson said.

Virgil drove back to the cabin and, on the way, called Griffin and, when she answered, asked what she was up to. "What I should have done a week ago: find the sleaziest people who might know about the Barbie doll makers and do a reverse auction—five hundred dollars for information, payable upon delivery of results. No? Six hundred dollars? No? A thousand dollars? No? Two thousand? I'll go to five grand, if I have to. Somewhere between five hundred and five thousand, I'll find my Judas. There's at least a few in every town."

"How are you going to do that?"

"Any goddamn way I can."

"Good luck with that," Virgil said.

The thought that she was right about finding a Judas—and she probably was—was moderately depressing, though Virgil himself had relied on more than one dirtball informant.

A t the cabin, Virgil got out a legal pad, listed all the people at the reunion meeting, and a few more—Justin/Justine's boyfriend, Marvin Hiners at the bank—and started writing down what he knew as facts about them. When he was done, he flipped through the pages, looking for connections. He didn't find anything particularly convincing.

At six o'clock he called Frankie, and they talked for half an hour. He learned that both Frankie and the dog Honus greatly missed him, and that a neighbor had gone in a ditch, rolled, and totaled his two-year-old Escalade. When he got off the phone, he stepped into the shower and got steamed up against the cold, dressed again, and drove across town to the steak house.

J enkins and Shrake knew Johnson and Clarice and approved of both of them. Shrake said to the table, as the drinks came, "We oughta start a pool on when Virgil solves this thing. I'm thinking three more days."

Johnson said, "That's what I'd take. If we're really going to do a pool, we'd have to cut the days into half days or something. Because if it's not soon, it's not going to happen at all . . ."

They were talking about that when Corbel Cain came in trailed by a woman who he introduced as Janey, his wife. She was a pretty, thin, and slightly fragile-looking woman. Virgil couldn't see her as the violent housewife who sparked off brawls with her husband, but he'd often been surprised in the past. Cain said that he was out on bail but hadn't given up on his search for Hemming's killer.

"Corbel . . ."

"That's the way things are," Cain said. He slapped Johnson on the shoulder and asked, "How're things going with the airplane?"

"Me'n Virgil are flying it back in April," Johnson said.

"You oughta invite me to go along. I could be a valuable addition to the crew," Cain said. "I used to fly myself. I could spell you at the controls."

"You still got a license?" Johnson asked.

"No, but who's gonna tell?" Corbel asked.

The Cains continued on to their own table, and Virgil, watching them from time to time, decided that they looked happy enough. They'd been there for an hour or so, whittling their steaks, when David Birkmann came in looking like a lost file clerk, in brown shoes, khaki Dockers, a blue shirt, parka, and a yellow ball cap. He said hello to Virgil, Johnson, and Clarice, then went off to a table by himself.

Johnson leaned across the table to Virgil and said in a low voice, "Birkmann's your killer. See that hat he's wearing? The little dots all over it?"

Virgil glanced at Birkmann's hat. A pale yellow with black dots. "Yeah?"

"He gives those hats out as promotions. I got one. If you look real close at those dots, they're actually little tiny bugs crawling all over. That, my friend, is nuts. He thinks it's funny."

"Well, he was the class clown," Virgil said. "He's supposed to have a good sense of humor."

"I say it again: goofy."

"You know that joke?" Shrake asked. "Mickey Mouse goes to his lawyer, says he wants a divorce from Minnie Mouse, and he explains why. The lawyer said, 'I'm not sure you should go for a divorce just because she's having a few psychological problems.' Mickey says, 'Psychological problems? I didn't say she was having psychological problems. I said she was fuckin' Goofy.'"

Virgil happened to glance over at Cain while Shrake was telling his musty joke and saw that Cain was staring past his wife at Birkmann's back. He thought, *Oh-oh* . . . but let it go.

Jenkins and Shrake had taken the last two available rooms at Ma and Pa Kettle's, probably the first time they'd all been occupied at once since the Great Flood of '27. Jenkins said that Margaret Griffin had asked that they be available the next morning for another raid. They would be.

"You know what she's doing?" Clarice asked. "She's

going around to people and offering a whole bunch of money for someone to rat out Jesse McGovern."

Virgil groaned and asked, "How'd you hear about it?"

"Everybody's heard about it," Johnson said. "Sandy Martinez told me that she put up a wanted poster in the Laundromat. One of two things is going to happen: somebody's going to rat out Jesse, or somebody's going to shoot Margaret in the head. Then you'd have two separate murder cases . . . or three."

"Ah, shit," Virgil said.

A s they were all leaving the restaurant, Johnson Johnson said he and Clarice would not be available for dinner the following evening because they had couples league night at Brown's Bowling Alley. Jenkins and Shrake asked about Brown's, Johnson filled them in and they decided they'd go by and bowl a few frames before heading to bed. They invited Virgil, but Virgil was thinking about his yellow pad and his murder case.

"I'm going to go back to the cabin, I'm going to lie on the bed and listen to Elmore James on my iPad, and I'm going to figure this out. If you guys get up a pool on when I'm going to crack this, you should take 'Tomorrow.'"

Jenkins looked at Shrake, Johnson, and Clarice and said, "Oooo. Wave."

The four of them did a football wave for Virgil, and he let them do it.

T he trip back to the cabin was slowed by the occasional snowpack on the roads. As was usually the case, the lead car in the line of vehicles going down Main Street was driven by the slowest, most cautious driver, who rarely ventured above fifteen miles per hour.

Virgil finally made it past the "Raccoon Crossing" sign and turned down the driveway and pulled up to the side of the porch. As he stopped the car, he saw a flash on the finger of land across the channel from the cabin and, a moment later, the truck jerked with a sound like *SPAT!*

There was a second flash and a second *SPAT!* And another. And Virgil realized that the truck was being shot at—that he was being shot at—and he jammed himself over the seat back into the second row and climbed through to the back hatch, as the truck continued to jerk, continued to *SPAT! SPAT! SPAT!* The truck was being hit, but it sounded like the shots were going into the engine compartment. Virgil reached back, ran the combination on his gun safe, got out the Glock, pushed open the back hatch, and climbed out and got behind a tire.

There was a last *SPAT!* and Virgil emptied the Glock, all seventeen rounds, at the last spot where he'd seen a flash, holding his gun at what he thought might be six feet above the flash. He had no real hope of hitting anything, but he might scare the shooter. He was slapping another magazine in the Glock when he smelled the gas . . .

He couldn't tell where it was coming from, then saw the reflection of fire on the snow under the engine compartment.

The gunfire from across the water had stopped, but the gunman might still be there waiting for Virgil to reveal himself. He took a chance, dashed around the back of the cabin, went through the little-used back door, having to kick a snowdrift out of the way before the screen door would open out. He ran through the cabin to the front door, went to his hands and knees, pushed the door open, reached out around the jamb until he got hold of the snow shovel he'd left there, pulled it inside.

He ran back through the cabin with the shovel, back to the truck. Fire was now dripping from the bottom of the engine compartment into the snow—a stream of burning gasoline. He didn't know exactly where the gas was coming from, but he began frantically throwing snow on the fire he could see, but it didn't stop. Still afraid of showing himself at the front of the truck, he dropped the shovel and, with freezing hands, called 911. When the operator answered, he told her that he had a bad truck fire and about the shooting. The operator knew where Johnson Johnson's cabin was and said that deputies and a fire truck would be on the way.

Virgil used the shovel to bank snow along the driver's side, popped the driver's-side doors, front and back, and began pulling gear out. The fire was close and hot, still confined to the engine compartment.

The truck was only ten feet from the cabin. Virgil thought about trying to shift the truck into neutral and rolling it down toward the river, but the front seat was now too hot, and fire broke through the dashboard above the gas pedal . . .

When the fire truck finally got there, six or seven minutes after his call, the entire front interior of his truck was burning. The firemen put the fire out in two minutes, hosing it with foam.

Virgil had hauled all his gear around behind the cabin,

and he sat on his duffel bag and watched them do it. When it was all done, one of the firemen came over and said, "Not looking so good."

Virgil said, "No, it really isn't."

The cops arrived a minute later, and when Virgil told them what had happened, they looked across the stretch of frozen river to where the shots had come from, and said, "Probably came in on the other side of the finger there, on the river, on a sled. Walk across that finger, probably fifty yards, wait until you show up. Long gone now."

"Are you sure that he's gone, so that we could run across and check it out?" Virgil asked.

The cop looked across the ice for a moment, shook his head. "Not by ourselves. We'd be sitting ducks for a guy with a deer rifle. Let's get some help out here."

He went to call for more cops, and, while he did, Virgil finally looked at the front of his 4Runner. He found four bullet holes but was sure that the truck had been hit more often than that. He got a flashlight and checked the mesh grille and found another hole. It was possible, he thought, that one had gone through one of the holes in the mesh without hitting the mesh itself.

The holes, he thought, looked to be .30 caliber. Virgil had gotten the impression that the shooter had been squeezing off shots one at a time—most probably working a bolt-action rifle.

A deer rifle, and not a .223, was the most popular firearm with gun enthusiasts. David Birkmann had said he had been a deer hunter, so he might have one. But in the

entire southern part of the state—good deer country—
such guns were limited to shotguns firing only slugs. Unless Birkmann traveled to hunt, he'd probably be shooting
a shotgun. A 12-gauge shotgun—about the only kind
used for hunting deer—would have a slug more than
twice as large as those that had hit the truck . . .

He would ask Birkmann about his gun, and who could
confirm it, but Virgil also had to consider the possibility
that he'd been shot at by Jesse McGovern's people.

As for the fire, one lucky shot probably hit the gas line
or fuel pump, spattering gas around the inside of the hot
engine compartment, or maybe one of the incoming
bullets had sparked off the iron engine itself. Whatever
had happened, the truck was done.

Twenty minutes later, six heavily armored deputies,
along with Jeff Purdy, had assembled at Johnson's
cabin, all of them armed with semiauto .223 black rifles.
Johnson's cabin faced out on a backwater of the main
river, a cul-de-sac. The opposite shore was a finger of
land, a narrow peninsula, that extended upstream to the
north. Virgil hadn't been out on it because it was low
and marshy and probably covered with poison ivy, but he
thought it couldn't have been more than a couple of
hundred yards across.

The deputies spread out along the near shore, always
three deputies with guns up, focusing on the far shore,
while two more, on the far ends of the line, hurriedly
crossed the open ice.

Those two moved along the far shore, closing on the
spot where the gunfire had come from. When they were

close, they stopped and set up, and the other deputies crossed two at a time. Virgil went with this last group.

When everyone was safely across, they moved slowly through the barren vegetation, powerful lights cutting through the brush, until they found the track of the shooter. As they'd expected, the shooter had walked, or run, to the other side of the finger of land to the river.

Then, as they hadn't expected, he had walked, or run, back down the finger to the point where it connected to the mainland. The tracks led up the riverbank, across the railroad tracks.

The buildings along the tracks and the river were either industrial warehouses or abandoned, with mostly empty parking lots, and all of them vacant at night. The shooter could have left his vehicle almost anywhere and it wouldn't have been thought of as out of place. He could have come and gone without being seen.

One of the deputies said to Virgil, "Don't quote me, but we're fucked."

TWENTY-FIVE

Virgil called Jon Duncan and told him that his truck had been burned to the ground, which was not an exaggeration. Duncan said, "Whoa! What are you going to do?"

"Go up to Winona and rent a Hertz, before anybody finds out what happened to my truck," Virgil said. "Talk to my insurance guy—I've got a law enforcement rider on it, so maybe I'll come out okay. Davenport's car got all shot up last fall, and he got some good money back."

"Well, do what you have to," Duncan said. "Is this gonna take much longer? I mean, either a solution or a dry hole?"

"A few more days, is my guess. I've got a lot of people stirred up, something will crack. Or not. Anyway, I gotta do something about wheels."

Virgil called Johnson, told him what happened, told him that the cabin was fine, and Johnson offered to loan Virgil a pickup. "Four-wheel drive, good heater, but the radio's shot, and it's got a big 'Johnson Johnson Timber Products' sign on the side."

"I'll rent," Virgil said, "if you can give me a ride up to Winona tomorrow morning."

"See you then."

There was no chance at all that anything could be recovered from the car by a crime scene crew—the bullets would have disintegrated as they ricocheted off the engine block. Virgil called Gene's Wrecker and Salvage and arranged for a wrecker to come pull out the 4Runner and hold it at the salvage yard until an insurance adjuster could look at it.

The wrecker showed up half an hour after he called, and Virgil went out and watched as the driver maneuvered the hulk up on top of the flatbed. The driver said, "State Farm? You'll get ten grand. Maybe twelve, if you put a gun to the guy's head. But I don't think twelve. Might try to stick you with eight."

Virgil went in the cabin to think about it. Had he been shot at by somebody involved in the Hemming and Moore murders or by somebody pissed off about the hunt for Jesse McGovern?

From the impressions in the snow where the shooter had been, it looked as though he'd been shooting while sitting, which was a good position, one that an experienced rifleman would use if he couldn't go prone. Yet, the shooter had hit nothing but the engine compartment: it was like he wasn't trying to actually hit Virgil.

On the other hand, he was willing to throw a lot of high-powered lead into the front of a truck with a man inside, so even if he didn't really want to kill Virgil, he was willing to risk it.

On the third hand, Virgil was higher up than the shooter, so the shooter, who was sitting at the waterline, was effectively shooting uphill and might not have been able to see much of the windshield, and, with the high beams on, might not have been able to even see the truck that well at all. He might simply have been shooting between the headlights.

No way to know, really.

And was it really a he? Virgil thought about that for a while and decided it probably was. The boot tracks in the snow weren't all that telling because the snow was so loose, but it appeared to Virgil that the boots were larger than anything a woman might wear. So probably a man.

Hadn't been Corbel Cain shooting at him, or David Birkmann, because they'd both been in the restaurant, still eating, when he drove back to the cabin. Whoever shot at him had been set up and waiting.

He was working through that reasoning when headlights swept the cabin. He got his gun, slapped the magazine to make sure it was seated, and went to stand beside the door. Johnson, he thought.

But it wasn't. A big man knocked on the door, and when Virgil peeked, he saw Elroy Cheever looking through the window glass. Both hands in sight.

Virgil opened the door and said, "Elroy?"

"I heard what happened," Cheever said. "About your truck getting shot up and burned."

"Yeah, it's a mess."

"I got that Tahoe out in the driveway, big guy. Ninety-seven miles on it. I'll throw in a free Class III hitch, with all the wiring, and the upgraded radio, for the same price we were talking about."

"Elroy . . ."

"Gonna make a sale, gotta strike while the iron is hot. Your iron was hot, judging from what I saw go by on Gene's wrecker," Cheever said. "What do you think? Want to go for a ride?"

Virgil felt vaguely embarrassed but he went anyway. He liked the truck, said he wanted to look at what Ford had. Cheever was pleasant about that, seemed to know all about Fords, was even complimentary, while letting Virgil know he was a fool if he didn't go for the Tahoe.

Virgil was at the wheel, going through town, when the sales pitch wound down. Virgil asked, "Tell the truth, who do you like for the murders?"

"Rob Knox," Cheever said without hesitation. "I wanted to talk to you about that, which is the other reason I came over. Look, Lucy and I had nothing to do with these murders. We're appalled. Honest to God, we really are. About the loan thing . . . Lucy and I are going to wind up as the richest people in town, because we know what we're doing and we're in the right business at the right time. Gina not giving us the loan was a blip in the process. It'd cost us ten thousand a year, but we're talking about five million in gross sales from the new dealership, once we get it running right. We'd like to have the ten grand, but it wasn't important, really. We sure as hell wouldn't kill anyone for it."

"We're not thinking that the murder was planned," Virgil said. "We're thinking it was an impulse. Like a slap, but with a bottle . . . by somebody who was angry."

"But that wasn't the case with Margot, was it? That was cold-blooded murder. And with Gina, somebody would have had to go *back* to kill her. They'd already left. That argues against impulse. Looks like intention to me."

"You're a smart guy," Virgil said. "Either the killer had to go back . . . or was new to the whole scene."

"That's why it was Knox," Cheever said. "I'm not saying that because he's gay. We're way past that, even in Trippton. There must be twenty guys who are openly gay in Trippton, and probably that many woman. Probably always have been that many, or more, in the closet. Most people knew that. Knew who they were. So nobody cares who's gay and who isn't, but it's money. It's money that's done it. Knox is an idiot, he's hungry for money, and, if the rumors are true, Justin Rhodes is about to come into a million bucks."

"I've had a couple other people suggest that to me," Virgil said.

"See? When you know a bunch of people in a small town like this, know them really well, you know who'd kill and who wouldn't . . ."

"You didn't see it in your school board," Virgil said. "The whole board turned out to be a bunch of killers."

"Well . . . that was nuts. But you're right. I never saw that. I never even suspected it," Cheever said. He stared out the passenger-side window, his face turned away from Virgil. "That was crazy. That was all about money, too. Millions of dollars. For me and Lucy, the amount involved was ten thousand a year, in interest, and after you write it off as a business expense, half that. Nothing. But for Knox, you're talking about a million or more. Serious money."

They worked that back and forth for a while. Virgil asked about Barry Long, the state legislator, Homecoming King, and greenhouse owner.

"Ah, Barry wouldn't kill anyone. Barry has one passion: politics. Nobody, and I mean *nobody*, will talk to him about it because he could bore the bark off a tree, once he gets started. He's a good representative because he knows all the ins and outs of state government and he brings home the bacon, but he doesn't have the . . . intensity . . . to kill somebody. Or anybody. He sure as shit wouldn't have come creeping up on you and tried to kill you with a deer rifle."

"Then who did? I've got two completely different sets of possibilities—the person who killed Hemming and Moore, or the people who are involved with Jesse McGovern in this Barbie-O thing."

Cheever's head bobbed up and down, considering, and said, "Look. Jesse gathered up a bunch of people who are really . . . backed into a corner. Can't live on welfare. We're talking people who might not have enough food to eat, even with the food shelf, not enough money to pay for heat. I've got a mechanic who's supporting his brother and his brother's family because his brother can't find work. Telling that guy to move to Texas to find a job is like telling him to move to Mars."

"Desperate."

"It's all over, in small towns. Hell, Trippton is better than most. Anyway, Jesse probably has fifteen or twenty working with her, all of them people like that. To have somebody trying to take away what Jesse's giving them . . . well, you want to talk about fear and anger and hate all stirred together, that's what you got."

Cheever offered to loan the Tahoe to Virgil over-night—he could drop Cheever off at home and take the truck to the cabin—but Virgil declined, and Cheever left him at the cabin a few minutes before eleven o'clock.

That night, Virgil lay in bed and tried to decide whether he'd been attacked by Jesse's people or by the murderer.

For the life of him, he couldn't decide one way or the other.

Jenkins called at nine o'clock, as Virgil was getting out of bed, and said he and Shrake had heard about the fire. "Somebody's trying to kill you, man. You gotta get out of there. Get a hotel up in La Crosse or something."

"I'll think about it," Virgil said. "What are you guys up to?"

"Waiting for Margaret to tell us—but something's going on. We know she was meeting with an informant last night. Apparently, somebody's taking her money."

"Keep me up to date," Virgil said.

Jenkins said he would.

Fuckin' Margaret S. Griffin.

Johnson showed up at ten o'clock, and, by eleven, Virgil was driving a Toyota 4Runner, with thirty thousand miles on it and a couple of dents. He didn't like it as much as he liked the Tahoe, but it was cheaper and felt more like a real truck. That is, less comfortable than the Tahoe. Something to think about when he had the time, which he wouldn't until he had the murders figured out.

When he left the Hertz agency, he followed Johnson back across the river to a La Crescent café, where they had breakfast, and Virgil stewed about the burning of his truck. Johnson had brought along a copy of the new *Republican-River*, and Virgil read with interest the story about the murders of Gina Hemming and Margot Moore, filled with quotes from Jeff Purdy, who was all over the case and who expected that an arrest would be made momentarily.

"What I'd like you to do," Virgil told Johnson when he was done with the paper, "is to call Jesse McGovern behind my back, since you obviously know how to get in touch with her, and tell her to call me again. I want to know who's shooting at me. I don't know if I can trust her, but I can at least get a start on working it out."

"I categorically deny knowing how to get in touch with her," Johnson said. "But keep your phone handy when you're driving back to Trippton."

"You're starting to piss me off," Virgil said. "I was shot at. With a .308, or something like it."

Johnson said, "You know I don't lie to you much, and I'm not lying now. I don't know how to get in touch with her directly. What I'll do is, I'll call a bunch of people who might know how to get in touch with her and tell them what you want. One or more of them can probably get in touch with her, but I don't know which ones."

"I need to talk to her," Virgil said. "Bad."

* * *

On the way back to Trippton, he called his insurance agent, told the agent that the car wouldn't be coming back to Mankato unless State Farm wanted to truck it back. "It's sitting in a junkyard and that would be the cheapest place to leave it," Virgil said. "It looks like it's been in a war zone. Bring your adjuster to the car, is what I'm saying."

He was twenty minutes out of Trippton when Shrake called. "Margaret thinks she's got Jesse McGovern spotted. She got direct testimony from her informant, and the governor got the AG to issue another search warrant. We're on our way there, if you want to join up."

He and Jenkins were north of Trippton, not more than ten or twelve minutes away, following Griffin out to another isolated farm. "Drive slow, I'm on my way," Virgil said. "We're also looking for a recently used .30 caliber rifle."

"Hope they don't use it on us," Shrake said. "Get my bullet allergy all in an uproar again."

Virgil didn't even think about trying to warn Jesse McGovern—he wanted to get the whole Barbie-O case done with, and if that meant slapping McGovern's ass in jail for a while, he was good with that.

The target farmhouse was up behind the bluffs, ten miles out of Trippton. Shrake called again and said Griffin was not going to slow down to wait for Virgil but was going straight in. "She's paranoid about them getting away again. About her source playing both sides."

"Coming fast as I can without wrecking the truck," Virgil said.

But he was late.

When he got to the farmhouse, Jenkins's truck was already in front of the barn, blocking the doors, and Griffin's Prius was right behind it. The side door of the farmhouse was open, but nobody was in sight. Virgil pulled in, hesitated, got his Glock out of the gun safe, and put it in his parka pocket.

As he was walking to the house, Shrake stuck his head out, held up a hand, disappeared back inside.

Virgil followed him in and found Jenkins, Shrake, and Griffin facing three women sitting on a broken-down couch in the living room. None of them was Jesse McGovern.

Jenkins said to Virgil, "This is the main factory. We got three or four hundred dolls, and boxes of parts out in the barn, more in here. The sheriff's bringing a van out here to take the Barbies and the parts. We're waiting for that."

Griffin added, "They've all been served, and we've got IDs on all of them."

"I'd like to look in the barn," Virgil said.

Shrake said, "I'll take you."

The three women on the couch, looking ragged and out of breath, all of them crying a little, hadn't said a word to Virgil. He followed Shrake out the door and, on the way, said, "I'd like to talk to those women without Griffin around. You think you could get her out here and leave me inside?"

"Sure. When the truck gets here, we'll get her out here

to certify the seizure," Shrake said. He added, "Can't remember when I felt this bad about doing my job."

"The question is, are we doing our job or are we running an errand for the governor because he's hoping for payback from somebody?"

"Could have gone all day without asking that," Shrake said.

The Barbies were housed in a variety of plain brown moving cartons, had been purchased individually in retail stores, and packed in the boxes for transport to the barn-factory. An assembly line had been set up on a rough plywood table, with four or five stools on each side of it, littered with batteries, tools, and surgically violated Barbies. A plastic bin of replacement parts was sitting in the middle of the table.

Virgil took it all in and thought about how sad it all was. "You guys going to arrest the women?"

Shrake shook his head. "Nah. Griffin says there's no point. She wants to stop the manufacturing, and this ought to do it. She's given everybody the cease-and-desist orders, so . . . I guess the Barbies go away, and that's the end of it."

"No sign of a rifle?"

"Really couldn't look," Shrake said. "Wasn't on the warrant."

There was an uncomfortable wait until the sheriff's truck showed up, which turned out to be a city public works department utility truck. Shrake said he'd stay inside with the women until the boxes were all loaded, to keep them out of trouble, and Griffin went out with Jenkins to supervise the seizure of the dolls and the replacement parts.

When Griffin was gone, Virgil said to the women, "We're not arresting you—but please, please don't go back to manufacturing the dolls. I don't want to come back to bust anyone, and I'll have to if you violate the court orders."

One of the women said, "You're Virgil." She was wearing a thin nylon babushka and looked like what Virgil thought a Syrian refugee might look like.

Virgil nodded.

"How in the hell are we going to eat, Virgil?"

"Don't ask me that," Virgil said. "Let me see what I can fix up with the town. Talk to the sheriff and see what can be done. I don't like this, and Jenkins and Shrake don't like it, but what you're doing is illegal, and with the court orders . . . I mean, we got no choice."

"You're just following orders," another woman said.

"C'mon," Virgil said. But, he thought, he was. "Listen, I know you don't owe me, but somebody tried to kill me last night. I need to know if it was somebody involved with you guys or if it came from whoever killed Gina Hemming and Margot Moore."

The third woman said, "Like you said, we don't owe you."

"You don't, but I'm going after the guy who did that . . . but maybe less hard if it was somebody trying to set me back a little, get me off your back. If it was the murderer, well, I'm going to be pulling up trees by the roots to find him. It'd help if I knew which was which."

After some sideways glances, one of the women said, "You know what? If I thought it would slow you down going after our people, I'd tell you. But I can't because we really don't know. Heard about it this morning down at Dunkin' Donuts, and we were talkin' about it on the way out here to work . . . but . . . don't know."

"All right," Virgil said. "You've got your legal papers there, don't violate them. When we're out of here, if one of you knows how to get in touch with Jesse, tell her to call me. She knows the number."

TWENTY-SIX

Virgil left the farmhouse to Jenkins, Shrake, and Griffin and drove into town, straight on through, and down Highway 26 to Lansing, Iowa, where he crossed the river and continued down Highway 35 to Prairie du Chien. Snowpacked spots on the highway, and the unfamiliarity of the new truck, slowed him down, and he was driving for two hours. On the way, he called the duty officer at the BCA and asked him to tell the Prairie du Chien cops that he was going to stop by and why.

He figured out the truck's navigation system as he drove, and the truck steered him right into the police department, which was housed in a white stone building next to what looked like, under the snow cover, a city park. The chief, he was told, was vacationing in Pensacola Beach, Florida, but Lieutenant Anderson Blaine was waiting and had been briefed on Virgil's problem.

Blaine turned out to be a tall, mild-mannered man, with black hair, black-rimmed glasses, and a black uniform. "Call me Andy. I understand you're looking for William Gurney, Mark Pendleton, and Son Davis," he said.

"Need to chat, unless one of them suddenly confesses to murder."

"Don't see that happening," Blaine said. "Let me get my coat. I'll walk you over to Le Café—it's a couple of blocks—you can talk to William and Mark."

Outside, Virgil asked, "This is a French restaurant?"

"Bastard French," Blaine said. "Started out with crêpes, steak-frites, baguettes, and cheese plates, ended up with really good coffee and banana muffins in the morning, chicken-fried steak, fries, and baguettes at night. The cheese plates stayed, of course, this being Wisconsin."

"Of course," Virgil said.

"I might mention to you, William and Mark are gay," Blaine said. "Not that there's anything wrong with that. They're a little flamboyant about it, but they're good guys, on the whole."

"Good information," Virgil said. "The guys I'm looking at up in Trippton are gay, too. Or something like that."

"Something like that? How are you something like gay?" Blaine asked.

"What do you call it if one guy thinks he's incorrectly gendered and is actually a woman in a male body, and he's dating a man? I mean, if he's a woman . . . and the guy's a guy . . . they're not gay, are they?"

"Beats the heck out of me," Blaine said. "I'm comfortable not thinking about it."

Le Café was crowded, for two o'clock on a chilly afternoon, but Gurney and Pendleton, two short men in late middle age, were willing to make some space in the work routine to talk to Virgil. They agreed that they knew Knox, who had patronized Le Café because, as a gay man, he felt more comfortable there than anywhere else in town.

"He took cooking classes from us, and he worked—for free—in our kitchen for a few weeks, at night, getting experience," Gurney said. "He hoped to open his own café somewhere, which he did. He hired a person who worked here in Prairie du Chien, and used to work for us, to be his main cook. Rob is still learning."

"Did he have a paying job here in town?" Virgil asked.

"Yeah, he worked at the Kaiser Inn as an assistant manager, which meant, you know, the night man," Pendleton said. "They serve meals there, morning and evening only. I guess he started making crêpes for breakfast . . . which was something beyond their regular cook."

"I believe he worked in hotels and motels for a while, sort of drifting around the country," Gurney said.

"You say 'I believe' . . . Does that mean you didn't know him all that well?"

"We don't, really." The two glanced at each other. "I hope you didn't come down here thinking that we had, or one of us had, a relationship with him," Gurney said. "Because we didn't. We knew he was gay, of course, but we didn't particularly care for him. He was on the make. A hustler."

"Interesting," Virgil said. "I'm most concerned about last Thursday night . . . he said he was here until late."

"I don't know how late he was, but he was here Thursday afternoon for one of our master classes. He's obviously picked up some practical experience, because he was cooking well," Pendleton said. "After the class, he

was gone for a while, but he came back for an early dinner, and we talked about his effort in Trippton . . . Le
Cheval Bleu? He said it was going well, but I have my
doubts."

"Why doubts?"

"Well, you have to know quite a bit to run a place like
this . . . It looks simple, but it isn't," Gurney said. "Like
baking. Mark is a great baker. We do a third of our business between seven in the morning and nine, and it's
probably the most profitable part. Coffee and bakery, it's
marked up more than alcohol. Rob didn't have a clue."

"And you say he was here for an early dinner."

"Yes, he came in at five o'clock, or maybe a bit after,"
Pendleton said. "Our early dinners are lightly patronized, so he could get in. But we had a birthday dinner at
seven, and his table was reserved for then. I can't tell you
exactly what time he left . . ."

They talked for a few more minutes, but Virgil came
away with the information that if Knox had driven directly back to Trippton from Le Café, he might possibly
have been there by nine.

Except, he thought, that it was snowing, and at night.
And Virgil had taken nearly two hours to drive down
during the day. On the other hand, Gurney and Pendleton couldn't say exactly when Knox had left. Could it
have been as early as six? No, not that early, they had
thought. But maybe as early as six-thirty . . .

Tight, Virgil thought. Very tight.

S on Davis, the third reference given by Knox, worked
at the Kaiser Inn and was leaving for the day when

Virgil and Blaine arrived. Knox had visited on Thursday after taking a cooking class at a cookware store, Davis said. But Knox hadn't had many friends at the Kaiser, Davis said, and had left after a few minutes. That had been around five o'clock.

Blaine summarized as they walked back to Virgil's truck. "He doesn't have a perfect alibi, but it would have been tough getting back to Trippton on that night in time to kill your victim."

"Yes. But it could be done . . . Maybe," Virgil said. "Gurney and Pendleton said he was a hustler—and there's a million bucks on the table."

"I wouldn't kill anyone for a million bucks," Blaine said. "But I'm glad nobody's offered me the chance. Heck of a lot of money."

Night was falling as Virgil crossed the bridge back into Iowa and turned north. Even driving in the dark, he made it back to Trippton in two hours—but without the snow factor. As a cop in southern Minnesota, he'd driven through any number of heavy snowstorms. In the daylight hours, it was easier, but at night it was sometimes impossible. He'd been forced off the road a half dozen times during blizzards, to wait it out in whatever motel he could find. He and a dozen other people had once spent a sleepless night in a convenience store in western Minnesota that its manager had kept open specifically as a refuge.

As he drove, Virgil kept running the numbers in his head: if Knox left Prairie du Chien at 6:20, say, he would have had two hours and forty minutes to make it back to Trippton to kill Hemming at nine o'clock. If he'd killed Hemming at 9:15 rather than immediately after nine, he'd have had almost three hours.

Of course, that assumed he'd walked up to Hemming's door, immediately whacked her on the head, and had left unseen.

A vagrant thought, as he looked over his high beams: why did Fred Fitzgerald's confession that he'd moved the body make Virgil think he couldn't have killed Hemming? Of course he could have—he'd confessed to the last half of the crime. But then, there was the whole left-handed thing, and the fact that they hadn't found the weapon at Hemming's house, at Fitzgerald's house, or in the Mississsippi.

All very confusing.

L e Cheval Bleu was open for dinner when Virgil walked through the front door. Only four tables, out of twenty, were occupied. If they'd offer a decent open-face roast beef sandwich, brown mushroom gravy, mashed potatoes with butter, and pumpkin or cherry pie, Virgil thought, or maybe hot fudge sundaes, they'd fill the place. Roast *beef*, and hold the *cheval*, French cuisine or not.

A waitress came to meet him, and he was about to ask for Knox when one of the few patrons, who'd had his back to Virgil, turned around, and Virgil saw that it was Justin Rhodes. Virgil didn't recognize the woman across the table from him, but Rhodes said something to her, dabbed his lips with a cloth napkin, got up, and hurried over to Virgil.

"Please tell me you're here for dinner," he said.

"I'm here to talk to Rob Knox," Virgil said.

"About what? . . . If I might ask?" Rhodes was anxious, twisting his hands.

"His alibi for his time down in Prairie du Chien doesn't entirely check out. We need to talk."

"Oh, boy—well, he's in back."

Two people were working in the kitchen, but not very hard, since there weren't many customers. Knox was wearing what looked to be a Japanese chef's outfit: a deep-bloody-red neck-high apron, with a banana-yellow bandanna wrapped around his head.

Virgil told him about his interviews in Prairie du Chien. "You told me you left quite a bit later than six-thirty," Virgil said. "Why was that?"

Knox objected. "I didn't leave immediately! I left Le Café after six-thirty because William reminded me that the table was reserved for an anniversary party or something . . ."

"Birthday," Virgil said. His phone buzzed with an incoming text. He ignored it.

"Yeah, birthday," Knox said. "So it wasn't six-thirty when I left, it was closer to seven, and I left because of the reservation. But no sooner did I get on the road than the snow started. I should have turned back, but I kept going, and I didn't get here until after ten o'clock, like I told you the first time. I was lucky to get here—it was really coming down."

He looked scared, Virgil thought. Too scared? He was being questioned about a murder, so a little fear was natural.

Virgil nailed down details about the trip back but couldn't shake him.

"Listen, there's a reason I went down there that I haven't talked about, that I didn't want to talk about." He stepped over to a roll of paper towels, ripped one off, and used it to wipe his sweating upper lip. "We're not exactly packing the place here. You might have noticed."

"I have."

"One reason I went down was to . . . take a close look at their menu," Knox said. "The American part of it. We're going to have to go more American here . . . and I was seeing how we could do that and still keep the French vibe."

"You were stealing their menu."

"Looking at it."

Virgil told him not to leave town. "I have to do more research, but we'll still have things to talk about. Like the million dollars."

"We don't need the money to make this place work! We don't!" Knox said.

Virgil left Rhodes and Knox standing in the kitchen and, on the way out, through the restaurant, glanced at the text message.

It came from Clarice. "Call me NOW."

He called, and she said, "Virgil, here's Johnson."

Johnson came on and said, "We're down at Brown's for couples league."

"Let me guess: you lost your balls."

"That's almost hilarious. Remind me to laugh. In the meantime, Corbel Cain was here. He'd had a few . . . like twelve . . . or something."

"Ah, shit, now what?"

"He told me, and everybody else, that he's figured out the murderer. Not only that, he knew where he was, and he was going to go over and face him down. He and Denwa had some more drinks, until Brown cut them off, and they left to confront Dave Birkmann."

"Birkmann? Why Birkmann?"

"Don't know, exactly. But, Corbel deduced it. They're on their way over to Club Gold. Birkmann's supposedly over there for karaoke."

"All right, I'm going."

Club Gold was six blocks away, straight up Main. Virgil had cranked the rented 4Runner over, ready to move, when it occurred to him that Rob Knox had told him something important. Maybe even critical. With Corbel Cain on his way to Club Gold, he couldn't wait to puzzle it out, but it was there, in the back of his brain. What was it?

He hadn't figured it out when he arrived at Club Gold. There were cars parked all along the street, so he went around back, to the parking lot, where he saw two men running across the lot to the back door.

Not running for their lives but running because they were in a rush to see something exciting. Like a fight. Like a confrontation between Corbel Cain and David Birkmann. Virgil stuck the 4Runner in the first parking slot he saw and hurried inside.

One step inside the back door, he could already hear the shouting. He jogged down the hall, past the restrooms, to the main barroom, where Cain, with Denwa Burke at his shoulder, was facing David Birkmann. A heavyset apron-wearing man stood between them—a bartender, Virgil thought.

They were surrounded by a dense crowd of happy on-lookers, most with beers in their hands, yelling encouragement to one man or the other. Virgil started to shoulder his way through the crowd when Cain pointed an accusing finger at Birkmann and stepped toward him, yelling something that Virgil couldn't make out.

Virgil shouted, "Police! Police! Let me through," but nobody paid any attention.

Cain suddenly launched himself toward Birkmann, fists held ear high; the bartender went chest to chest with him, but Cain grabbed him by the shirt and spun him away and turned back to Birkmann.

Birkmann was standing, red-faced, in front of the karaoke stage, and he shouted something back at Cain, then turned to the stage and grabbed a microphone stand. When Cain charged him, he swung it at him. The microphone came whizzing off the top of the stand and broke something on the back wall, something glass, and Virgil pushed through the circle of bar patrons, who continued to watch with an interest that positively bordered on delight.

Cain saw the microphone stand coming at his face and blocked it with one of his heavy forearms.

Which wasn't quite heavy enough.

WHACK! The impact sounded like a butcher cutting a leg bone in half.

Cain yelped with pain and staggered away while Birkmann looked wildly around the bar and shouted something at Burke, who stumbled over his own feet and fell on his butt. Birkmann looked at the microphone stand in his hands, tossed it back on the stage, and ran his hands through his hair . . .

Virgil broke into the open circle of patrons, pointed at Birkmann, and shouted, "Sit down! Sit on the stage."

Birkmann said, "He was going to kill me," as Virgil passed. Cain was holding his left arm across his chest with his right hand and arm, and Virgil asked, "You okay?"

"Busted my arm," Cain said.

"Why? What are you doing?"

"He killed Gina," Cain said, and several pain tears leaked out of the corners of his eyes. "I can see it clear as day."

"How do you know that?" Virgil asked.

"Process of elimination. When you know nobody else did it, it has to be whoever is left."

Virgil couldn't believe it. "That's it? You were going to beat him up because you'd eliminated all the other possibilities? In your own mind? Which is soaked in vodka?"

"Beer, mostly. And that was good enough for us," Cain said.

"Ah, for Christ's sakes," Virgil said, turning back toward the crowd. He shouted, "Everybody, go away. Go back to what you were doing."

Not many moved. The bartender was there, and he pointed at Cain and Burke and shouted, "You! You! You're permanently banned."

Burke said, "Hey, Doug, I didn't do nothing."

"You're banned. Permanently," the bartender shouted again.

"For how long?" Burke asked.

"Until . . . February."

The crowd laughed, people slapping one another on the back. Virgil asked Burke, "Are you sober enough to drive Corbel down to the clinic?"

"I don't think so. I'm kinda . . . liquored up."

"All right." Virgil gave Cain a thumb. "Out in my truck." He pointed a finger at Birkmann. "I'll talk to you later."

Birkmann said, "He was going to kill me."

"I was only going to slap him a little until he confessed," Cain said.

Birkmann: "See? I just wanted to sing."

"All right." Virgil turned to the bartender. "You got this?"

"Yeah, the cops are on the way. But it's over if you get Corbel out of here." He nodded at Burke. "And this asshole." To Birkmann he said, "You owe us for a microphone."

Birkmann said, "Okay, if it's broken."

Burke said, "I need a drink."

Virgil left Burke standing in the parking lot, loaded Cain in the passenger seat of the 4Runner. On the way to the clinic, Cain said, "My arm hurts like hell. I never broke one before."

Virgil said, "Shut up."

"What, you're pissed at me, too?"

"You're an asshole, Corbel. You deserve a broken arm. You're lucky he didn't bury that microphone in your fuckin' skull."

"Yeah, he was crazy mad."

"Wouldn't you be if some drunk started pushing you

around in a bar and told everybody that you'd murdered Gina Hemming?"

"Yeah, but I wouldn't have busted his arm."

Virgil had calmed down by the time they got to the clinic, but as they walked to the door he told Cain, "You're an alcoholic, Corbel. You're a binge drinker, which is the worst kind, because you don't believe that you're an alcoholic. You'll eventually kill somebody, either in a fight or driving drunk. Then you'll dry out, because they don't serve drinks in prison. You want to visit Stillwater for a few years, keep on drinking."

"You really turned into a Debbie Downer," Cain said. He laughed. "That goddamn Birkmann. He broke my arm. I gotta give it to him, I didn't see that coming. Not at all. Didn't think Bug Boy had it in him."

TWENTY-SEVEN

Virgil waited until Cain's arm was x-rayed and the duty doctor confirmed that it was broken. "Simple fracture, not terrible. We'll put a cast on it. Probably be on for three or four months, depending on how fast you heal."

Cain, who was rapidly sobering up, said, "I got to quit this shit."

The doc agreed and asked, "Aren't you the guy who got beat up by Ryan Harney's wife?"

"Yeah, I guess. Been a bad week," Cain said.

The doc said that because Cain had been drinking, and because he was going to need some painkillers, he wanted to keep him overnight until the alcohol had worn off. "I'm going to supervise the analgesics myself. I don't want you overdosing and dying, which would get me sued."

"That's nice, worried about getting sued while I'm dying," Cain said.

The doc said, "People die all the time. I can live with that. It's the lawsuits that are a pain in the ass."

A nurse came in and said to the doctor, "We got more

business coming in. Some out-of-town woman got in a fight up at Tony's Chicago Style. She's burned. Some other woman got a broken arm."

Virgil had an instant bad feeling. "What out-of-town woman?" he asked.

"Don't know. Guy on the phone said there was a brawl . . . The out-of-towner broke the other woman's arm with some kinda pipe or something . . ."

"Ah, shit . . ."

S ure enough.

Margaret Griffin was the first through the door, helped out of a pizza delivery truck by a worried man wearing a white paper chef's hat. Griffin was holding a wet white towel over her face, saw Virgil, and said, "I been burned, bad. Woman threw a slice of red-hot pizza at me."

The doctor left Cain in an examination room and took Griffin to another. Virgil said, "I need to talk to her," and the doc said, "You can come in, if she says it's okay."

Griffin said, "It's okay."

The doctor peeled away the towel. The pizza had stuck to the bridge of Griffin's nose, to her forehead above her eyes, and to a quarter-sized patch of her cheekbone. The doc said, "Yeah, you're burned."

"How bad?" Griffin asked.

"Second-degree, superficial. You've got some blistering. I need to clean you up. I'll give you some ointment for the pain because it *will* hurt."

"Will it scar?" Griffin asked.

"No, it shouldn't. You're lucky it didn't get in your eyes. That would have been a much larger problem."

"No thanks to her," Griffin said.

The nurse came back. "We've got the other one. Where do you want me to put her?"

Griffin said, "Bring her in here—give me a shot at her other arm."

"Ah . . . maybe not. Stick her in the first room," the doc said. "Both the breaks will probably be overnight."

"How did this happen?" Virgil asked Griffin.

"I went into the pizza parlor. I was standing in line, and this woman was sitting at a table. She'd gotten her pizza, and she looked at me and asked if I was the private detective looking for the Barbie dolls. I said I was. And she picked up a slice of pizza and threw it at me. Boiling hot cheese. Stuck to my face. I pulled it off fast as I could . . ."

"You hit her with your baton?" Virgil asked.

"Yeah. She was going to throw more pizza at me, but I got to her first."

"Jeez, Margaret, I'm sorry. We need to get done with this Barbie thing . . ."

"You get me Jesse McGovern and I'm gone," she said.

"I'm trying to get in touch with her now," Virgil said.

Virgil went out to the lobby and called the sheriff's office, told them what had happened, and a deputy said that she'd come down and interview Griffin. "After she's made her statement, I'll check with Lanny up at Tony's and if he backs her up we'll charge the other woman with assault."

"Thanks," Virgil said. He went back and told Griffin what he'd done.

Griffin said, "I'll give them a statement, but I'll be damned if I'm coming back here for a court date. Maybe if she'd scarred me . . . But if I heal up okay, I'll take the busted arm and call it even."

The doc said, "You'll be back to normal in a couple weeks. If you broke her humerus, it could take her a year to get back to normal."

"Good. She can spend the year thinking about why she's fucked up. Could have blinded me."

"I gotta stop this shit," Virgil said. "Margaret, time for you to go home."

"Tell me about it."

Virgil didn't care either about Cain or the woman who'd gotten her arm broken but stayed with Griffin until she was cleaned up. The doc put a dressing on her face, gave her some pain ointment that included an antiseptic, told her that her biggest potential problem was infection, and told her where to go to pay for the treatment.

Virgil drove her back to Tony's Chicago Style, where she got in her car and said, "Fuck this place."

Virgil went back to the cabin, easing the new truck down into the fire-charred slot beside the cabin. He went in the back door, just in case, sat down, got back up, fished a Leinenkugel's out of the refrigerator, sat back down again to focus on the beer.

Johnson called five minutes later and said, "I heard Birkmann won."

"Nobody won, Johnson," Virgil said. "It was another full, flat-out Trippton clusterfuck. Not only that, somebody messed up Margaret S. Griffin."

He gave Johnson the details and then said, "Call up all the people who might know Jesse McGovern. I want to talk to her. Tonight."

"I'll try," Johnson said.

McGovern didn't call until much later; Virgil had given up, turned off the lights, and pulled the bedcovers up to his neck, when his phone buzzed.

She said, "This is Jesse."

"Goddamnit, Jesse, you know what happened last night? And tonight?"

"I know what happened last night—your truck—but I don't know what happened tonight."

"One of your women ran into Margaret Griffin down at Tony's and threw a slice of hot pizza in her face. Burned her face bad. And if that cheese had gotten into her eyes, it could have blinded her. Your employee now has a broken arm."

"Oh, God. All right, you got most of our Barbie stock in that raid this morning," McGovern said. "Not enough left to make it worth the trouble. I'll close it down now. You can tell Griffin that we're all done and we won't do it again."

"Was it one of your people who shot me up last night?"

McGovern said, "Virgil, I don't control them. I got

eighteen people working for me part-time and most of them got husbands or wives, and they're hurting. I don't know if one of them shot you up last night, but there was quite a bit of . . . I don't know what to call it . . . Glee, maybe? . . . There was quite a bit of glee this morning at the other barn, where we were building the dolls. They were talking about it and laughing, but they all said they didn't know who did it."

"And you believed them."

"No. I think somebody in that group knew who did it, but I couldn't tell you which one," McGovern said. "They won't tell me, either—they're protecting me from knowing. I've told them that they're hurting us, not helping, but . . . they've got some thick heads."

"If I catch the one who did it, he or she is going to prison," Virgil said. "You tell them that. That should cut the glee."

"I'll tell them," McGovern said.

McGovern: "I gave you a tip on the murders and you haven't done anything with it."

Virgil: "I tracked down your tipster . . ."

"I heard about that . . ."

"She says the guy in the van was blond. There are two blonds driving those vans. They both have solid alibis for Thursday night. I've also been told, privately, that Bobbie Cole might not be the most reliable witness. She sometimes gets confused about exactly what time, or what day, she might have seen something."

"Huh. I have to say, that might be right," McGovern said.

"So . . ."

McGovern said, "Do you believe she saw anything at all? The van?"

"Yeah, she might've seen the van there sometime, but exactly what time . . ."

"Well, what other day would one of those vans have been parked in front of Gina Hemming's house at nine-thirty at night?"

Virgil said, "Uhh . . . I've got no answer for that."

"Maybe you ought to get one."

"I'll try. This number—will it be good for you?"

"No," she said. "This is a borrowed phone, and I'll be giving it back, so you won't be able to track me with it. I'll borrow another one and call you tomorrow afternoon, see what Griffin has to say."

"I'll be talking to you," Virgil said.

Virgil lay in bed in the dark but spent no time at all consulting with God. He spent it, instead, in contemplation. He'd never formulated exactly what he thought about contemplation except that it was superficially like meditation. You found a quiet, dark place—a bed would do fine—and worked with your brain. Instead of attempting to empty your brain, as you did with meditation, you filled it with a particular subject matter and stirred it around, making new connections, as ridiculous as those connections might be.

Lucas Davenport, Virgil's old boss, had a friend named Kidd who sometimes worked with tarot cards. Kidd argued that there was no supernatural aspect to the cards, but when you selected one at random, and used the tarot "meaning" as an angle with which to examine a problem, you often achieved a new clarity. The tarot forced you out of the worn ruts of your thinking. Sometimes, he said, it even worked.

And that was, Virgil believed, another form of contemplation.

Lying on the bed, near sleep, opening his eyes every once in a while to peer up into the rafters, he came to a realization: Rob Knox, Justin Rhodes's boyfriend, had told him who the killer was.

Something he'd said had given the whole game away— but not about himself. Knox and Rhodes were both innocent, Virgil realized, but he didn't know why he was so sure of that.

Having solved that part of the crime, Virgil went to sleep.

At nine the next morning, Johnson Johnson called and woke him up.

"You're still in bed? I wish I had a job that let me sleep that late."

"I was up late last night, contemplating," Virgil told him.

"Did it do any good?"

"Yeah. I know who knows who the killer is. Rob Knox knows. He just doesn't know he knows."

"He doesn't know he knows and you don't know—do I got this right?"

"More or less," Virgil said. "I'm gonna go see him. You think Clarice could come along?"

"I guess . . . Why Clarice?"

"I wanted another unfogged mind to hear what Knox has to say," Virgil said.

"Wiseass. Okay, I'll come with you."

"I was hoping you'd offer. I gotta get cleaned up, get some breakfast, and think about it some more. The restaurant serves lunch, so I'll see you there at eleven. We'll catch him before they get busy."

Virgil took his time getting ready now that the end of the hunt was in sight. After shaving and showering, he dressed and called Margaret Griffin and said, "Jesse McGovern called me last night, on a borrowed phone. She was upset when she heard about the truck getting shot up, and more upset when I told her about you getting burned. The woman who attacked you will be the second of her people to go to court, so she's calling it all off. She says she's shutting down the operation."

After a moment of silence, Griffin asked, "Do you believe her?"

"Yeah, for no other reason than she said we got most of her doll stock in the raid," Virgil said. "But, I think she's worried about the violence, too. If they'd shot me the other night, the town would have been filled with BCA agents, and there's a chance that Jesse would be doing a few years in jail as the head of a criminal conspiracy. I think she knows that. Same if you'd been seriously hurt last night. Then we wouldn't be fooling around with cease-and-desist orders, we'd be talking felony arrest warrants. So, I believe her."

"Okay. I'll talk to my contact in Los Angeles, see what they think," Griffin said. "We've got people monitoring the Internet sales offers, and if those end, I think they'll probably call me back home."

"That would be good," Virgil said. "Jesse's supposed to call me again on another borrowed phone, so I won't be able to track her, and if she does I'll tell her to make sure the Internet stuff stops. I don't know if she'll be able to stop resales, but the new sales—she should be able to call those off."

"Keep me informed," Griffin said.

"Will do."

At eleven o'clock, Virgil found Johnson Johnson talking with Justin Rhodes at Le Cheval Bleu. When Virgil walked in, Johnson said, "Knox is in the back, whipping up a crêpe. Wait—did I say 'whip'?"

"Shut up, Johnson," Rhodes said. And, "He did NOT have anything to do with the murders."

"Yeah, I know," Virgil said. "But he knows something I need to know."

"What?"

"I don't know."

Rhodes and Johnson glanced at each other, and Johnson said, "Same old Flowers shit. You gotta ride with it."

Knox was talking to a guy in a tall cook's hat. When he saw Virgil, he broke away from the cook and asked, "What?"

"Tell me what you said the other night."

"What?"

"Tell me what you said."

"You know what I said," Knox said.

"Yeah, but maybe not exactly. How did it go? What exactly did you say?"

Knox rubbed his forehead between his eyes and shut his eyes and began to recite what he remembered of their conversation. When he was finished, Johnson looked at Virgil and asked, "Well?"

"Nothing," Virgil said. "Maybe I was wrong. Maybe there wasn't anything."

He'd pulled up a kitchen stool to listen to Knox and now he stood up and said, "But that's not right, there was something."

Knox said, "Maybe you should talk to a shrink. Maybe get hypnotized or something." He pulled on his red Japanese apron and yellow bandanna and said, "I gotta help cook, if you're done."

Johnson followed Virgil out through the restaurant to the front door. As they left, Rhodes said, "Feel free to come back and eat anytime."

Outside, in the cold, Johnson said, "Well, that was a total waste of time. And I won't be eating there any time soon. I suspect ol' Rob might hock a loogie into my crêpes susanne."

"*Suzette,*" Virgil said absently. He was staring out into the street. "It wasn't a waste of time. He told me what I needed to know."

"What?"

"I got it. This second. I think I know who killed them," Virgil said.

"Who?"

"Don't tell anyone until I pile up the evidence."

"I won't, except maybe Clarice," Johnson said.

"Well, tell her not to tell anyone. This is gonna take the rest of the day to figure out."

"Who is it?" Johnson demanded. "And how do you know?"

So Virgil told him and Johnson gaped. "That's all you got?" He looked through the window into the restaurant. "You figured it out because of a hat?"

TWENTY-EIGHT

Virgil said good-bye to Johnson and called Jenkins. "You back in St. Paul?"

"Yup. What's up?"

"I want you to run out to Stillwater," Virgil said. Stillwater was the state penitentiary. "There's a guy out there named Buster Gedney, doing five years on the school board murder case—he was manufacturing silencers and making full-auto modification kits for .223s. I need you to ask him a question about who he sold a silencer to."

"I can do that. When do you need it?"

"Today."

Even knowing who the killer was, Virgil had a major problem to deal with: it was perfectly possible to know who committed a murder without any chance of getting a conviction.

Virgil didn't count on getting much from Gedney, a sad-sack machinist who'd been out on the periphery of the board murders. But Margot Moore's friends who were at her house at the time of her murder said that the sound of the shots that killed her were as quiet as hand-claps. Knowing whether Gedney sold a silencer to Virgil's major suspect would be another good piece of the puzzle.

Virgil had realized something else: everything in the case depended on working out the *precise* time line Hemming was killed.

The Moore murder, on the other hand, had been so efficient that he'd have to name and arrest the killer be-fore he could hope to find any evidence, because the only evidence would be the gun that was used to kill her, a semiautomatic .22. Semiauto .22 long-rifle pistols were made by a variety of manufacturers, including Ruger, Browning, Walther, Smith & Wesson, Sig, and Beretta. Ruger also made a semiautomatic .22 rifle, probably the most popular .22 in America, though Virgil doubted the shooter used a rifle. The firing pin's impact mark made on the .22 shells found by the crime scene crew might give them the brand, which could be important.

But he had to get enough evidence to obtain a search warrant before he'd find the gun . . .

Virgil got on his phone, called Lucy Cheever. "You were absolutely the last to leave Gina Hemming's house. If you had to make your best guess, what time was it? Down to the minute."

Cheever said, after thinking about it, "Three or four minutes to nine."

"*Before* nine o'clock?"

"Yes. People started leaving probably around eight-thirty or quarter to nine, but nobody stayed much longer after that. Gina said a few things to Margot and to Justin at the last minute, and then we had a few words, but I still think it was probably before nine when I left."

"Did you make any phone calls or anything while you were driving home?"

"No. No, I didn't. I was only a few minutes away; I drove straight home. If you really need an exact time, Justin is always on his phone, and I left before he'd gotten all the way down to the street. He might be able to tell you closer than I can . . ."

V irgil called Rhodes.

When he left Hemming's house, Rhodes said, he'd driven home to continue reading *Remembrance of Things Past* in Knox's absence. "I was probably halfway home when I called Rob to find out if he was on his way back to Trippton in the snow. He said he was . . ."

"Look at the 'Recents' on your phone and tell me what time the call went through."

"Okay, hang on . . ."

A few seconds later, Rhodes said, "The call went through at nine-oh-two."

"You were halfway home?"

"Well, maybe not exactly. I was driving home . . . I mean, I didn't call him the minute I left Gina's . . . It was some ways."

"What time do you think you actually walked away from Gina's? What time did you leave Lucy Cheever there with Gina?"

"I . . . guess . . . maybe eight fifty-five? If the call was at nine-oh-two, I had to walk down to my car and I said something to Margot, who was ahead of me a little, getting into her car, saying good night . . . so, yeah . . . eight fifty-five or thereabout."

Virgil called David Birkmann. "When you left Hemming's house, did you make any phone calls? Anything that would tell you the exact time that you left?"

"No . . . I didn't have anybody to call. I just drove down to Club Gold. There were a bunch of people there who could probably tell you when I got there . . . Probably ten minutes to nine. Something like that. Why?"

"I realized I have to nail this time line down. I hadn't understood how important it is."

"Well, I walked down the driveway with Sheila. Maybe she made a call."

"Thanks, Dave, I'll check."

Club Gold was closed when Virgil got there, but a couple of people were working inside. He banged on the glass door until an impatient man came trotting over— Jerry Clark, the manager. He opened the door and asked, "Virgil?"

"Yes. I need to talk to you about last Thursday."

"Ooo-kay. Uh . . ."

Virgil followed Clark back to the bar's office, closed the door, and said, "I don't want you talking about what I'm going to tell you. 'Cause you could get killed."

Clark was a thin man with a weathered face and knife-edge nose. His Adam's apple bobbed a couple of times, and he said, "I won't talk to nobody."

"I'm trying to nail down a time line and I need to know what time David Birkmann got here. Is there any way we can do that?"

"Depends on how close you need the time."

"How close can you get me?" Virgil asked.

"We do videos of the karaoke. We start at about eight o'clock—maybe not exactly, but close—and we run the camera continuously until we quit at eleven or so. Sometimes we run a little late, or quit a little early, depending on how many people we get singing," Clark said. "We could run the video forward and see exactly how long it runs before Dave came on . . . but I don't know if we started exactly at eight, so we could be a few minutes off."

"Where's the video now?"

Clark pointed to a shelf hanging on a side wall. "Right there. We keep them on a hard drive. For ten bucks, we'll email you a copy of your performance. You'd be surprised how many people ask."

"Let's take a look."

Clark hooked the hard drive to a laptop, found the video from Thursday, and ran it fast-forward until they found Birkmann, who was climbing up on the stage, smiling and sweating. The video took in that part of the crowd, sitting at round metal tables in front of the stage. Other patrons walked back and forth in front of the camera from time to time. The audience gave Birkmann a brief round of applause and then he did a reasonably creditable version of "Pretty Woman."

"Well . . . he was up there singing at nine-forty, give or take," Clark said, looking at the time line running at the bottom of the video. "Probably not five minutes one way or the other."

"Could he just walk up and get on the stage?"

"No, he would have had to sign up . . . but sometimes there isn't much of a wait. It's sorta like a party. We don't have one person right after another; some guys sing three or four times . . . We don't always stick right to the list, either, depending on who's ready to go. He wouldn't have to wait long."

If Birkmann went back to Hemming's house after he was sure that everybody else was out of sight—say, five minutes after nine o'clock—he would have had to kill her, let the body bleed into the carpet for a couple of minutes at least, move the body and arrange it, and get out of there and down to the bar and start singing, all in half an hour. A decent defense attorney would chop that time line to pieces, looking for every excuse to add a few minutes—like with the falling snow. Birkmann would have been driving carefully . . . A good attorney would stick an extra five minutes in there.

While Virgil was thinking about that, Clark muttered, "Let me see if I can . . ."

He ran the video backward, then forwards again, until he found a heavyset blond woman climbing up on the stage. "Okay," Clark said. "Let's see if Carroll's in the crowd. He usually is."

"What are we doing?" Virgil asked, looking back at the video.

"Looking for Carroll Wilson. That's his wife, Jeanette, up there singing. Carroll's usually . . . Yeah, there he is." He stopped the video and tapped the head of a man who was sitting at a table below the stage but near its center.

When Jeanette started singing, Carroll stood up and took a photo with his cell phone.

"Thank you," Virgil said. "Where can I find Carroll?"

"He's got the Stihl chain saw dealership. We can call him."

Carroll Wilson had the photos of his wife on his phone. The first one was taken, he said, right after his wife started singing. The time stamp at the top of the photo said 8:44.

"Don't mess with that photo, we'll want to save it as evidence," Virgil said. "I'll come by later to talk to you about it."

"I'll be here," Wilson said.

Virgil didn't say so, but when he said he'd come by to talk to him about it, he meant that he'd give Wilson a subpoena and take his phone away from him.

He and Clark went back to the video, marked the photo at 8:44, and ran the video forward to Birkmann's appearance onstage. "We must've started a little late," Clark said after they figured out the time line. "If Carroll took that picture at eight forty-four, Dave started singing at nine fifty-one."

"I'll need to take the hard drive with me," Virgil said. "I'll give you a receipt."

"Okay, but I'm kinda into this now," Clark said. "Let me roll back . . . Let's see if we can spot Dave with his parka on . . ."

They couldn't. The first time they saw him was when he moved into the video and climbed up on the stage, and he wasn't wearing the parka.

"So he'd already hung it up," Clark said.

"Do you have the sign-up sheets?"

Clark shook his head. "Threw them away as soon as we were done. They're down at the landfill by now."

They couldn't think of any more ways of spotting Birkmann's entrance to the club—no security cameras covering the parking lot—so Virgil was left with the video showing him getting onstage.

In his initial interview with Virgil, and the quick phone interview earlier that afternoon, Birkmann had suggested that he left Hemming's house at around 8:45 and had driven directly to Club Gold and, shortly after, had begun singing. He hadn't. In fact, if he'd been telling the truth about when he left Hemming's house, he'd have been at the club for an hour before he went onstage.

Again, a good defense attorney could make a hash out of that. A guy goes to a bar, talks to people, has a couple of beers, signs up for karaoke . . . Who would know exactly how long you'd been there. An hour might seem like fifteen minutes.

Virgil sat in his truck outside Hemming's house, eyes closed, and tried to imagine the string of events if the killer was David Birkmann, as he now thought likely.

Birkmann goes back to the house for some reason. He and Hemming have a quick and ultimately violent argument—money or sex, Virgil thought. Give them ten minutes for that. She slashes him with her nails, he hits her with something round or cylindrical, takes it with him when he leaves.

Give him an additional ten minutes to react to her death, move the body, run out of the house. According to that time line, he's probably out of the house by 9:30, down at the bar by 9:37. Fred Fitzgerald arrives at 9:40 . . .

Tight, but workable . . . But he'd need more to get a conviction.

A confession would be good.

Virgil opened his eyes, sighed.

He'd been badly fooled by Birkmann's very vulnerability. His obvious and genuine depression, the fact that the Hemming's murder had left him distraught. When Virgil asked him about the GetOut! truck seen by Bobbie Cole outside Hemming's house, he hadn't tried to deny it—he'd actually insisted that it was probably his and let Virgil decide that Cole was an unreliable witness who'd gotten the time wrong.

He couldn't have untangled that before Moore was killed—he still hadn't untangled what that killing was about. Was it possible that it really was a separate problem?

But, no. It wasn't.

He still had a few more people to check: Birkmann's employees—the non-blonds. He had their names in his notebooks and he spent two hours that afternoon tracking them down. Because Hemming's murder had been a sensation, all three men knew where they'd been the night of the murder.

Two of them had been at home with their families. The third had been with his girlfriend at the movies in La Crosse. Virgil checked on the La Crosse alibi with a phone call to the girlfriend, while he was still sitting with Birkmann's employee, and the girlfriend confirmed it. That wasn't airtight, but Virgil believed it anyway: all three said that they had little previous contact with either Hemming or Moore and had never done business with either of them.

Virgil was back in his truck when Jerry Clark, Club Gold manager, called. "I, uh, told my wife about talking to you. I figured when you said don't tell anybody, you didn't mean her . . ."

"Well . . . she can't talk, Jerry. Honest to God, there've already been two murders, one in absolutely cold blood."

"Yeah, okay. Anyway, she said that she's sure she saw Dave come in from the parking lot with Cary Lowe. She said he still had his parka on. I don't have Cary's number, but he works at Home Electric and Appliance here on Main. You might check with him."

"Great. But don't tell anyone else."

"I won't. Promise."

Virgil had seen the Home Electric store, did a U-turn, and went back to it. The store did both sales and small engine and electric repairs, and Lowe, the store's assistant manager, was alone in the store's workshop when Virgil arrived. Virgil asked about Birkmann.

"I do remember that," Lowe said. "I didn't see him come in from the parking lot, but I ran into him in the men's can."

"Was he still wearing his parka?"

"Yup. I remember that because there's not a lot of room between the urinal and the sink, and your coats can kinda overlap. Dave was washing his hands, and I had to pee a little sideways to make sure I didn't spray his coat."

"Did you make a phone call around then? Something we could use to tell the time?"

"No, but it was probably . . . nine-thirty? Something like that?"

"Nine-thirty. Definitely after nine?"

"Oh, yeah," Lowe said. "Thursday is store night in Trippton, and I was working until nine. There was no one in the store, so I locked up right at nine. The club's only two blocks down, so I walked over, had a beer, was watching the karaoke, went back to pee, and ran into Dave in the men's room. So that was probably . . . nine-thirty, give or take."

"And he'd just come in from the parking lot?"

"I don't know that; I didn't see him come in. He had his parka on, though, and the club's always warm."

"Thank you," Virgil said.

Virgil called Pweters, the sheriff's deputy. "You working tonight?"

"Yeah, I'm three to eleven. You got something?"

"I'll tell you about it when I see you. I've got some

stuff to think about, so let's plan to get together about five o'clock. You know where Johnson Johnson's cabin is?"

"Yeah."

"Meet you there at five."

The cherry on the cake arrived a few minutes later when Lucas Davenport called Virgil from the Twin Cities. Davenport was now a federal marshal, no longer working with the BCA, but he and Virgil still talked.

"Jenkins called me," Davenport said. "He wanted me to tell you that Buster Gedney didn't sell any silencers to any of the people on your list."

"That's not good," Virgil asked. "Why didn't he call me himself?"

"Because he remembered something, despite being hit in the head a lot. He remembered that when I was doing the Black Hole investigation, that one of the guys involved in the murders had been a pest control officer."

"Yeah?"

"Yeah. He had a silenced Ruger .22 semiauto pistol that was made especially for sale to pest control officers. I don't know if Ruger still makes them, but they did for a long time."

"One of my suspects—the leading suspect—runs a pest control company," Virgil said.

"Jenkins mentioned that. Now that we've solved your case for you, for which we plan to take full credit, I'd recommend that you go over and pick the guy up."

"I'll do that," Virgil said.

Cherry on the cake.

TWENTY-NINE

When Virgil called that afternoon, David Birkmann was sitting in his van outside the Corsair Motel in Rochester. They spoke only a few minutes, but Birkmann thought Flowers was working on an idea and that that idea would take him to Birkmann as the killer.

Birkmann knew as much about guns as the average Minnesota small-town male, which was actually quite a bit: he'd owned two 12-gauge shotguns and a .22 rifle and had shot a dozen deer over fifteen seasons of hunting.

As far as pistols were concerned, he'd forgotten about his father's old Ruger until he needed it. But if you'd handled other guns, its operation was simple enough, and an hour on the Internet gave him all the information he needed about cleaning and servicing the .22.

It'd worked faultlessly when he killed Margot Moore.

Still, one thing he knew for sure was that if he were going to kill himself, he wouldn't do it with the .22. Three shots in the forehead might reliably kill, but his research on the Internet suggested that a suicide attempt with a .22 might leave him as a vegetable rather than painlessly dead.

One of the shotguns would work, of course, but they'd blow most of his head off. He wanted something tidier than that: he was thinking a .38. A cheap gun would be fine because he didn't plan to target-shoot with it or even shoot it more than once.

He'd also considered going up to the I-90 bridge and throwing himself off. The fall onto the ice would kill him instantly. But . . . he was afraid of heights. The idea of looking down to the point of impact made him nauseated even thinking about it.

This is where he'd gotten to a week after he'd killed the only woman he'd ever really loved and killed another woman who really hadn't deserved it. He'd killed Moore when he still had fantasies of getting away with it all . . .

The fantasies were going away, and he was going to kill himself. He couldn't bear the thought of being led into the county court in an orange jumpsuit and chains, his friends and neighbors peering at him in disbelief.

Birkmann had been to gun shows several times—they were social events in Trippton—and the show in Rochester was like all the other ones, if larger. Private dealers worked out of individual motel rooms, usually showing ten or twenty weapons of a particular type. The "big room" had fifty dealers set up on a spiral of tables, selling everything from T-shirts and bumper stickers—"Honk If You've Never Seen a Gun Fired From a Vehicle," "If Babies Had Guns, They Wouldn't Be Aborted"—to tiny derringers for ninety dollars and massive .50 caliber Barretts for ten thousand.

He circled past the T-shirt, decal, bumper sticker, and knife sellers in the big room, looked in confusion at the array of AR-15 parts, watched a woman demonstrating a speedloader for a .44 Magnum pistol as long as her forearm, and eventually found what he wanted in one of the private dealer rooms: a table full of Ruger revolvers.

He knew he wanted a simple .38 but, being Minnesotan, wound up with a diminutive chrome Ruger revolver that would shoot both .38 specials and .357 Magnums.

"No tax on that; this is a private sale," the dealer said. "Won't have to fool around with the background check, so you can put it right in your pocket and take it home. Plus, of course, it chambers those .357s for home defense as well as .38s for practice."

Birkmann made himself smile, a rare thing for the past week, when he went for the .357 because it would shoot both rounds. In other words, a deal: two for one. Not like he really needed the bargain, if he was only going to fire it once, but if you were Minnesotan you went for the deal.

Birkmann bought the gun and a box of .38s, which would be more than sufficient for a suicide, and, without exactly putting his finger on the reason why, a box of .357s. He'd almost gotten away with it, he thought. That didn't make him much happier.

David—he thought of himself as David rather than Big Dave, Daveareeno, Daveissimo, D-Man, Chips, or Bug Boy—didn't consider himself a killer.

Not a real killer. Even when it came to suicide.

* * *

Birkmann drove back to Trippton, whimpering from time to time, with the gun on the passenger seat, tricking up the truck with dark energy. And he thought about the past week.

Gina Hemming, the rich, arrogant, divorced bank chairwoman of the board and president of the Second National Bank and Class of '92's Most Likely to Succeed, and David Birkmann, financially okay divorced owner of GetOut! and a Main Street donut shop, '92's class clown—one of them carrying a spectacularly unrequited love . . .

Then Margot Moore . . . He'd been at the Dunkin' Donuts store when Moore jogged across the street from Moore Financial wrapped in a business jacket, good enough for a quick two minutes in the cold. They'd talked for a while about Hemming's murder, because everybody was talking about it, and they talked about Virgil Flowers's investigation.

"He's pushing everybody. He's heard about stuff that nobody else ever knew about, about who's been sleeping with who," Birkmann confided to Moore. "He even asked me about that spanking thing, the D and B . . ."

"B and D," Moore said, correcting him. "I think what he's basically doing is working out a time line to see who was the last to leave Gina's place, who might have gone back, who might have seen somebody else driving around . . ."

Birkmann shook his head. "Don't know about that. By nine o'clock, I was already down at Club Gold, doing the karaoke."

Moore frowned. "I thought you left after me. I thought your van was still there when I pulled out."

Birkmann shook his head. "Naw, I was out of there

early. I'm not a meeting guy. Tell me what to do and I'll do it. Make me run around in circles with a committee and I get this need to escape."

Moore nodded, and they talked about the possibility that Hemming's death was an accident. There'd been rumors she'd fallen down the stairs.

Even as they talked, Birkmann's heart felt as though somebody had gripped it in his fist and squeezed. Moore remembered that he hadn't been gone at nine o'clock, that he'd been the last to leave. Sooner or later, Flowers would hear about that.

He hadn't wanted to kill Moore—he liked her—but it was a matter of survival. He hadn't deserved what had happened to him with Gina Hemming, it had been an accident, but there was no possibility of walking away from it. At least with the .22, it had been quick.

Three shots and he was off . . . panicked, hiding out at home, the .22 wrapped in rags and stuffed behind some rafters in the basement. He heard the next day, at the donut shop, that there had been two women in the kitchen when he killed Moore at the front door. That was a shock, but . . . nothing happened.

Nothing. Had. Happened.

Then Flowers had come asking about a blond man sitting in a GetOut! truck after nine o'clock at Hemming's house. Birkmann wasn't blond, and he had no idea why Flowers was looking for a blond, but, sooner or later, he'd be back to Birkmann.

But Birkmann would be gone . . .

Wouldn't he?

THIRTY

Pweters showed up exactly at five o'clock and found Virgil fitting new batteries into his twin voice recorders. Fred Fitzgerald's statement about moving Hemming's body had been transferred to the prosecutor's files, and had also been transcribed to paper.

"What're we up to?" Pweters asked. His face was red with the cold. He brushed snow off his shoulders and added, "Starting to snow again. Wish it would quit for a while."

"We live in Minnesota," Virgil said. "We're gonna go see David Birkmann and see if we can bullshit him into a confession."

"Birkmann?"

"Yeah. He lies well, but I worked my way through it," Virgil said. "I'm ninety-seven percent that he killed Hemming and Margot Moore. I don't know exactly why he killed Moore, but I suspect it was to cover up something."

"Well, shoot. Didn't actually see this coming," Pweters said. "You want to tell me about it?"

Virgil told him and Pweters said, "A hat? I mean . . ."

"Not only the hat. It's the silenced .22. It's the fact

that he was in love with Hemming forever—according to George Brown anyway—and she . . . disdained him . . . and that can lead to violence. When Corbel Cain accused him of killing Hemming, what'd Birkmann do? He grabbed a microphone stand and broke Corbel's arm with it. If he'd hit him on the head, Corbel would be dead. So we know Birkmann's capable of violence . . . And, like I said, he's been lying about the whole time line."

Pweters walked in a slow circle around the cabin's living room, then said, "If we just go up there and bust him, what are the chances he'd be convicted? On what you know now?"

"That's the weird thing—if he's put on trial here, I wouldn't be surprised if he walked. If we put him on trial up in the Cities, where nobody knows him, I think we'd probably get him."

Pweters nodded at that. "You're right. Everybody here knows him, and they'd go in thinking that good ol' Dave Birkmann would never kill anyone . . . He'd walk."

"So we keep the recorders out of sight—I've got some lapel mikes that we can clip to the bottom of our coats—and we get him talking. Maybe scare him a little by reading his rights to him."

"If he asks for an attorney?"

"He won't," Virgil said. "He's shocked and freaked out by what he's done. He's gonna talk about it some. If he talks about it even a little, we'll have him."

B irkmann had a beer, and he had another, and he twisted the top off a third. He'd loaded the new pistol with the .357 shells, but he'd left it on the kitchen counter, glittering away, catching the eye, like a rattlesnake among the cups and plates. He wasn't drinking as a way to work up to shooting himself; he was thinking it over.

He'd seen gun suicides in movies, and, a couple of times, the man about to die wrapped a towel around his head to minimize the mess. The movies made it look like the civilized thing to do, but really? He kept visualizing the two scenarios: one without the towel, his brains splattering all over the wall, and one with it, with his face wrapped like a mummy, the sudden blotch of blood on the outside of the towel . . . and the masked face, the mummy, found by the cops.

Should he leave a note? A confession? Should he say something about the way Hemming had treated him?

And he wondered what would happen when he pulled the trigger. He wouldn't wake up in heaven, he thought, he wouldn't give himself that. It would be, he thought, like somebody turned off the TV. He'd go wherever a TV picture went. Shouldn't hurt . . . should it?

But what if he sorta *missed*? What if he blew out half his brain and spent the rest of his life as a vegetable, deep in pain and no way to tell anyone? That's when he put in the .357s.

He sighed. No point in moving too soon, he thought. If he was going to kill himself, he had plenty of time. All the time in the world.

He was tap dancing, he knew, the same way he'd tried to tap-dance around the fact that he'd killed Hemming and later had murdered Margot Moore. Maybe something would happen that would help him out . . .

* * *

Virgil and Pweters walked out to their trucks. They'd drive up separately, they decided, and if Birkmann wasn't home, they'd hit the downtown bars until they found him.

Virgil led the way up the bluffs and, from half a mile out, saw lights in Birkmann's house. Pweters would see them, too. Virgil rolled up into the parking area, Pweters a hundred yards behind him. As Virgil got out of the truck, he saw a curtain moving in what he knew was Birkmann's kitchen.

"Looks like he's home," Pweters said a minute later, stepping across the new half inch of snow.

"The curtains moved. I think he's seen us," Virgil said. "Let's knock. Is your recorder turned on?"

"Yeah, I'm all set," he said, and "Sweet Jesus sitting on the curb eating a peanut butter sandwich, I've never walked up to something like this."

They knocked, and a moment later Birkmann swung the door open, looming in the doorway. He was in stocking feet, jeans, a plaid shirt, a heavy wool cardigan. He frowned and asked, "What's up? Virgil? Luke?"

"We need to talk," Virgil said. "We need to come in."

"Well . . . okay. Have you figured it out?"

"I think we have," Virgil said. "We need your help with it."

Birkmann didn't react. He said, "Come in, then. Snowing again, huh? Like the night Gina died."

He led the way up the short flight of stairs to the

kitchen and around the corner to the living room. He'd been drinking, Virgil thought: he could smell the beer. There were three chairs in the living room, two facing the television, more or less, the same two they'd sat in when Virgil first interviewed Birkmann. Birkmann pulled around a third chair, across from the other two so they could all face one another, and sank into it.

"Who did it?" he asked.

Virgil said, "Well, Dave . . . you did."

Again, no immediate reaction. The silence stretched taut, and finally Birkmann asked, "How do you figure?"

"Before I tell you all that, I need to tell you exactly what your rights are here . . ." Virgil said.

Virgil recited the standard Miranda warning, hesitating long enough for Birkmann to reply but no longer than he had to, and continued with, "We have the evidence, Dave. What we haven't been able to figure out is why you killed Gina. And, for God's sakes, why did you kill Margot Moore? What'd she ever do to you?"

"Why do you think it's me?" Birkmann asked.

"Because you have yellow hats."

"What?"

"Because Bobbie Cole got off at the Harvest Store at nine o'clock exactly, stopped at Piggly Wiggly, and saw your van parked outside Gina Hemming's house on her way home after she left the Piggly Wiggly—and that was way after nine o'clock. She said the man inside was a blond, but I cleared both of your blond guys. Then I saw somebody put a blond cap on his head . . . and I remembered sitting down in the steak house and you were wearing a yellow hat that night . . . a blond hat."

"That's it? A hat?"

"No, we've got a lot of other stuff now," Virgil said. "Once we knew it was you, we began looking at your alibi more closely. We have a videotape of your first karaoke song, and you didn't go on almost until ten o'clock that night. You'd told me it was more like nine o'clock. We found a guy who took a leak at the same time as you, back in the men's can, and he didn't leave work until nine o'clock, and he had time to walk down to the bar and have a beer before you arrived. And we know about the silenced .22. I suspect it was probably your father's."

Birkmann said nothing for a while, finally nodding and saying, "Yeah, it was Dad's. I'd forgotten all about it until I thought I needed it. It just jumped out of the closet and bit me on the ass. Like it wanted to be used."

"Why?" Virgil asked. "You know, you might have beaten the Hemming murder, but you can't beat Margot Moore's. That was a completely cold-blooded murder. Why did you have to do that?"

Birkmann shook his head and said, "I didn't think I could beat Gina's death. Even though it was more like an accident than anything else . . . She'd come after me with her fingernails and I was trying to fight her off . . . And Margot saw me there too late for my alibi. She mentioned it to me and I knew eventually it'd get back to you. I was still hoping to get clear of everything."

"Tell us about Gina Hemming," Pweters said. "We were told that you loved her . . ."

"The only woman I ever truly loved," Birkmann said sadly. "I'll tell you something else. I loved her and I thought I loved my ex-wife, at first anyway, but none of them ever loved me. I was Bug Boy. Who's gonna love Bug Boy?"

He went on, told them about the killing of Hemming, about the murder of Moore, and, when he was done, began to weep.

Virgil said, "Dave, I gotta arrest you."

Birkmann held up his left hand and said, "Sit down, Virgil. Please."

Halfway through his confession, Birkmann had put his hand into his cardigan's pocket, pulled out a wad of tissue paper, and used it to soak up the tears that had been running down his face. He put his hand back in the pocket and pushed himself out of the chair. When he pulled his hand out of the pocket a second time, it held a chrome revolver. He said, "I think there's some possibility that I'll be able to shoot my way out of this."

That was no .22 in his hand, Virgil thought. That was a much bigger gun.

Pweters said, "Dave, don't even think about it. Not unless you want to die right now." Virgil risked a quick glance at Pweters. Pweters's parka was open and his hand was near his holstered pistol, but really not close enough, and he was still sunk in the easy chair, an awkward position from which to draw a gun.

"I actually bought this gun to kill myself," Birkmann said, wiggling his gun hand. "Whether I do it or you do it, what does it matter to me?"

"Because it would be more pointless killing," Virgil said. "We didn't come rolling up here without telling anyone. We told Jeff Purdy what we were doing and asked him to get us a search warrant for the .22. Speaking of which, and before you decide to shoot us . . . what did you hit Gina with?"

"I took over a bottle of champagne," Birkmann said, looking over at Virgil. "She even laughed at the champagne. I thought it was good stuff, but . . . I guess it wasn't. She made fun of it and she started screaming at me—what an asshole I was, what a loser—and when she slashed at me with her fingernails, I . . . swung. I didn't want to hurt her . . ."

His gun hand moved. He said, "Virgil, I'm sorry it's come to this."

"David, don't bring that gun up," Virgil said. "I've got a pistol in my jacket pocket and my hand is on it, and if you start to bring that gun up, I'm going to shoot you in the guts."

Birkmann looked a little sadder as Virgil said it. "You know what, Virgil? One thing everybody in town knows is, you don't carry your gun. You keep it locked up in your truck. Everybody knows that."

"But not now," Virgil said. "I'll shoot you in the guts, David."

Birkmann hesitated but then jerked the revolver up, and Pweters went for his gun.

Before either one could pull a trigger, Virgil shot Birkmann in the guts.

The blast from the gun was barely muffled by the nylon fabric on Virgil's parka and, inside the small living room, sounded like a grenade. A split second later, there was a second earsplitting *BOOM!* and Birkmann took two stumbling steps backward, tripped over the arm of his chair, and fell on his back. The revolver fell from his hand, and he groaned once, and when Virgil got there and kicked the revolver away, Birkmann looked up at him with surprised eyes but said nothing at all.

Pweters said, "I shot my gun."

Virgil: "What?"

Pweters was there with his gun in his hand. He looked at Birkmann and put his pistol back in its holster and five seconds later was talking to a woman at the 911 center, getting an ambulance and more cops up to Birkmann's house.

The ambulance was there in eight minutes, the first sheriff's car in nine. In the intervening time, Virgil sat on a hassock next to Birkmann and said, "Dave, close your eyes and don't talk. You're going to be bleeding bad and you need to save everything you've got."

Birkmann's head twitched once in acknowledgment.

Pweters said, "I shot my gun. I shot it right through the side of the house. I'm lucky I didn't shoot myself in the freakin' leg."

Birkmann was on his way to the clinic in fifteen minutes, and one of the EMTs told Virgil that he'd be flown by helicopter to the Mayo at Rochester; the local docs would simply plug the hole as best they could and get him on his way.

Virgil called Jon Duncan at home and told him about the shooting, asked him to get a crime scene crew to the house. "How solid are we?" Duncan asked.

"We read him his rights and recorded his confession,"

Virgil said. "It was afterwards that we got into all the excitement."

"I'm sending everything, man. Right now. They'll be there by midnight. Uh . . . what about the Barbie-Os?"

"Jon, I want you to take this in the gentlest, most caring way," Virgil said. "Go fuck yourself."

Virgil and Pweters kept the deputies out of the scene of the shooting, but Virgil took a quick look around the kitchen and spotted an oversized bottle of champagne sitting on a countertop. The paper label on one side was damaged, and there was a hair stuck to it.

He pointed it out to Pweters, who said, "Let's hope to hell it stays stuck until your crime scene gets here."

It did.

When Birkmann was gone, and the shooting scene safely blocked off, Pweters started running his mouth while pacing around Birkmann's kitchen. He didn't stop talking even when he looked in Birkmann's refrigerator and took out a carrot, which he munched on as he talked. He'd never seen a shooting take place, he said, although he'd seen a couple of aftermaths. "I mean like, holy shit, here I was sitting in the chair, and he had that fuckin' cannon in his hand . . . You see that? It's a freakin' .357. It would've made a hole in you that you could push an orange through . . . I was trying to stretch my leg out so I'd have a chance at getting my pistol loose after he shot you . . ."

"He didn't think I had a gun—he would have shot you first," Virgil said.

"Whoa! I didn't think of that. Man, I was like this far away from going for it." He held his thumb and forefinger an inch apart. "And then when you shot him, and I thought he'd fired—I was still alive, and nothing hurt—but I didn't know what the heck had happened and I yanked my gun and damn near shot myself in the leg getting it out. I got my finger in there on the trigger and I was in this huge hurry and I yanked . . . Man, I'm lucky I didn't kill somebody . . ."

Virgil let him talk.

After a while, Pweters ran down and said finally, "I thought you never carried your gun. Like Dave said, everybody knows it."

"Not never," Virgil said. "I knew he had a gun that he'd used to kill Margot Moore. I'd seen him try to hit Corbel with that microphone stand. So I put the gun in my pocket."

"Shot him in the guts," Pweters marveled. "Old Bug Boy won't be easy on the toilet for a few months. He's lucky he wasn't totally . . . exterminated. Know what I'm sayin'?"

THIRTY-ONE

A cop-involved shooting was always messy.

The Buchanan County sheriff's deputy who was serving as the temporary crime scene investigator got them to reenact the shooting, filmed it, took a thousand more still photographs, put crime scene tape on everything that didn't move, and froze the scene until the BCA crime scene crew could get back to Trippton.

Virgil turned his pistol over to Jeff Purdy, who didn't want it but would hold it for the BCA shooting team that would be down the next morning. The team would take statements from everybody and collect Virgil's pistol and the two recorders. The crime scene crew would be right behind them. Birkmann's pistol lay on the floor where it had fallen and wouldn't be moved until the BCA crime scene crew picked it up and bagged it.

Birkmann was given preliminary treatment at the Trippton Clinic, along with a couple of units of blood, and was flown to Rochester. The Mayo surgeons did the best they could to put his guts and hip back together, although he lost a couple turns in his small intestine. His spine had not been involved, as the rapidly expanding bullet narrowly missed the sciatic nerve and knocked a quarter-sized chunk out of his ilium and a big piece of meat out of his butt.

The Mayo docs said when he came out of anesthesia, he wouldn't respond even to medical questions and had begun weeping.

He would get better, but it was gonna hurt and it would take a while.

Virgil got back to Johnson's cabin after midnight and found Johnson and Clarice waiting.

"Heard all about it," Johnson said. "How come you didn't shoot him in the heart?"

"I didn't have a lot of time to perfect my aim," Virgil said. "Or even get my gun out of my pocket. I ruined a perfectly good parka."

Clarice said she'd have been happy to patch it for him, but she didn't know how to sew. "Maybe Frankie does."

"I don't think she does, either," Virgil said.

Every time he stuck his hand in his parka pocket, he pushed his finger through the bullet hole and looked down to see the finger wiggling at him. He couldn't seem to help himself, and the hole was slowly getting larger. Even when he resolved not to put his hand in his pocket, he did it anyway. He took the coat off and hung it on a peg by the door.

Johnson asked, "Are the cops going to investigate you tonight?"

"Not any more," Virgil said. "Why?"

"Because we've got an excellent bottle of wine, a

2014 Christopher Creek Pinot Noir, which I could have one glass of, and you and Clarice could finish, but I don't want to do that if somebody's coming over to test your alcohol content," Johnson said.

"What, you guys are wine freaks now?"

"Johnson is. Turns out the only wine he likes is expensive," Clarice said. "I'm good with any old sangria, as long as it's got ice cubes in it."

Johnson broke out the wine, and Clarice got giggly, and Virgil got as mellow as he could get a few hours after shooting somebody in the gut, and they traded theories about David Birkmann and what love could do to you.

"I'm not sure it was love," Clarice said, as she drank down her second glass of wine. "Maybe he just wanted her, you know, trying to get some status in the old hometown after all those years of being Bug Boy. What sparked him off was, she told him he couldn't have her. That he was Bug Boy and that he was going to stay that way forever."

"Dave did tell me he didn't know much about sex," Virgil said. "I'm not ready for a psychiatric analysis of David Birkmann vis-à-vis Gina Hemming, but I'd really like to know about him killing Margot Moore. He was friends with her . . . sort of. They used to talk over at the donut shop, I know that."

"Yes, that was . . . weird. Awful," Clarice said.

"What I think is, Dave got used to killing stuff over the years," Johnson said. "Bugs, coons, rats . . . whatever. You do it long enough, and casually enough, snuffing them out without thinking, that'd make it easier to kill a human being."

Virgil: "You really think so?"

"I do," Johnson said. "Not if a guy goes out and knocks over a deer or two during hunting season—I know a lot of hunters who jump through their asses telling themselves that it's all right, it's the way of the world and all that, and they feel kinda bad about the dead animal. But I think if you kill things every day, day in and day out, for years . . . you get some calluses."

When the wine, Johnson, and Clarice were gone, Virgil called Frankie and told her all about it and that he felt bad about it. She might have had a callus or two herself, Virgil thought as they talked. She had a harsh, clear view of justice, and she wanted it done. "Virgil, wake up: maybe the guy started as an accidental killer, but he wound up as an assassin, with a silenced pistol, killing a woman who'd never done anything to him. And if you hadn't shot him, he'd have shot you and Peters, and there would have been two more people murdered and he'd still be on the loose," she said. "Besides, he's not even dead. If it'd been me, I might have put a couple more bullets in him."

Virgil said, *"Pweters."*

"What?"

"His name is Pweters, not Peters."

"Probably a misspelling on his birth certificate," Frankie said. "Nobody is named Pweters. God, I wish I could get my hands on you right now."

"I wish you could, too," Virgil said. "But it's going to be another day or two."

"Maybe I should drive over," Frankie said.

"Nah. You don't take your chick to the gig," Virgil said. "I'm gonna be stir-fried in bureaucracy and I'm gonna be in a bad mood. Couple of days, sweetie."

The shooting team, two senior BCA agents, showed up the next morning. Virgil knew both of them and thought they were capable investigators. They interviewed Virgil and Pweters separately, recorded everything, then walked Virgil through the investigation that led up to the shooting.

When it was all done, one of the agents, whose name was Russell Roy, told Virgil that they would take his Glock back to BCA headquarters for a test firing to harvest slugs for comparison with the one that had buried itself in the wall behind Birkmann and would return the gun to him the following week. "You're temporarily suspended, with pay. Don't tell anyone I told you this, but you're not going to have a problem as far as we're concerned. Good investigation and the shooting was fully justified. Jeff Purdy agrees."

"Thank you," Virgil said.

Roy glanced around—they were in Birkmann's house, where the crime scene crew was at work—and said quietly, "Jon Duncan says he's arranged for you to be suspended for three weeks, with pay . . . if you get my meaning."

"Excellent," Virgil said.

"One more thing," Roy said, again the lowered voice. "Jon said that since you're suspended . . . you're done with the Barbie-O investigation."

"Aw . . . man. Yes. Yes."

*   *   *

Virgil told the reporter/editor/publisher of the *Republican-River* that he couldn't comment on a continuing investigation, but neither Purdy nor Pweters had a problem with talking.

Purdy said, "We've worked hard to train our men to be the best law enforcement officers in the region," thus taking credit for the overall quality of the work, "and I feel Deputy Pweters certainly met our standards," thus subtly suggesting other well-trained Buchanan County deputies under Purdy's command would have done at least as well, and that while Pweters met the standards, he possibly hadn't exceeded them.

Pweters said, "I can't talk too much about it, but I have to say I've never encountered a situation quite as desperate as what I faced with Agent Flowers at David Birkmann's house. We were seconds from being murdered ourselves, and if Birkmann had been a tiny bit quicker with his .357 Magnum, the outcome might have been a tragedy rather than a victory for Buchanan County law enforcement," meaning him.

His statement somewhat obscured the question of exactly who shot Birkmann, and the first couple of paragraphs of the *Republican-River*'s story reported that Birkmann had been shot in a confrontation with Deputy Luke Pweters and BCA Agent Virgil Flowers, further obscuring the issue. The *Republican-River*'s reporter/editor/publisher clearly understood Flowers wouldn't be buttering their toast after the next election, but Pweters might be.

*   *   *

Margaret Griffin was told by her employers that they were satisfied with Jesse McGovern's statement to a Minnesota state law enforcement officer—Virgil—that they wouldn't manufacture any more dolls, and she was recalled to Los Angeles.

She tracked down Virgil the day after the shooting and said, "Congratulations. Sounded like a regular old Trippton rodeo. I'm glad you weren't hurt."

"So am I," Virgil said. "This is an unusual town."

Griffin had white patches on her forehead, nose, and cheek where she'd been burned by the hot pizza. "You okay on the shooting?"

"Looks like," Virgil said. "Are you headed home?"

"As fast as I can get back to the Twin Cities. I've got a flight out this evening." She looked around at Main Street. "It's been . . . real. Wish I'd found that goddamn McGovern."

"You take it easy, Margaret," Virgil said.

"I will. Hello, Santa Monica." She pronounced it Son-ta Mo-NEE-ka.

Later that afternoon, on her way up to Minneapolis–St. Paul International, Griffin hit a patch of black ice with the Prius's slick hard tires and skidded off the road backward into a shallow ditch north of Rochester. She wasn't hurt, but the car had to be towed, and statements made to Avis, and all the flights the next day were full. She wound up staying two extra days in Minneapolis, with temperatures in the minus teens.

Virgil didn't laugh when he heard about it, but he may have smiled.

*   *   *

Fred Fitzgerald was told by a county judge to keep his nose clean after the county attorney announced that Fitzgerald would not be prosecuted on the gross misdemeanor of interfering with a body because the information he voluntarily gave to authorities was instrumental in solving the murders of Gina Hemming and Margot Moore.

He walked.

Elroy and Lucy Cheever got their loan from the Second National Bank of Trippton and bought the Ford dealership. By the end of the year, they'd driven the Dodge dealership out of business. The bank itself was sold a few months later to Wells Fargo, and Marvin Hiners stayed on as the manager of the local branch.

Rob Knox, as it turned out, had a greasy thumb: over the next year, he added fried chicken, open-face roast beef sandwiches, and Jell-O with carrot shreds to the menu of Le Cheval Bleu, and the restaurant began to prosper. Mac and cheese with truffles . . . mashed potatoes with brown mushroom gravy aux chanterelles . . .

Justin decided that he wasn't female but *was* gay, and their relationship continued.

Virgil planned to leave town the third day after the shooting. The night before, he had dinner with Clarice and Johnson Johnson at the steak house. Johnson was unusually subdued, and finally Virgil asked Clarice, "What's wrong with Johnson?"

She lifted her hands above her head and waggled them and said, "He just . . . he just can't leave well enough alone. It's like that goddamn airplane . . ."

"It's purely a business deal," Johnson said.

"It's morally reprehensible, in my opinion." Clarice said to Virgil. "Although I'll probably still sleep with him, if only to give my horses a barn to live in."

"Tell me," Virgil said.

Johnson had been making inquiries, having noticed that Margot Moore had no living relatives to sue Birkmann for her murder. "I talked to Hemming's sister . . . she's not going to sue, either. She said all she wants is to be done with it all. So Birkmann's got some assets . . ."

"How does this affect you?"

"Dave's gonna need some money for his defense," Johnson said. "His extermination techs are already talking about getting together to buy the business from him."

Clarice rolled her eyes, turned to Virgil, and said, "Johnson thinks he can pick up the Dunkin' Donuts franchise. Cheap."

Virgil pointed his fork at Johnson and said, "Johnson, you don't know a fuckin' thing about running a donut shop."

"Neither did Dave," Johnson said. "All the employees transferred over to Dave from his wife's lover. They'd be transferred over to me—everybody needs jobs. I'm thinking, 'Donut King of Trippton, Minnesota.'"

Virgil said, "Hail to the chief."

The deal closed in May. Johnson FedExed a dozen

Bavarian Kremes to Virgil, and they were only a little squashed when they got to the farm.

Virgil left on the third day after the shooting. He stopped at a Kwik Trip in La Crescent to get cheese-and-peanut-butter crackers and a Diet Coke and was backing away from the cooler when he bumped into a woman coming down the aisle behind him.

He said, "Excuse me," and noticed the gold-flecked green eyes, and the woman smiled at him and said, "That's okay."

The voice sounded familiar. He took another look at the auburn hair and the freckles and the foxy face, now some fifteen years older than when he saw it in the yearbook: "Jesse?"

"Do I know you?" she asked, turning back to him. She was nearly as tall as he was.

"We've spoken."

She took only a second. "Virgil?"

Virgil nodded. "I hope you're not going ahead with the i-Phone-eeeO. I don't want to come down here again."

"You couldn't catch me *this* time . . . unless you're doing it now."

Virgil put up both hands. "No. Nope. No way. I'm going home, and Margaret S. Griffin should be back in L.A. by now. The thing is, if you go with the iPhone-eeeO, Apple will probably put out a hit on you. Those guys won't be messing around with some low-rent PI with court papers. They'll send out some guys with thick necks and they'll cut your head off, and I'll be down here on another murder."

"How long do you think those two guys would last in Trippton? With my girls?"

"Okay . . . you got me. But I'm begging you, wait until I'm on vacation or something."

She laughed, a happy sound, then cut it off and said in a hushed voice, "David Birkmann? I can't believe it. It's like saying a duck did it."

"He has . . . issues," Virgil said. "The whole thing would be a tragedy, if it weren't basically so slipshod and stupid."

They walked up to the counter together and checked out, McGovern with a Ding Dong and a Pepsi, Virgil with a Diet Coke and his crackers.

In the parking lot, she said, "I'd give you my new phone number and tell you to call me up the next time you're in town, except you'd use the number to trace my call."

"Well . . ."

His parka was open, and she caught the placket of his shirt with a forefinger, gave it a tug. "You take it easy, cowboy."

"You, too," Virgil said. Being the enlightened feminist that he was, he would have denied checking out her ass as she climbed in the truck, but he did and found it seriously acceptable. When she backed out, he read off her truck license plate and wrote it down when he got in his rented 4Runner. Not as good as a phone number but useful nevertheless.

Frankie, of course, freaked out when she saw him. *"What happened to you? You didn't tell me . . ."*

"Got beat up by some women; they moved around

some cartilage," Virgil said. "I'm basically okay. I know I look a little funny."

The dog was bouncing his forepaws off Virgil's chest, and Virgil gave him a thorough scratch, and Frankie pointed Virgil at a chair and said, "Tell me every bit of it. From the time you left on Sunday."

He did, and at the end she said, "You were crazy to go in that house without your gun in your hand. I don't care if you had it in your pocket. You knew he was a psycho."

"A mistake," Virgil admitted. "Though if we'd gone in with guns, he might have lawyered up, and we wouldn't have gotten our voice recordings."

"All right. Does your busted nose hurt so much that you're off kissing for a while?"

"I don't believe so," Virgil said.

So then they did all the things you do when you get home from a trip, all the dirty clothes wadded up and tossed in the washing machine, the bag put away. Virgil told Frankie about his three-week suspension, with pay, and she suggested that they take a trip somewhere.

"We could run back over to Trippton," he said. "Ice fishing, snowmobile riding, we could shop for sex toys in Bernie's Books . . ."

"I'm thinking Phoenix or Los Angeles. Someplace warm and dry."

"We'll talk about it . . ." he said. "Hell, let's do it. We'll call for tickets tonight."

At three-thirty, just before dark, Virgil walked Honus through some of the neighboring streets. When he was sure that nobody was looking, he let Honus take an oversized dump on the lawn of a guy neither of them particularly liked. Virgil kicked some snow over it, and the two of them went on their way. A fine Minnesota tradition, he thought. There'd be layers of well-preserved dog poop in the guy's yard come spring, and he'd be rolling along with his lawn mower and *SKAT!* Dog shit everywhere.

Honus looked up at him, and they both laughed at the thought.

That night, he and Frankie fooled around again, then read in bed, Honus curled up between their feet. They slept in the next morning, Virgil finally crawling out at nine o'clock, Frankie rolling over for another five minutes.

He was shaving when she came in, stared in the mirror for a minute, said to herself, "Hello, gorgeous. You seem to look better every day. How do you keep it up?"

"Gotta be the great sex," Virgil said.

She said, "Huh," opened the medicine cabinet, and fished out her birth control pills.

Virgil said, "Give me those." He took them from her fingers, dropped them in the wastebasket, and continued shaving.

She blinked a few times and said, "No way."

"*Way,*" Virgil said.

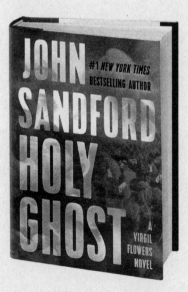

ONE

Wardell Holland, the mayor of Wheatfield, Minnesota, was sitting in the double-wide he rented from his mother, a Daisy match-grade pellet rifle in his hands, shooting flies. His mother suspected he let the flies in on purpose, so he could shoot at them. He denied it, but he was lying.

He was tracking a bull-sized bluebottle when the doorbell croaked. Like most other things in the place, there was something not quite right with the doorbell, but not quite wrong enough to fix. In this case, the doorbell probably indicated that the beer had arrived. The kid had taken his own sweet time about it; school had been out for an hour.

"Come in!" Holland shouted.

The fly tracked out of the bedroom and lazily circled through the living room and toward the kitchen. He picked it up over the sights and the kid outside yelled, "Don't go shooting . . ."

POP! A clear miss. The fly juked as the pellet whipped past, then circled around the sink and out of sight. The pellet ricocheted once and stuck in the fiberboard closet door by the entrance.

"Hey! Hey! You crazy fuckin' pillhead, you're gonna put my eye out."

Holland shouted, "He's gone, you can come in."

John Jacob Skinner edged through the door, keeping an eye on Holland, who was sprawled on the couch, his prosthetic foot propped up on the arm, the rifle lying across his stomach. Skinner, who was seventeen, said, "Goddamnit, Wardell . . ."

"I won't shoot, even if I see him . . . though he is a trophy-sized beast."

Skinner eased into the room, carrying a six-pack of Coors Light. "You want one now or you want it in the refrigerator? They're cold."

"Now, of course. I shoot better with a little alcohol in me."

"Right." Skinner pulled loose two cans, tossed one to Holland, put four in the refrigerator, popped the top on the last one and took a drink.

Skinner resembled his name: he was six-foot-three, skinny, with long red hair that never seemed overly clean, a razor-thin face, prominent Adam's apple and bony shoulders and hips. He had about a billion freckles.

He'd shown a minor talent for basketball in junior high, but had quit the game when he went to high school. He told friends that he needed non-school time to *think*, since it was impossible to think when he was actually *in* school.

The coach had asked, "Now what in the Sam Hill do you want to *think* for, Skinner? Where's that gonna get you?"

He didn't know the answer to that question, but he did know that being the second man on the lowest level, 1-A Border Conference would get him nowhere at all. He'd thought at least that far.

"One of these days," Skinner said to Holland, "you're gonna catch a ricochet in the dick. Then what? Army gonna give you a wooden cock?"

"Shut up," Holland said.

Holland had been elected mayor as a gag played by the voters of Wheatfield on the town's stuffed shirts. What made it even funnier was that after an unsuccessful first term, Holland was re-elected in a landslide. He'd run for office on a variety of slogans his minions had spray-painted on walls around town: "No more bullshit: we're fucked," "Beer Sales on Sunday," "I'll do what I can."

All of which outshone his opponent's "A Bright Future for Wheatfield" and "Happy Days Are Here Again."

This, in a town whose population had fallen from 829 in 2000 to 721 in the 2010 census and now probably hovered around 650, leaving behind twenty or thirty empty houses and a bunch of empty apartments over the downtown stores. Half the stores were themselves shuttered and some had simply been abandoned by their owners, eventually and pointlessly taken by the county for lack of property tax payments.

This in a town where, fifteen years earlier, the city council had purchased from the then mayor, in a corrupt deal, a forty-acre tract on the edge of town. The town had run water and an electric cable out to it and adver-tised it on a lonely I-90 billboard as the Wheatfield Industrial Park (WHIP.) In fifteen years, it had not attracted a single business, and, in the estimation of voters, never would.

Therefore, Holland.

Holland, a former first lieutenant in the Army, had lost a foot in Afghanistan and lived on a military disability pension, which, in Wheatfield, was good enough. He'd refused the thirty-dollar-per-meeting mayor's salary and had rented out the industrial park to a local corn farmer, so the forty acres was finally producing a bit of money. Sixty-eight hundred dollars a year, to be exact.

When he was feeling industrious, Holland would limp around town with a weed-whacker, trimming weeds and brush from around stop signs, fire hydrants, and drainage ditches. Once a month or so, he'd run the town's riding lawn mower around the local park and Little League ball field, which was more than any other mayor had done. None of that took too long in a metropolis of 650 souls.

Skinner asked Holland, "Remember how you said you were gonna do what you can for the town? When you were elected?"

"I was deeply sincere," Holland said, insincerely.

"I know."

Skinner dragged a chair around from the breakfast bar, straddled it backwards, facing Holland on the couch, and said, "I was walking by the Catholic Church last night."

"Good," Holland said. And, "Why don't you open the door and let a couple more flies in? I'm running out of game and that big bastard's hiding."

"There was some Mexicans coming out of the church,"

Skinner continued. "They're meeting there on Wednesday nights. Praying and shit."

"I knew that," Holland said. He was distracted, as the bull bluebottle hove into view. He lifted the rifle.

Skinner said, "Honest to God, Holland, you shoot that rifle, I'm gonna take this fuckin' can of beer and I'm gonna sink it in your fuckin' forehead. Put that rifle down and listen to what I'm saying."

The fly reversed itself and disappeared and Holland took the rifle down. "You were walking by the Catholic Church . . ."

The church had been all but abandoned by the archdiocese. Not enough Catholics to keep it going and not enough local hippies to buy it as a dance studio or enough prostitutes to buy it as a massage parlor. There was a packing plant forty miles down the Interstate, though, with lots of Mexican workers, and the housing was cheap enough in Wheatfield that it had lately attracted two dozen of the larger Mexican families.

The diocese had given a key to the church to a representative of the Wheatfield Mexicans, who were doing a bit to maintain it and to pay the liability insurance. Every once in a while, a Spanish-speaking priest would drop by to say a Mass.

Skinner: "I got to thinking . . ."

"Man, that always makes me nervous," Holland said. "Know what I'm saying?"

"What I thought of was, how to make Wheatfield the busiest town on the prairie. Big money for everybody. For a long time. We could get a cut ourselves, if we could buy out Henry Morganstat. Could we get a mortgage, you think?"

Holland sighed. "I got no idea how a seventeen-year-old high school kid could be so full of shit as you are. I really don't. A hundred and sixty pounds of shit in a twelve-pound bag. So tell me, then finish your beer, and go away, and leave me with my fly."

Skinner told him.

Holland had nothing to say for a long time. He stared across the space between them and finally said, "Jesus Christ, that could work, J. J. You say it'd cost six hundred dollars? I mean, I *got* six hundred dollars. I'd have to look some stuff up on the Internet. And that thing about buying out Henry . . . I think he'd take twenty grand for the place. I got the GI Bill and my mother would probably loan me enough for the rest, at nine percent, the miserable bitch, but . . . Jesus Christ."

"I'd want a piece of the action," Skinner said.

"Well, of course. You came up with the idea, I'll come up with the money. We go fifty-fifty," Holland said.

"That's good. I'd hate to get everything in place and then have to blackmail you for a share," Skinner said.

Holland's eyes narrowed: "We gotta talk to some guys . . ."

Skinner said, "We can't talk to *any* guys. This is you and me . . . If we . . ." He realized that Holland's eyes were tracking past him and he turned and saw the fly headed back to the kitchen. "Goddamnit Holland, look at me. We're talking about saving the town, here. Making big money, too."

Holland said, "We'll have to tell at least one more person. We need a woman."

Skinner scratched his nose. "Yeah. I thought of that. There's Jennie. She can keep her mouth shut."

"You still nailin' her?"

"From time to time, yeah, when Larry isn't around."

"You know, you're gonna knock her up sooner or later," Holland said. "She's ripe as a plum and I'd guess her baby clock is about to go off. What is she, anyway, thirty-three? When that red-haired bun pops outa the oven, you best be on a Greyhound to Hawaii."

"Yeah, yeah, maybe, but she'd do this, and she'd be perfect. Who else would we get, anyway?"

"I dunno, I . . ."

The fly tracked around the room again and Holland said, "Shhhh . . . he's gonna land." He lifted the rifle and pointed it over Skinner's shoulder toward the sink. Skinner lurched forward onto the floor to get down and out of the way, as Holland pulled the trigger.

The fly disappeared in a puff of fly guts and broken wings.

Holland looked down at Skinner and whispered, "Got him. It's like . . . it's like some kinda *sign*."

TWO

Five months later, Mayor Wardell Holland told Virgil Flowers that there weren't any available motel rooms in Wheatfield and not even over in Blue Earth, down I-90. He'd checked. "Your best bet is Mankato. It's an hour away."

"I *live* in Mankato," Virgil said. "That's my best shot?"

"Well, we've only got one operating motel, Tarweveld Inn. It's booked solid five months out, with a waiting list. There's a Motel 6 coming online in a couple of months, but that won't help. You need to get down here. And I mean, *right now*. Today!"

"I didn't know things were that tight," Virgil said. "I can do it, but it'll be a pain in the ass, driving back and forth every day."

"Okay, had a thought," Holland said. "Let me make a call—gimme ten minutes."

Virgil hung up, dropped the phone in his pocket, dragged a spoon through the stove-top pot of Cream of Wheat, and shouted, "It's ready!" At his knee, Honus the yellow dog looked up anxiously, always worried that he wouldn't get his fair share, although he always did.

A moment later, Frankie Nobles eased into the kitchen, barefoot, wearing a pink quilted housecoat straight out of Target. She was a short blond woman, busty, with a slender waist, and normally rosy-cheeked. On this morning, her face was a greenish white and she had one hand on her stomach. "Why don't I remember these parts? Five kids and I never remember."

Morning sickness. She burped and grimaced.

"Bad?"

She thought for a moment, said, "About a four on a scale of one to ten. That's not too bad. When I get to a seven, you'll know it."

Virgil was spooning the Cream of Wheat into a bowl: "Tell me when."

"Keep going," she said. "I'm starving. At least I can keep that stuff down."

All three of them, Virgil, Frankie, and Honus the yellow dog were eating Cream of Wheat, and two of them were reading different pieces of the *Free Press* when Holland called back. "Okay, I got you a place. Mother-in-law apartment of the local hairdresser and her husband. Separate entrance and you get a refrigerator and a microwave. Nice folks. Fifty bucks a day. Extra ten for housekeeping if you want it."

"Aw, jeez, I dunno," Virgil said. "What happened to the mother-in-law?"

"Dead. Choked to death on one of those vegan fake-meat burgers, that was a few years back. And listen, this place isn't exactly what you might think—it's not a dump in the basement. They've been renting it out to pilgrims, fixed it up nice. I've seen it. The only reason it's available is, Roy's picky about who they rent it to."

"All right. I'll take it," Virgil said. "I'll be there by noon. Where will I find you?"

"I run the local store," the mayor said. "We're a block north of downtown, across from the Catholic Church. Skinner & Holland, Eats and Souvenirs. You can't miss it."

"**W**hen will you be back?" Frankie asked, when Virgil was off the phone.

"Any time you need me—it's only an hour from here," Virgil said. "With lights and siren, fifty minutes, max."

"I'll be out at the farm, the boys can take care of me," she said. They were sitting in Virgil's kitchen, the May sunlight streaming through the window over the sink, a pretty Sunday morning in Mankato.

Less than a month away from summer and the longest day of the year, the spring so far had been cool and generously wet without being offensive, and through the window they could see the pink blossoms on the neighbor's apple tree. "It'll be a nice drive down there. You be careful. I always worry when you're dealing with a nut."

"We don't know he's a nut. Or she," Virgil said. "Could be a woman."

"Not likely. When was the last time you heard of a random sniper who was female?"

"Don't even know he's a sniper," Virgil said. "There might be a motive that ties the two shootings together. That would make him a shooter, but not a random sniper."

"You said 'he' and 'him,'" Frankie pointed out.

"That's because you're right," Virgil said. "It's a guy."

*   *   *

Frankie went to shower and get dressed while Virgil got his traveling gear together, which, as usual, bummed out Honus. Honus was a yellow dog of no specific breed, although there had to be some Labrador DNA in the mix: he loved to go out to the swimming hole. That wouldn't happen for another few weeks, as the water coming out of the uphill spring was essentially liquid ice.

Virgil gave him a scratch, then roughed up his head. He was getting neurotic about the dog, which the dog took advantage of. Frankie never made him feel bad about going out on a case, and she loved to hear about them afterwards. Honus, on the other hand, always acted like This Was It: Virgil was ditching him, never to play baseball again.

Virgil was a tall man, thin, athletic, with longish blond hair and an easy smile. He was wearing a "got mule" T-shirt, purchased in the parking lot at a Gov't Mule show a year earlier in Des Moines; an inky blue corduroy sport coat; and boot-cut blue jeans over cordovan cowboy boots.

As an agent of the Bureau of Criminal Apprehension, he should have been wearing a suit with a blue or white oxford-cloth shirt, a dull but coordinated nylon necktie and black high-polished wingtips. What the BCA didn't know, he figured, couldn't hurt him.

Since he'd be close to home, he packed only one extra pair of jeans, with five days' worth of everything else. To the clothing he added added a pump shotgun and a box of shells. A Glock 9mm semi-automatic pistol went in his Tahoe's gun safe with two extra magazines. If he needed more than fifty-one shots at somebody, he deserved to die.

When he was packed, he considered the boat. He rarely went anywhere in Minnesota without towing the boat, in case an emergency fishing opportunity should jump out in front of him. This time, though, he decided to leave it. There wasn't fishable water anywhere near Wheatfield, unless you liked carp and bullheads, and he was only an hour from home. If he really needed to, he could always come and get the boat.

Frankie reappeared to kiss him good-bye and give him a few more minutes of essential advice: "Don't get shot: really. With your rug rat chewing on my ankles, I'm gonna need your help."

"I'll be back for the ultrasound, even if I haven't gotten anywhere on the shooting."

"Better be," she said. The ultrasound was scheduled for the following week.

Virgil rubbed his chin on Honus the yellow dog's forehead and then he was on his way, turning south down Highway 169 and out of town.

Virgil had passed through Wheatfield a couple of times, but had never stopped. He knew little about the place, other than what he'd read in the newspaper stories, of which there had been many in the past few months: it had been settled by Dutch pioneers in the nineteenth century, who gave the town its name: Tarweveld, which meant "wheat field." The Dutch were followed by a bunch of Bavarians and finally a few Irish, few of whom could correctly pronounce the town's name. By 1900, even the inhabitants were stumbling over it, and in 1902, the name was officially changed to Wheatfield. About every other lawn had a miniature Dutch windmill on it, the product of a manic carpenter who loved building windmills and insisted on doing it.

Like a lot of prairie towns, Wheatfield had been dying. Minnesota and the surrounding states had plenty of jobs—Minnesota's unemployment rate was three percent, and Iowa's was even lower, down in the two's. The problem was, the jobs were in larger towns, and the small towns had little to offer their residents, especially the younger ones.

Wheatfield had reached its peak population of 1,500 as a farm-service center after World War II. The Interstate had severely damaged its businesses—it was too easy to get to larger towns—and regional Walmarts had pretty much finished them off. There was still a cafe and a gas station and a hardware store and a couple of other businesses, but they'd been moribund as well.

Not anymore.

The previous winter, on a Wednesday night between Thanksgiving and Christmas, the Virgin Mary had appeared at St. Mary's Catholic Church to a congregation of mostly Mexican worshippers, with a few devout Anglos mixed in. Unlike other Marian Apparitions, as her appearances were called, this one had been documented by numerous cell phone cameras.

The night after the first apparition, the church had been jammed with worshippers and the simply curious, as word of the miracle spread. There had not yet been a priest in attendance, so a deacon was presiding when the Virgin appeared the second time, floating in the air behind the altar.

The Virgin spoke. According to commentators in Mexico City, she said, "Bienaventurados los mansos, porque ellos heredarán la tierra," or, "Blessed are the meek, for they shall inherit the earth." The same commentators said the Virgin didn't have a very good accent in any dialect of Spanish that they knew of, but somebody quickly pointed out that she couldn't be expected to, since her native language would have been Aramaic; or, perhaps, she was speaking a form that would have been closer to Latin. A few skeptics suggested a more local accent, more of a oodala-oodala-oodala Minnesota version of Spanish.

A panel of experts convened by CNN agreed that the Virgin's appearance could cost Donald Trump three to four percentage points in the next presidential election by encouraging meek female voters who wished to inherit the earth. A similar panel on Fox argued her appearance would certainly increase the vote for Donald Trump, possibly by as much as five percentage points, by encouraging the religious right.

A television reporter from the Twin Cities had been interviewing people outside the church when the second apparition occurred, and when worshippers began screaming, she rushed inside. Her cameraman tripped and fell going up the stairs, was nearly trampled by people fighting to get past him. He managed to get video of only the very end of the apparition as the figure of the Virgin faded away.

But he got *something*.

The reporter herself had seen and heard the Virgin.

At the end of her report, she had tearfully confessed, "I came to St. Mary's as a nonbeliever, but now . . ." She fell to her knees: "I *believe*. I BELIEVE!"

She went viral, and a week later was offered a job as a weather girl on an LA television station, an offer she accepted.

JOHN SANDFORD

"If you haven't read Sandford yet, you have been missing one of the great summer-read novelists of all time."
—Stephen King